I0823733

A GARDEN OF TREES

ALSO BY NICHOLAS MOSLEY

Accident

Assassins

Impossible Object

Natalie Natalia

Catastrophe Practice

Imago Bird

Serpent

Judith

Hopeful Monsters

Efforts at Truth: An Autobiography

Children of Darkness and Light

The Hesperides Tree

Inventing God

The Uses of Slime Mould: Essays of Four Decades

Look at the Dark

Time at War

Experience and Religion

God's Hazard

Paradoxes of Peace, or The Presence of Infinity

NICHOLAS MOSLEY

A GARDEN OF TREES

DALKEY ARCHIVE PRESS
CHAMPAIGN / DUBLIN / LONDON

Library of Congress Cataloging-in-Publication Data

Mosley, Nicholas, 1923-
A garden of trees / Nicholas Mosley. -- 1st ed.
p. cm.
ISBN 978-1-56478-718-7 (cloth : acid-free paper)
I. Title.
PR6063.O82G37 2012
823'.914--dc23
2012003304

Partially funded by a grant from the Illinois Arts Council, a state agency

www.dalkeyarchive.com

Cover: design and composition by Sarah French, painting by Ilya Repin (*Apples and Leaves*, 1879)
Printed on permanent/durable acid-free paper and bound in the United States of America

INTRODUCTION

This was my second book, a novel, written in the late nineteen forties and early fifties when I was still trying to settle into peacetime life after fighting in the infantry in the Second World War. My first novel, *Spaces of the Dark*, was a sad story about a young soldier coming home and being unable to settle, being haunted by a particularly traumatic wartime incident. This book was published by Rupert Hart-Davis and was reasonably well received. My second, *A Garden of Trees*, was turned down by Hart-Davis and another publisher. I was told—It is not unusual for a young author to write a good first novel about his personal experiences; but then with his second he is apt to go off into rigmaroles about a crazy world where a reader is not drawn to follow him. I argued—But are not the rigmaroles of a crazy world in everyone's personal experience?

A publisher did eventually agree to publish the book, but by that time I was eagerly finishing my third novel and was reluctant to go back myself to worry about *A Garden of Trees*. So I put it to one side, and the typescript has languished on musty shelves ever since in various houses I have moved between during the last sixty years. Until now, that is, when I am too old to consider starting anything new, but when being on the brink of moving to another new house the old script has unexpectedly popped up as if giving me a nudge. And I have wondered if there might be some interest in a story of that chaotic time so long ago.

When I was writing *A Garden of Trees* I had been out of the army for three or four years: I had married, had gone on a long honeymoon to a small island in the West Indies where I wrote much of *Spaces of the Dark*. My wife and I would listen on a small crackling radio to the world news, the main items of which were all about the likelihood of a third world war: Russia with its vast conventional forces and occupied satellite states was said to be threatening to invade the West. So now there were suggestions that since we and the Americans had atomic bombs and the Russians as yet had not, would it not be wise for us to drop a few of our bombs on Russia first before they got theirs, which soon they surely would. Well, was there not enough evidence here for people to experience the world as mad?

My wife and I might have stayed on our tiny island but we did not want to feel quite cut off from even such a world; but we also did not want to feel part of the functioning of madness. So when we got home we looked around, and bought a small hill-farm in North Wales, in an area where my wife had been happy as an evacuee in the war, and for which I had saved up enough money during the war from the income from a trust made by my mother's family in America. We hoped we might thus find some life of sanity away from the belligerence of a confrontation-obsessed world.

We had a go at running our farm as if it were some Garden of Eden—with cattle and pigs and a small flock of sheep thrown in. I supposed it was unlikely that we would have made much of a success of it anyway; but soon my wife Rosemary became pregnant; and there was no piped water to the farmhouse, and electricity came from a water-wheel in the village that froze up in winter. And there were no pregnancies in Eden.

We took a break in London for the birth of the baby, and then returned with a helper to our idyll of a stone cottage with its wild mountain stream rushing past the back door. But then Rosemary became pregnant again, and this time there were signs of a threatening miscarriage. Rosemary's family now stepped in with resolute sanity and arranged for her and our child to be taken by ambulance to her grandmother's vast house in Hertfordshire, where they could be attended by nurses and doctors. And here eventually the new baby was born, and flourished. But I had to return to our hillside fastness alone, to see the gradual disposal of our animals. And to get on with the writing of *A Garden of Trees.*

The story concerns a sister and a brother slightly younger than myself, and the narrator and a slightly older man. We were all of us—author and his four characters—trying to find a pathway of sanity in what seemed an insane world. And we were all discovering—what? that one cannot create one's own Garden of Eden; one can have such a vision, but then has to work for whatever fragments of it one might be able to make real. What one sees around one as the madness of humanity is simply an aspect of the way in which life works: nature is savage; evolution is ruthless and not within one's control. Love is usually for what one has not got, not for what one has. What one has, one can learn to cherish, but what one plants in one's garden is apt to be knocked down like skittles.

One of the blessings or banes that is likely to crop up in such a setting is religion. This is experienced by the characters in *A Garden of Trees*: it was experienced by myself, that lonely autumn at the farm with hopes and expectations falling like leaves around my head. I had a letter from my oldest friend from childhood and the army saying that he was planning to become a monk. I replied that I thought he was insane. Correspondence swirled and eddied to and fro. My sanity, and that of the scenes I was writing in my book, bobbed up and down like a small boat in a rough sea. It takes a while for such a voyage to discover—perhaps never stability, but some buoyancy.

It used to be a tenet of the fashionable literary world—and for all I know still is—that the experiences of a writer's life have no bearing on a consideration of his work. This has always seemed to me a source as well as a symptom of insanity. With the cropping-up of this old script, there should at least be no such danger from my own clumps of trees.

NICHOLAS MOSLEY, 2012

A GARDEN OF TREES

I
THE BEGINNING

1

It was at a political meeting that I first saw Marius. Sixty policemen went past me in a bus—an extraordinary sight. A double-decker bus, the policemen piled on top of each other in rows, like vegetables, prize-winners surely. They all had their helmets on and seemed identical. Or like pelicans, perhaps, with their hard domed heads; but within the little glass cases of the windows more lifeless and remote. The bus was momentarily held up in the traffic and the crowd turned to stare at it. Nobody laughed. Then the traffic moved and the bus swam on—a queer intent-looking fish with its belly-load of sixty dispassionate Jonahs. I wondered if it would ever spew them out.

Marius was on the edge of the crowd, on a corner. He watched the bus go by with an expression of grim and happy amazement. He was a huge man, hearty, standing in an old stained raincoat with his hands in his pockets and his tallness leaning forwards to where his head, thrust downwards, seemed to collect the shadows. It was this that I remember in him. The projections of his face—his cheek-bones, jawbones, eyebrows—appeared to gather the darkness round them as in a too emphatic photograph. It was as if the light came only from the other side of him, although the street was pale and clear with the impersonal glaze of February. His hair too—curly or straight, I couldn't tell which—seemed to dull the light, absorb it, lying thick upon his head with a quite incidental neatness. He was like some figure in an early silent film. I could not imagine him speaking.

The bus had stopped again a little beyond him, and he went up to it, peering, like a child examining the fish in an aquarium. He walked up the line of windows and then back again; the policemen never moved. Backwards and forwards like the judge at the show. Then he stepped back onto the pavement and smiled.

There was the sudden blast of a loudspeaker. I had come to the meeting idly, as a spectator, because I wanted to see how such affairs were conducted. I was not interested in politics; but I had wanted to see what life there was here, in the streets, among the people who had to make a business of it. I had not found much in the life that I knew. This was the end of the nineteen forties, not long after the war. The loudspeaker was booming, insistent, like a bell rung close to the ear. It surged and eddied on the air in waves, the rolling swing of a bell hitting the ear physically, to pierce it. It knocked the mind off its balance as the rollers of the sea knock the body off its feet. I had no idea where the noise was coming from. The words were unintelligible.

Marius and I were on the edge of the crowd, in the wrong street perhaps, but to have approached the noise any closer would have been like walking into a cave where the waves break over the opening. So we stood still, resisting it, while the crowd wandered past us blankly, edging nearer and nearer to the center of the noise. Like stirred-up mud sinking back to the bottom of a pool they drifted; and we were like stones becoming visible out of the murk.

I stayed by Marius because even from that first sight of him I wanted to know him. In the sepulchral dirtiness of the streets he became defined as something living; in the graveyard of East London he was an intruder, like a tree. He seemed to spread his roots around him like an aura upon which the weeds of the graveyard would not grow. The crowd, as they went past him, circled him deferentially and left a space between their bodies and his. He had a power either of the plague or the angels. I wanted to know which. Or if it were both.

The crowd were scurrying now. They were all small beside him. Tiny, wiry men like bantams; men in caps, men with their trousers hitched so far up that they had to step jerkily, like ducks, walking from the waist. Then fatter, smoother men hustling along busily like balloons when the air is expelled from them; rotund dominant men blowing along by the pressure of their own innate distention; with prominent hips, tight hips, their legs working from their knees and no waist at all. And then the youths, all oily, hair like seaweed, all hair, nothing but dangling greasy heads on matchstick bodies and heads nodding, clamorous, their mouths blindly and ferociously demanding attention like wounds. And then Marius.

Marius was like a monster in the land of the damned. But there did not seem to be life except with him.

The crowd took us at last. There was a rush from behind, and we were carried, unresisting, up a side street. There we could see the loud-speaker. Six great trumpets stood on top of a van like some immemorial gramophone; cones which might at any moment, surely, be turned into blunderbusses to scatter us with grapeshot. And the sound bellowing out of them in waves; more steady than a gramophone, more persistent; a giant's loudspeaker and a giant's voice and a man in a grey suit on top of the van, his hands on his hips, speaking quietly.

At first that was all I could see. The light was failing; in half an hour it would be dark. I was jostled into the front garden of a house; and then, by raising myself on the railings, I could see further. I saw the small circle of men placed round the van; hard, serious men, standing at ease, in raincoats. Marius had been wearing a raincoat. I wondered if he might be one of them. But Marius had disappeared. And outside the small circle of henchmen were the police, scores and scores of them, just standing motionless between the guardians and the crowd.

I looked for Marius. He must have pushed past me when I had stepped into the garden. The crowd was beginning to surge. Some women complained.

I liked the women better than the men. They were more individual; the older ones solid, controlled, exercising judgment. They were on their own mostly, despising the herd-nervous flotsam of the men. The tide rolled about them and left them calm. Short women, rather square, with handkerchiefs round their heads and carrying shopping-bags although it was a Sunday. And every here and there was a young girl, on tip-toe, with the savagely pretty face of a fox or squirrel—one of those childishly confident East End girls whom one expects to be a gangster's moll or a rich man's mistress but who never are because they are so respectable. Girls with wide cheek-bones and slanting eyes and reddish hair piled up on their heads in tiers, brown coated and skirted (long coats, short skirts, so that only a small and surprising band of skirt was visible), and stockinged in the best, the very best, silk. From a distance they were beautiful.

And then someone began to sing. At first it was only a group of youths opening and shutting their mouths, silently, because nothing could be heard above the unending boom of the loudspeaker. But gradually, as the group solidified itself around a suddenly upraised banner like one of those legendary squares amid the chaos of Waterloo—the banner bounding slightly above their grease-plumed heads to give assurance to their movements and indeed some conformity to the otherwise haphazard opening and shutting of their mouths—the singing became audible; tentative at first, like the preliminary murmurs of chickens in a thunderstorm; then taking strength; and during a momentary pause of the loudspeaker it suddenly rang out clear and strong, shockingly almost, a solemn tuneless song grated out with the unholy desperation of hymns that are sung in lifeboats or in earthquakes, a frail yet determined demonstration of will that threatened to defy even the eternity of the loudspeaker. And then there was the clatter of horses, and a line of mounted police came trotting into the crowd.

Until that moment the scene had presented at least the semblance of order, even if it did not possess the purpose I had been looking for. But with the arrival of the mounted police all action and order failed. At Waterloo the squares were supposed to have held, I believe, against even the most extravagant charges; but these did not, and this was hardly a charge—more like a jogging up the Mall to an opening of Parliament or some equally redundant traditional procedure. But in the Mall the crowds were guarded by two lines of soldiers; they were safe from the lovely, the terrifying horses; and here, where the horses were on top of them, they were not.

And they were lovely horses. Big bays and chestnuts; big snorting geldings edging into the crowd sideways, stamping, crouching rather; beautiful horses beautifully kept with fine, shiny coats and the skin jerking up and down around their withers; big mares clattering, slipping slightly, their eyes wide, haunches trembling, prancing in tiny controlled steps into the crowd who wobbled and fell back as if elephants were upon them. It was not a panic, not a rush—just a queer boiling hubbub of wrestling compliant; a nervous instinctive fear such as people have for mice or toads, not the fear of tigers, of the jungle. But the horses went on edging in, remorseless, beautiful; and then a child went down, and a woman after it, and then the quick balloon-blown hustling of the men went over them, and the shouting rose, crescendoing. Then a whole row of women seemed to trip over at once, like ninepins; and the men backed eddying round them, pausing, bending to help them up. But the horses came on, shuddering, insistent, and knocked the bending men on top of the women, and then it was near to panic, suddenly there was fear. From under the delicate bone-brittle hocks of the horses people picked themselves up, picked the children up, turning kneeling with their hands up in front of their faces and then hurrying, feverishly, out of the way of the monsters. And it was then that I saw Marius again—he was standing as if wedged between the tail of one horse and the head of another, standing quite unmoved and serious and staring into the horse's eye as if he had already appraised its physical points and was now more concerned with its character, its temperament; staring at the horse and then looking down to see a fat demented child on the ground at his feet and picking it up and with one swift and exaggerated movement lifting it clean over the horse's head into the arms of a pedestrian and bewildered policeman; then turning to find the mother screaming for it from behind the barrier of flashing hooves and bridles and going over to her to offer her his hand, politely, to lead her through the burning ring of flesh and leather, Brunnhilde-like, and introducing her to the policeman who was indeed showing signs of impatience with the howling child who had bitten him on the finger. The mother seized the child and ran; and then the horses were past us. In a few moments the street was almost deserted.

I had been behind the railings and was apart from the disturbance; but why had it started? The crowd had been orderly, systematic;—at least no more heedless than a Saturday afternoon football crowd. And the singing, so frail, no more than a Salvation Army demonstration. So why the cavalry? What orders had been given to reduce the evening to sterility? This had happened when the singing started, but it was the horses that had caused the disturbance, nothing else. And now the meeting was over. The streets were cleared, the loudspeaker quieted. There was nothing except the policemen and Marius and me.

What was Marius then? Perhaps a plain clothes detective, perhaps some secret agent; or perhaps he had come to study horses for a zoo.

"That was a strange business," I said.

"Yes," he said. He spoke quite naturally, hardly bothering to look me up and down.

"I can't see why they wanted to break it up."

"Oh well," he said, "I think they always want to break things up, don't they?"

"Do they?" I said.

"Yes."

"But why?"

"Well," he said, "it's the fashion. It's what people want. The extraordinary thing about this country is that people always seem to get what they want."

"But they don't seem to want anything."

"No," he said. "That's another extraordinary thing."

We walked down the darkening street. He did not seem to be sarcastic. He talked in an offhand way, rather distant.

"But they want things for themselves," I said.

"Yes," he said.

"Comfortable things, crazy things."

"Yes."

"It all seems rather a mess to me."

"Yes," he said.

Such a strange man, with his agreements. I was sure he wasn't being sarcastic. At that time (I was still quite young) I thought that I could always get to know people by talking to them, by saying the things that would please them, and as a rule I had been successful with those I had wanted to know. At least, I thought that I had known them. But I had no idea what to say to Marius. I felt, rather foolishly, that when I spoke to him not only were my words wrong, but my whole tone of voice, my expression too. It was almost as if on my old formula I was incapable of knowing anybody. So I kept quiet.

"So," he said, "I expect that they even want you to think them a mess!" He peered at me amicably.

We were getting back towards the crowd. I could see the bus parked in a side street, like a whale washed up in a dockyard. The horses were gone. A line of policemen on foot was pushing the crowd back, advancing wearily upon them, causing grumbles. The crowd retreated, keeping clear of the police, not wanting to touch them. Then suddenly a man detached himself from his neighbours, wrapped his raincoat around himself, scraped his feet along the ground once or twice like a boxer in his corner, and charged the policemen. He ran like a man approaching the long jump, leapt, and was bounced back deftly by restraining arms. It seemed a quite dispassionate performance. He tried it once again, a little more wildly this time, burrowing his head slightly, almost diving. The police took little notice of him. He bounced comfortably. Then he rejoined his friends. It was as if he had to make some purely ritualistic effort to assert himself, to ensure his self-respect; as if it were some animal instinct within him to make him hurl himself thus; like a monkey that hurls itself against the bars of its cage, catches itself, and then returns to its corner to scratch. He was a tough, rotund little man—one of the balloons. There was certainly nothing purposeful about him.

"There," I said to Marius. "That's what I mean."

"That?" he said. "Yes."

We went up a side street. We were on the inside of the police cordon, alone. The street at first was empty, with doors closed, giving the impression of enormous events elsewhere. Then, at the far end, some men appeared, running, looking over their shoulders like fugitives. When they were clear into the street they stopped, hopping sideways, and tried to appear at ease. A number collected, forming a column. They were demonstrators who, having evaded the police, were about to demonstrate. They huddled into their column and came marching down the street in a thin line, wispily, all bedraggled and out of step. They trilled some chant about killing. A schoolboy crocodile on the trail of its schoolboy prey.

"Perhaps you'll see something else," Marius said.

Along the other side of the street came a girl and boy, carrying newspapers. The crocodile saw them, paused, seemed to shiver along its reptile length and then broke, setting upon them. The boy and girl went down, crumpling, and then were out of sight. They were buried beneath the reptile bodies. There were some youths jumping up and down on the edge of the crowd trying to get a look, to be in on it, their hands rested friendlily on their companion's shoulders. It was all quite quiet—just the whispering of feet, the feet of the insects, the scurry of cockroaches towards their hole, their refuge; and their refuge was this, the beating up of the girl and the boy. Marius was walking towards them steadily, his hands coming out of his pockets, I following him; and when he reached them he made a way dispassionately through the crowd until he came to the girl and boy, the flailing arms and the plunging movement of fists fading down before him, the youths stepping back, tossing their hair, wondering; then he was above the two crouching figures on the pavement and the boy had his arms wrapped round his head and the girl was gripping the railings as if she were chained. But they were unhurt, unscratched even—after the fists and the kicks they were not even so greatly perturbed—for the boy, seeing Marius above him, stood up quickly and ran, and then waited about twenty yards off: and the girl, pulling herself up by the railings and shaking herself seemed more concerned with the state of her stockings than with any bodily harm. She pulled at her clothes angrily, and then turned to the crowd, shouting something unintelligible at them, but as she marched off proudly to join the boy they did nothing to stop her except follow her with jeers, and at the end, when she was almost past them, snatch her papers from her and hurl them into the air from which they fell, rather damply, upon a neighbouring doorstep. The boy ran to pick them up, and the crowd lurched threateningly; but he got them, and tidied them, and the two of them proceeded on their way down the street. So it was all a game after all, I thought; they are only children and these are only children's tears. And then a brick hit Marius.

It hit him on the temple, obliquely, so that his head jerked round and he staggered rather, then felt for his forehead with the back of his hand and was examining the blood on it while the echo of the brick still clattered against the stones. He dabbed at his forehead again, cautiously, and he was reaching for his handkerchief while I was advancing futilely upon the crowd trying to alarm them with my fear; and then they left us. They reformed their column. Someone grated an order. They wandered off like prisoners into the dusk. Marius was carefully folding his handkerchief into a pad.

"Are you all right?" I said.

"Yes," he said.

"I should like to murder the lot of them," I said.

"I should like a brandy," he said.

We went to find a pub. Marius looked as he always looked, but then he never looked quite as if he belonged to himself. I wondered why he had been the only person to get hurt. Perhaps they had felt that he was more than a child and a gamesplayer, and had resented him. They had certainly left him quickly enough when he had been standing dabbing his forehead at the side of the street.

We got through the police cordons. The crowds were now spasmodic, wandering in groups. It was cold, heavy evening, full of damp.

"What time is it?" he said.

"Six o'clock," I said.

"Then I must ring up."

That was all he said. His head had stopped bleeding. We walked into a pub and he went through to the telephone.

The bar was tough, crowded, frightening. I ordered two brandies. The others were all drinking beer. They were old men mostly, hard grizzled men, quiet in their authority. The pubs were probably the only places in London where their authority still prevailed. Outside it was the rule of youths on the pavements, middle age in the offices, women in the homes. The old men left the rackets to the outsiders. In the pub they were patriarchal like priests; and even some of the racketeers, intruders at the bar, seemed aware of their own vulgarity. For the old men were tough. Seeing me and my two double brandies one of them said to me, "There's a door marked gentlemen for the likes of you."

"What?" I said.

"I said there's a door marked gentlemen for the likes of you."

"Oh," I said. I was nervous and did not know what he meant. I was thinking that he must be a nice old man to be talking to me so.

"And do you know what there is when you get through it," he said. He was smiling slily into his beer.

"Oh yes," I said.

I eventually understood what he meant. I stood gripping my two double brandies at the bar, unable to retreat and unable to reply. I wanted to answer him, to win him round, to expose this gentlemen rubbish; but I knew that if I opened my mouth I should sound either querulous or superior. I felt that this failure was somehow Marius's fault, and I wanted Marius to return to deal with it. Meanwhile I could feel them all grinning at me, all being drawn into the joke, all waiting happily for the hopelessly one-sided skirmish between the cockney and the toff. It was all according to form. I must be easy with them, I thought, and then they will accept me. I grinned stupidly at the old man and his beer. But it was no use; I was only doing it through cowardice, so that they should accept me. The old man was winking to his companions, they were gathering round; I was twirling my brandy glasses for the hundredth time and trying to force my face to assume a less ridiculous expression; and then Marius returned.

The old man looked Marius up and down. "I was saying there's a door marked gentlemen for the likes of you," he repeated. I found myself hating him. I wanted Marius to rub him in the dirt. I hated his glib complacent repetitions.

"What?" Marius echoed.

The old man repeated his statement yet again, and I wanted to sneer at him.

"For me?" Marius said. "But I don't want it." He was looking round vacantly for the door marked gentlemen.

"It's all the likes of you are fit for," the old man said. He was still winking and grinning and one of the intruders began to copy Marius's voice in the unbearable music-hall version of the Oxford accent.

"Well I'm drinking brandy and you're drinking beer," Marius said, "and I expect you'll have to use it before me." He drank his brandy and the intruders giggled.

"There's some would like to be drinking brandy but can't," the old man said.

"Well I'll get you a brandy," Marius said. "And then you'll be happy, because you won't have to go through the door marked gentlemen."

He ordered three more brandies and the old man accepted his silently. Now I did not hate the old man, I loved him, and I wanted him to love Marius. His companions were making faces rather desperately; they were losing their grip.

Marius looked genial and unconcerned. "Why all this talk about lavatories?" he said.

"You're all right," the old man said.

Marius laughed.

"Yes," Marius said.

"And I know what I'm talking about," the old man said he was swaying slightly with his elbow on the bar and his eyes watery.

"You are lucky," Marius said.

"I know what I'm talking about," he repeated.

Those who had seemed to be intruders at the bar were giggling. The old man advanced on them suddenly and swore at them with effortless ferocity. They protested, alarmed. Then the old man flung back his arm, clearing a space around him, and waited.

"I think we'd better all have a brandy," Marius said.

"No," the old man said, "beer." He leant across the bar and made signs at the barman like a tic-tac man.

"This is mine," I said.

He looked at me. "All right," he said. "But beer will do."

We all drank. The intruders were silent. They let their glasses stand for a moment and then they lifted them ceremoniously and drank in unison. I did not know how Marius had done it. After the sneers and the antagonism it was as if we were all suddenly in love.

"Hooray!" the old man said.

"Yes," Marius said. The old man swayed forwards and touched him on the arm.

"What do you think will happen?" he said.

"Perhaps something like this," Marius said.

"Out there? In the streets?" The old man looked round for somewhere to spit.

"Every now and then," Marius said.

"Not in my lifetime," the old man said.

"Sometimes."

"Ah, you're still young."

"It makes no difference," Marius said.

We were gathered round Marius as if he were a prophet. The old man still had hold of his arm and I could see his fingers move as if he were stroking him.

"You watch out then," the old man said. "You watch out it doesn't work the other way."

"On me?" Marius said.

"Yes. They'll hate you. I'm telling you. You'll see."

"Well . . . " Marius said. He seemed to think for a moment and then put his glass down and turned to me. "When you say it's a mess," he said, "I know what you mean and it is: but you don't see that none of this matters. Nothing now matters except the way in which you and the mess affect each other. You don't like your point of view because it doesn't really give you a view at all. And if it's a view that you're looking for then you want to reach a point from which the view will not be your own. I think that is what matters." And when he had finished he laughed and took up his glass again and the old man was already making tic-tac signs for more beer.

I do not remember him saying much more than this. I do not remember any of us knowing him or understanding him. The intruders were watching their manners and the old man was drunk and I was knowing nothing except some quite impersonal feeling of elation; yet between the time that he had rung up and the time that the girl arrived we were all in some way giving him our worship.

When the girl came in she came through the door like a ghost, like a thing that goes through solid objects. I saw her in the mirror at the back of the bar, and one second it was Marius and the next second it was her, and she was coming up to us quick and direct and I could see the alarm of her eyes where they stretched like an animal. I do not remember what she wore, except that it was something bright and plain, and I don't remember what she carried: I do not remember if at that moment I thought her beautiful, but I know that she was frightened and that she smiled and that she came into the room not as a girl or a person but a ghost.

"I say," she said. "Have you seen that bus with all those policemen?"

"I was afraid you might have trouble getting through," Marius said.

"But are they going anywhere?" she said. "I mean is there a conductor or anything to start them and stop them?"

"Have a drink," Marius said.

"What would you like?" I said.

"Water please. But do you suppose they have any tickets?"

She was a medium sized ghost with medium hair and everything else about her quite exceptional and then, standing close to me, she became flesh and blood—a tough straight flesh like a tulip and blood which gave her the nervousness of an animal. She had a wide mouth and soft brown eyes and when she spoke she spoke with the whole of her body as if there were some violence within her to make her dance. It was as if she would respond to a touch or even a presence. She took the glass of water from me, and when it was in her hand I half expected it to bubble over and spill.

All the people in the pub were watching her. I supposed people always watched her. The barman was wiping the bar and lifting up the glasses to get at the underneath of them, and as he leaned forwards with the cloth he was watching her and Marius out of the tops of his eyes. Everyone was silent. And then suddenly she laughed, and some of the water did spill, and this time I did expect the glass to fly out of her hand in some uncontrollable spasm of amusement.

"But how did you get up here?" she said.

"I've been hit on the head by a brick," Marius said.

"Oh dear," she said.

"A small one," Marius said.

"Your poor head," she said.

The old man solemnly raised his glass to her. She responded to him, quickly, as if he had touched her. They drank.

"I knew a man once who was hit by a brick," she said. "But I think it was on his elbow. So I supposed that's different."

"Yes, that's different," Marius said.

"It's dreadful," she said. "I never can tell a story."

"That story was all right," the old man said. "I'm telling you. Never you mind it being a bad story."

"I think it's because my mouth gets so full of dribble," she said.

I could not think of anything to say. I had never met such people. I began to be afraid that without such people I had never met anyone at all.

"I've been trying to buy a musical box," she said.

"Oh," I said.

"It's for a wedding present. Do you think a musical box is a good wedding present?"

"Yes," I said. Again I could think of nothing else.

She turned to Marius. "There," she said, "he thinks it's a good wedding present." Marius was drinking. Her voice and her body moved back to me. “Thank you,” she said. The corners of her eyes were wrinkled like flowers. “Were you hit on the head by a brick?”

“No,” I said.

Outside in the street there were some children playing. I could hear the noise of them each time the door opened to let someone in. They were playing soldiers, playing war behind the dustbins. They were banging old tins and shouting, and then one of them put his head round the door and pointed a stick at Marius and made a sound like a gun going off. He was a small boy with an old army cap on his head, and he stood there grinning. The barman shouted at him and he swung his stick backwards and forwards like a machine-gun and then he ran off back into the street. He had surprised us.

“Them kids,” the barman said. “You'd have thought we'd had enough of it without them kids going round playing soldiers.”

“Yes,” Marius said.

“And what's going to happen to them?” the old man said. “What's going to happen to the kids in the streets?”

“I suppose they'll continue,” Marius said, “until it kills them.”

“It's a dirty game,” the old man said. “It's a dirty rotten game to be out in the streets chucking bricks around and chucking bombs around when you get too big for bricks.”

“How are you going to stop it?” Marius said.

“I don't know. I'll be out of it before the next one comes. I've had enough of it. It's you who'll have to do the stopping.”

“I can't stop anything,” Marius said.

The girl was standing close to him as if she wanted to impart something to him without telling him, without looking at him even; trying to impart something serious just by the way she leant and the way she became impersonal so suddenly when she was serious.

“What can you do?” I said.

Marius laughed. “What can I do?” he said to the girl.

“Can't you make them frightened?” she said.

“*I* can't frighten them,” he said.

“No, but I mean, can't you make them frightened for themselves?”

The old man put his glass down on the counter and stretched towards her. "Come here," he said: "Come here a minute." She was nervous. His fingers stretched out to her like the branches of trees. "But they are frightened," he said: "of themselves; — they are frightened."

"Oh no," she said. "I don't think they are. Not really frightened."

"Come here," he said.

"Not frightened for themselves. I said for, not of." She spoke in a queer flat voice, different from before. Her serious voice, I supposed—her impersonal voice; the voice that she used perhaps when she was making people frightened for themselves. I did not know then what she meant, but I felt it. And I think the old man did too, for he let go of her suddenly and swayed back again and said, "frightened of hell, perhaps," and she said,

"Yes!"—a grave and unearthly monosyllable like a clap.

There was a moment's silence, a silence throughout the room, and then there was a scraping of a chair and a laugh and Marius was taking it up and turning and ordering more beer even as the girl looked at me with her queer soft alarming eyes and her mouth half smiling, and then her face became twisted and her eyes went down and she left the smile somewhere in the spaces between us, and it was lost, and I was frightened, as if I myself were a ghost.

We were there for another quarter of an hour, but I do not remember much about it. Marius was joking with the old man most of the time, and the girl joined in with one or two of the others, although I do not think she had her heart in it quite like Marius had. I was thinking about what she had said, and I was frightened, frightened for myself. I wanted to get away on my own to think about it, for I found that I could not speak to them any more. I had wanted to go on with them, to ask them to dinner perhaps, but now I could not approach them. I felt separated from them by enormous distances, the distances by which they had separated me from my past life, the distances in which her smile had got lost. For I felt separate from everybody. I had felt earlier that my old contacts were worthless, and now I knew that as yet I was not capable of having contact with them. As I looked round the pub I became aware of it for the first time as a place—a place of loneliness. The bottles and glasses on the shelves seemed to be symbols of infinity, the infinity of distance between others and myself. The bottles touched, but there was no contact. Only the cold chink of glass, the surface scratch, the brittle breakable aloneness of objects. Even the light was reflected: there was no contact. I could not speak to Marius and the girl because I was hard like glass and was afraid of breaking.

Before they left the old man handed something to Marius, a charm, I think—some seated figure carved in wood. Marius tried to refuse it, but the old man pressed it on him, pressed it into his hand, honouring him. So Marius received it. They had their contact. Then the girl held out her hand to the man and said goodbye. As he took it he looked as if he were crying. Then she shook hands with me, and she was nervous, not looking at me. Marius followed her to the door and he waved at me and then went out. I went to the door to watch them. As they turned the corner the small boy with the army hat jumped out from behind a wall and waved his gun at Marius. They paused, and I think the girl looked back at me, but I could not be sure. Perhaps she was only looking at the boy. It did not matter much anyway because the distance was so great.

2

I did not see either of them again for about a year. I went abroad, writing a book, traveling alone through France and Spain and trying to pretend that loneliness did not matter. Then I got on a boat and traveled further, and by the time I came home I had almost forgotten what it was like to live in company, to have contact with people. On the homeward voyage I shared a cabin with an Australian—a man who had something to do with fruit I think—and he did his best with me.

I liked him, but we had nothing to say to each other. I had really got out of the way of talking to anyone.

At Southampton there were a number of people on the quay to welcome us. The ship edged in sideways through the floating scum, and the people stood on their toes and waved their handkerchiefs. Above them the cranes were like skyscrapers. There was a small child holding a Union Jack and shouting, but they could none of them be heard. It was a slow business. The tugs were pulling in opposite directions, and men with ropes seemed to be fishing in the sea. After a time the people on the quay gave up trying to make themselves heard. It is difficult to keep up the appearances of a welcome for an hour and a half. They sank back quietly into the shelter of the cranes, and soon stopped smiling. It was a windy day, and they had to hold their hats.

I was leaning on the rail of the ship, and I could feel my cabin companion lurking behind me, wanting to talk.

He came up to me. "Well," he said, "there's nothing like home." He was a thin wedge-faced man, with a small moustache.

"No," I said.

"And you've been away a long time. A year's a long time to be away from home."

"Yes," I said.

"But you needn't worry. I've been away longer."

"No," I said.

He was rolling a cigarette, smoothing and flicking it with deft fingers and then dabbing at it with his tongue. He had two gold teeth, rather savage, and his close-cropped head was like fur.

"You'll be going to your people then? Your people's here?"

"Yes," I said. "Well no, not exactly."

He tapped the damp cigarette with his thumbnail, and then lit it. The paper burned fiercely in spite of the wet.

"You know," he said, "you're a funny bird."

"Funny?"

"Yes," he said. "You know something? I don't like you English. I don't like you because you're so damn cold. And you're about the coldest person I've ever met, but I don't mind you. And that's funny."

"Yes," I said. The ship was into the quay now, effortlessly, without a sound. There was an attempt at renewed enthusiasm from the welcomers, but it was carried away like paper in the wind.

"Look," he said. "You come out and do the town with me to-night. You're coming up to town?"

"Yes," I said.

"Well you'll come out with me. You'll be better for it."

"I'm afraid I can't," I said. "But thank you all the same."

"You don't mind my asking you?"

"No," I said.

We leaned on the rail, side by side. I hated Southampton, and wished that I did not have to leave the boat. From where we stood we could see the factory chimneys, and the white steeples of the churches quite dwarfed, like toys. I wished that I could have said to this man: You come out and do the town with me, and I will introduce you to my friends; but I did not know what my friends were called.

"You got friends in town?" he said.

"One or two," I said, "but I don't know what's become of them now."

"You're a funny bird," he said.

A gangway was pushed into the side of the ship. A line of officials lingered on it like caterpillars.

"You ever get lonely?" he said.

"Sometimes," I said.

"You got a girl, I mean? Anything like that?"

"Not much," I said.

"Well I don't know," he said. "You're a funny bird."

I had often thought of Marius and the girl during the time that I had been away. I had hoped that one day I might know them again, in order that I might find out about them. For having met them once, I knew only the unreality of that meeting; and it was an unreality that seemed to have spread to every other situation that I approached. And yet I thought that it could only be through them that reality could be regained. For as I had traveled I had built up fantasies around them, and they had haunted me. It seemed at times that my conception of them lived a life of its own with me—a recurring dream that ran its course on unknown levels of my mind but which rose, every now and then, into consciousness through some fissure of emotion. And it was through these fissures that I thought I had to probe. I remember a time when I was among some Roman ruins in the South of France and I had gone to sleep in the sun, and when I woke up the place was empty, quite empty, but I was sure they were there, and I ran down the old white rocks looking for them, the girl and Marius, the dead white rocks in the dusty sun, and of course they were not there, there was nothing there, nothing but centuries, and the heat of the sun that was insistent like a noise.

"I like a bit of company myself," my companion said.

"Yes," I said.

Or there was a time during the carnival in Trinidad when the people were out dancing on the savannah, they were dancing in masks and wild dresses, banging the lids of dustbins for drums, hammering; and I was amongst them walking through them and the noise was in discords like something breaking, the surface breaking, like a drill on the road; and through the clamour of the crowd I was looking for Marius and the girl and feeling for them and the noise with the heat was beating against the ground seeming to lift me up and carry me and I was floating; and I did not find them and of course they were not there although several times I felt their presence like this and wondered.

"Don't you ever let your hair down?" my companion said, grinning.

"It's long enough already," I said. He looked at me and began to laugh.

There was some coming and going on the gangways now. The deck was deserted. Below us the passengers were proceeding in jerks along the quay. They could move only a few yards before they dropped some of their luggage. I pointed to them.

"Like a sack race," I said.

My companion was still laughing. I was surprised. "You know something?" he said. "You're dry, you're really dry. I didn't think you were, but you're dry." He was bounding his head up and down and showing his two gold teeth, and from the tone of his voice I think he meant it as a compliment.

In London the crocuses were out in the parks and the spring was early. People were taking off their coats and lying on the grass, but they kept apart from each other, aloof, and their eyes were cautious as if they did not trust the sudden sun. In the streets they hurried past with their gaze on shop windows, on the advertisements, or on their clothes, like people who are intent on avoiding unwelcome friends. In the buses they were neat and inscrutable as if the avoidance had been detected, as if they were nursing some insult with the indifferent face of pretence. They were somehow on their dignity, as if the world had offended them; and this attitude was reflected in the popular headlines of the day. "Demand your rights," they shouted; "Every decent man and woman deserves the best"; and when the best was not forthcoming—"It is an insult to every Briton in the land." This was the attitude. The ordinary people had demanded a cult of ordinariness and now were indignant that it had not given them extraordinary things.

Faced with this I almost regretted that I had not stayed with the Australian. He at least had been open, and smiling, and even if I had had nothing to say to him I could sit with him comfortably in silence. Now the silence was oppressive. The Australian belonged to the new world in which ease of manner was still instinctive; in the old world it seemed that instinct had reverted to a desperate necessity to keep up appearances, without requiring either that the appearances should be pleasant or that people should know what they were hiding. I felt that I should have liked for one night to have done the town with the Australian in the new-world, careless way.

One of the first of my old acquaintances whom I met in London was Alice Kerr. I had known her for several years in an intermittent way, and we usually got on well together. She was older than me, divorced and childless, and she was said to be beautiful. I was glad to meet her because I thought that she at least would not be suffering from this strange bewilderment, and I remembered her encouraging ability to greet one after an absence as if one had never been away.

I met her buying cigarettes in Fulham Road. She was delving languidly into her bag and agreeing absentmindedly with the complaints of the tobacconist. When she saw me she said, "They've only got these small ones, isn't it ridiculous?" Her eyes were tired, and her face had the pale transparent quality of wax.

"I'm so glad I've met you," I said.

"I can't bear these ghastly small ones," she said.

She paid the tobacconist and took her Woodbines. When we were outside I said, "I should never have had the courage to come and see you on my own."

"How ridiculous," she said. "Why wouldn't you have had the courage?"

"I've been away so long. I don't seem to know anyone now."

"How ridiculous," she said. "You're looking very well." We walked up the street. She was wearing a huge coat with a stiff collar jutting up the back of her neck, like armour. This was fashionable. "Have you got one of those machines?" she asked.

"What machines?"

"Those sun-tan machines."

"No," I said.

"Everyone seems to have a machine," she said.

Talking to her had always been like playing a game in which only she knew the rules, but now a tiredness gave the impression that even she was playing it more in boredom than for fun.

"I've been to the West Indies," I said.

"How dreadful."

"I've been trying to write a book," I said.

"People are always writing books," she said.

"And I wanted to be somewhere on my own."

"Men always want to be on their own," she said. "It's so depressing."

I followed her up the steps of her house. Formerly, when she had played the game of conversation as a game and nothing else, I had liked to watch her play it, although I could not play it myself. It had then seemed strange and amusing; and there had been none of this quick sliding off the subject in peremptory denial. Now she was like someone who is learning how to skate and is frightened of being spoken to in case she will fall down. The game seemed to have turned into a rather desperate attempt to keep one's balance.

As she opened the front door she said, "I suppose you must come in, but I do think it's dreadful of you to say that you hadn't got the courage to come here on your own. I should be so ashamed."

Inside the house my inability to play the game became, as always, oppressive. I had hoped, if it was to be at best a matter of keeping one's balance, that we might give up playing altogether; but we had to have some sort of conversation and I think that this was the only sort of conversation that we knew. It was my fault that it failed. She went to make some tea and we talked through the open door in the kitchen.

"Now tell me what you've been doing," she said.

"I've told you, I've been . . . "

"Now don't start telling me about your book, for heaven's sake."

"No. Well I've been traveling . . . "

"Nor your travels. It's dreadful that no one can talk of anything except their travels. As if places mattered."

"What does matter?" I said.

"What a stupid question," she said.

She brought the tea and we drank in silence. I wondered what this thin ice was upon which everybody was skating, this frightened unmanageable surface which forced the people in the streets into a useless pose of dignity, and Alice into a nervous refusal of any offered contact. As I drank my tea I thought that perhaps she was just bored with me, but then she said: "How nice it is to see you. You're looking wonderfully well."

"Thank you," I said.

"It's such a relief to see people who are well. Most people are so dreary." She had lit a cigarette even before she had finished eating, and she was trying to brush crumbs off her skirt.

"People in London seem to be frightened of something," I said. "What is it?"

"Frightened?" she said. "What do you mean?"

"I mean that they seem to expect to be offended by something, and are trying terribly hard to appear at ease."

"People are so tired of serious things," she said.

"Then why are they serious?"

"They are not, it is only you who are serious."

"It is as if they are always looking over their shoulders to see what is following them, and there always is something following them, because they drag it along."

"Oh all this talk," she said.

"But why are they frightened?"

"Well why shouldn't they be frightened? Aren't there enough things to be frightened of? God knows I don't blame them."

"What things?" I said.

"What things? You've only got to read the papers, and then you'll see."

I did not expect this. She was standing up and brushing her clothes with the hand that held her cigarette, and the ash was spilling on her shoes. I had not thought of Alice as a person who took much notice of the papers.

"Do you mean Russia and the Bomb and that sort of thing?"

" . . . and the strikes and communists and food and everything, oh good heavens, don't you use your eyes?"

"But people aren't really afraid of all that, are they?"

"They're crazy if they're not," she said.

"I'm not."

"Well you're a baby."

I changed the conversation. I was thinking how it seemed impossible to talk to anyone now—first the Australian whom I liked but with whom I could not be at ease, then the people in the streets who were unapproachable behind their facades; and now Alice whose words seemed to rattle like skittles knocked down by every statement that I made. So I tried to talk to her of friends and acquaintances and gossip, which was familiar ground between us, but it was she who quickly returned to the conversation as if there were something in it that fascinated her in spite of her apparent distaste, as if the skittles had to be put up again and the game to continue because skittles was the only game that mattered. She had carried the tea things through to the kitchen, and she interrupted me to say: "You don't understand people at all, or else you would not be surprised that they are worried."

"I'm surprised because I didn't think they thought about serious things," I said.

"They don't talk about them, thank God, but that doesn't mean they aren't worried. You only notice things on the surface, which is why you are so stupid. People never show anything on the surface."

“I agree with that,” I said.

“And you aren’t worried because you haven’t noticed what is going on at all, not at all, or else you have done and are fool enough not to admit it.”

“But all this is on the surface . . . ” I began.

“Oh nonsense,” she said. “Absolute nonsense.”

I did not know quite what we were arguing about. She emerged from the kitchen and I watched her standing bleakly in front of the window. “But you,” I said, “you personally—are worried by it?”

“By what?” she said.

“Well, by the food and the strikes and the communists.”

“Yes,” she said. “Of course I am. It’s like always having someone behind you with a knife in your back.”

“Then why don’t you do something . . . ” I began.

“Oh,” she said, “you’d never understand. I can’t explain it to you if you don’t understand.”

I left her soon after this. We had nothing to say to each other. As I walked away down the street with the lights coming on like small explosions I thought that perhaps the loneliness that I felt was felt by everyone, that we were all cut off from each other by a failure of the expectation that once had been between us. For although I had been skeptical of Alice’s examples of fear, I had felt some truth in her perception; for in a way it was the unease of this age which, by denying any optimistic or even possible view of the future, had taken from the present its reality and meaning. And so we were all on the surface, on the thin ice surface, and time had become the fear of falling on our backs. Time was anxiety and space was a sliding sphere, and all we could expect was the unexpected. It was as if for the first time the universe had become real to us, as if we felt ourselves like fragments on the edge of relentless stars: and although I had said that this did not worry me, worry is a condition that can exist apart from care. For myself I did not care if there should be no future and no certainty, but others did, and I think it was their concern that had set the distances between us. For in every meeting and every relationship there must exist some ground upon which contact is established, and this ground had slipped into darkness with a turn of the sliding world. Those whom I met knew no means other than the old ones of custom, and I myself, at that time, knew no means at all. I only knew that those around me were on dangerous ground, alone, their eyes closed in a kind of panic, not daring to look too closely at what might lie beneath their feet; and that I, more lonely than most, could not even imagine where I was standing. But above all this I had in front of me the image of Marius and the girl, Marius and the girl who had shoved me on to the ice-rink and who were now the only people who could get me off. I was looking for them as one looks for the arm of some friendly professional, but I did not know where to find them and I did not even know who they were. I was afraid that they would forever have to remain as images, and that, in the way of images, they would grant me no more service than I could grant myself. And it did not seem, as a fragment under the starlight, that I could do very much for myself.

3

But I did meet Marius, and it was through Alice that I found him. A few days after our tea-party I received a postcard from her saying, "If you would like to come here this evening I am expecting a friend who might interest you." Just that. So I went round early and found Alice alone.

"Who is the friend?" I said.

"What friend?" she said.

"You said something on your postcard about a friend."

"Oh did I?"

"Yes."

"Well he may turn up."

I guessed from this that the friend was of some importance to her and that she hoped he would impress me. Since I hate arranged meetings where impressiveness is expected, I awaited the arrival of the stranger with some anxiety. When the doorbell rang and Alice went to answer it I propped myself defensively against the wall and prepared for the worst. And then Marius came in.

He looked younger than when I had seen him last. I think that each time I saw him throughout his life he appeared to be younger than I remembered him, as if time, in deference to his changing moods, had allowed him to reverse the process of age. He must have been very old I thought, and was now approaching youth with an energy that was apparent in the small movements of his hands and his laughing eyes. Alice introduced us, rather proudly, and I still did not hear his surname. He looked at me and put a hand to his mouth as if to hide his smile.

"Yes," he said, "we've met."

"Oh you've met, have you?" Alice said.

"Yes," I said.

"Oh dear. Men always seem to have met." She moved away from us and I could see how disappointed she was. She liked playing the game of the experimental hostess. Marius sat down abruptly and she offered him a cigarette. "Where did you meet?" she said.

"I was being lynched," Marius said.

"I'm not surprised."

"No. And then we went to a pub. It was rather strange."

"Oh very strange," Alice said.

"Men are always being lynched," I said. Marius laughed loudly and Alice looked at me with patience.

"You're right," she said. "You're right, but you'd never know it."

Marius looked from her to me and back again. I knew that this was going to be a difficult evening, but it did not seem to matter. Marius said, "Are you being lynched, Alice?"

"No," she said.

"But I'm sure you imagine you are."

"This is really a very boring conversation," she said. She opened the door of a cupboard and produced bottles and glasses.

"Alice thinks there's someone behind her with a knife," I said. I had a great desire to giggle, and I nearly overbalanced as I leaned against the wall.

"A knife?" Marius said. "A sharp knife?"

"Yes."

"Good at cutting things?"

"Yes."

"How useful," Marius said.

"Are you drunk?" Alice said; for in my efforts to maintain my balance I had toppled against some fire-tongs which fell heavily in the grate.

"Perhaps he thinks there's someone underneath him with a poker," Marius said.

Alice poured out the drinks. She looked tired. Marius continued tentatively "I should like very much to have someone behind me with a knife. I never know anyone who has a knife . . . "

"Marius," Alice said, "if you go on like this I shall scream."

"Dear Alice," he said, "I should not like you to scream."

Alice went out of the room to get some ice. Marius moved as if he was going to follow her, and then he changed his mind and came back to me. "I am afraid that Alice is upset," he said. "I think it was rather a disappointment to her that we had already met."

"Yes," I said. He was pacing up and down the room with his hand still up to his mouth.

"I think that now she will want us to hate each other," he said.

"Hate each other? Will she?"

"She may do. I think she had been expecting something from this meeting. Something else she likes . . . Do you know her well?"

"Not very."

"She is a kind person, very kind."

"Then why . . . ?"—But Alice had returned, and I could say no more.

Alice gave us drinks and Marius was polite to her. And then, in a strangely subtle way, he tried to get her into a good humour. He said all the things that she must have wanted him to say—all the things that I could never remember; and gradually, as he talked, saying nothing but saying it pleasantly, she came round to him and appeared at ease again. I listened to them, and I wondered how sincere Marius was being, and whether indeed Alice was accepting his efforts sincerely. I could not tell what was behind their formal interchange of jokes and gossip, but I sensed, as the evening progressed, that there was some battle between them that was being fought out on ground of which I had no knowledge with forces that were camouflaged from the uninitiated eye. They circled round each other like rival celebrities, but in spite of Marius's efforts—or perhaps because of them—I felt that Alice's geniality was a trifle forced. I did not bother to enquire into this too closely because sincerity did not seem to matter on an occasion like this, and besides, I was too bewildered by the surprise of meeting Marius again. I felt as I had felt the first time that I had met him—as if in some way I was separate from myself—and my only care was that this time I should be able to stay with him and learn about him, and if possible find the girl. His conversation with Alice was quite unreal to me. The battle between them touched me, however, whenever I was left alone with either one or the other of them—the first occasion having occurred when Alice left the room to get some ice. Later, when Marius had gone out to meet a friend of his, as he had said, and we had arranged to join him again in a few minutes, Alice turned to me and carried the battle for another short skirmish into the open.

"What do you think of Marius?" she said.

"I like him."

"Do you admire him?"

"Yes, I think I do." Admire was not a word that had occurred to me before.

"I can't think why everyone admires him," she said. "I think it's ridiculous. It shows what children people are."

"Does everyone admire him?"

"Oh yes. All your sort of people. I can't understand it. If you only knew what my friends, my real friends, think of him, how they laugh at him!"

"Why?"

"Really laugh at him!"

"Then they must envy . . . "

"Oh envy, that is all you can think of, as if anything were so obvious . . . "

"But . . . "

"You're so serious, so silly, but I should have thought that even you would have seen through Marius!"

"Then why did you ask me to meet him?"

"I didn't."

"Oh."

And then, when we had gone to meet Marius in the inevitable pub round the corner, I was able to leave Alice temporarily and join Marius and his friend as they stood at the bar in conversation. Marius glanced at Alice over his shoulder and then looked at me in a mocking, knowledgeable way, as if again there was in him a tendency to laugh which, owing to exigencies of the battle, he had to suppress; and when I rejoined Alice I felt that I had been drawn a little closer into the struggle although I still did not know what it was about.

Alice was restless. She made no pretence of geniality with me. She kept on glancing at Marius and his friend, and she was tossing her hair back from her face in a gesture that I knew was one of annoyance. "Look at them," she said. "What on earth are they talking about?"

"I don't know," I said.

"Fancy coming here just to talk. About themselves, too, I expect. Creeping out like moths after dark to talk about themselves."

"What is Marius's history?" I said.

"History? I don't think he has one. I wouldn't dream of asking him, anyway. It's only people like you, darling, who would ask people their history."

She had never called me "darling" before. I went on hurriedly: "But what does he do? What did he do in the war, for instance?"

"I don't know. I don't suppose he does anything. I think he only came here after the war. What does it matter anyway? Why do you want to know about him? Do you think you can understand people just by finding out about their lives?"

"Yes," I said.

"Well you can't. And if you want to know about Marius look at that man who's with him now. You can find out more about a person from small things like that than from the story of their lives."

The man was rather sinister. A thick fair-haired man with an expressionless face and tiny intent eyes: a fair moustache and grey flannel trousers and the musty military look of a staff officer. He was talking to Marius and smoking delicately, like a woman. Marius was watching him.

"What on earth can they be doing?" Alice said; and then, drawn irresistibly to attack them, she called out "Marius, can you get us a drink?"

Marius turned to her, and his companion looked sullen. Alice was smiling serenely like someone expecting to be photographed. Then Marius murmured something to the man and they came over to us. Marius introduced him as Mr. Jackson.

"How do you do," Alice said. "I hope we didn't interrupt your conversation."

"Not at all," the man said formally. He wore a thin striped tie, and his face had the rough scrubbed look of a rubber sponge. He reminded me of the men in raincoats at the political meeting. He did not sit down.

"Do go on talking if you want to," Alice said. "I am sure you must have terribly important things to say to each other."

The man stood stiffly, hating her. Marius said to him quietly, "I am sorry that there is nothing more I can do."

"You will not be there?" the man said.

"No," Marius said.

"How exciting!" Alice said. "It sounds like a robbery!"

The man went on hating her out of his small scrubbed eyes. "You will be expected," he said to Marius.

"Yes," Marius said.

"With the guns and the dynamite?" Alice mocked.

The man turned his back on her. He nodded abruptly to Marius. "I will leave you to this," he said. Then he walked out of the room. Marius sat down.

Alice began, "God, what a man. I could smell him, literally smell him. I've never met such a sinister man in my life."

Marius said nothing.

Alice turned to me and went on "Darling, now you see what it's like when men get together, how dreadful they are, how creepy, really, I think that nowadays men would rather go out with each other than with a woman."

She was speaking to me, but the battle was with Marius. He said nothing, and she went on:—

"Darling, how glamorous you look. I'm sure you wouldn't rather go out with a man like that, would you darling. Look at Marius now, isn't he dreadful, I think he must have caught some terrible disease."

Marius was sitting thoughtfully, twirling his glass, and I wondered if in these silly moments I was going to lose the chance of knowing him for ever. I wanted Alice to go, I wanted to be alone with him, but Alice seemed to be carrying the battle on to indefensible territory so that Marius would have to retreat and I should lose him in the chaos. All these 'darlings', these sneers at Marius, were part of her tactics; and I remembered how Marius had said that she might want us to hate each other. I was powerless, and it seemed that Marius was powerless too: but then Alice, incensed by his silence, blundered. She spoke to him.

"Marius," she said, "what on earth were you doing with a man like that?"

"What?" Marius said.

"That's a man who would stick a knife into you quicker than a piece of meat."

"A piece of meat?" Marius said.

"Oh don't be so dull."

"He's a vegetarian," Marius said.

Alice turned away. She shook her pale dangling hair from her forehead, and I wanted to cheer.

"He's head of the greengrocer's guild," Marius said. "He's called Munroe."

"Oh dear," Alice said.

"The last time he ate meat," Marius said, "he was fined forty shillings by his union."

"Marius," Alice said, "if you go on like this I shall leave."

"He was very upset about it," Marius said. "He told me that it felt as if there was someone always behind him with a carrot."

"I warn you," Alice said. "I can't stand it when you are so dull."

"He said it was worse than being a donkey," Marius said.

"I'm going," Alice said.

"I'm sorry," Marius said. "Thank you very much for asking me round."

Alice waited a moment and then stood up. "Goodbye," she said. Marius looked very sad. I was staring at the table not wanting to see her, for I could feel her expecting me to make some move. "Goodbye," Marius said. Then she walked away from us, and I was sorry. We both stood up and she went to the door and was gone.

Marius sat down. He remained very still and then he sighed and said "It was a pity, that, but I'm afraid I couldn't think of anything else." He scratched his head with a gesture of dismissal and pushed his half empty glass of beer away from him. "I was rather put out by that man," he said. Then he looked at me and said "Come and see Annabelle, she would love to see you," and at once I forgot about Alice and the queerness of the battle and any sorrow at our victory, for I was thinking—Annabelle, I must remember Annabelle—and I followed him into the street.

I walked a little behind him, feeling like a puppet, a puppet worked by strings. Marius was the player and the lamp-lit street our stage, and as I walked I noticed the things around me as the setting for a play, objects slung together for the purpose of illusion, and beyond us, outside the perimeter of the arc-lights, an unseen audience whose presence was felt like rain. In the gutter a man selling matches raised his head and muttered across the pavement; and a woman, dragged by dogs, swept past him like a ship. Marius stood on the curb and held his hand up for a taxi, and one swung to his bidding as if he had pulled it with a rope. We climbed in and Marius murmured instructions, and we drove away. It would not be very far, I thought—Kensington or Sloane Street, the homes of Annabelles and Mariuses—but in Knightsbridge the taxi turned right and took us up into the park. We emerged opposite the big ship-like shapes of the hotels in Park Lane, and the taxi drove between them and stopped in Grosvenor Square. Marius paid it, and we walked through the hall of a large block of flats. The floor was thickly carpeted and there were flowers on the walls: real flowers, in carved vases, and the smell of scent. We got into the lift and went up to the fourth floor. The flat where Annabelle lived was large and hot and very expensive.

The door was unlocked and Marius pushed it and went in. In the drawing-room Annabelle and a man with golden hair were sitting at the piano playing chopsticks. The man was humming and not getting the playing right. As we came in he stopped and said "Ha!" at Marius, and Annabelle went on playing the bass. Marius said, "That's Peter." He nodded to me.

"Can you play chopsticks?" Annabelle said. "No one else can." I remembered how the corners of her eyes were wrinkled.

"Yes," I said. I sat down on the stool with her, and we played. She played very quickly to try me out, and I kept up with her. I could see her laughing to herself as she went faster and faster, and she put out her tongue between her teeth. The golden-haired man watched us and tried to join in at the top of the piano, but he couldn't get it right, so he thumped on the keys with his fists. It was a huge piano, and it made a lot of noise. Marius was standing by the window holding a corner of the curtain back and looking out like a detective. Then Annabelle stopped playing suddenly and sat back with her hands in the lap of her bright red dress. "You play very well," she said.

"It's not very difficult," I said.

"No." She lifted her hand and pushed a curl from her cheek behind her ear. We were close to each other on the stool, and I was leaning away from her rather twisted. "Can you play properly?" she said.

"No," I said.

"Play something," she said, still sitting, with her hands back in her lap.

I played an old waltz, which was the only thing I knew. I played it badly, thumping it. I had learned it at school. I got some of the notes wrong.

"How impressive," she said. "Can you play anything else?"

"No," I said. "Can you?"

She played the same thing as I had done, but beautifully, as it should be played.

"How rude," said the golden-haired man. "Don't you think my sister is rude?"

"Is she your sister?" I said.

"Yes," he said. "My beautiful sister."

"I hope you are pleased," Annabelle said, finishing off with a flourish.

Peter turned away from us, and Annabelle sat sideways so that I could see her throat. "Marius," Peter said, "come away from that window. There is nothing to see."

Marius smiled and came into the middle of the room and watched us.

"The great thing about Marius," Peter said, "is that he never speaks. That's a great thing to learn. It's always so inspiring. The only time that I have ever inspired anyone was when I had an infected larynx and couldn't speak. It was at a dinner party and I never said a word. They all thought I was marvelous."

"We haven't seen you for a long time," Annabelle said to me.

"I've been away," I said.

"I'm sure Napoleon never spoke," Peter said. "I'm sure he never said a word. Do you think he did, Marius?"

"I'm sure he did," Marius said.

"I don't think so. Of course it's foolish to speak. You can never say anything so wise as what people think you might say if you don't."

"It depends what you look like," Marius said.

"I look like a lobster," Peter said, staring at a mirror.

Annabelle said to me "I am so glad you've found us. I was wondering if we would ever see you again."

"I was wondering if you would remember me."

"Oh yes," she said.

Peter was walking round the room. He was saying "Of course it's all right for you. You've got the face for it. People think you are like a God when you don't say anything. And Gods have got to be silent, or else they would make fools of themselves. What on earth could a God say that would make any sense?"

"I don't know," Marius said.

"Nothing. They can't make sense so they don't say anything. Very sensible. How terrible it would be to be a God!"

"Why?" Annabelle said.

"Because of their conscience. Think of God's conscience! Man's is bad enough, but think of God's!"

"You can't," Annabelle said.

"I can. And it makes me sick."

"That's silly," Annabelle said, and again I saw something frightening in her alarming eyes.

Marius sat down. "I have seen Mr. Jackson," he said.

"And finished it?"

"Yes. Mr. Jackson was a communist," Marius said to me.

"Oh," I said.

"I was rude to him and then we were rude to someone who perhaps is his opposite. Mr. Jackson is quite right, it is difficult to find any other alternative."

"It is easy to look," Peter said.

"One is, sooner or later, rude to everyone. One is rude until there is no one left to be rude to. Then one is rude to oneself."

"Why don't you stop?" Annabelle said.

"But we are only just starting!" Peter said. "It is impossible to start anything until one has been rude to everything. Now you have been rude to this communist you are rid of him. When we are rid of everyone we will begin!"

"Begin what?" Annabelle said.

"Whatever happens. We have to be rid of things first. We have to stop worrying about things that don't matter."

The telephone rang. Annabelle went to answer it. I watched her as she walked across the room. She stood holding the receiver loosely to her ear, with her thigh propped against a table. She was looking at Marius who was sitting in a chair with his overcoat on. She spoke vaguely into the receiver—"Oh hullo, yes no . . . no I can't, not to-night . . . if you like, yes, do . . . oh just Peter and one or two other people. All right, we'll expect you then." The red of her dress was vivid against the paleness of the room, like a rose-leaf floating in a bowl of silver. She put down the receiver and unhitched herself from the table. "Freddie," she said, "Freddie Naylor." She walked over to Marius, pushing the curls to the back of her long white neck.

"Now," Peter said, "we can be rude to him."

"He's all right," Annabelle said, standing in front of Marius and trying to tell him something.

"He thinks he's still at school," Peter said. "He will still think he's at school for the rest of his life."

"I think I know him," I said.

"He is like a dead bird."

"Yes."

"Not even stuffed." Annabelle and Marius were looking at each other like conspirators.

"He might at least have the decency to get stuffed," Peter said.

Annabelle went up to him. "Shall we have something to eat," she said, "before they come?"

"We'll get stuffed," Peter said.

Annabelle went out of the room. Marius sat in his chair as if he were asleep. I think they had been trying to say something about Peter, but I could not be sure. Peter was walking up and down. He said, "People are either schoolboys or clowns. People are always unhappy. Do you know why clowns are unhappy? Because if you make a business of laughter your leisure can only deal with tears. That is all there is left to you. I think I must be a clown."

"There is ham and lettuce," Annabelle called from the kitchen, "and a few potatoes."

"And the rest are schoolboys. A schoolboy is someone who doesn't know the difference between business and leisure, who has never laughed and never cried. They function because the rules instruct them to function, and they are blessed with the inability to ever question why."

"And lots of bread and butter," Annabelle called.

"Supposing," Peter said, "that one made a business of tears, would one then be able to laugh in one's leisure? Would it be possible? Is that what you do, Marius?"

"Do what?" Marius said.

"That is what God does. I am sure that is what God does. That is why he deals in tears. Marius, when you are silent, when people think you are a God, do you want to laugh or cry?"

"You talk too much," Annabelle said, coming into the room with a tray.

"I know," Peter said, "that is what I am talking about."

"Well don't," Annabelle said, going out again.

"Have you ever been unhappy, Marius?" Peter said.

"Yes." Marius said.

"When?"

"When I am hurt."

"That isn't an answer. Gods never answer. I don't believe that Gods are ever unhappy. I'm sure that I couldn't tell whether Marius was unhappy or not, could you?" he said to me.

"No," I said.

"Gods can be hurt," Annabelle said, coming in again with some sandwiches. She passed Peter without looking at him.

"Yes," Peter said. He watched her. Then he went to the window. "I should think so," he said. "I should think a God's about the most hurt thing there is. He should be. He asks for it. Bloody fool." He stood with his back to us. "How many people think you're a God, Marius?"

"I don't know," Marius said.

"And how many people think you're a bloody fool?"

"I don't know."

"Oh." Peter opened the window and leant out into the night. "God's a bloody fool," he shouted. Then he closed the window and drew the curtains and took some sandwiches from Annabelle's tray.

The door-bell rang. No one went to answer it. "Now I have been rude to God," Peter said. Annabelle stood sadly in front of her sandwiches as if she had suffered some momentary loss. Then Peter shouted, "Come in, come in, you unstuffed owl," and he filled his mouth with a potato. There was no reply. Annabelle went to the door and I could hear her talking in the passage, and then she came in again followed by three people. One was Freddie Naylor. Behind him came a delicate prancing man wearing a bow tie, and with them a smart girl carrying a handbag like a drum.

"Hullo Peter," Freddie said. "You know Nancy, don't you. This is Hilton Weekes."

"How do you do," Peter said, munching his potato.

"We've all come along," Freddie said. "I knew you wouldn't mind. I heard your father and mother were away, so I knew you'd be well in. I see you are." He opened his mouth and made a noise like someone blowing their nose.

"Have some lettuce," Peter said.

"Well in the liquor," laughed Freddie. He was looking round for drinks.

The smart girl was chattering to Annabelle and was writhing her mouth as if she were putting on lipstick. Her bag was suspended from straps around her neck, and every time she moved it bounced against her middle. Annabelle was watching her carefully. Hilton Weekes was flitting round the room looking at the pictures.

"I'm afraid I don't know your name," Peter said, introducing me. I told him.

"Oh yes," Freddie said. "Weren't you in the Regiment?"

"Yes," I said.

"I thought I remembered you."

"I'm afraid I left it," I said.

"Oh yes," he said. He looked away. Peter was introducing the others to Marius. Marius stood up and shook hands. The prancing man was poised beside him with his head on one side, and the girl was approaching like a one-man band. Peter was doing some joke about introducing Marius as a cardinal.

"You have been in England long?" the prancing man said. He spoke meticulously, as if to a foreigner.

"Yes," Marius said.

"You have come over to . . . ?"

"To . . . ?"

"I thought . . . "

"No," Marius said.

"Oh." The girl was staring at Marius open-mouthed. Above her head two feathers swayed like wireless-masts, and her earrings clashed faintly like cymbals. Peter began to sing, "Ta-ra-ra-boom-de-ay."

Freddie advanced impatiently upon Annabelle. "Why don't you come out with us?" he said. "We were going to have some dinner. Why don't you?"

"I can't." Annabelle said.

He caught hold of her arm in an awkward, lurching way, and she stood turned away from him while he held her. "Why not?" he said. "Come along. Don't let's have any nonsense." He pulled her arm and Annabelle swayed, letting her arm go, but her feet did not move. He looked stiff and ugly beside her.

"She doesn't want to." Peter called out. "She hates your guts, Freddie, she hates your guts."

Freddie laughed. He gave another pull at Annabelle's arm and she overbalanced, crossing her feet to steady herself. I could not see her face. The prancing man was standing in front of Marius and Marius was looking over his shiny oiled head towards Peter. "I don't know about that," Freddie said in his thick, throttled voice, "but she's going to have dinner with us, aren't you?" He squeezed her arm and I could see how he wanted to hurt her.

"You're a sadist, Freddie," Peter called. "Has anyone ever told you you're a sadist?"

"Oh are you?" the prancing man said brightly.

The smart girl swung round and caught him on the hip with her drum. The she went writhing up to Freddie. "Why should she come?" she said. "Why should the poor thing come if she doesn't want to?" She stood with her soft powdered face stretched loudly up towards Freddie's. Freddie did not look at her. Annabelle swayed on one leg with her head down, and Freddie's starched white cuff showed up against her skin like a bandage.

"Why don't you go to a girl's school?" Peter called. "Why don't you pinch Nancy, she's longing for it." Nancy became convulsed with giggles, clutching her drum to her middle.

"Come along," Freddie said, furiously.

"If you pinch Nancy," Peter said, "she'll make a noise like a hunting-horn."

Freddie took a step towards Annabelle so that she straightened out on her feet. "Well what are you going to do to-night?" he said. "What else are you doing?"

"I'm having dinner," Annabelle said. She stood miserably.

"Oh," Freddie said. He let go of her. She stood where she was. Freddie walked over to Peter. "Let's have your drinks then," he said. "Where are they?"

"No drinks," Peter said. "Only lettuces."

"On the wagon?" Freddie sneered.

"No, they've arrived," Peter said. He began to laugh uncontrollably.

Nancy was plucking at the prancing man's sleeve. "We'd better go," she said. "Don't let's stay if Annabelle doesn't want to."

"We'll stay," Freddie said. "We'll have some lettuces." He stood obstinately while Annabelle cut him some ham, and I felt rather sorry for him. Peter was still laughing, and Hilton Weekes was holding a book up, saying, "I say, has anybody read this?" and no one was taking any notice of him.

There was a silence. Freddie was chewing his ham. Then—"Annabelle has become very superior, hasn't she?" he said speaking to no one in particular.

"Oh yes," Peter said, "she's become religious."

"Oh religious," Freddie said. He looked at Marius and then at me. I suddenly realized that I was copying Marius, although I could not do it as he did. He was leaning on the back of a chair and I was propped against the piano, but I felt a fool when Freddie looked at me. Marius was smiling faintly at the carpet, but he did not look a fool. "Do you mean to say she goes to church?" Freddie said, watching Marius.

"No," Peter said: "the Church comes to her." He began laughing again, and Annabelle put a hand in front of her eyes like someone very tired. Then Peter saw her, suddenly, and he stopped laughing, so that the noise between them died.

"Oh," Freddie said. Hilton Weekes coughed nervously; he was looking for somewhere to deposit his book. The girl was by the door, a powder-puff in her hand, holding it arrested in front of her nose like a handkerchief. She looked as if she were about to sneeze. Then she said "Oh do let's go, please," in a kind of despair.

"We certainly don't seem to be very welcome here," Freddie said.

Peter looked miserably at Annabelle, who still had her hand in front of her eyes. Then he went up to Freddie. "But you *are* welcome," he said, "really; won't you stay and have a drink?"

"We'll go," Freddie said.

"But I think you're terribly nice," Peter said. "Really Freddie, I am sure I can find you a drink. Do stay."

"No," Freddie said.

"I was joking," Peter said. "I am always joking." He looked very sad and quite sincere. "You should know that I am joking." Then he turned to the girl. "I think you're terribly nice too," he said. "Can't you show us what you've got in that lovely bag?"

"Oh just one or two things," said the girl, happy now, starting to struggle with the clips.

"Do let's see."

"Come on," Freddie said, swearing furiously from the passage.

"Just the few things that I always carry about with me . . . " She was like a child showing off a new toy.

"How exciting!" Peter said.

Freddie seized the girl and dragged her into the passage. Now that Peter had become friendly he was determined to go. I supposed he thought it was a joke. I did not blame him. Hilton Weekes followed them quickly. On the landing the bag burst, scattering a few dainty objects on the floor. The girl and Hilton Weekes knelt to pick them up, and Peter was hovering round saying, "That's a nice one, that really is: I've never seen one like that before;" and Freddie was looking as if he was going to burst too. At length they gathered themselves together and went. We could hear Peter's voice following them pleasantly down the passage.

We waited uneasily. Then Peter returned. He went straight to Annabelle. "I am so sorry," he said. "So sorry, sweet Annabelle." She took her hand from her eyes and smiled. "You were quite funny," she said.

"I am an ass and a pig," he said, "and I am going to pour ashes on my head." He went into the bathroom.

"Let's go for a walk," Marius said.

"Yes," Annabelle said.

Peter joined us. His hair was neatly brushed. We set out. In the lift I had a feeling of elation that I had not felt before in my life. Peter touched Annabelle gently on the shoulder, and when she looked at him I saw that she had tears in her eyes. Marius's head was bowed as if he were asleep again. As we stepped out of the building into the night I felt as though I wanted to do something for these people because they were so peculiar.

The square was huge and moonlit. A statue stood folded like the wings of a bird. Peter said, "I should like to get out of England because England is dying."

Marius said, "You do not leave a deathbed, you go to it. You go to it because a deathbed always has meaning while life very often has not."

"England will not admit that it is dying," Peter said. "That is what makes it unbearable. There is nothing so ugly as a sick-room in which the patient has to pretend that he is well."

"There is meaning even in that ugliness," Marius said. "I do not care much about beauty and ugliness, I only care for meanings and the sadness of the world."

"I don't," Peter said. "I am too close to it. All I hate is ugliness and all I want is beauty."

Annabelle walked a little ahead of us with her coat thrown carelessly over her shoulder and the cold wind blowing against her neck. Her arms and legs were white like water, and as she moved her dress became darker than her hair which the moon made icy.

"There is no beauty without meaning," Marius said. "You may make an image of your own and call it beauty, you may give it your praise and worship all your life, but in the end it will fail you. On a death-bed it will fail you. You cannot die beautifully without meaning."

"Die beautifully?" Peter said.

"Yes. And that is what faces us. Did you not say that England was dying? Well then, you die beautifully, and that is what always faces people, as individuals, at any time in history, whether or not a civilization is dying as well."

"We should be beginning," Peter said.

"Our world is old, and with the arrogance of age it is complaining. You cannot praise it and you cannot pity it, because praise and pity are reserved for achievement. It has built its images and has seen them broken, and on its knees it is searching for the fragments that it loved. It finds them, sometimes, among the rubble of cities—a pedestal, a memory, limbs of old glories that are dug from the dust and refastened with wires to give an illusion of solidity. And then illusion is there, for some: a civilization will worship its images until there is no one left to worship them. But when there is no one left then few will ever have known what their ending has meant. And you, you hate the world, but it is you who are part of it. You want your images, you want your shapes; and your complaint is the same as the complaint of the world, the complaint that what is breakable has been broken, that what is temporal is not eternal, that what is of the earth is no more than the earth and crumbles. You have seen the pretty castles that were built in the sand, and now you are lamenting that the tide has run over them. But the tide is greater than the castles, and if it is beauty that you want then you should see the beauty in the tide. Praise and pity are the noises of history, they are not the noises of life. The noise of life is the tide. Why will you not hear it?"

"I hear you," Peter said, "but I do not hear the tide."

"Your complaint is the complaining of the body whose blood has grown thin, but the body is not the meaning and still you can love it. You look at the body and you see that it is drowned, but when you look why do you not say 'The tide has gone over it' instead of 'The body is ugly'?"

"What is the tide?" Peter said.

"That is for you to say."

"The body is ugly," Peter said. "The tide has gone over it. I will say what you want me to say. But there are still some things that are beautiful."

Annabelle stepped up the small wooden railing that separated us from the grass, and as she swung herself over she became for a moment like a dancer on her toes. "Beginnings are never beautiful," she said.

"What you want," I said, "is a place that has died many years ago, a place in which there is no movement and no meaning except that which exists in a fossil or a stone."

"And is there such a place?" Peter said.

"I believe so."

"Where?"

"I have lived in one. I have left it. It is an island in the south. There is nothing living except the cactus and the crabs, and the people are only shadows on the faces of the rocks."

"And you left it?" Peter said; "Why?"

"Because it was too old," I said. "It was too old and too dead and too dry. Our world may be ageing, but a grave like that is uncanny. It is too close to the sun. The sun is not the God of life—that is nonsense. The sun is the God of eternity. One cannot live under a sky so old."

"Rain is the God of life," Marius said, "rain and dampness and softness and dew."

"Of which there was none. Have you ever lived in a place in which the only softness is rotten? You find it strange. You become frightened of touching things in case your finger goes through."

"You need not touch things," Peter said. "You need only look. You cannot touch beauty, it must always be apart from you. And it must be hard so that it will remain apart from you and you may not be tempted to stroke it."

"That is the old beauty," Marius said, "the beauty that is dead."

"Then I want it!" Peter said.

"The new beauty," Marius said, "is the sound of a swan's wing and the beginning of fear."

"Look!" Annabelle said. "Look! There is a shooting star!" Some million miles beyond her pointing finger a star shed out its light some million years ago and vanished.

"There are always shooting stars," Peter said. "Whenever you look into the sky you see one. That is why people think them so exceptional."

We walked around the square with our collars turned up around our ears while Annabelle, in front of us, swung her coat down from her naked shoulder and swept it about on the ground at her feet sending little swirls of leaves wandering wearily into the darkness.

After a silence Peter said, "Tell me more about your island."

"The only things living," I said, "are in the sea. Beneath the water blue and gold fish swim among the coral, and you cannot touch them. The island itself is like a sphinx in the desert, and the natives who come there come only by day and by night it is silent."

"And do they speak?" Peter said.

"They shout and they laugh," I said, "but I do not remember them as speaking."

"Oh Marius," Peter said, "let us go to where they only shout and laugh and where the land is like a sphinx in the sea!"

"We could not shout," Marius said. "And I think that to live on a sphinx would be sacrilege."

"But you love sacrilege!" Peter said. "To you sacrilege is so beautiful!"

Marius frowned and said nothing.

"You could be a sphinx," Peter said.

We stopped beside the statue. "One cannot live in eternity," Marius said. "One can only live in memory of it. I know this island. It is we who are too old for it."

"Older than the sphinx?"

"Older than palm trees in the desert. Once the world was a garden and we sat by water and now it is no longer."

"It is a desert?"

"Except by imagination."

"We could find new springs."

"The same trees would grow. We could not sit beneath them."

"We could climb among the branches."

"We are too old, too heavy, they would not carry us."

"There must be a new beginning."

"There has been an old one."

"A new one that would carry us like an island in the sea."

"Like a grave in a churchyard."

"There is no beginning in graves."

"You do not know," Marius said.

"What is memory?" Peter said.

"Memory is a graveyard."

"Oh Marius, Marius, how I hate this world!" Peter walked away from us into the darkness.

Annabelle put on her coat and we sat on the small stone parapet beneath the statue. There was the sound of water beside us, and the moon made distances solid like ice.

"There is water here," Annabelle said.

"When you go out of the garden," Marius said, "you remember what was in it and the death you died there. If you remember this always then the desert is beautiful. If you do not you cannot live."

"There should be fishes," Annabelle said.

"If you cannot live you will pretend that you are living. This is the imagination of dreams. But if you remember you will not be dead. This is the imagination of reality."

"Did you love your island?" Annabelle said.

"I loved it except that I was alone," I said.

"And did you mind that?"

"I should have gone mad."

"You go mad with people too."

"Why?"

"Because you cannot touch them."

"You can," I said.

"If you remember," Marius said—"if always there is before you this sight of yourself being born in blood, and if you say that that birth was the first death I died because of the agony . . . "

"Can you?" Annabelle said.

" . . . then you will be able to touch people for a time even if you cannot touch yourself. People can only touch each other in the face of love or tragedy."

"And yourself?"

"Oh, you can never touch yourself except through others. That is a later development."

"That is what Peter wants."

"I can see him talking to a dustman."

"He will be talking of the moon."

"He would desire the moon without knowing what to do with it."

"There is the moon in this water."

"That is as near as anyone will ever get to it." Annabelle put her finger into the water and the moon came to life in waves. "One could lie in it," she said.

"You see, because it is a reflection."

"Can you only touch reflections?"

"Only those that are true to the things that they reflect."

"And will they have meaning?"

"They will have reality."

"I don't know if that is true."

"I don't know what we're talking about," Marius said.

Annabelle splashed her hand into the fountain and ripples of laughter seemed to ease across the stillness. "You do, but you're so crafty," she said. "And what was it that stopped you going mad?"

"Stopped?" Marius said.

"Yes."

"Grapefruits."

"Grapefruits?"

"Yes." We began to laugh. "I will tell you about it. When I was a boy we used to play a game with grapefruits. My friend would go up to one of the top windows of the house—and it was a very tall house—and he threw grapefruits down at me. I would catch them. It was a very extraordinary feeling and it stopped me going mad."

Annabelle and I laughed so much that we had to stand up.

"Have you ever caught a grapefruit?" he said. "A grapefruit falling from a very great height?"

"No," I said.

"You should try it. It is a very extraordinary feeling. And when you miss it, you see, it hits the ground and bursts, and that is tragedy." Annabelle was making so much noise that he had to stop.

"And when you catch it?" I said.

"Why, you catch it," he said, putting his hands together gently. "Like this. It is so soft and heavy. And the sound it makes is like love."

"Love!" Annabelle said, indignant.

"And you had plenty of grapefruits?" I said. "Then where did you live?"

"Where you did," he said. "On an island in the West Indies."

I had not imagined this. For an instant it was as if I had a premonition of disaster. In the moonlight Marius's face had almost assumed the features of a negro or a half-caste—the queer brooding stillness of them that lies at the centre of their laughter. "Which island?" I asked.

He told me. I remembered it. I remembered the dead-smelling town beneath the dead volcano, the deep green of the vegetation that was deeper than seaweed, the tall ruined sugar-cane factories that waited among the trees like monoliths. I had stayed there for a while and had been disquieted by it. It seemed alone among the islands. It was all softness there, all untouchable, the sea deep and dark, unfathomable, alarming to swim in; no boats on it, no slanting square sails to give it colour, no fish; just the deep unending stillness of rottenness among the mountains, and in the town the static garbage smell around the twisted people and above them the bells of the cathedral.

"But there," he said, "I agree with you. It is impossible to live."

"How strange that I should never have asked you where you were born," Annabelle said.

"You don't ask many questions."

"No." She sat down and shivered for the first time in the cold.

"And will you ever go back there?" I said.

"I shall go back when there is something to do. I should not know what to do there at the moment."

"What is there that you do here?" I said.

"Not much," he said.

"No."

Peter came towards us across the grass. "I have been talking to a beggar," he said.

"I thought he was a dustman."

"He was a beggar," Peter said. "He is selling shoe-strings. I asked him why he did not work and he said why should he? He was standing at the entrance to some fashionable club from which bachelors were emerging after their evening's game of squash. Well, why should he?"

"Why do you call them shoe-strings?" Marius said.

"Because shoe-strings are what one tries to lift oneself up by when there is nothing else to lift with. No one bought his shoe-strings. Do you suppose it is possible to lift oneself up by one's feet?"

"No," Annabelle said.

"It is true that there is no reason to work. There is not even the reason of making money if one can get it by begging. He said he made ten pounds a week. I am sure if one tried hard enough one could lift oneself up by one's feet."

"Try it," Annabelle said.

"I'm always trying it. I am a nonconformist. Sooner or later I shall do it or I shall break my back."

"And what will you do when you have done it?" Marius said.

"I will be God. What more need I do? Those bachelors, now, why do they not try it instead of playing squash? It would be better exercise. Why does no one try it except me?"

"I knew you would be talking of the moon," Annabelle said.

"No one is serious. I cannot bear that no one is serious. There is only one thing in life that is of any importance, and that is to get oneself off the ground. If there is nothing to lift you you must lift yourself. That is what I mean by shoe-strings. He realized that. He was a poetic beggar. He realized the enormous importance of doing nothing but dealing in shoe-strings. He is going home to-night to practise getting himself off his feet."

"He will be wasting his time," Annabelle said.

"Why?"

"Because he won't know whether or not he has done it."

"I knew a man," Marius said, "who tied himself to a towel-rail."

"When you try to lift yourself there is nothing to judge it by, you will end by pretending and not knowing that you pretend."

"What happened to him?" I said.

"He was burnt," Marius said.

"What is there to judge it by? Pretending is a disease, you do not know when you have got it. Does it matter so long as you try?"

"Disease can be cured."

"How?"

"By other people."

"Oh love, love, you are always talking about love. Will you cure me, Annabelle?"

"Yes," Annabelle said.

Peter took off his shoes and socks and sat down on the parapet with his back to us so that his feet were in the water. He began to sing, and then stopped. He said: "The world is diseased, the disease is infectious, the infection is pretence. Should one not isolate oneself from infection? Everywhere there is madness. The people in the streets are no less mad than the people in palaces. The world must be changed or be renounced."

"What do you remember?" Annabelle asked.

"Man must be changed or be destroyed. If he is not changed he must change himself. If he is not destroyed he will certainly destroy himself. I remember the future."

"I remember the present," Marius said.

"One day something will happen. We will get off the ground for a moment. It is only a moment that matters. Then we will be changed. It is the future that matters."

"In the future," Marius said, "we will break our backs and die."

"There are four of us," Peter said. "We will put strings under each other's feet and pull. We will stand at the four corners of a circle and we will build a totem pole in the middle and the pole will have pulleys and we will raise ourselves. Is that what you call love?"

"Yes," Annabelle said.

"You are right," Peter said. "We must have a pole. The world has given up its totems, that is why it is on the ground. The world is too solitary. Will you tell us when our pole is built and we can pull?"

"If it were we who built it we still should not know where we were going."

"You would," I said.

"We still should not know what we were."

"You would," I said.

"We never know about ourselves."

"A totem does not work unless a sacrifice is made to it," Marius said.

"Then make a sacrifice," Peter said. He looked to the sky. "One day I will jump off that roof and will either fly or be a sacrifice."

"You know about yourselves," I said.

"There are sacrifices in the present, always," Marius said. "Then tell us when to honour them. The world must be changed. Annabelle, what do you judge things by?"

"By not judging," she said.

"How do you know what you are without pretending?"

"By not knowing."

"How do you know where you are going?"

"By believing."

"And that is what you judge things by. Now, now, a star, and then it is you who we can believe in."

"We are still children," Annabelle said.

"Will you tell us when to begin?"

"Yes," Annabelle said.

We all looked to the sky, but the stars had become veiled with clouds. It was as if we were alone on top of a mountain. Peter splashed, the water touched us, it might have been rain that fell upon us equally. I felt, suddenly, that I might have been any one of them. "I must go," I said.

"Must you?" They looked at me.

"Yes," I said.

"You will come back and see us?" Annabelle said.

"You will come back and stay?"

"I will come back soon," I said.

"Good."

I left them. I walked away hurriedly. I hoped that they would understand. I walked up flat rectangular streets without seeing anything. I had nowhere else to go and no one was expecting me, but I felt that if I had stayed with them much longer I should have either lost what I had found or else found something which at the moment would have been too great for me.

II
CHILDREN

4

Emotion is not describable. The words have all been used, and they are tired. What I felt about Marius and Annabelle and Peter I thought was a new feeling, but I suppose it was really as old as the words with which I could not describe it. But every experience seems new to the person who experiences it, while the words are old to everyone. So the words can only explain.

When children are children they are either on their own or in company, but wherever they are they are not faced with the problem of solitude. To the child the problem is either unknown or it is an agony, and an agony cannot last for long. It is cured by unconsciousness or comforted by love, and there are a million mysteries by which its pain can be diverted. Children are never religious and they are never hypocrites, and religion and hypocrisy are two of the answers to the problem of solitude.

When children are no longer children they become conscious of solitude. Then, if there is love, it is all the answer that it was when they were children; but if there is no love, then there is fear, because unconsciousness has gone and mysteries have become fearful instead of diverting. Then the fight against solitude begins, and it may be fought by either denial or remedy. Denial is hypocrisy and remedy is faith. There can always be the attitude of not fighting it at all, but that becomes a descent into non-existence.

The world chooses denial because denial is easier. Denial is the easiest thing imaginable, because it does not even require imagination. And few people have imagination, so that hypocrisy begins.

Hypocrisy is pretending that you like people when you don't, pretending that you are happy when you aren't, pretending you are doing things for others when you are doing them for yourself, pretending that you are getting somewhere when you are going round in circles. Hypocrisy is living negatively and pretending that it is positive. Hypocrisy works because for a large number of people it is the only thing that can work, and something has to work or else people cannot believe that they exist. Hypocrisy is not wrong, it is just unlucky. It is unlucky because under its terms belief in existence remains only a surmise and not a reality. But it is necessary because some belief in existence is necessary, and an unreal belief fulfills at least the necessary functions of a real one. Belief in existence is automatic, it has to be; and for some reason belief in existence cannot be maintained without love or religion or hypocrisy. That is a condition of being human.

In solitude one does not exist because one is not human. And so there is no real solitude, only the fear of it. If the fear becomes answerable by the usual means then one goes mad. But that, too, in its way, is an answer. Madness occurs when the normal means fail.

Of the normal means hypocrisy is the easiest even for those who have imagination because it is possible to recognize hypocrisy and loathe hypocrisy and yet still be a hypocrite. In fact for the majority of people who have imagination this is the usual condition because love and faith are difficult to come by. They know that they are hypocrites and yet they have no means of ceasing to be hypocrites. To exist in solitude is impossible and to go mad is undesirable. So in spite of themselves they are hypocrites and knowing it they are never quite at peace. For imagination contains the expectation of truth.

This is the human predicament. And a person who has imagination will find, if he remains in the predicament for long, that he loses his imagination. That is why older people will usually admit the predicament less readily than the young. For the mind which both condemns the notion of hypocrisy, and yet is aware of the unalterable existence of it in itself, is an uneasy mind; and if hypocrisy is thus recognized it will ultimately be defeated in its purpose. For the purpose of hypocrisy is the maintenance of belief—a peaceful belief even at the cost of truth. So that after a time the hypocrisy is no longer recognized, and the apparatus of the mind which once did recognize it becomes withered and dead. The imaginative awareness of solitude becomes, in time, like the acceptance of solitude, impossible: and the imagination dies.

But to those who are in the predicament and are fighting it and who cling to their imagination with an inherent desire almost as strong as that with which they cling to their belief in existence, there are the remedies of faith and love. But these remedies cannot be approached either intellectually or through an effort of will. If they are, then it is likely that the attempt will result in hypocrisy. One of the cruelest qualities of the predicament is the impossibility of intellectually discriminating between hypocrisy on the one hand and religion and love on the other. What is called religion is often a facet of hypocrisy, and so is what is called love. The intellect has no power to say, "This is or that is not hypocrisy," because the intellect is concerned only with rationalisations after an assumption and not with the assumption itself. The intellect cannot stand outside itself and judge itself because it has nowhere to stand. But there is something that stands outside the assumption, and that is emotion.

Emotion is that which makes belief a reality. For, when the question is put, "Why should not emotion be a facet of hypocrisy?", the question has lost its force. It has somehow become meaningless. It is not even frightening. Emotion is that which hypocrisy is not.

That is because emotion comes from outside a person and is not in its origins part of them. It is the only reality that is unchallengeable because it is objective. A person cannot make himself love and he cannot make himself hate, and he cannot give to himself the conviction that is religion. That is why an effort of will in this direction will often lead to hypocrisy. But although it is emotion that makes conviction possible, that stands outside the assumption and gives validity to it, it is for this very reason the most difficult thing to come by, because it is unpredictable and uncontrollable. The fact that it is in its origins outside a person is at once its triumph and its misery.

A man cannot make himself love. A man cannot give himself faith. He can only wait till the chance of love comes, and when it comes be ready to receive it. If it does come, he at least has the chance of it. If it does not, then he will have lost his battle. This is why hypocrisy can be called merely an unlucky position, and love a lucky one. Love and faith are really the same thing.

It is possible that love will come to everyone who is ready to receive it, but that, again, is an intellectual conjecture, and cannot finally be judged. It is impossible to know why love does or does not come.

It is thus that the problem of solitude stands at the centre of man's existence. It is the problem of life or death, and love is the only answer for those who would keep their imagination. Love is the only remedy to solitude, love is the only means to keep alive. For without love a man loses his imagination; without imagination a man soon ceases to be human: without humanity a man does not exist.

When I left Annabelle and Marius and Peter in the square I realized the force of this only dimly. All I knew was that I was feeling something that I had never felt before in my life and which in fact had seemed to turn me into a different person. I did not think about love and did not question it: I knew neither what it meant nor what it entailed nor even that it would last. But the feeling was that for the first time in years I was not faced with the problem of solitude. Before this I had fought with the problem and had found myself being beaten by it: I had even learnt, in some frightening way, the meaning of that phrase, "the descent into non-existence." But now it was the problem that had ceased to exist. And I, perhaps, had begun to exist. It was the force of this that had made me leave them so suddenly. When one becomes a different person at the age of twenty-three it is a shock that has to be suffered apart from the cause of it.

5

Alice rang me up the next morning. I had slept late, and was still in bed, and I went out sleepily onto the landing. Alice sounded cheerful. I could not concentrate upon what she was saying, but I agreed to have lunch with her. Then I went back to bed.

By the time I arrived at the restaurant I had remembered that my last meeting with her had not been successful. Marius and I had been rude, and she had left us angrily. I now wished to make up for this, and for more besides; because it struck me suddenly that in all my friendship with Alice there had been something degrading for both of us. I had liked being with her because as a character she fascinated me, and by watching her I thought I was learning about people as a whole. I liked listening to her oddities and contradictions—expressions of a character that seemed to exist so much on the surface, flashing out in different directions like the facets of a diamond, indicating a centre hidden and obscure. She seemed to behave with the unswerving superficiality of an older generation; and yet, being really of my generation, to be possessed by none of the older people's righteousness and cant. Thus I could both approach her and at the same time try to find out what this life on the surface meant—why it was necessary for so many energetic people to spend their energy like this—whether they recognized their oddities and contradictions and practised them purposely, or whether it was merely some instinct within them which made them function as they did. But in approaching her like this, as an object of experiment almost—to be observed and analysed as an excellent example of what I wanted to understand—I was treating her as a machine and not as a person, and it was this that was degrading. It was degrading for me because to treat people as machines is to become a machine oneself, and it was degrading for her because she tried, in her own way, to like me, and yet found me, I suppose, because my way was different from hers, unexpectedly dull and inhuman. It was this that I wanted to change.

Alice had arrived at the restaurant before me. She was sitting at the best table by the window and was ordering wine. When she saw me she waved, and as I sat down she put her hand on top of mine. "Darling," she said, "how wonderful to see you." Her eyes were the colour of a smart bright swimming-pool. "This is *my* lunch," she said. "I am sure it is going to be a wonderful lunch."

"It is very kind of you," I said.

"How nice you look," she said. Her hand as it lay on top of mine was pointed and thin with long smooth nails, and two silver bracelets jutted up from her wrist like hoops. I wondered why when she stood up they did not fall off. Her arm against the table-cloth was white like wax.

"You look very nice too," I said.

"Darling," she said, "you don't mean it, but still."

"I do mean it, you know, but I can't say it," I said.

"Why can't you say it?"

"Because it doesn't sound right when I say it."

"Darling, if you meant it it would."

"It somehow doesn't," I said.

A waiter approached. He produced two menus the size of magazines. "I have ordered lunch," Alice said. He flicked at the table languidly with a cloth. "And claret," Alice said. "Can we please have it soon?" The waiter bowed to her and departed. "I hope you like claret," Alice said to me.

"I do," I said.

"I'm sure you really despise it, darling, but you should get to know about claret, you know."

"Yes," I said.

She took the skin on the back of my hand between her finger nails and gave it a pinch. It hurt considerably. I wanted to giggle, as I thought how funny it would be if I put my other hand on top of hers and we played the game of pulling the bottom hand out from underneath and slapping it back on the top of the pile. But I did not think that this suggestion would amuse her. I had to say something quickly, however, as the pain was becoming unbearable, so I said "Why is it, do you think, that we find it so difficult to talk to each other?"

"Darling I don't know," she said, stopping pinching.

"I mean, what do you like talking about with other people?"

"With whom?"

"With your friends, your real friends, as you once said."

"Darling, we just talk."

"You're not going to get angry if I go on?"

"No," she said, pleasantly, but taking her hand away from mine.

"Because, you see, you seem to talk about things that I could never say."

"You're so young, darling," she said, and I was afraid that she was going to withdraw from me again.

"I don't think it's being young," I said. "What is it that you want from people when you talk?"

"To be amusing, charming, gay, surely."

"I don't think I do, you see."

"Why, what on earth do you want?"

"I don't know," I said.

"To be serious?" she sighed tremendously. "Darling, don't you want ever to stop being serious?"

"I can't ever begin," I said.

"Now I think you are trying to be clever," she said.

The waiter brought soup. Then the claret arrived and there was the ceremony of opening the bottle and tasting it. I had a momentary fear that Alice was going to send it back, but she didn't. Her hesitation was only a successful ruse to impress the waiter. We sipped it appreciatively.

"I was wondering," I said, "why is it that you and I mean different things by being serious and gay."

"It really is being young, you know. I really can't explain it." For the first time since I had known her she appeared to be entirely serious.

"Do explain it," I said.

"Well, you see, I think life just becomes a business when you are older."

"But you surely still feel things? Unbusinesslike things, I mean?"

"Darling, what you feel hasn't got much to do with life."

"It has everything to do with it, surely . . . "

"Not life, not living it," she said. We drank our soup while I thought this over.

"Then you are like me," I said; —"what you feel you can't express."

"Good heavens, I'm not like you," she said.

"But you see you are, because what you feel is different from what comes out, which is business."

"Not very nice businesses come out of you darling," she said.

"No, but that is the difficulty you see, to live what you feel."

"You can't," she said. "Not possibly."

"Why not?"

"Because you can't." She obstinately finished her soup.

"What can you live then?" I said.

"You can have fun, darling," she said. "Have you ever thought of that?"

"I can't have fun when I don't feel like it. Why not make a business of what you feel?"

"It really isn't so easy," she said. She reached into her bag for a cigarette. "Besides, you don't know anything about businesses, darling."

"I think I am beginning to," I said.

"Why?" she said.

"Because we have been talking for ten minutes without you getting angry. Isn't that good business?"

"It's because you have been so terribly gay, darling," she said, with an enormous smile.

"So serious," I said.

"But you see, your face is nice, which makes all the difference."

"And it hasn't been before?"

"No," she said.

The soup was taken away and meat appeared. We waited while the vegetables were ladled out, and I was thinking what a success the lunch was, how we were enjoying it, and then Alice said in a casual voice, "What did you do after I had left you last night?"

"Last night?" I said. I remembered suddenly our rudeness to her, and my remorse. I wondered why it was that until now I had forgotten it; perhaps it had been Alice's business to make me forget it—the business in which she was so practised and clever. So that it might have been that the success of the lunch had nothing to do with me at all, and then why had Alice wanted to remind me of my rudeness now?

"Yes," Alice said. There was an awkwardness between us. She was looking out of the window and seemed to be waiting for something.

"I stayed with Marius for a while," I said. I found that I did not want to tell her about Annabelle and Peter. We were both of us uneasy. "Do you know where Marius lives?" I said, remembering that this was something that I wanted to discover from her.

"No," she said.

"But you must do, you got in touch with him last night."

"Oh did I?" she said.

"Yes."

"He is staying in Grosvenor Square, I believe, with some friends."

"Oh," I said. I had not imagined him as living there. "Do you know the friends?" I said.

"No," she said.

"Marius isn't . . . ?" I began.

"Isn't what?"

"Nothing," I said. For a moment, and for some inexplicable reason, I had wanted to ask if Marius was married to Annabelle. But knew that he wasn't.

There was a silence. Alice's heavy beautiful face looked unutterably sad. While I had been wondering about Marius I had not thought of what she might be wanting herself. As she looked out of the window I could see the reflections of the traffic in her eyes.

"Darling," she said, "for God's sake say something, can't you tell me about last night?" She looked so tired.

"We went round to Grosvenor Square," I said.

"Oh you did?"

"Yes. I can't think why I didn't tell you about that before."

"That doesn't matter does it?"

"What?"

"But what happened, darling?"—I could not quite discover what we were saying.

"Isn't it strange to live in Grosvenor Square," I said.

"Is it?"

"I mean I didn't think anyone did now . . . " I said, and then I talked off, lost, and Alice went on staring out of the window with her heavy blue wax-work eyes.

We ate in silence. Plates were removed and fresh ones came, and I still did not know what Alice was wanting. I tried to talk of inconsequential things, but the sadness remained around us like damp and I could not deal with it. I remembered what Alice had once said about it being impossible to learn anything about people by talking to them, and I realized that this was at least true when applied to her. I could not ask her what she wanted, and I could not tell without asking what it was that made her sad or happy. I thought, perhaps, that I really knew nothing about her at all.

"You would like Marius's friends," I said at random. "They are a brother and a sister, and I am sure you would get on well if you met them."

"I'm sure I would, darling," she said, turning her eyes on mine.

And then it was all right. By this time we had finished lunch; before I left her, I had promised to arrange a meeting between her and them. Alice was smiling, letting her eyes rest on me, and she talked with a quickening energy that I had not seen in her for years. But I did not know what it was all about, what the lunch was about—whether she had arranged it and been pleasant merely in the hope of this promised meeting, or whether we had really made some contact in the things that mattered between ourselves. I did not know whether it was my effort to be nice to her that had been successful—but as we were about to leave each other in the street and I was thanking her for the lunch, she turned to me suddenly and said, "You are getting quite good at businesses, darling: perhaps you are growing a little older after all"; and then she squeezed my arm and walked away.

For a few days I saw no one. I stayed in my room and tried to write, but what was there to say when people were such mysteries? The sun shone and the children shouted in the streets, but men and women were shuttered in basements behind the light.

Men and women were like shops, with their goods in the windows, what they had bought and what they offered to sell. The display was all that was visible, the display of words and behaviour in which they trafficked and grew rich and sometimes grew bankrupt, the figures of their businesses recorded in ledgers around the shelves; but what the men and women were like, were really like, apart from the businesses, was never known. The customer never penetrated through to the back parlour where the shop-keeper lived, the shop-keeper so courteous and impassive, where he took off his smile and slept. The customer never got down into the basement where the efforts were weighed, the businesses balanced, where the question was judged, finally—this is or this is not what matters, this has or has not been worth while.

And Alice was a dealer in mysteries: this I knew. It was her way of dressing the shop window, of introducing novelties, of keeping the public amused. To cloak her pretences she used to patter like a conjuror, to catch the audience guessing she made slips with her hands. But the slips were false slips, they were pretences at pretending, the reality was behind them and the audience was fooled. Trying to understand Alice was like trying to work out a sentence with too many negatives; the sense became lost, baffled, in the cancellation of meaning. In Alice there were layers and layers of possible cancellations, but the audience never knew what was intended and what was not; how much she was bluffing others and how much she was bluffing herself.

And it was not only professional conjurors who played tricks with their audience. Every audience was at a distance demanding to be amused, and everyone, in this way, was a conjuror. The tricks were demanded and the tricks were performed, but the audience was supposed not to see the reality. The only difference between the professional conjuror and the amateur was that the professional at least knew himself how the trick had been played and why; while the amateur did not.

All amateurs, I thought—and that included Annabelle and Peter and Marius. But with them, somehow when they were among their audience, the tricks appeared no longer as tricks but rather as demonstrations of a reality that lay behind them. When they produced a rabbit out of a hat they did so because they wanted a rabbit; when flags came out of their mouths instead of words the words were not needed and the flags were used to wave with; when pigeons flew out from their coat-tails it was because they wore coats that pigeons lived in. With them what they acted was an expression of what they felt. In their shop windows lay only that which they loved, and so it was not a shop, for there was no buying and selling. They only gave and received, and lived there, and the shop and basement were one.

And I, in my room, a hired room, a washstand disguised as a writing desk, a curtain for a cupboard, a gas fire demanding shillings that I seldom possessed, a chest of drawers, two beds, a table in the middle, the walls the colour of brown papers, the covers of the chairs and divans like the woven remains of dust—this was my basement, my home, the cell wherein I slept. But this was not where I could live—(were the basements of others the same?)—there was nothing of myself in this solitude—(was there anything of themselves in others'?)—were all basements then a sham and was there nothing but the windows? Lying on my bed and watching the gradually yellowing ceiling where it ran into the frieze above the walls I knew that it was not here that I could work. And now in the evenings, out of doors, I could not yet go round to see Annabelle and Peter. Because, if the world is a dressed window and the eyes of the customers go no further than the window it is not as a customer that one should ask for more than the world. If I went to Annabelle and Peter and knocked at their door I should be approaching as a customer, my smile would be the smile of consciousness and their welcome would be frozen by the formality of my words. Going like this, being accustomed to the world, we could not have helped it. For me, at least, having grown so rooted into loneliness, it would have been inevitable. So that in hoping for more than the world, hoping for reality, I looked for a different approach. And I could find no other approach, because the entrances to reality are through the world's windows.

In Grosvenor Square, when the sun shone, the typists came out from their offices to eat their lunch beneath the statue. They sat on the parapets with their paper bags, and soldiers came in twos and threes to sit opposite them. Mothers arrived with their children, prams were handled up the steps, straps were unfastened, the children ran, clattered, splashed in the fountain, hurried about their business of having fun among the stones. A man lay on his back with a handkerchief over his face: a woman with thick legs took her shoes off. A soft silence of sweat rose dropping through the light, and here I came for lunch to eat my sandwiches.

A small boy was riding a bicycle up the path. The place was different in the daylight. A tiny bicycle, like a toy, a fat tiny boy with a peaked cap and spectacles. I looked up to where the façade of the block of flats where Annabelle lived rose pink and pale and majestic. The small boy swerved, some typists screamed, he straightened himself: he was like some turn at the circus, imperturbable and whirling on his jerking wheels. There was a window high up in the flat pink surface where a curtain hung limply into the daylight. The silver wheels twinkled, the soldiers joined in: lurching between their legs he was like a rabbit dodging trees. I did not know which was Annabelle's window: I did not mind.

Sun and solitude and nothing to do. I will sit here, I thought, until something happens. The small boy was arrested by a keeper. One of the windows was hers: out of the door there was a chance that she might come. A paper bag exploded like a pop-gun. I could sit here for years, I thought: there is nothing to stop me. An old woman like a Rembrandt was being photographed: some Americans were focusing in groups of three. A wave of laughter ran through the crowd. A soldier was inflating another bag, his eyes were like cherries, his cheeks blown tight. As he burst it the girls put their hands to their ears and wailed. Her eyes will be like an animal's, I thought. The soldier beckoned towards the girls, he moved his body with his hands along the parapet, he patted the vacant stonework by his side. She will be dressed in red, she will have her hands in her pockets, when she walks she will not appear to be moving. The girls squirmed, protested, placed their fingers in front of their faces in reproof. Then one of them rose, advanced tentatively, was pushed from behind, and collapsed uproarious upon skirted knees. She will not appear to be moving. Then another girl made the attempt, stepped gingerly, held her skirt like a paddler. She was half way across and then suddenly, with a rush, was beside the soldier with a bun from his bag. She stretched her legs out in front of her, lay back on her elbows. The two sides cheered. It was like a game of French and English.

"If she comes out of the door": but she might never. The soldiers and the girls were intermingled now—so easily. What were they saying? Nothing. The words were cries without the necessity of meaning. A lunch with sandwiches, a seat on the stone, and they were no longer strangers. So easily. An arm was slipped round a waist, a body leaned sideways, hair fell downwards on a shoulder. That evening they would meet again, they would go dancing, in alleys of darkness they would see each other home. The façade of the home where Annabelle lived was as impersonal as a factory. That evening they would touch, skirmish, circulate in couples. Suddenly the high-up window with the curtain hanging out was closed, silently, and now there was nothing to suggest that the surface had any more depth than a photograph.

I stood up. There was no reason that she should ever come this way. They were munching sausage rolls from communal fingers. No reason at all. To get together you have to have paper bags, you have to burst them, you have to deal in giggles and the arching of eyes. I moved away from them. They were arm in arm beside the fountains. She might never. It was not possible for me to go up because formality was necessary, and it was not possible to stay because to others it so apparently was not.

I walked to the National Gallery. The street was cluttered with the crowd. I minded now. Stepping on and off the pavement it was as if there was someone by my side. A string of bubbles descended from an advertisement: they were iridescent and oily like drops from a melted rainbow. In Trafalgar Square the fountains again were playing. They were soft and spectacular, the mist hung whitely, the scene was extended to a faintly distorted size. Here the stones were black, the groups in hundreds, the pigeons thick and myriad like ants. It was as if the lunch-hour picnic by the statue had been commercialized into the feeding of a thousand waiting mouths.

From beneath the great portico the birds chattered clamorous and invisible. Inside there was silence, and the vision of wings. A dim brownness, a watery stillness, an aquarium of eternity looking outwards to the light. The light was on the walls, the people were fishes, observing their observers they were sleepy like the sea. Paintings do what churches do, by stressing one's insignificance they make possible self-repose. Squares of light, windows of eternity, solitude supported upon golden tides of foam. Swimming through the stillness I came upon a red velvet chair like coral. I sat in it. Sleepy with opaqueness I closed my eyes. When I opened them again I saw standing in front of me a girl whom I thought was Annabelle.

Of course it wasn't. It was just a girl in a red coat looking at a Michelangelo picture and standing there with some of the poised intensity of the figures in the painting, a poise which I had recognized as being characteristic of Annabelle. She was standing with her weight on one leg and her head turned over her shoulder, the whole force of her seeming to be concentrated upon the point of her hip. I got up and walked round her to see her face, and it was a sad face, rather old and puffy, but it was the girl in the red coat who made me realize how much I loved Annabelle. It was funny, I thought. A stranger in a red coat with dark untidy hair.

So I walked away. I walked out down the steps with the chattering of birds beginning again, and in front of me the traffic like a furnace of machines. I wondered where I could find her, where I could come across her as if by accident. In the street it was dirty, there was a hammering of metal, a noise of steam and scorching and the arid smell of dust. I walked past St. Martin-in-the-Fields and down into the Strand. Where I could touch her, stand beside her, watch her face as it turned. But the noise was too insistent. It was enveloping, ferocious, like a forest fire. I could not think. I turned back furiously the way I had come, the afternoon like smoke and my body choked to breathe it, and then, as in a shaft of daylight, I saw Peter on the other side of the road.

A click of vision. The noise retreated. Quietly the cars ran gliding on their way. He was on the edge of a small crowd at the back of the National Gallery, an audience collected to watch the street performers' turns. I could hear a man shouting his patter to get the crowd to give him money. Peter was throwing him pennies. I crossed over to him. He was leaning forwards, impatiently, like a child at a circus. "Oh look," he said, "have you got any pennies?"

"Yes," I said.

"Do lend me them, you see, this is a man who bends bars on his forehead."

I gave him what I had. He threw them all with a clatter onto the pavement, and the man picked them up like a sparrow hopping for crumbs. Then he held them up warily to the light and examined them. "Like a five pound note," Peter said: "What an extraordinary man!" The man had thrown his cap down on to the ground and was jumping up and down on it, and all the time he was gasping out his thick unintelligible patter when suddenly, with no change in his voice, he picked up a large iron bar, rolled up his shirt sleeve, and began beating the bar heavily against his forearm. The flesh on his arm turned yellow, and then blue, and gradually the bar became bent. He was now making a noise like a boiler before it bursts. Then he stopped, just as suddenly, rolled his sleeve down, put his cap on his head, picked up the assortment of bars, mostly bent, which were on the pavement beside him, pushed his way hurriedly through the crowd, and disappeared down the steps of a gentlemen's lavatory. I could see a policeman coming sauntering towards us.

"But his forehead!" Peter said. "He didn't do it on his forehead!"

"Does he beat it on his forehead?" I said.

"No," Peter said. The crowd was shuffling away before the policeman's advance. "Do you think he can beat it on his forehead?"

"I don't suppose so," I said.

"He just bends it, you see." Peter was standing scratching his head, and the policeman was viewing us suspiciously. "But we must find him," Peter said. "You can't possibly go away without seeing his forehead." He moved towards the lavatory.

I followed him. A desire to laugh was like an itch in my throat. Going down the damp stone steps Peter said, "he must bend them back again, I suppose, sometime, unless he has a great many bars." Inside the lavatory the cubicles were spaced out along one wall like a row of miniature loose-boxes. There was no sign of the man. "He's engaged," Peter said. We stood in the middle of the floor peering at the notices on the doors. The lavatory attendant came out from his room and stood watching us over his spectacles. He was a small bald man in a dirty white coat. "Perhaps he lives here," Peter said. "Perhaps he stays here and bends all these pipes." The attendant came forward and stood behind Peter, his head coming up to Peter's elbow. "Here he is," Peter said: "He's at home." We went up to one of the doors and knocked.

"'Ere," said the attendant.

"I want him to bend them back," Peter said.

"Who?" the attendant said.

"I will give him ten bob," Peter said.

"You will?"

The attendant worked his spectacles up and down on his nose with a movement like someone eating spaghetti. Then he went over to the door and banged on it loudly. "'S all right Charlie," he said. "'S not the cops. Bloke 'ere wants to give yer ten bob." A cautious utter came from inside the door.

"Ten bob to bend 'em back again," said the attendant. "Take it or leave it." He strolled back to his room by the entrance. There was a noise of an exploding boiler again and then the man emerged defensively from his cubicle with a cluster of bars in each hand. He looked like a prehistoric plumber. He was a savage square man whose neck was about twice as thick as the top of his head, like the hero of a strip-cartoon. The veins on his forehead stood out softly. Peter tried to explain what he wanted, while the man stood opposite us whistling through his nose. Then he took the ten shilling note that Peter offered him, stuffed it into his pocket, and selected a bar about half an inch thick. He handed this to Peter, who took it and tried it out once or twice on his knee without making any impression on it and handed it back politely. The man braced himself, threw his head back, raised the bar ceremoniously and placed it on his forehead. The veins bulged horribly. He clasped and clasped his hands several times on the end of the bar like a mountaineer feeling for a hold on a rock, and then he jumped with both feet off the floor, uttered a muffled grunt, and heaved. The bar straightened considerably. He paused, jumped again, and heaved; and this time the bar slipped coming scraping down the front of his face and taking skin off his nose. Peter said, "Good heavens!" and the man stared stupidly in front of him. He hit the bar once or twice like a petulant child, and then smacked a hand on to his face sending blood splashing in drops around his ears. He held his hand up staring at it. Then he smacked his hand on to his face again, and finally uttered a tremendous bellow. The attendant came hurrying out of his room.

"Did 'e 'it yer Charlie?" the attendant said. "Did 'e 'it yer on the nose?"

"Good heavens no," Peter said, backing away nervously.

"This is a convenience," shouted the attendant. "A respectable convenience!"

"I'm sure it is," Peter said, stumbling over a mop and pail.

"Wot's up?" yelled the attendant, putting his mouth about an inch from Charlie's ear. "Wot's up with yer face, Charlie?"

Charlie muttered into an enormous brown handkerchief that he had produced from his pocket and was now holding clasped upon his nose.

"The bar slipped," I explained. "It slipped and scraped his nose."

"It did, did it?" yelled the attendant. "Slipped and scraped his nose, did it, slipped and scraped his nose?" He repeated this at the top of his voice.

"That's right," Peter said, but was unable to make himself heard.

"I'll give yer slip and scrape yer nose," reiterated the attendant.

Just then Charlie removed his bloodstained handkerchief from his face and uttered another great bellow. Peter was walking round him patting him anxiously on the back, but the attendant sprang forwards and this time really let himself go. " 'Ush it up, Charlie," he roared: "For Christ's sake 'ush it. We'll 'ave the cops down with all this bloody noise." The sound of his voice in the enclosed space was like a landslide.

And then, as the echoes cleared, there was the sound of heavy boots descending the steps. The attendant acted with speed. He pushed the bleeding Charlie back into his cubicle, slammed the door on him, and turned to us, saying, "In you go, quick, I don't want no trouble in this convenience." Propelled by his whisper we made a rush for two locked doors and pushed against them futilely. "No pennies," Peter said. "Charlie's got the lot." The attendant whirled us round and pushed us into a cubicle at the end which was unlocked. "Into the free," he whispered viciously. "It's the free that's good enough for some." He slammed the door on us. "And others too," we could hear him adding, repeatedly, as the policeman or whoever it was arrived at the bottom of the steps.

I was laughing so much I couldn't breathe. I leant against the wall and Peter pulled out a handkerchief to mop his face, but he seemed to remember Charlie's, so he put it away again hurriedly. We could hear the policeman's footsteps going sedately along outside, and I was holding my breath so tightly that I thought the wall would fall down. After a long pause I let my breath out quickly, and then couldn't get it in again. Peter leant over and whispered very seriously, "I say, what's a free?"

I couldn't answer. I sat on the seat and wondered if I should ever get my breath back and then Peter whispered again, more loudly, "What did he mean by a free?"

I tried to speak, but after a few syllables my whisper cracked into a squeak but I was able to go on laughing. "What a wonderful idea," Peter said. "Why doesn't everybody come here?" He was peering round trying to read the writing on the walls. From somewhere on our right I could hear Charlie's interminable mutter; but the sound, all steam and rumblings, seemed to be in keeping with the place. I was more concerned with my laughter, which seemed liable to explode again at any moment. Outside, the policeman was talking to the attendant: we could hear his boots creaking as if he was standing still. The attendant was putting him off cleverly, uttering high-pitched grunts of innocence. I was beginning to breathe more easily when Peter leaned over towards me again. "I say," he said, "do you realize that it is a criminal offence for two Englishmen to be found together in a lavatory? It is the only thing the public cannot stand." And then we were both laughing.

I don't know how long we stayed there, but eventually the policeman went, and the attendant came to let us out. We wanted to see how Charlie was doing, but the attendant would not let us. He drove us out, heedless of our apologies. In the sunlight we felt very stupid and exhausted. As we walked away we could hear the attendant and Charlie greeting each other below the earth. The noise they made was like the beginnings of a water-spout.

Peter was meeting Annabelle for tea, and I went with him. As we walked I asked him, "Do things like that often happen to you?" and he said, "They seem to," and after a while he added, "They do if you look for them, you know. They seem quite often to happen to me."

And I suppose they did. Looking back on the days that I spent at this time with Peter and Annabelle and Marius, it seems that something like that was always liable to happen; wherever I went with them the expectation of an extraordinary incident followed us like a ghost, even quite normal occasions being turned by this sense of anticipation into moments of oddity. It was all happy at first, while the laughter of the ghost was a benevolent laughter. It was only later that the ghost, as if in the passing of time he had grown tired of such childishness, became malevolent. It was then, as Alice had said, that life demanded to be taken as a business. But we were all young when I first knew them, and we did not look ahead to the future.

As I walked with Peter I thought of how it seemed that whenever I was in the presence of any of them I ceased to be conscious of myself as an individual and became, for the moment, a working part of the function in which we were engaged. And it was in this guise that the feeling of myself as an individual, as apart from consciousness, became actual. Going up the street through the sunlight I existed as a movement of the passing afternoon, but the existence was a real one, an experience that demanded neither thought nor question, a certainty that was very different from the dreams and self-enquiries of my moods when I was alone. I wondered if this was what Alice had described as fun, but the function of childishness would not have been fun to her. And then there were moments when the oddity was too mysterious for laughter.

Peter led the way into a store in Regent Street, up in a lift to the restaurant where the air was warm and scented, and as I looked around me turning with the heat of the room I saw Annabelle sitting with Marius at a table for four. We went across and sat opposite them, Peter facing Marius and Annabelle facing me, and Peter began telling Marius the story of the man with the iron bars. There was a band playing wearily in the corner, and Peter's words seemed to swim among the music like a child splashing gaily in an oily sea. Annabelle was not listening to the story, nor to the music, and as I watched her her eyes went down from Peter, down to the table-cloth which was blue and chequered and on which two knives lay, and she took one of the knives in her smaller pointed fingers and spun it, carefully, so that it flashed under the light like a catherine wheel. I was watching her hands and her wrists as they disappeared into the sleeves of her dress, and all the time she was looking downwards so that the lashes of her eyes were visible like fringes against her cheeks. Peter was saying, "A free lavatory, just think of it, a free lavatory," and Annabelle was leaning forwards with her hair falling down over her forehead and the neck of her dress open slanting against her throat. The warm oily water of the restaurant lapped around us, and Marius was laughing at Peter as he splashed, and Annabelle and I were floating like two bubbles in the sea. As she sat I had the impression that her clothes were quite separate from her, they were drapings of a statue unveiled and alone. At the centre there was darkness, the darkness of a cave: and as the sea broke over her, as the bubbles were devoured, the openings at her wrists and throat were yet caverns which the waves dared not enter, chasms of infinity in which the swimmer might drown. I wished that all might dissolve, become one with the waters; and Peter was saying, "No, not comic, tragic: just think of the tragedy of that poor man's nose."

"The irony of it," Marius said.

"Oh Marius," Peter said, "what a dreadful joke!"

The sea and Annabelle. Somebody laughed. "I saw Alice the other day," I said to Marius.

"Oh did you? I wondered which one of us she would continue with."

"Who is Alice?" Peter said.

"One of your enemies . . . "

"I have no enemies," Peter said. "Perhaps she is in love with you, Marius."

"Oh always love . . . " Annabelle began.

"I have only those whom I understand and those whom I don't understand. Is Alice old?"

"Not very. She is someone who tries to keep one jump ahead of you like an electric hare." Marius gave a short description of Alice.

"That is what I don't understand. Isn't it extraordinary how they behave?"

"This silly 'they,'" Annabelle said.

"But it means something. 'They' are the one-jump-ahead people—the gay, the superficial, the successful. I envy them. They deal exclusively with ambition and seduction."

"Alice is an oddity," Marius said.

"I envy them. I understand no one except ourselves. Everyone else I have met belongs to 'they.' They think about power, bed, clothes, and servants. Why? One might as well collect matchboxes. They are the army of the great irreligious."

"Are you religious?" Annabelle said.

"I think about it. I wish I didn't. I tell you I like these electric hares. Life must be very pleasant for them. But they must be distinguished. It is not good pretending that someone who is obsessed with power and bed and clothes and servants is the same as someone who isn't. Do you know, they often fly a hundred miles for a game of cards and a thousand for a horse-race?"

"Would you like that?" Annabelle said.

"I should like to enjoy it. I am afraid it would depress me terribly. But I should like to study them, perhaps to get one jump ahead of them. What do they think about in the aeroplane? I should like to ask them that."

"It is too much of a battle," Marius said. "A whole-time job."

"That's why they do it. They have no other whole-time job. I have never had a job in my life, but I should never have time to play cards."

"Big battles," Annabelle said, "and war."

"Nobody has a whole-time job anymore. Only a few have a whole-time life. The rest have to kill time. Have you ever thought what a good phrase that is—killing time?"

"A frightening one," Annabelle said.

"Yes. But I should like to meet this Alice. Why not ask her round?"

"She wants to meet you," I said.

"She does? Perhaps we have a glamour for them too. We will have a battle. Is this the first jump?"

"And who's the greyhound?" Annabelle said.

“I told you she was in love with Marius.”

“Perhaps she is in love with you,” Marius said.

“With me? How spectacular!”

“No.”

“Oh, well then, how spectacular for you,” Peter said to me.

“I feel quite fond of this Alice,” Annabelle said.

“Why, are you too?”

“No . . . ”

“Well that’s a pity.”

“Well yes, but I mean . . . ” Annabelle was suddenly blushing.

“Of course,” Peter said.

The people at the next table were watching us. There was a heavy blond woman with an enormous hat who sat very still so that it would not fall off, and two neat, reserved men with careful clothes who nevertheless looked shoddy. Every now and then they would raise a cigarette-stained finger to their faces to smooth some feature—a moustache, a lip, or an eyebrow—and then they would go on looking at us out of their musty, impassive eyes.

“Alice has much in common with the communists,” Marius said. “Do you remember what we were saying? They have the same obsessions. Opposites often resemble each other. If you want to pick sides you will not find many people on your own.”

“All the more space to jump,” Peter said.

“You will not even find the religious. Catholics and communists and social-conventionalists will all join hands to fight an individual. They all have a ready-made version of truth, and with this in common they can respect each other. The one thing they never respect is a person who has no truth, who is searching for it. This is the devil that is anathema to all of them.”

“You said that Alice was expecting something from our meeting,” I said.

“Yes, but on her terms, you see, and when it was not on her terms I suppose that she would have rather that we had not met at all. Alice at heart is such an idealist.”

"And now?" I said.

"Perhaps she wants it even on our terms, but I don't think we've got any."

"No terms?" Peter said.

"The trouble is," I said, "that if one has no terms then this one-jump-ahead business is so bewildering one cannot even pretend to be a greyhound."

"I've got plenty of terms," Peter said.

"But do you want to be a greyhound?" Annabelle said.

"I am a greyhound," Peter said.

"No," I said. "But one has to be something. And Alice makes it difficult for one to be anything."

"You might be one of those men who walk behind the greyhounds with a shovel," Peter said.

"That's the game," Marius said. "That is how she is able to be something herself."

"They wear bowler hats," Peter said.

The people at the next table were listening to us. The woman had a hand up to the corner of her open mouth and was scratching it with a long scarlet finger-nail, and the two men had their elbows on the table, their hands clasped, discreetly.

"You see," Marius said, "the greyhound never does catch the hare. If it did, the whole purpose of the game would be destroyed. And the hare would be destroyed too. So no one ever does catch Alice up."

"No one ever loves her?"

"But love means something different to someone like Alice. It's a part of the race."

"Like a French novel," Peter said. "The hero chases the heroine for the first half of the book, and then they find they have changed places and she is chasing him. And so on till they drop."

"What happens when they pass each other?" Annabelle said.

"The usual," Peter said.

"But I mean, that's all right."

"No, because the one who's being chased is so dazed at being passed that she doesn't get back into her stride again until she's doing the chasing."

"But then . . . "

"Then the boot's on the other foot; or rather, the bowler hat is on the head of the man with the shovel. He's behind you see."

"What happens if the man with the bowler hat catches the hare?" Marius said.

"He's electrocuted," Peter said.

"Who is this man with the hat?" Annabelle said.

"Well, he has to go behind you see with a shovel in order to . . . "

"I know, but what is he to Alice?"

"As a matter of fact, she says there always is someone behind her," I said.

"There you are then."

"Where?"

"In the dung-cart," Peter said.

I could see the people at the next table becoming annoyed with us. The two men were leaning towards each other nodding their heads and making derogatory noises in their throats, and the woman was looking rather forlorn like a lost baby.

"The point is," Marius said, "that if the races ever stopped then several thousand people would have nothing to do in the evenings. So they go on, and time is killed, and a few other things are killed in the process."

"The heart is killed," Peter said.

"Yes, but you see, the heart of the hare would be killed anyway, so the hare dare not stop. That is what is frightening."

"What has happened to the heart of the hare that it should ever have started running?" Annabelle said.

"But Annabelle," Peter said, "you cannot expect the hare not to run when the dogs are after it."

"Then it is you who are the dogs," Annabelle said, "and it is you who have taken away the heart of the hare."

"Is it?" Peter said. "Is it I who have asked it to be a hare?"

"It is no good blaming anyone except yourself," Annabelle said.

"You said once that we can never know about ourselves," I said.

"No, but yourself is the only person that you can blame."

Peter looked sad. "I cannot blame myself for the pride and seduction and prostitution of others," he said.

"Perhaps not, but you cannot blame the others either."

"I don't," he said. "You know I don't."

"You are such a terrifying moralist," Marius said.

We stood up, preparing to go. The people at the next table looked down at our feet. Annabelle wore no stockings, Peter had a hole in the leg of his trousers, and Marius wore enormous brown shoes that were curiously flat like kippers. The men looked pleased. As we went down in the lift Peter said, "Why not ask Alice round to-morrow?" and Marius said, "Alice has had a rather heartbreaking life, you know." Peter said, "Why?" and Marius said, "Well, you must wait till you see her," and Annabelle and I stood with our arms close in to our sides, not touching. In the street Peter said, "Shall we expect you to-morrow?" and I said, "Yes," and as I walked away she did not look at me and it was as if there was some string between us that was breaking.

6

Alice had got herself well dressed up. Tall, thin, with a coat like a cape hanging in folds, her smooth drooping face very pale above it, in the taxi she talked incessantly in her lilting emphatic way. "How exciting," she said. "I never go out, you see. Are you anxious then? Why are you so silent? I promise I won't disgrace you in any way."

We were going round for drinks. The taxi rattled like a cocktail shaker. Drinks were the meeting-ground for social England. Tea in the villages and gin in the cities. Hands would have nothing to do without a cup or glass to fiddle with, mouths would lose their power without a liquid to drown the silences. A façade had to be erected: for Alice and the people with Alice meetings would be unbearable without a barrier. For Peter and Annabelle on their own it would not be necessary, but even they could not deal with social England without a façade.

In the room at Grosvenor Square the drinks were there, ready, on a silver tray by the window. Alice sat opposite them, talking, her face soft and pallid in the reflected light. Only her eyes were hard—brittle and metallic like the fragile flash of glass. She was making an impression, putting her act over, getting power. Our entrance had been a success. She did it so cleverly, there was such artistry behind it, she had already turned the ground into a battlefield. I was sad that the battle had begun so quickly, almost automatically, as Peter had predicted. I wondered why Alice had wanted to come. She fought efficiently, with the power that she knew, the power of her bright steely eyes like the polished sights of a machine-gun. Gentleness had gone, and quietness had gone: she hated silences. Silences to her were uncanny. So she carried her eyes all gleaming and bright and she quite steadily shot people down with them. Her voice was only an accompaniment, like the noise of bullets. It was her eyes that fired, hitting, and her words were the echo.

"So you have come to live in England?" she was saying: "And your father is still abroad? I should have thought that it was better, surely, to be abroad nowadays than in England."

"I agree," Peter said.

"Then why don't you go? It would be easy for you, wouldn't it?"

"It's Marius's fault," Peter said. "He wants to stay."

"But good heavens, you don't have to do what Marius wants, do you?"

"Oh yes, I think we do."

"Why? How dreadful to be dependent on Marius!"

"Yes it's terribly sinister isn't it?" Peter said.

Alice turned away. I wondered if it was possible that Peter might defeat her, if defeat was what he wanted. He was nervous, being under fire, and after all it is difficult not to fight back against machine-guns. But I did not particularly want him to win.

"Of course," she said, "you are terribly lucky to be living here. It really is delightful. I should not mind London so much myself if I could live in a place like this."

"Do you mind London?" Peter said.

"Doesn't everyone? No servants, no fun, no food . . . "

"Surely there is plenty of food?"

"Of course, to you, who can eat in a restaurant, who can get anything . . . "

"What I meant was to you," Peter said.

"To me? Of course to me. I didn't think you'd understand."

"I try," Peter said.

Annabelle was in the background, Marius had not yet come in, and Peter was doing his fighting with a cautious indignation that was still quite pleasant, but which I was afraid at any moment might turn to alarm. Alice rattled on with unceasing attack.

"You know," she was saying, "really anything can happen to you anywhere nowadays, the other day I was in a taxi, it is too dreadful, and we stopped at a stoplight, and a man got in beside me, just got in, a perfect stranger, just sitting there beside me without even saying a word."

"Yes?" Peter said. "Yes?"

"He really might have done anything, he might have cut my throat; it is terrible to think that one is at the mercy of people like that, that they are quite on top of you, everywhere."

"And what did he do?" Peter said.

"I told you, he came and sat in my taxi."

"He did?"

"Yes. And then people get drunk the whole time, and they come round knocking at your door, or ring you up, and you have to spend hours with them, literally hours, trying to get them away, and you have no peace any more, that is the terrible thing, you have no peace."

"But the man in the taxi . . . "

"But peace . . . " Peter and I both started talking at once, and then stopped, and Alice darted in quickly.

"It is like living in a workhouse," she said.

"A workhouse!" Peter said, as if shocked.

"But surely these people . . . " I began again.

"Of whom are you talking?" Peter said to Alice.

"Of everyone," Alice said.

"You make me almost contented," Peter said. I saw Annabelle look up at him quickly.

" . . . it is because they can't stand peace," I went on.

"Contented?" Alice said, ignoring me. "How can you say that, don't you feel it, don't you know what I mean, they have power over you, absolute power, in a million ways, and you can't get away from them, all the fuss, and the dreariness, it is on top of you like a fog, don't you know what I mean?"

"No," Peter said.

"Well, good heavens, what sort of idea can you have of life?"

"I still don't know of whom you are talking," Peter said. "You personally—why does it strike you as a workhouse?"

"It is what one is deprived of," Alice said.

"And what is that?"

"Why—fun, easiness, easiness, yes, nothing is ever easy anymore, people are too frightened to be easy: they are starved, really starved, of all the things that make life bearable."

"It is not ease and fun that make life bearable," Peter said. "As indeed most people know who at the moment have too much of it."

"Too much of it?"

"Yes, and the ones who haven't at least have more than they ever had before, and they are the majority. The ones who have less are the minority and them I don't know about, except that I shouldn't think that the fun and ease that they had once ever did them any good, so that they are missing the point when they complain of the lack of it."

"Of course they complain, they are suffocated, sat on, there is no gaiety any more."

"For whom?" I said. "For you who still have money enough to create your own gaiety, or for those who have money for the first time and can't?"

"And who are they sat on by," Peter said, "other than the man in the taxi?"

"You are being ridiculous," Alice said.

"I never did get the harm of that man in the taxi," Peter said.

There was a silence. It seemed that the battle would drift on, interminably, and that no good would come of it. I realized, with surprise, that I had expected good to come of it. There is always the hope of results before a war. And now it seemed that at the end, as always, there would be no results except the weakening of all participants. I looked to Annabelle, but she was still withdrawn from us. I had given up trying to change the direction of the conflict myself. I regretted bringing Alice into such futility, and regretted even more that Annabelle would not help me. She seemed to be waiting for something. Peter was now doing the attacking with a persistence that was little different from Alice's.

"I don't trust all this gaiety stuff," he said. "Cheap food, cheap drink, cheap talk, cheap women, cheap life—oh, I don't believe in that sort of gaiety at all!"

"It was better than living in a dreadful concentration camp like this," Alice said.

"A concentration camp?" Peter said. "Oh no, you can't say anything about that, how can you talk about a concentration camp?"

"Don't you know what I mean?" Alice said.

Marius came in. He said something about being sorry he was late, and sat down. Annabelle was kneeling on the floor in front of the fire, and she moved to make room for his legs. Alice watched her. Peter was standing by the piano, and it seemed then that what was happening was of more importance than a social battle. The nervousness had gone from Peter's face, and in its place was a certain comical sadness which is the look of someone who has been hurt and is hiding it. I wondered how it was that Alice had hurt him, for her remark about a concentration camp had been no more, surely, than what he would expect; and then I realized, painfully, that the things that Alice had been saying—her phrases even—were those which Peter might well have said himself.

Realizing this, and watching Annabelle rather than Peter (she still had her back turned; why did she not speak?), I saw the alarm of having words thrown back at one in a way that made them hateful. Peter had spoken against England, but he had spoken against its pride and its complacencies, not its suffering. And now Alice had taken the words he might have used and had turned them into a complaint against the irrelevant lack of amenities. By doing this she had defeated him on the terms which they had accepted. The terms would now have to change—I did not know into what—but I found myself hoping.

"Oh Marius, darling," Alice was saying, "thank heavens you are here. I am having another of these dreadful serious arguments with your friends. Do try and be amusing, darling, because this is such a lovely room. One really should not be serious in a room like this." She turned to Annabelle. "Do you know what I mean?"

"We have not been so very serious, have we?" Annabelle said.

Alice laughed. "How right, how terribly right you are," she said. "Oh Marius, darling, do give me a cigarette."

The ground had already changed. Peter was out of it, solitary, and Annabelle and Marius were being engaged. Marius was getting the "darlings" as I once had done. Then Marius had been the enemy and the weapons of jealousy had been used against him. Now they were being used against Annabelle. She was sitting on the ground with her elbow touching Marius's knee. I did not think words would hurt her.

"Do you know what suffering is?" Peter said.

"Tell me," Alice said to Annabelle, "how long have you been living here?"

"About a year," Annabelle said.

"And where were you before that?"

"We were abroad, with my father."

"Oh yes."

"There is no suffering except physical suffering," Peter said.

"Nonsense," Alice said. And then to Marius as he offered her a match—"Isn't it nonsense, darling?"

"Sometimes," Marius said.

"These cigarettes are like brown paper, where on earth do you get them?"

Peter walked over to me. He pointed at Marius. "He is betraying me," he whispered loudly. Then he went back to the piano.

Alice was saying, "I am sure that sooner or later one will be poisoned by the cigarettes and drink that people give one."

Peter played a note on the piano. "Anything but physical suffering you can change," he said.

"A friend of mine went blind, literally, from drinking gin."

"Then change it," Annabelle said. Peter did not seem to hear her.

"He had to stay in bed for a week."

"Suffering is when you can't even die," Marius said.

"How pompous, darling."

"Yes," Marius said.

Annabelle had gone back into her silence. Alice was looking at her restlessly as if she resented this. Peter banged again on the piano. "I expect he was blind already," he said.

"Tell me," Alice said, "does this go on all the time?"

"Not all the time," Annabelle said.

Peter played a chord. "Did he think he had been put in a concentration camp when he drank the gin?"

"Doesn't it get terribly on your nerves?" Alice said.

"We have no nerves," Peter said furiously, shutting the lid of the piano.

"Marius," Alice said, "how is your wife?"

The air had suddenly become difficult to breathe. There was a shock, an alarm, an embarrassment in the room that dared not be looked at. Annabelle had turned her head so that her hair fell downwards across her face, shutting it away from us, as if she were hiding herself from the thing that Alice's words had created. Peter walked over to the window where he became a silhouette either approaching or receding, and it was only Marius who smiled into Alice's eyes.

"I wondered if, when you saw her, you would give her my love."

"Thank you," Marius said.

I did not know about Marius's wife. I did not know what anyone knew about Marius's wife. The air was unbearable.

"I wondered how often you saw her now," Alice said.

"I often see her," Marius said.

"She is so lovely." From where Alice was sitting she could not see Annabelle without turning to her, so after a while she did turn, and Annabelle was still leaning with her hair like a curtain over her face. "Don't you think she is lovely?" Alice said.

"I have never seen her," Annabelle said.

"Oh," Alice said. "Oh haven't you?" She gazed at Annabelle heavily, like a jealous sister.

I did not know who would ever speak next. I could not speak myself, for I did not know what was happening. The three who were sitting seemed frozen, enclosed, as if their hearts held their muscles rigid with waiting. Peter, by the window, seemed to be moving; although he never got any closer and never any farther away. He was like a ship on the horizon, which only proceeds when you cease to watch it. I looked down at the floor and tried not to think of Marius's wife, not to feel anything, until I should know about her. I tried to think of how the embarrassment might be ended, but every second that it lasted seemed to show that the situation was final, the battle over, we had been defeated and there was nothing more to be done. I found that I was saying these words to myself over and over again—we have been defeated, we have been defeated—not knowing what I was meaning but feeling that the defeat was greater than on the simple terms on which we had begun. I felt that it was a vital defeat, a large-scale defeat, a defeat on our own terms (for why should there be such disaster at the mention of Marius's wife?), and I was sensing the ruin of this, the outrage, when Annabelle shook the hair back from her face and stood up and walked over to Peter.

The others did not hear what she said. I did. "Now you can begin," she said.

She went past him, and waited, and again I had the impression of movement that was not visible. They both had their backs to us. Then Annabelle was coming towards us again and it seemed that Peter almost pushed in front of her. "You are right," he said.

He sat on the arm of Marius's chair, facing Alice. "You are right, we have nerves, we live on them." His smile fluttered towards Alice's jealousy like a bird. "Don't mind when we rest them." Alice did not look at him. "I, of course, not we," he said. "I know nothing of suffering." Alice flicked the ash from her cigarette into the fireplace. "But I know what you mean," he said. "Perhaps you know what I mean too."

Alice did not answer him. Peter put his head in his hands. The bird, wounded, trailed its wings across his face. "I wonder why one ever speaks," he said. "Speaking gets things wrong, and it doesn't get them right again." He looked up at Alice. "What one says means nothing, and what does mean something when there is nothing to say?"

"Darling, it seems that you know the answer to that," Alice said.

Annabelle was coming forwards carrying glasses and Marius stood up and they were both talking suddenly as if a spring had been released. We were on new ground and could breathe again. Annabelle was offering a drink to Alice who was reaching for it and chatting, I couldn't hear what about, with her eyes bright, pleasantly, and Marius was nodding his head at her and grinning. Peter was sitting with his hands on his knees looking up at the ceiling and Annabelle came over so that she stood by my side. The scene, instead of a battlefield, was now a conversation piece: with each one of us appearing to be posed according to the balance of the grouping. The talk ran, all at once, nonsensically, like water; with Marius in the lead, charming, controlling it, saying—

"Alice, do you remember, when we first came to London, and I stayed with you, how funny it was, when you used to go out to the shops in your dressing-gown, and you were so annoyed, because no one thought it was a dressing-gown, but a coat." "Quite untrue, darling," Alice said. "And the woman next door sent you flowers." "She sends me fish now, darling." "And came to you for advice, why fish?" "They have holes in them, why do they?" "And you gave her such cruel advice, you are the sort of person people always come to with their troubles." "She had a lover who was a bicyclist, do you remember?" "But really no reason to discourage him so." "I am sure it would have been unhealthy," Alice said.

And Annabelle: "Bicyclists can be extraordinary, you remember Nancy? Well, she was picked up by one on the Portsmouth Road." "That can become a terrible habit," Alice said. "She was going to Chobham, and the man refused to put her down, simply refused." "Why was she going to Chobham on a bicycle?" "She wasn't, you see, but she ran out of petrol, and the man took her for miles to his lodgings, and she had to ring up for her father." "Oh, a motor-bicycle," Marius said. "Yes, wasn't yours?" "No, he couldn't keep his legs still for a minute," Alice said.

And Alice: "It is because they travel so fast that you can never get away from them." "And what did her father do?" "In France they come past you even when you are traveling in a car." "He got hold of the chief constable and the Fire Brigade." "It wouldn't be so bad if they didn't appear to be pedaling upside down." "Did they manage to put her out?" "They usually carry a small extinguisher with them, I believe." "Yes, they did, after a time," Annabelle said.

And Peter: "I believe they have holes in them because . . . " "Then why did she ring up her father?" "I don't know what it can be if it isn't that sort of fish." "To tell him that she was in Bagshot instead of Chobham."

And Alice, finally: "Marius, darling, give me one more cigarette, and then I must go."

Peter tried to make her stay, but she wouldn't. Then Annabelle asked if she could come to see her house, and they arranged some meeting. They were kind to each other, and rather effusive. As I accompanied her to the door I said, "Why won't you stay?" and she said, "It's all right for you, darling, but really not any more for me": and on the landing she added, "You will see, later, what I mean." We all said good-bye. I did not know whether to go with her, to follow her into the lift, to get her a taxi, to stay with her perhaps. "Thank you so much for my evening," she said. "Thank you so much for coming," they said. Marius went on past me and took her arm and they went along the landing together and stood by the lift. They were still talking. Then the door closed and we were shut off from them, and I regretted something for Alice, but Marius was with her and it was all right. Peter picked up a paper and went quietly along to the bathroom. We turned. The scene seemed to be littered with the fallen petals of flowers. For the first time I was alone with Annabelle.

She sat down by the fire.

"Has Marius got a wife?" I said.

"Yes," she said.

"Who is his wife?"

"She is someone who is dying."

It was strange how in a room so warm we kept ourselves close to the fire.

"Dying?" I said.

"Yes. She is in hospital. I have never seen her. She came after the war, with Marius, to London. She has been dying a long time."

"Do you know what is wrong with her?"

"Yes," she said, but she said nothing more.

We could hear Peter singing in the bathroom. He was singing a song in German at the top of his voice.

"I should like to see her," I said.

"Marius may take you. But she doesn't want to see people now."

"I should not ask him."

"No."

"And he would not take you?"

"No," she said. "Not me."

I wondered what it was that gave Annabelle her calmness and assurance as if no wind ever came to disturb the fallen petals of her life.

"If Marius had no wife," I said, "would he marry you?"

"I don't know," she said.

"And would you like to marry him?"

"I don't know," she said.

But the petals had fallen, because I could see the shadow of them beneath her eyes.

"Peter, shut up," Annabelle shouted. The singing ceased.

"Has Peter ever seen her?" I said.

"No. I don't think he ever asked about her."

"Why not?"

"I don't think it ever happened to concern him." As she said this I felt that it was untrue. It was one of the few untrue things she ever said.

"So it does concern you," I said.

"No," she said. "Not now; not a bit any longer."

Peter came back into the room. He was wrapped in a bath towel. "Why?" he said. "Why shut up?"

"We were talking about Marius's wife," Annabelle said.

"Oh yes," Peter said. "Of course." He looked towards the door, standing in his bath towel, steaming rather, looking like the hero of an amateur Shakespeare play. Then Marius came in, and stopped in the doorway, watching him, and for a while they gazed at each other craftily like actors who have forgotten their lines. On their faces were expressions of amusement, and yet uncertainty; as if they had much to say to each other, but had neither the knowledge of what it was nor the means to say it. And then Peter, as if the necessity of expression had become too much for him, suddenly snatched the towel from his body and began to dance, heavily, on the carpet. He thudded up and down, waving his towel round and round him like a cloak.

Marius watched him. Peter continued. Then Marius raised an arm and grimaced at him, wickedly, like a gargoyle. Peter retreated. Marius advanced, tentatively, like a lion-tamer, and Peter went dancing away round the piano and then he suddenly made a dash for the open door and was out on to the landing trailing the towel behind him and his feet thumping softly on the scented floor. He stopped in the middle of the silent heated square of carpet onto which opened the doors of the other flats and the lift, and he stood there, naked, holding his towel on the ground like a victorious matador.

Marius watched him. "He will be arrested," Annabelle said. I could see the panel of lights by the lift shaft starting to flicker, which meant that the lift was ascending from the floors below. Peter stood there. "He is such an exhibitionist," Annabelle said. The lift was approaching the floor upon which Peter stood, and there was a large glass window in the door where it might stop. "We'll all be in the Sunday papers," Annabelle said. The lights flickered up, uncertainly, and then the lift itself came into sight, through the glass window, like the raising of a blind. It did stop. A woman's face was at the window, peering vacantly at Peter. Peter was motionless and imposing, like a statue. "Perhaps she'll think he is one of the decorations," Annabelle said. The woman's face hovered, despairingly, like a moon. She put up a finger and tapped discreetly on the glass. Peter stood there. "She will, after all, never believe it," Annabelle said. The moon blinked, pathetically, as if there were a fly on its nose. After a few seconds it retreated inside the lift and the blind descended. "She will now have to be analysed," Annabelle said.

Marius had picked a flower out of a bowl that stood on the piano, and he walked to the door where he held the flower twirling in his fingers, and then he said, "Peter, can you pick a flower up with your toes?" Peter unhinged himself from the pose he had adopted and approached us slowly and said, “Yes, I can,” and raised his foot. Marius dropped the flower on the floor, where it lay, an ugly dark chrysanthemum, with a long green stem, rather spiderish, its head soft and heavy; and Peter picked it up with his toes. He lifted it carefully, balancing on one foot, transferring it from his toes to his opposite hand and then holding it out towards Marius. Marius took it. Peter lifted the towel and wrapped it around his middle and then went back to the bathroom. The door closed and Marius twirled the flower in his fingers so that it wobbled as if it were alive. “Alice once tried to kill herself,” he said.

“Is that one of your tragedies?” Annabelle said.

“Yes.” He came into the room and sat down. He looked serious, aloof, as if he were employed in some business. I had not seen him like this before. “Alice knows what she is talking about,” he said. “The man whom she loved was killed in a motor accident in which she was driving. The man whom she married was mad. It is really only people like Alice who know what they are talking about at all.”

“About suffering?”

“About hopelessness. Which is more to the point, which requires a creative fit to get out of, and that is what Alice hasn’t got. Perhaps the world hasn’t.”

“Do you have to have tragedies before you can talk?”

“There is always a tragedy. You have to see it. What did you say to Peter?”

“Not much. Did we do it all right?”

“I think so.”

“Alice has to fight.”

“That is better than nothing. Perhaps that is creative. She keeps herself from dying.”

“And the world?” I said.

“Keeps itself. If you can’t see the tragedy that is there all the time you create your own tragedies by fighting. It doesn’t help much. But people seldom see things unless they hit them on the nose.”

I was thinking all the time of Marius’s wife who was dying.

"How did Alice begin?" I said.

"By being poor. Did you realize that? It gave her a start. It is true that the future of the world is with those who have to work."

"Did you have to work?"

"If you can call it that."

"And the future is with Alice?"

"She knows what it is about. She doesn't fool herself. Perhaps she has changed herself too much either to want it or to do much about it."

"Why didn't you stay with your communists?"

"There are other things besides the future of the world."

"For those who don't have to work?"

"There is the present. Nothing to do with the world. The eternal present."

"Which is more important?"

"Both. The present, I think, to us. You and I are already dead to the world, you see."

"The world is not dead to us."

"Of course not."

"What is this hopelessness?"

"Mixing eternity with the future. The future is what will happen, beyond our control, beyond our living. That is what is the world to those who work. Eternity is what might happen, what is in our control, what is in our dying. We can create it."

"Hopelessness is hunger and drudgery," Annabelle said. "It is nothing else."

"With hunger and drudgery there is the future. There is always hope. Where there is no hunger or drudgery there is also the hope of the present. This is the same as eternity. There is only hopelessness when drudgery looks to the present and idleness looks to the future. Alice is idle and looks to the future, but she remembers drudgery. That is her mixture of fact and hopelessness."

"I don't understand," Annabelle said.

"Neither do I."

"Begin again."

"To do anything with life or death you have got to be creative. To be creative you have got to see tragedy. Those who work, who are poor, see the tragedy of the work. It hits them, they see it, they are the world's future. This has nothing to do with truth, nothing to do with eternity. The idle are the world's past, but to everyone there is the tragedy of man and eternity. This is what has to do with truth, and what is seldom seen."

"When idleness is despised it will hit the idle. That is what is happening. Bricks at the public schoolboy may save his soul."

"They may save his future. But his soul? He will only have ceased to be idle, dodging bricks."

"I don't care about this boy," Annabelle said. "I care only that miserable people should not continue in their misery."

"Do you mean misery or do you mean hunger and drudgery?"

"I mean either. For us they are the same. You said that the world was not dead to us. Aren't we talking about souls?"

"Are you?" Marius said.

"You once said also that we could not touch ourselves until we had touched others. We cannot help ourselves until we have helped others. This is talking about souls."

"That is the present, then."

"All right. Whatever misery is, it is for us to do something."

"For us, yes. To be creative. Was it that this evening?"

"So you can begin," Annabelle said again.

This conversation was spoken in a flat, quick way as if we were reading from a book. It was like a verbal exercise, I thought: or like the statements and responses of a service in a church. We were strangely formal with each other.

"Peter was very clever," Marius said. "It was almost frightening."

"He was always good at games," Annabelle said.

"He got rid of the right things this time."

There was a sudden shout from the bathroom, and the noise of a fall. Neither Annabelle nor Marius moved. I wondered if all that Peter had done that evening—when he had danced out to the landing, for instance—was designed to get rid of embarrassments. Even now I could feel the formality loosening. Then there was a cry from Peter saying, "I am hurt, I have got concussion." Annabelle stirred, unhurriedly. "Oh dear," she said.

She got up and went to the door. Peter appeared, still naked, his bath towel rather sodden, his hand up to his head. "What happened?" Annabelle said.

"My towel fell in the water," he said.

"I mean what happened to your head?"

"It hit the ceiling," he said.

He tottered towards us. "I was doing a jump," he said. "I had the impression that I could not come into the room without a jump. So I was practising. I went up like a balloon. I had to make my entrance, you see."

"No," Annabelle said.

"I could not have come in without my entrance. I was a greyhound. And now I am unconscious. Do you think I am unconscious?"

"No," Annabelle said.

"And perhaps I should have a warm blanket to cover me and a little brandy perhaps."

"I will get it," Annabelle said.

Peter lay on the sofa. He covered himself with cushions, so that only his feet and head were visible. Annabelle sat on his legs. He sipped his brandy. There was no formality now. He said—"What does that Alice mean by our serious conversations? She is the first person I have had a serious conversation with in my life."

"We have been talking about Alice," Marius said.

"I heard you. And what are you going to do about it?"

"About what?"

"About Alice who is so difficult to help and your boy who has not yet had bricks thrown at him and the hungry who are not fed and me who has concussion on a comfortable sofa?"

"Are you really hurt?" Annabelle said.

"No," he said. "But life is such a donkey. What can you do with it?"

"You can sit on its back," I said.

"I don't like riding donkeys."

"You might as well get around."

"I know too much," he said. "I know what donkeys are. I know so enormously much."

Marius stood up and began to walk around the room.

"How can one help?" Peter said.

Marius stopped by the window.

"Because that is the problem," Peter said. "That is what you said. On a donkey you are alone, and that is no good. You're not really living if you stick to your donkey. Because if you get more than one person on a donkey you eventually break its back."

"We have all sat on its back together," Annabelle said.

"For moments. For four of us. But time separates us and there are more than four people in the world, and for the best part of our lives are we then condemned to a lonely education in riding?"

Marius said: "If we are then it is because we are at the beginning and only as individuals can we begin things."

"Begin what?"

"Begin to learn how not to be alone."

"Yes," Peter said. "But might it not be possible that we, the four of us, might continue?"

"We have got to find out so much more before even that is possible," Marius said.

"And then?" Peter said.

"Then I do not know," Marius said. "But I do not think that even then there will be a chance of being together until in some way, in some degree, what we have found is treated as an instinct."

"By other people?" Peter said. "Is that necessary?"

"Until it is accepted," Marius said, "—until what we are looking for has become an instinct, a convention, we shall always be separate from other people. So long as to us life remains a donkey, there will only be room for one person on its back. It will be this combination, always—the individual versus the donkey—until some new convention is born. Some new relationship, that is;—the symbol of which will not be the individual and the donkey. Some new feeling, so that life may be more than an education in riding; some new behavior, so that the symbol of the donkey may die; and then something new may rise in its place."

"A horse?" Peter said, with a wild and miserable laugh. "Do you mean a horse?"

"Not a horse," Marius said.

"Do you mean love?" Annabelle said. "And if you do, then that is nothing new and we already know about it and indeed it is as old as the world."

"I do mean love," Marius said.

"Tell me," Peter said.

Marius stood with his back to us, by the window, looking out into the dark. There was a quietness in the room which had come with the night. "I mean this," he said, "that the old love is dead. It is dead because the means that it had to express itself are dead. I don't know if they ever existed. I am talking about love of people, love of humanity, the love between several individuals. The old love said, 'Love thy neighbour,' but it didn't say how. And it is the 'how' that matters, it is the only thing that matters, and it never said how. It might as well have said nothing. Because everybody wants to love their neighbours, of course they do, but they can't. They find it impossible. They don't know how to set about it. So they are stuck, and they fail, and they hate each other. The world is turning to hate because it has forgotten the means of love.

"They tried, of course. They said all the words. But if you go to your neighbour and try loving him in the old way he will think you a fool. He won't want it, in the old way. And I am talking about the best kind of neighbours, too—the people who are still in the hope of love, who have not yet become bitter through failure. But they still won't want the old love. If you offer it to them they will feel hollow, enclosed, indifferent, they will think you are getting at them, they will be bored with you, that is the terrible thing, bored. They *won't* accept it from you. The old love is meaningless to people now."

"The old love did not say, 'Love thy neighbour,' first," Annabelle said.

"I know, but it said it second, and it did not say how. That is why it has failed. It is just words; it leaves people empty; it is a statement of the self. Yes this is it," he said, turning towards Annabelle, "—when you talk about love in the old way you are making a statement about yourself, nothing more. The statement on its own has no relevance to the people to whom it is addressed. And the old behaviour, too, that has no relevance either."

"That's right," Annabelle said.

"Well?" Marius said.

"But what is this old love that you are talking about, and what was it that the old love that I am talking about said first?"

"Well?" Peter said.

"It must be something new," Marius said. "A new behaviour. An entirely new means of expressing love." He said this obstinately, as if for the first time he and Annabelle were in disagreement.

"But how?" Peter said. "That is your question."

"I don't know," Marius said.

"You do," Peter said.

"I don't." He was still looking at Annabelle.

"The old love that you have been talking about has never been love at all," Annabelle said. "And the old love that I am talking about did not make the statement 'Love thy neighbour' on its own."

"No?"

"No," Annabelle said. "But go on with what you were saying."

"Go on," Peter said.

"I was going to say this," Marius said. He spoke slowly, as if his mind were only half on his words, and half on a problem that lay somewhere beyond them. "I do not know what love either has been or will be, but I know what it is not. It is not the statement of desire. It is not the behaviour of the imposition of desire. It has nothing to do with the self at all. The means haven't. It is the means that I am talking about. For the means of loving the self must be dissolved."

"Into what?" Peter said.

"Look," Marius said. "This." He spoke more quickly now, as if the problem beyond him, which lay somewhere in the distance between him and Annabelle, had now come into sight. "Into what you have created. This is similar to the creation of an artist. There is no communion between the artist himself and his audience. The artist has to create something beyond himself in order that there may be communion. When a great dancer dances he is not himself, he is his part, he becomes his part in order that he may project himself upon his audience. He loses himself, and he creates something new;—and this created part is the only meeting-ground between audience and dancer. Once this meeting-ground has been created, then, and only then, will there be communion. And it is the same with love. A lover must lose himself in order that his love may be communicable. He must create something out of the loss of himself in order that his love may be acceptable. What his technique is—how it may be defined—I do not know. It may be different in every instance. But I know this:—that every successful creation is a reflection of eternity: the technique will deal in symbols which are reflections of reality. Reality is what one desires—it is not what is. To create it there has to be movement which is in awe of eternity. One has first to be aware of the tragedies of eternity, and then to reflect them. So that two things are necessary:—to have the eyes of a man who sees these tragedies and the technique of a craftsman who can create their symbols in terms which will reach to others. Then what is becomes what one desires. Technique is the throwing of reality across the ground that separates loneliness. Perhaps, in memory, in the loss of self which is execution, one could throw communion across these spaces like one throws a ball."

Annabelle said: "The meeting ground has already been created. What is needed is the technique of finding it, not the technique of creating it oneself."

"Of finding it then. It doesn't matter. The act of creation has to be created again in each individual before he can find it. It doesn't matter. Lose yourself and draw your symbols from the subconscious or the superconscious or call it God, if you like, it's all the same—any old tragedy will do. I know that you must have your God. I know what you mean by your first commandment. Have it then. But I will tell you this, that the technique is something different to that of the churches. The churches have never answered the question of technique. But art has tried to, and dancing has tried to, and we must go back to the savages for that. But savages have something of the technique without the desire to use it: or rather, they use it for fear. And we have the desire without the technique. It is this that one should study, perhaps—this subtlety of movement and attitude, this darkness of laughter, and use it for love. It is there, somewhere, hidden; and that is what will be new."

There was a silence, and then Annabelle said: "Yes, but God is more than a word, and the first commandment is at least half of the technique, and although you may say what you like about churches there is another meaning of that word which might explain even more about the technique if it ever exists as more than a meaning."

"Which it doesn't," Marius said.

"I don't know. But it exists as a symbol, and that is my symbol. Whether it exists as more I don't know because I have never tried it."

"Tried what?" Marius said.

"Tried to lose myself in the meeting-ground which is not just a word but which is the first commandment."

"Oh hell," Peter said. He sat up suddenly. "And I'll tell you this, that it is easier to get lessons in dancing that it is to love God. Three guineas in Oxford Street and you can jump like a bloody savage. But three prayers to God and all you get is a crick in the back. And a kick too, most likely. I know because I've tried it."

"You haven't," Annabelle said.

"I have. And I tell you that I can jump but I can't love God, and I don't always hit my head on the ceiling, either."

"It was you who asked the question," Annabelle said. "How to help others and how not to be alone."

"And it is you who have not answered it. You say you must lose yourself, Marius says through dancing and you say through God, and I say that if I have to choose between being a savage who cuts up his children and an ascetic who cuts up himself, then I would rather stick to my donkey and try to train it into a horse. I stick to that symbol, and to hell with the rest."

"As a matter of fact," Annabelle said, "you do not stick to your donkey, and you do care about other people, and you could not bear it if you were on your own."

"To hell with the rest," Peter said.

"You said at the beginning that you are not living if you stick to your donkey. You know that that is true and that you yourself would always live for other people and in fact do more for other people than you will ever admit or imagine."

"To hell with everything," Peter shouted. "And to hell with me. If you dare to flatter me I shall cry."

"I suppose we shall behave now as we should have behaved anyway," Marius said, "whatever are the words that we have used."

"Then give me the brandy," Peter said, "and to hell with words."

"It is you this evening who have danced and who have loved," Annabelle said.

"I told you I should cry," Peter said. "And now will you play the piano, please, very sadly, so that my tears may be mistaken, as they will always be mistaken, I hope, for the tears of either brandies or pianos. And let us behave, for a little, as you say, as we should anyway behave, but won't, because of our symbols and our nonsense and the things that we can never understand and can never even hope to. You can play a psalm and Marius can croon like a negro and I will make a noise like a lonesome and tragic ass. Then, indeed, we will have created a reflection of eternity. And I still think that I know more about life than the whole bloody lot of you put together."

Annabelle played the piano.

7

In the days that followed I was with them, often, meeting for coffee in the mornings as a substitute for breakfast, and buns in the afternoon as a substitute for lunch. I do not think we ever ate properly except in the evenings, when Annabelle would cook us large quantities of buttered eggs in the flat, or we would go to some foreign restaurant which Peter had heard was excellent, and there eat the chopped cabbage, the skewered gristle, the queer pancakes, in which such foreign restaurants excel. Meals are the standard by which the duration of the day is timed, so that with the neglect of eating the days themselves became haphazard, passing quickly, almost unnoticeably, and becoming muddled with the nights. Emerging from a door, or drawing the curtains of a window, it was often a shock to find that the dawn, or the dusk, had crept up on us without warning, and that the scene we had expected had been transformed into either the candle-light of evening or the pale arena-like glare of early morning. Marius usually was away during the day, engaged upon some business about which I never quite discovered, but he would join us at night wherever we were, and he had a fortunate faculty for interpreting the garbled and often contradictory messages that we left behind us at the flat. Whether we were with him, or away from him, it was always the same. I think that in all our lives this spring was a queer interlude in which time became a vacuum, and we were all waiting for something to happen, whatever it would be.

Of our lives before this time we never talked, although we seemed to talk of everything else, and it was not until long after that I learnt some of the details of Peter's and Annabelle's childhood. I never learnt much about Marius's. He was older than us, and always mysterious. I think he was about thirty when we knew him. I learnt something about him, later, from his wife. But from the other people who knew him before he met Peter and Annabelle I never discovered a thing. They told me a lot about themselves, about how they reacted to Marius, but they never answered questions about Marius himself. He had that effect on people. He made them think about themselves, but never gave anything away.

He had lived most of his life in the West Indies, in a big house by the sea. He had come over to England in the war, as Alice had said, with his wife, and his wife was ill, and she had gone to hospital. Then he had lived alone, busying himself with a number of things that interested him, and being taken up by people who dropped him as soon as he disappointed them, and who usually returned at intervals to dig him up again only to retire in increasing bafflement when he would not submit to their plans. He intrigued people and at the same time infuriated them, for although they sensed that he was an extraordinary person they could not tell where his power lay. I have heard people talk of him as if he could have been anything, or again as if he were a wastrel without any power at all. But he was the kind of person who all his life is treated as a celebrity, although I do not think he was anything of a celebrity until the end.

When he had met Annabelle and Peter he went to live with them. I do not suppose that they talked much about this, either; he just stayed one night in the spare room of the flat that belonged to their parents and went on staying there on and off for the next six months. Their parents were away—their father was at that time the governor of some colony in Africa—and they had left their home in London for the use of their children. Annabelle was eighteen and Peter twenty, and Peter had come home previously to do his service in the army. This he had done, and Annabelle had come with him to look after the flat, and to be introduced to London by a series of relations.

When Annabelle had first moved into the flat these relations had done their best to move in with her, or at least to persuade her to move in with them. They had said that it would be more proper. But she had held out against them, and in this she was supported by her parents, who showed their regard for their children by letting them do as they wished. So Annabelle kept the flat and cleaned it and did the cooking with the help of a woman who came in each day, and it was there that Peter had come during his week-ends and his leaves from the army, and it was there that Marius came during the holiday that Peter had before he was due to go to Oxford.

For a while the three of them lived there together, and Marius stayed ostensibly as a friend of Peter's. But when Peter went away there was talk about Marius staying on in the flat alone with Annabelle, so for a time Marius had gone away out of deference to this talk; but Annabelle's scorn toward such scruples was so prolonged and vehement that eventually he moved back again out of deference to her. The talk had continued, anyway, even when he had gone: for people argued that he would not have left if he had not had something to hide. As Annabelle said, to run one's life according to the theories of others is a business too contradictory to be considered even out of kindness. So Marius stayed, and the necessary attempts at explanation were made, and the parents had not minded. And anyhow, Peter was not away for long.

Peter had gone to Oxford and had hated it with all the fury of which he was capable, and had walked out before the end of his first term. He said to me once: "Oxford is like a flea-circus: you can suspend a flea from wires and pretend that its struggles are acrobatics, but it can never get off the wires and it can never stop being a flea." In all this talk of Oxford he used phrases like these, as if the only people he had met there were either parasites or puppets, and the pride that drove them only the parade of greed. But his talk was always exaggerated, and I do not know what was in his heart. In the army he had been happy, because he had expected nothing from it, and yet in spite of the drudgery he had found something, with surprise—the simplicity of simple people doing things that are supposed to be unpleasant. And at Oxford he had expected something, because he had been told to expect it, and he had found only the complications of complicated people doing things that are supposed to be pleasant. He had been taken up by the societies, by the clubs, by the serious young men with portfolios: he had sat in the junior common room and had been smothered by smoke and tea: he had felt the heaviness of the jokes and the lightness of the discussions: he had written his essays as judgments and been told that he was not in a position to judge: he had studied other people's judgments and decided that there was no one in a position to judge. He had gone to some lectures and had not heard them, to others and had not understood them, others again and had wished that he had neither heard nor understood. At first he had tried to work, but in his mind all the time was the conviction that his work was irrelevant, that it was a fraud, that several thousand people were playing logical acrostics and were claiming that they were dealing with philosophical truth. This was what obsessed him—the knowledge that what he wanted was judgment and truth, and the fear that what he was getting was instruction in crossword puzzles. He wouldn't have minded, perhaps, if this had been admitted. But it wasn't. The instruction was solemn, circumlocutory, and ceaseless. The instructors were as grandiloquent as emperors or saints. He even heard, one evening, during a sermon by the Master, his college described as a temple in which men's souls were kept pure by the bright virginity of scholarship. This was a schoolroom where they played lexington and lotto! A barrack-room housey-housey fitting numbers into squares! He walked out of the sermon, because he felt ill, and then he stopped trying to work.

He shared a room with a man of thirty, who was married, and who could not afford to stop working. This man made noises in his throat while he worked; and when he was not making noises in his throat he was knocking his pipe out on his boot or blowing through it like a whistle. So Peter went out. He would have had to have gone out anyway, he said, because the room was so cold, and because the only arm-chair had a loose spring in it that hummed like a harmonium. Also the ugliness was aggressive: the wallpaper brown, the carpet green, the upholstery muddy. So he went out to parties, and he gave parties himself, and he was quite taken up by the party-going people.

He gave gramophone parties that were stopped by the Dean, river-boat parties that were stopped by proctors, dance-hall parties that were stopped by the police. He climbed up over walls, along across roofs, down through windows. He fell through buttery skylights into bursars' arms. At tea time he picked up girls with their evening dresses tucked up beneath their coats, at breakfast time he returned them re-tucked to their colleges after a celibate night in the streets. If he was locked out after midnight he could not get in before dawn, if he tried to sleep in the daytime he was disturbed by traffic and bells. Indeed, he said that it was the bells that finally drove him to leave. There was one that exploded just outside his window every quarter of an hour, and he claimed that it broke his tooth glass and did not even give accurate time.

And throughout all this period there was the gossip, and the intrigues, and the jealousy;—the strain of social pleasure revolving like bicycle wheels in the street. Bicycles whizzing up Broad Street, whizzing down St. Giles, with the gossip whizzing secretly on tyres of whispered words. Peter played, pedaled, and went faster than the rest. For a time he was rumoured to be engaged to three girls at once, and men spent sleepless nights explaining his success in terms of snobbery. He bought a car, and they said he was a millionaire; he sold it, and they said he was bankrupt. They followed him to Woodstock, they followed him down the Thames; they followed him voraciously, in a swarm, and then suddenly he stopped. The bells, for the last time, had broken his tooth glass.

So he left Oxford, and he came away hating things, for he felt that Oxford was a microcosm of the world. His memories of the army were no use to him, for he knew that what one finds in the army does not exist outside its ranks. He hated in general, in theory, the work, the play, societies and systems—but he never really hated individuals. I think that individuals were too precious to him; and there was too much love in him also beneath the fury, and it was this that made him so violent. There was more love in him than in most of the people I have known and it was always trying to come out, so that his indignation had to fight to squash it. His indignation won because the world in which he found himself invites more indignation than love on the surface, and he could not get beneath the surface because he felt so uncompromisingly about the evidence of his ears and eyes. He judged himself on his actions, and so he judged the world on its actions, and he judged fiercely, ruthlessly, with a desperate overworking of his conscience that could not tolerate mistakes. This, of course, was the biggest mistake of all; as he had been told at Oxford, one is not in a position to judge the world. Also, if he had paid more attention to his own shortcomings, as Annabelle had told him, instead of those of the world, he might have made fewer mistakes himself and thus eased the strain on his conscience. But with all his feelings turned outwards from himself, outwards towards evidence about which he felt so strongly that he had to judge it, he had to rage against it or else the strain upon his conscience would have broken him. He could not accept things. He was a sensitive person, and in his way an unselfish one. That is what gave him his talent for funniness, his talent for laughter and making other people love. But I think that the only people he ever loved himself were Annabelle and Marius.

Being turned outwards, and suffering, he had to have a God, and his god was Marius. I believe that Marius was a god to several people, but to none so strongly as he was to Peter. Peter took Marius as a god because he was free not only from all the things that Peter hated, but also from the hatred that was in Peter; and perhaps it was this hatred that obsessed Peter most of all. I know that Marius never hated. I don't know if he ever loved, either, in a human, passionate way; not even Annabelle. The word seems to bear a different relation to him. There is a meaning of the word in which it is abstract, inhuman; as if it described the state in which love might be possible, rather than the fact of love itself. This meaning, I think, was more applicable to Marius. Of course, Marius was not entirely like this, but he seemed to be at moments; and looking back on him this seems to be the best way to explain him.

It is difficult to explain him further. I heard him called a saint, once, at the end of his life, but he was not a saint. Saints are solitary, emotional people, whose force is emotional and who as a result are often embarrassing. Saints are crucified by the world because people get fed up with them, because they are too much of a good thing, not because the world feels a challenge from them. Marius's force was not emotional: he was too restrained, enclosed, static. It was not intellectual either, because I think he despised the intellect: he never gave much time to arguments that were logical. Another word is needed to describe the force that Marius possessed, and I do not think that the word exists. It was something to do with the subconscious, something frightening without the emotion of fear and true without the validity of reason. One always felt that Marius was right, like an oracle, even when one disagreed with his words. It was this that was frightening. His force, his whole understanding, seemed to come from a different level of consciousness to that of other people. Being in this presence was sometimes like the feeling that one gets when one is alone in a forest—a hard, impersonal, unbelievable feeling, like losing consciousness. I thought of him once as a tree, and I remember this feeling. Primitive peoples are said to worship trees because they imagine that there is something supernatural about them. There is nothing emotional or intellectual about this sensation. It is different from that—on another level.

And the world did feel a challenge from Marius. They felt him as a witch, not as a saint, and they resented him. The peculiarity of witches, as opposed to that of saints, is that they are usually burned without having done anything. Saints have to do a lot before attention is called to them: witches need do nothing. Saints are condemned for their unnatural actions: witches for their unnatural personality. Marius did not have to do anything. He maddened people by doing nothing, by his aloofness. And those who did not see him as a god often saw him as a witch, and they wanted to burn him. They said he was inhuman, and so he was. Humanity depends upon the conflict between good and evil, and I do not think that there was often a conflict in Marius at all.

And Annabelle? I cannot describe Annabelle. She has seemed to me to be most things in her time.

In the days that we were together, then, after our meeting with Alice, we moved around London with the impetuosity of people who have not known each other for very long, people who have been thrown together on a holiday that might end at any moment or go on for years, people who keep moving because to sit still is a waste of time. Peter, waiting for news from his father, had nothing to do: I, being idle and disorganized, had nothing to do: Marius and Annabelle, although they disappeared regularly—she to the shops and kitchen, he to no one knew where—did not let what they had to do intrude upon the irresponsibility that seemed our special province. I have never again been happy in this province, but I was then, and I think it was this very fact that we were waiting, as if on a holiday, and the fact that we really knew each other so little, that made this happiness possible. I had built up myths around them, and perhaps they had built up their own myths too, and one can live by myths quite easily so long as circumstances do not combine to mock or shatter them. For me the circumstances were propitious for myths, because my knowledge of the reality was so limited. There were many unanswered questions that lay around us, for instance—questions about Marius's wife, about Marius's relations with Annabelle, about hers with him, about Peter's attitude to whatever these relations were. There was also the question about myself—about why they should be content that I should spend so much time with them. This question was never even asked. Nor, indeed, were the others, but they hung in the air around us like the mysteries, the riddles, that are the guardians of myths. The question of Marius's wife, especially, was often present in my mind; but instead of causing the uncertainty that might have been expected, in some way it helped, by the fact of its secrecy, to mitigate the irresponsibility and make possible the fun. Since we did not know what it was that we ought to worry about, we waited for a time when we might; and in the meantime did not worry at all. It was as if, under the shadow of secrets, we were able to live more freely beneath the sun that might otherwise have weaned us. The power of myths usually resides in their mysteries.

It was this power that determined my feelings at that time towards Annabelle. I loved her, and I knew that I loved her, but it seemed impossible that I should ever make this known. I felt that she belonged to Marius; that there was so much established between her and Marius in their attitude, their behaviour, and their past, that any intrusion on my part would be sacrilege. It never occurred to me to try to establish a separate relationship between the two of us on our own. Whenever we happened to find each other on our own by chance, the situation at once became awkward, alarming, as if we were treading on forbidden ground; threatening the myth, coming close to breaking some taboo. We would make polite conversation, not looking at each other, and wait for the others to return. I became strangely aware of myself at these moments—aware of responsibility and the stretching length of time. But the others always did return, and then we would greet them, and the fantasy, shaded from its dangers, could continue on its levels out of time and out of thought. I did not know the nature of these taboos, these mysteries, but I remember them. Whatever love there was between Annabelle and me at that time belonged to them. I think it was the existence of Marius's wife that was perhaps the cause of them. She was the fifth person amongst us, always, absent and unknown, who by her presence and yet her absence made the relationship between the four of us so imaginary and yet so strong.

So we lived on the surface, and the surface was movement, and the movement was fun. Alice was right, I thought; it is fun that matters. Fun as a business, fun as a life, fun as an attitude that is graceful and creative. There were days when nothing mattered but this, and these I remember.

Peter walking up the street with his golden hair bounding, his jacket open, his tie over his shoulder, his shirt rucked up around his waist: Annabelle with a hat like those that Spanish men wear when they come in to towns for the festivals, a black stiff hat with a wide flat brim and a crown on top like a cake tin: Marius on the corner, always slightly dramatic, always posed, his hands in his pockets, watching. Peter running through the traffic, running for a bus, everything flying, his arms, his legs, his elbows, waving: Annabelle swaying with long quick steps with her chin tilted up above the soft black strap that ran from her hat past her cheek-bones: Marius standing, watching us catch the bus, following from a distance discreetly in a taxi. Peter wore old clothes, clothes from his school days, but he wore them with a peculiarly careless elegance. Annabelle made her own clothes, made them from stiff jutting material that went in capes and folds, reminding one of bustles and epaulettes and bodices. One never noticed what Marius wore.

Peter protests: "Annabelle, that hat is preposterous; you might be in the chorus of the Chocolate Soldier." "They wore busbies, surely, or those cardboard things like jugs." "Yours is like a cheese dish." "We haven't eaten for twelve hours," Marius says; "Let's go in here."

But we don't, we go on, to the park, perhaps, where the band is playing (Peter: "Give us a song, Annabelle, you look like Lily Langtry"); or to Lords, for the last few overs of the day (Marius: "What we want is something revolutionary, a bowler who can send the ball up very high and get it coming down vertically on the stumps"); or to Kew, for the flowers (Annabelle: "I don't think anyone will see you if you go into the bushes").

At Kew the flowers are out, some children are playing with a brightly coloured ball, the nursemaids are knitting beside their prams. The ball rolls to our feet, Peter picks it up ("Look out for the greenhouse"), he kicks it, it shoots up over the trees like a rocket. We spend several minutes trying to fish it out of the river, we borrow a walking-stick from an old man asleep. The children watch us, severe, reproachful. We are so much younger than they. Peter gets the ball to the edge of the river; he slashes at it, wickedly, with the stick; it disappears gracefully over the trees from whence it came. The children seize it, the old man dreams, Annabelle smells a petal from a blossom like snow.

In the park we meet friends, friends of Annabelle's, they want us to go somewhere, they have several cars. We climb in. It is a garden-party day with garden-party people, some boats on the river, fireworks, games. Annabelle walks through the crowd like a reaper through an orchard; she is in grey, and takes her hat off, because other women are in purple and have cherries in their hair. The men are tightly waisted, carrying gloves and rolled umbrellas. The day is hot. Peter undoes more buttons as the others mop their brows. We glide away, discreetly, seeing a fair-ground in a field. Crossing over a bridge above an ornamental garden we are like willow-patterned people on a plate of painted green.

There are swing-boats, and we swing, and the earth slips sideways like the tumbling of a tray. Annabelle is above me, her hands are towards my head, the rope pulls her arms and her arms go with it, her hair is flung to the sunlight like the rising pulse of flames. She pulls, standing upright, her body is like a bird; she comes downwards, down upon me, then beneath me, as if she were drowned. The bird flies, falls to the water, she floats like a swimmer stretched laughing on the sea. As I stand up to pull, my knees touch hers, her body is like the waves upon which seagulls rest, and I am the bird.

Peter is by the cocoanut-shy. "I say, these things are stuck on with glue." "I know, old man, but you can't expect to win every time." "I haven't won once." "I know, old man, but you're honestly not supposed to."

Annabelle props her elbows on the counter of a booth. She is given an air-gun, loaded. She leans forwards so that her waist is against the edge of the counter and the black band of her belt seems to cut her body in two. I stand behind her. Her dress is pulled forwards in tiny wrinkles from her armpits and her skirt curves outwards with the softness of skin. One foot is against the upright structure of the counter and the other is back with her toe just touching the ground. I can see her breathing. Then she holds her breath, and the muscle in her leg tightens, and she shoots a clay pipe from a shelf.

Peter is rotating dispassionately on the end of a chain. "Rather dull, this." We encourage him, and he stands on his head. The machine is stopped. "Sorry, old man, but it's strictly anti-rules." "I say, do all you people talk like this?" "Like what, old man, but you might get a nasty flesh wound." "Flesh wound be damned, I might get killed."

As we go back in the cars I am alone with Annabelle. We sit looking out of our respective windows. The road passes. Time passes. We do not speak. The car is a tiny boat which has to be balanced very still. The road is dark, and the lights from other cars blind us. If only I could see into the dark, I think, and if other people did not blind me, I might not be so alone when I am alone with Annabelle.

It was at Lords, finally, watching the cricket, that I met the Australian with whom I had shared a cabin on the boat. We were standing by the tavern, and Marius and Peter were having their protracted argument about the ball that should come down vertically on the stumps. ("You could hook it." "Not if he pitched it dead on." "He can't have it both ways." "Neither can you unless you sit on the stumps.") The Australian came out of the Tavern with a mug of beer, and he did not see me at first. He was listening to the conversation. Annabelle had now joined in. ("Why shouldn't you sit on the stumps?" "Danger of L.B.W." "But the umpire never could tell unless he was up in the sky like a balloon." "No reason why he shouldn't be." "He might get biased in a wind.") The Australian had his head on one side and was grinning, incredulously. He began to roll a cigarette with the quick, damp movements that I remembered so well. The talk went on. ("It all depends on getting it very high." "It sounds to me just like your grapefruits." "You couldn't hook a grapefruit, not at Lords." "You might hook a lemon at the Oval." "Oh Marius, really, what a dreadful joke.")

Then the Australian saw me. I detached myself from the group and greeted him. "Well," he said, "and so you haven't got any friends?" His gold teeth were showing, and I was glad to see him. "We were trying to find some way of beating you Australians," I said. ("It would burst." "Not if you glided it." "You couldn't glide a banana." "If you avoided the slips." "Oh Marius, really, what an utterly dreadful joke.") "You certainly have got some friends," said the Australian. "Yes," I said. ("You might pull a plum." "Like Little Jack Horner." "Would that be L.J. Horner, Sydney, second test?") "Yes that would be Christmas," said the Australian, joining in. I introduced him. "He must have been quite young at the time," Marius said. "Yes that was the game when Old King Cole was called on to bowl," said the Australian, leaning back on his heels and roaring with laughter.

The Australian was a great success. He said that Annabelle was a corker, Marius sharp, and Peter dry. He called Peter's bluff, and outwitted him in complexities. With Marius he got involved in a discussion on the cultivation of fruits. We never knew when he was serious. He paid Annabelle elaborate compliments, and we drank a lot of beer. He played our game like a professional—one of those new-world professionals who take sport so devoutly. As we talked with him and followed him through the maze of his serious jokes, in spite of the laughter and the success of the day, I had the impression that we were only amateurs at this sport, that we would never make a business of it as he did; and after we left him it seemed we could retire unhurt. And just before we parted he came over and said to me, grinning all golden with his teeth: "And you said that you hadn't got a girl."

III
A GARDEN OF TREES

8

So, in a playground, as children, we waited; there was talk but no action because there was nothing to do. In the playground there was no responsibility, no conflict—it was a small enclosed existence in a corner shut off from the world. The sun shone and we did not look over the railings. We thought we knew about love because Marius had talked about love, we thought we moved in awe of our secrets because they were secret: but our emotions, however real they appeared, were emotions of the imagination. We created our rituals—the swings, the see-saws, of the children's mind—but they were symbols which went no further than the confines of our waiting. We remembered our words; we thought we saw a tragedy here, a reflection there, eternity in our secrets; but so long as they remained words and not actions they had little relevance to living. Enclosed thus we could have continued but for the prevalence of time. Time came in, like a nursemaid, with the demands of reality; and on a summer morning Marius asked me if I would like to see his wife.

It was a windy day. I had slept badly on a sofa in the flat, and my eyes were heavy as if drained of moisture. Marius came early, before the others were up, and when he asked me I did not think of what to expect. I dressed, and had breakfast, and followed him. We went in a taxi, I did not know where.

The day seemed blown with the litter of ages. Driving through the wind it was as if we were leaving our past behind like paper. Out beyond the railings, across the waiting world, I felt little except the numbness. And yet there, at the end, was the centre of the mystery. Marius's wife had always seemed to me the guardian of our secrets. Stepping out of the taxi and standing on the threshold I might have been some novice on this edge of another life.

A mottled, unpretentious building, one of a row, more of a nursing home than a hospital, with large knobs of bells on either side of the door. We waited. Inside there was an atmosphere of caution combined with disregard. Silent, neat officials lurked behind half-closed doors, watching yet oblivious, not caring to hide and yet not willing to help. Marius led the way, ignoring them, steadily, like a soldier marching through an occupied town. I followed him up the carpeted stairs and along the vanishing rubber-tiled corridors. There was a silence like that which precedes an action. Then he stopped and knocked on a door. Again we waited.

This was a private nursing home, I could see; quiet, rich, discreet; suffering muffled behind doors of polished wood, the privacy of richness observed as in a bank. At the far end of the passage nurses glided, carrying objects shrouded under heavy white cloths. Disease, dying, was well camouflaged here, white-painted with cleanliness, scrubbed with optimism—the buoyant, determined optimism of a healthy pretence. As we waited a figure emerged upon the passage like a ghost, a disheveled old man in a dressing-gown, lost, flat-slippered, poling his old thin neck out of his garment like a tortoise, peering and bewildered. A nurse saw him, and seized him, and steered him flip-flap down the passage to the bathroom. He seemed dingy and crumbling in the stiffness of the building, as if he had strayed from the housemaid's cupboard where the dustpans and brushes are kept. The patients often seem out of place in a nursing home. Marius became uneasy waiting outside the door, so he pushed and went in.

A white, bright room, with flowers. A lot of painted steel, painted girders, like the cabin of a ship. A high bed, hard yet somehow crooked, and a whiteness, a terrible whiteness, like snow.

And the woman in the bed was part of it. She was hard, stiff, quite motionless, white skin against the white pillows; silent, and lined, and erect; nothing of the old man's decay, crumbling; no shuffling, flip-flap shuffling, no age, softness; just hard and white and a creaking, somehow, with the tension of being alive. The being-alive creaking against the not-being.

Her hair was black, and her eyes were black; still no colour. Blackness was only the intensifying of whiteness, and whiteness remained. A young face, petrified; a terrible thinness stretched over bones like a sheet over iron spikes. Arms and shoulders covered, draped; just the neck fluted like a pillar and the fragile, staring, breakable china face. Such a beautiful face. And one hand curved up on the counterpane like a sun-dried, brittle, fossilized shell.

"I have brought a friend," Marius said. "Do you want us?"

Her eyes moved, and her head slightly, and she whispered, "Yes."

"Here is a chair," Marius said. I sat on it. Marius leaned on a table by her bed.

"It is kind of you to come," she said to me, whispering; the fragile, unblinking black eyes staring at me. Then her eyelids closed, for a moment, with an almost imperceptible movement, like the falling of a drop of water, and when she spoke again her voice was clear, defined, like the echoes of a flute. "You are a friend," she said. "I have not seen you before."

"No," I said; "I am sorry." I did not know what I was saying.

"Marius has brought you," she said. "I do not see many people now." She spoke liltingly, with great precision. She blinked again. Then her white, cockle-shell hand fluttered up towards Marius. "Marius," she said; "why have you brought him?"

"Would you like to talk?" he said. "Shall I go?"

"Yes," she said. "For a minute."

And Marius went.

In the quietness I could hear the distant, cavernous sounds of the traffic of London. There was no sound from the building, no sound at all. Facing the white blinding stare of the woman amongst the pillows I felt that I was dead.

"Tell me," she said, "when you first met Marius."

I told her of our meeting, and after.

"And was he alone?" she said.

I told her of Annabelle.

"Tell me more about her," she said.

I told her. And then I told her about Peter, and the flat, and what I knew of them.

"Thank you," she said. She lay for a while, not heeding me. Then she moistened her lips, and I saw how incredibly strong her teeth were, a young woman's teeth, like lilies. "Do you always tell the truth?" she said.

"No," I said.

"Perhaps you do. I am sorry to ask you so many questions. There are just one or two things I wish to know, you see, that Marius cannot tell me. The truth anyway is not something that can be told."

"No," I said.

"I am dying," she said. "Has Marius told you that?"

"No," I said.

"Has he told you anything about me?"

"No," I said.

"Perhaps that too is something that cannot be told. And what do you think of Marius?"

"I think . . . " I began. My voice sounded thick, artificial, like a buffoon. It rose upon the air like some inflated condescension. My throat would not obey my ears, and I could not bear it. "I think a great deal," I said.

"Do you?" she said. She seemed to frown, as if in embarrassment. Her hand fluttered up towards her eyes. "I want to know that Marius will not be destroyed," she said.

It did not seem that there was anything now that I could say. The room had become like a box in which bodies are preserved for centuries. Around us hung the dust in the shapes that life had given it, the eyes and hands and tongues that are moistened into movement, that are dried again in tombs until a breath can collapse and shatter them. In front of our throats stretched a tension of gossamer that only the note of a reed could pierce. When she spoke her voice was clear as a needle: it did not harm. But for me, I could not speak as men speak, with their faces, because the noise of impurity would have scattered the dust. But there was something that had to be said, and when I heard it it was not as if it had come from me, but rather from outside, from where men, in another age and another existence, seek to ravage the tomb with the clink of their axes. I said, "What was it that happened to you?"

"Has Marius ever talked to you about love?" she said.

"Yes," I said.

"And did you agree with it?"

"I don't know," I said. And then again, as an echo, as the sound of a pick in the stillness where dead men have not heard a sound for centuries, I said, "What was it that happened to you?"

"Me?" she said. "Shall I tell you?"

I looked away from her. The sounds were clearer now. Sand began to fall between the corners of the girders, a trickle like an hour-glass when the earth is rocked. "Yes," I said.

"I said that it was something that cannot be told. I shot myself. Is that what you want?"

"No," I said.

"Marius came into the room and I hit him. Marius was a shadow. There is nothing to believe in when people are shadows. Is that what you have found?"

"No," I said.

"There is a futility that is deathly. The weight of it kills you and there is nothing to be done. It was that with Marius."

"With Marius?" I said.

"I have told you," she said. "I went out onto the sand."

"The sand?" I said.

"We lived there, did you know?"

"Yes," I said.

"My hand waved in the wind. I was not good at it. What else shall I tell you?"

"Tell me why you hit him."

"Because I was afraid."

We sat side by side like monuments, our hands folded, our eyes in front of us with the blindness of marble. "Why?" I said.

"Why is one afraid? I do not know. Do you? It is a place that is much older than its people. Perhaps that is what makes one afraid. Have you been there?"

"Yes," I said.

"We lived under the sun. A large house, by the sea, where the wind blew. We saw no white people, only fishermen and servants. Marius sat on the rocks and did not do anything. We loved the place. I did. I have never loved any other place."

"Love?" I said.

"I will tell you," she said. "I have never told it to anyone before. Marius talks about love. We talked about love when we were married. I was rich, and a European, and Marius was not. I hated Europe, I always have done, and I married Marius. When the war came we stayed there. I would not have minded. Europe could have destroyed itself. When we talked about love it sounded something new."

"And it was not?"

"Marius sat out beneath a palm tree. It is wrong to talk about it. It is easier to talk than to believe. When you talk there are only shadows and they deceive you. Have you found this?"

"No," I said.

"The men built Marius a shelter from the wind, and he had a table in front of him on which he wrote. When the war came he folded the paper into a dart and sent it floating through the trees like a bird. I remember how I watched it. He sent the war floating away from us. It was like the dove that went out of the ark, and we were alone."

"And you were not?"

"We never talked about the war, nor about Europe. We thought that there were other things to talk of. Marius tore up the paper that was left beneath the palm tree, and he dropped it into the water where the fishes came to nibble at it like bread. When we had no more to say we said nothing. That is what happens. Why are you frightened, do you know?"

"No," I said.

"Marius went out each day onto the rocks, and I watched him. He was quiet as a rock himself, and he let the sea come up to him and wash him. There was nothing to do. Then he stayed out at night even, sleeping on the beach where the crabs ran, and I came out to join him, and the house was empty, behind us, with the servants running it, quite silently, as they do, and us on the rock in front of the palm trees."

"And Marius?" I said.

"Then he went away from me, searching for something. I did not know what was happening. When you have put your trust in shadows there is nothing that is real. Have you found this? He went with the fishermen in their boats as they sailed after the flying fish, he went with them into the hills and stayed in their villages. They treated him as their god, their personal god, but he did not do anything. That is what happens when nothing is real. The nothingness destroys you. The weight of it grows. The estate was mine, a huge rotting estate with sugar-canes and fruit trees, but it was he who became part of it, who decayed with it, who felt it. He sat with them in front of their huts and ate their food and watched them. He sat for hours with his hands among the grasses and there was a silence about him like death. He never did anything. I did not see much of him then. In the evening it grew cold and I went back to the empty house where no fires were laid and I sat there. There was a futility that was timeless, that was worse than death. I felt sometimes that it would strangle me. I remember the sounds that came down from the hills."

"The sounds?" I said.

"I remember them. There was a day when the wind stopped. Marius came down and sat with his back to me, on the verandah, in the darkness. It was an evening of unusual heat. I waited for him. There was a futility that was deathly. Love, I remembered. Then he went away from the house towards the sea and I followed him. He sat on a rock and dropped stones into the water and he watched them become silver and seem to burn beneath the surface. 'That is the phosphorous,' I said. I sat down beside him. 'What are you going to do?' I said. He put his arm into the water so that it shone like something molten. 'Who am I?' he said. I thought he was mad, then. I am sure I thought him mad. This is what happened."

"What happened?" I said.

"If he did not know how could I persuade him? There was a despair that crushed me. The moonlight was behind him and his eyes went black. 'I am nothing,' he said, and he lifted his hand out of the water so that it dripped like a baptism."

"What happened?" I said.

"I tried to know what he was feeling. Why are you frightened, do you know? It is the emptiness that kills you. His shape in the darkness was like wings, like animals, and it was not he, had he not said so? I am not, he had said. And that is what I knew, that he wasn't, in the darkness."

"And you hit him . . . "

"There is a fear which is of damnation. When a person is a person no longer there is death in his place. As he sat on the rocks crouched heavy like a devil it was as if he were a mirror and I was he and there was nothing between us except what was going outwards into what was not bearable. All that he had said and had not said was hollow like a skull. What it meant was nothingness. It was not then that I hit him. He dived into the sea and swam away from the moonlight."

"And you went out onto the sand . . . "

"When he came into the room I did not expect that there it would follow me. He came in with the thing that was not him and the death and the corruption and when I cried he shouted to drown me but it was not him that I wanted to kill. I ran for the door and he slammed it in front of me and it was then that I hit him. Whatever it was that was taking me into eternity and would have taken me if I had not run it was not that that I could kill but rather myself before it could take me. When love is nothingness and words are empty and what you have trusted is a lie there is nothing else to be done. I went out onto the sand where the sea was crying."

"And you shot yourself . . . "

"Living as we had done what else could I do? With one of us mad and nothing but the two of us I only wanted to end it. There was nothing but the two of us in the whole of the world. With emptiness there is terror and you cannot escape it. Outside it was raining. Everything was a shadow and the shadow was a lie. That is what you must remember when you talk about love. By the sea there was a wind and I was not good at it."

"The wind had stopped," I said.

"Yes," she said. "The wind had stopped. The rain was soft and heavy with tears."

"And is this true?" I said.

"True?" she said. "I have told you that what is true cannot be told. This is a story of love and Marius."

As we sat the sounds from outside from very far away had grown and the slow disintegration of the tomb had scattered the dust trickling and sliding inwards and downwards piling gradually in particles around our feet expelling the web that had held us for centuries, the airless stillness falling to nothing as the earth came crumbling mounting up on us our eyes our hands our tongues crushed in on us so that now when there was light there was also no shape and the achievement of the pick looked down upon a desert. "What is there now?" I said.

"Now?" she said. "Is not that for you to tell me?"

"Yes," I said. I sat in the shape of a thought that has been forgotten.

"And can you tell me?"

"No," I said.

"Perhaps you do tell the truth," she said. "Perhaps that is why Marius brought you."

"Yes," I said.

The light from the room was white like an arc light: time had come in on us like an awakening into snow. The eyes emerging out of darkness and birth were pained and blinded by the weight of the sky. I looked towards the door beyond which shadows ran softly. "I will tell you tommorrow," I said.

"Thank you," she said.

I stood up. Her face was still like paper and her hands like shells. "Goodbye," I said.

"Goodbye," she said.

Outside it was raining and the wind had stopped.

Marius was standing beneath a lamp post at the end of the street. I joined him. "Let's walk," I said. He followed me round the corner to where the road ran down like a switchback. "Why was it not love with her?" I said.

"Because she was afraid of it."

"Why?"

"Because it is frightening."

"That is not the point," I said.

"No," he said. When he spoke he spoke quickly as if his life depended on it.

"Then why was it with her?"

"Because to her there was nothing else except the two of us."

"That is what she said. Have you then worked it out and arranged it like a plea all stamped and docketed and legal?"

"And are you prosecuting me?"

"Yes," I said. We walked beside the buses that crawled like something wounded.

"I did nothing," Marius said. "I just stood there."

"And to you there was something else besides the two of you?"

"That is not for me to say."

"That is what she said. And if you had not stood?"

"What?" he said. "And what should I have done?"

"I don't know," I said. "I don't know at all."

"Neither do I," he said.

At the bottom of the hill there was a crossroads in which the buses were wedged like lice. "Would you have stopped it if you could?" I said.

"That is no question," he said. "It happened. I stood there and she destroyed herself."

"Did not you destroy her?"

"I tell you again, it happened."

"Then tell me," I said.

"What?" he said.

"Oh nothing, nothing . . . "

"I tell you," he said, "I had been thinking. For months I had been thinking. Don't other people think?"

"Oh yes," I said.

"And I discovered something. Well?"

"And she destroyed herself!"

"Yes."

"Why do you put it like that? Is it necessary to defend yourself?"

"Yes," he said. "It is."

"Then I hate you for it."

We walked in silence. It seemed to me that I was destroying everything.

"Listen," I said. "I am not saying that you destroyed her. I am saying that what you had discovered did."

"What does this mean?" he said. "Some men are destroyed when they look on death. Is that death's responsibility?"

"You cannot talk about death's responsibility," I said.

"All right then."

"But what happened was wrong. And you can talk about man's responsibility."

"All right."

"And you are a man."

"How comforting!" he said. I suddenly realized how much he was suffering.

"So that it is your responsibility," I said. "And are you trying to say that it was worth it?"

"I will not use your words," he said.

"Then what words will you use?"

"None," he said.

"You have used them to justify yourself."

"Because you were attacking me."

"I am attacking you now," I said.

We walked on. "What is it that you are asking?" he said.

"I am asking whether you hold yourself responsible for the effects that you have on others."

"I hold myself responsible for my actions," he said, "but not for what I am."

"And you define your actions rather easily," I said.

"It is not a difficult definition."

"It is a limited one. And why do you not hold yourself responsible for what you are?"

"Because I believe in God."

"God?" I said. "Why not the devil?"

"Because the devil is concerned with actions."

"And what you are is the concern of God?"

"Yes," he said, "fundamentally."

"That must give you comfort," I said.

He turned on me furiously. "Listen," he said, "There are things in which you believe, in your inmost soul you believe, and they are the concern of God. If you have searched into your soul and have found something, if you have reached and can reach no further, then there, what you have found, that is God. You cannot deny that. You cannot deny that God. You may be wrong, for you may not have reached far enough, and you may forget what you have found, but if you believe something honestly then that is your God for you, and you can never deny it, never, no matter what may be its effects and its catastrophes."

"Is it not by its effects that you should judge it?"

"I do not judge," he said. "How can I judge it? There is a law and a truth that is beyond judgment. What you are trying to make me say is that my belief is a belief of the devil because a person was destroyed when she looked on it. You hold responsibility as a judgment against my belief. And I am saying that I accept responsibility for every decision at every time, but with judgment I am not concerned. The belief is God's and the judgment is God's, and the catastrophes are just what happen."

"What then is your responsibility when your wife is destroyed?"

"My responsibility is that I will not tell you, but it is not to deny my God."

"Why will you not tell me?"

"Because you would sneer."

"And are you frightened of that?"

"I am not frightened for myself but for you."

"Are you frightened for me when you would destroy your wife and pray to your God all in one breath and in the name of love?"

"Yes I am frightened, and yes then that is my responsibility to pray to my God, and I will tell you this, that you do not know what love is, you have no conception of what love is, you do not know about love at all."

"Do you?" I said.

"Ask someone else," he said.

"Your wife?"

"Yes," he said; "Ask her, ask my wife," and he turned away from me and walked off violently into the crowd where he disappeared like a bubble in a swirl of water.

I stood at the crossroads. I thought: There is madness, now. Outside the playground there is nothing but madness. Secrets should never be told. Secrets should never be told. Secrets should never be told. I repeated this, endlessly.

The world went past me. What Marius has talked about is madness. The secret is horror, horror is at the centre, there is nothing but horror. Perhaps it is myself who is mad.

The rain was green as if the world was drowning. All this has happened too quickly, things do not happen so quickly as this. Out beyond the railings, across the waiting world, time has foundered like a wreck on the rocks. They say that to a drowning man time is speeded so that all his life is in one second. What is it that he remembers? Marius said it was eternity. Perhaps, after all, he only remembers what has been left undone.

What is Marius? He said it was tragedy. He said that nothing can happen until there was tragedy. Once there were no conflicts and now that there is a conflict what can happen now? Perhaps conflicts are of the imagination, like the games of children. That is one thing I should have learned, from the sense of madness.

So there is tragedy. A conflict is irrelevant, because I do not know. I do not know what I am feeling. Emotion is not like this, it is what is known. Get rid of the conflict and then I shall know. This is the one thing I have learned. Now, at every moment, there is something to do.

I rang up Annabelle. The glass was broken in the window of the call box, so that the noises of the street came in in waves. "Hullo," she said.

"I want to ask you something, something about Marius."

"Where are you?"

"When Marius told you about him and his wife, what did he say?"

"Can't you come round here or can I meet you?"

"I don't think so, I'm sorry, I have to get back . . . "

"Are you there now, at the hospital?"

"I have been, I have to . . . "

"Can't I see you?"

"No."

A pause, then: "He told me that when . . . "

"I am sorry, I can't hear you."

"Surely it is not what happened then but what happens now," she shouted.

"What?"

"I said surely . . . "

"I hear you. But what can I do now when I do not know what Marius is?"

"Don't you know what Marius is?"

"No," I said.

"You do, you do, and you must not . . . "

"I can't hear you."

"I said you must not take a failure . . . "

"Did he say it was a failure?"

"Of course he did. Wasn't it a failure?"

"He seemed to think . . . "

"Is not everything both a failure and not a failure, and what has that got to do with it?"

"Everything . . . "

"No nothing, nothing, surely, you know what you feel about Marius, you know what Marius is, you cannot judge . . . "

"If I cannot judge what can I do?"

"Do? Can't you do what you have to do and it is not a quibble over words that will decide you?"

"What have I to do?"

"What you feel and what Marius is to you, isn't it?"

"Yes," I said. "I'll see you." I went out of the call-box and walked among the streets.

A green day. Emotion is not describable. But if I cannot judge what is a failure and what is not a failure what is there to judge and what to know? And if I cannot know what is a disaster and what is not a disaster can I judge what is right and wrong just by looking inwards to the inmost soul, he said, but we can never know about ourselves, she said, and what is there to do? But can we know about others then, what to do at least and thus to everyone yes everyone but Marius especially who is close to me and who has helped me and who has given to me these days and this part of him this whole of him and this should I, I know, but can I? And what is this failure except that everything both is and isn't, and to him what am I to do but give—he who has been five years with a dying wife, who saw her die, who saw her kill, who saw him kill, five years looking inwards to ask a question that cannot be answered, a question like that, too, was it or was it not, am I or am I not, O God, and what can he do except pray to his God O God if it was then it was and I did, and if it wasn't then it wasn't and I did, and the prayer is the same whether it was or wasn't. And forgiveness is the same, too, so that it doesn't matter except that he asks to be forgiven, which he does, from his God, and from me too, from me, and who am I to walk about the streets asking a question that even his God does not answer because it is not necessary to be answered but only to have something done about it, and this is what I can do here and now because I have seen this suffering and hers too and it is not for me to ask about it but only to help it. This I accept and must do although I do not know how and I do not know why and I do not even know if it will be right or wrong, but that doesn't seem to matter any more, I don't know why, it is the doing that matters, and for the how and why and right and wrong I trust to luck and whatever there is between us and whatever there is between everyone in the world and that indeed he has given me. What they have done for others I can do for them. It is a green day. I must do for what he is and what he requires.

I went back to the hospital. "I hope I am not disturbing you," I said.

"I did not expect you," she said.

"No." She raised herself.

"Why have you come back?"

"I have had a row with Marius," I said.

"A row? Have you?"

"Yes."

"I did not mean . . . " She looked frightened. "I am afraid I was rather dramatic this morning," she said.

"So was I."

"Perhaps after all . . . " She paused, and I knew that I had to begin.

"It is a fault of mine—being dramatic," I said.

"Yes?"

"It is what happens when you don't know what should be happening really. Why can't you get well?"

"Because they say so."

"Who?"

"There is a man called Dr. Livingstone."

"There is? I shall make you laugh. When was the last time you laughed?"

"Why do you want me to get well?"

"Isn't that what matters?"

"Is it?"

"Perhaps because I am in love with Annabelle," I said.

"Oh," she said. I knew that it was imperative that there should be no silence.

"Do you know what Peter said once? That if one makes a business of tears then one is free to laugh at one's leisure."

"Did he? And does he laugh?"

"No, he makes other people laugh, he is the clown that cries by night."

"And what are you?"

"Just at the moment I don't know."

"Why did you say that about Annabelle?"

"Because I have got to think of a joke."

"That wasn't a joke."

"No, that is the terrible thing, I can't think of a joke."

"Please, it is not necessary."

"It is, I am sure, I am like the fools that prattle in tragedies, they have to think of jokes. I hope they find it easier."

"Is this what Marius has done to you? Is this what happens now?"

"I think so, yes. This room is like a diving-bell. Shall I send you flowers?"

"Marius brings me flowers."

"Marius would bring you a wreath of last year's laurel. What do you do with them?"

"I have them taken away. I do not like to see them out."

"You can have them in pots. I will bring you a tree planted in a tub."

"A tree would wither in a room like this."

"It would not if you liked it. It would be your tree. When the nurses came they would get caught up in its branches like Absalom."

"They would look funny without their hats."

"Yes. And Marius could sit in it and then he would look funny too."

"Marius has never looked funny. Perhaps that is what . . . "

"Yes, we must make him look funny."

"He would not look funny in a tree."

"He would if you laughed."

"I laughed about the nurses," she said.

I sat by her bed. It was as if I were dreaming. "Marius is all right," I said.

"What can you do for him?"

"I will do something," I said.

"And Annabelle?"

"I will do what I can."

"You are too good to us."

"No," I said.

"It is worse for him than for anyone."

"He has been very good to me."

"Has he?"

"Yes, he has made things possible."

"For others?"

"Yes, yes, for others, and by that and nothing else for himself."

"Does he suffer?

"You know about that sort of suffering."

"It won't destroy him?"

"It didn't destroy you," I said.

She looked at me. I know what it was that I had to answer. "And if I should die?" she said.

"You won't die," I said.

"If I did?"

"He would remember."

"I do not want him to remember."

"Then he would have Annabelle," I said.

"He would?"

"Yes."

"You are too good to us," she said again.

"No."

"You are."

"That is the only point of anything," I said.

After a while I went to see Dr. Livingstone. He was a quiet, impressive man. "No," he said, "she can't get well." He explained something technical. "If I had had her at first . . . " he said. "But she was abroad, wasn't she? Are you a relative?"

"No," I said. "Will she die then?"

"That is not for me to say," he said.

"But will she?"

"She may do. The bullet may move and that would kill her. She is here under observation. I cannot operate."

"Why can't you operate?"

He explained. Again something technical.

"Might I get other advice?" I said.

"I have had other advice," he said.

"Oh. And what about moving her—out of this place, I mean. Is that possible?"

"I have told all this to her husband," he said.

"Yes?"

"She is paralysed all down one side of her body," he said. "She is paralysed below the waist. She either cannot eat or will not. She is kept alive by drugs. She needs constant supervision. It would be madness to move her. I have told her husband this."

"And is she in pain?" I said.

"We do all we can," he said.

"Great pain?"

"Sometimes," he said.

"And what would make the bullet move?" I said.

"Now look here . . . " he said.

"I'm sorry," I said; "I didn't mean anything by that."

"Listen," he said. "I don't know who you are, but I'll tell you this. She is a very remarkable woman. I don't know how she's kept alive so long. She must have had something to live for or else by now she would have died."

"Yes," I said. "I think she has wanted to find something out."

"I don't know," he said. "She never will see anyone except her husband."

"No," I said. "Thank you, doctor, for your help."

"And I will tell you this too," he said, "That when she wants to die she will die, and I don't expect she will till then."

"No," I said. "Thank you, doctor. Thank you for your help."

When I got back to her room she was sitting up in bed and was almost smiling. "Well," she said, "did you like Dr. Livingstone?"

"Yes," I said.

"And did he tell you that I could not get well?"

"Yes," I said.

"I am so sorry about Annabelle," she said.

"Oh God," I said. I wanted to cry.

She went on quickly, "I should like a fruit tree, I think. And you must get a little can to water it with."

"You could have an aquarium," I said.

"Yes, that would remind me. I should like those fishes that are striped like silk."

"You could grow sponges in the wash-basin," I said.

"I am sure that would not be necessary. Marius used to dive for sponges and he got very deaf."

"Did he really swim? Now he is so stately. I am sure I should laugh if I saw him swim."

"What effect does he have on the others?"

"On Annabelle and Peter? They do not have much to do."

"They may have one day, you know."

"Yes," I said.

"You have given me such a clever answer," she said.

"Not an answer," I said. "It is what we have to do now."

"Why is it only after one has stopped thinking oneself important that one feels important at all?"

"That's what's funny," I said. "There has to be someone else too."

"And something else besides the someone else. Isn't that what Marius said?"

"Marius talks so much he would have to have a committee to listen to him anyway."

"Yes," she said. She laughed. "What else shall we do to this room?"

"Perhaps pictures and a gramophone and we can all wear paper hats."

"That is never funny. What about birds?"

"Birds will come when the tree is enormous."

"Yes," she said. Then: "There is something else that I should like you to bring."

"What?" I said.

"No," she said, "it doesn't matter."

"What?" I said.

"Never mind," she said. "I think I can get it myself." I did not know what she meant but I felt too tired to think.

"Marius told me to ask you whether he knows what love is," I said.

"Is that what you asked him?"

"Yes," I said.

"Yes. And do you know what you are?"

"No," I said. "That is something that I think I shall never know."

"Perhaps that is what I should tell you to ask Annabelle and what she need not answer."

"Why not answer?"

"Because I have not answered, have I, but haven't you?"

"I don't know," I said. "Both of us have. The whole lot I don't know at all. What I am wondering is how to get an aquarium and a tree up those stairs without being arrested as a lunatic."

"That is a more important question," she said.

"Yes."

"Perhaps if they thought you were a lunatic they would help you with them up the stairs and put you to bed with them and then we could both be lunatics together."

"Yes," I said.

"That is a very comforting thought," she said.

When I left her I felt so tired and had such a headache that I forgot to ask her again what it was that she wanted and what she had not asked me for.

9

Outside I found that it was evening. There was an enormous moon on the roof tops that looked like a jellyfish. I was cold and rather feverish. The moon looked so heavy that I was sure it could never rise. I went round to Annabelle, and found her alone. "Do you know where Marius is?" I said.

"No," she said. "He hasn't been in all day."

"I feel like a jellyfish," I said.

"Have something to eat," she said.

"No," I said; "I don't think I could have anything to eat."

"Have something to drink," she said.

"Yes," I said; "I will have something to drink."

"You don't look like a jellyfish," she said.

She brought me a large glass and filled it. She was wearing a velvet dress which changed colour as she moved.

"Did you go back?" she said.

"Yes, I went back."

"And was it all right?"

"I hope it was all right. I think I must get drunk," I said.

"Do," she said. "What did Marius say?"

"We went in and Marius went out and I was alone with her and I got very excited and then I went out to find Marius. Can I have another drink?"

"Yes," she said.

"Marius said what the hell and you said what the hell and then I said what the hell. This really is a very good drink."

"Yes," she said.

"And now she says what the hell too, and I have got to find an aquarium and a tree."

"A tree?"

"A fruit tree, which is where it all started, I suppose, in a garden of trees."

"I suppose it did," she said.

"I never understood that story," I said, "and I don't understand it now."

"That is where she and Marius started," Annabelle said.

"Was it? Yes. Do you really think it is all what the hell?"

"No," she said.

"No. But I mean, what is your responsibility?"

"To choose to do the best thing in every circumstance, isn't it?"

"I don't know what's best," I said. She moved again, and the lights on velvet altered like shadows on a hill. "I don't know how to know what's best."

"Your conscience, isn't it, and what you are?"

"That's what I don't know," I said.

"Don't you?"

"No." I remembered what had been said at the hospital, and the shadows rustled across the hills like fingers. "Why do you suppose Marius took me to see her?" I said.

"Perhaps because nothing would surprise you and you could be what she would like."

"Is that what I am then?"

"I don't know," she said.

"Or because I am curious and dramatic and like putting my finger into other people's pies?"

"People's pies need a finger to lift them."

"Do they? I never know what will lift and what will break the pie to pieces."

"Don't you?"

"No. For instance, when you should say what you are thinking and when you should not."

"It depends on what is important," she said.

"It is very important," I said.

She came over to fill my glass and she looked at me with her green and grey cat's eyes and as she leaned over me there were circles like hills, and then she seemed to draw herself inwards as if she were ashamed.

"I am in love with you," I said.

"Are you?" she said.

"Yes," I said.

She walked away from me and stood beside the door of a cupboard and all the time it was as if she were trying physically to withdraw herself, to hide behind squares what was circles and light.

"Where is Peter?" I said.

"He is at a party," she said.

"Why is he at a party?"

"I don't know," she said. She looked as if she wanted to disappear into the cupboard.

"Let's go to the party," I said. "Are you invited?"

"Yes," she said.

"Would you like it then? Or am I too drunk? I am so sorry, I am making excuses, you see."

"No," she said; "you are not too drunk."

She came away from the cupboard and for a moment there was the violence within her that I had seen the first time at the pub, the uncontrollable spasm of amusement and energy that this time made her clutch at her skirt with one hand while the other was curved up sharply behind her back, her feet set apart with one ankle overturned on the carpet awkwardly, her green and grey cat's eyes laughing into mine and her smile caught up all over her body as if she were being tickled. "I should love to go to the party," she said.

"I must change," I said.

"What about Marius?" she said.

"Marius, apparently, is none of our responsibility."

"You must wear Peter's tails," she said. "He is wearing his dinner jacket."

"Marius is God's responsibility."

"Do you want a bath?" she said.

"Do you?"

"No."

"Then I don't. That is your responsibility."

She led me through to Peter's room. "These are his shirts and his ties," she said. "Is there anything else that you want?"

"Love," I said. "But that is my responsibility."

"You'll have to do the best you can," she said.

"I am," I said.

"I mean, I hope his collars fit."

"That is his stud's responsibility."

"Hurry then."

"This is where it all started," I said. "In a garden of trees." She went out and closed the bedroom door behind her.

At the party we had some difficulty in finding Peter. He was in the kitchen playing French cricket with the cook. We got him back to where they were dancing. "Why on earth are you wearing tails?" he said.

"I had to borrow them," I said.

"They look rather moth-eaten."

"Yes."

"Is there anything interesting in the pockets?"

"There are some very peculiar things," I said.

"Do let's see. Why, those are my things!" he said.

"Yes."

"I say, that is a peculiar thing."

We followed Annabelle into a gilded room where glasses reflected the tops of bodies and feet were shuffling in a wedged parade. A group of men detached themselves from a pillar like clothes being taken off a hook in the wall, and clustered round Annabelle. She was leaning away from them, quietly. "Annabelle looks so precarious," Peter said.

She was turning from one to another of them, cautiously, and every now and then they touched her, and she was holding her hands in front of her, holding a handkerchief, holding herself in, looking exposed and fragile in her dress with her eyes flickering and her mouth half failing and her arms and shoulders outrageous in the light. "Annabelle is like a lamp-post," Peter said.

"Is everyone in love with her?"

"They are all dogs," Peter said.

"I am in love with her."

"And I am the dog in the manger," Peter said.

She went to dance with a wooden-faced man in his uniform. She danced with her hand entwined in the folds of her skirt and her head turned sideways looking down towards the floor. There was the rustle of silk and the smell of lavender. The man was stiff and Annabelle seemed caught up to him like a child in the arms of a wicked uncle. "They are all leg-lifters and tail-waggers," Peter said: "and Annabelle is a tree."

At the end of the dance she came back to us and the man rejoined the group and they were talking about Peter and Peter was restless. Annabelle looked anxious pushing her hair behind her ears. When the music began again I asked her to dance and we waltzed away narrowly between obstacles of knees.

A smell of lavender, the memory of bundled bags that hang in dressers, her movements exaggerated, the curve of her back steady but herself circling with no ordinary grace, the violence and energy always there from the downlooking eyes, the lashes enormous, the mouth open to teeth and tongue and the neck parted in down-hanging curls which were soft and fair, the unseen movements beneath my hand revolving determinedly, the body always bending away from me, swaying as if eager to swing from control. I laughed.

She stopped. "Why do you laugh?" she said.

"You waltz like a boxer," I said.

She straightened herself and we began again and she let her skirt go so that it swung out and away from us and she held herself so that I saw beyond her and we made huge circles on the floor like a tide. We became balanced like a top with her uprightness clutched by my hand at her waist and her ribs not breathing, controlled and spinning; and then it happened as one always wants it to happen, we became quite still while the room was revolving round us, we became quite alone while the crowd was only colours, we became quite together while the huge skirt enfolded us on the top of the turning earth.

"You waltz very well," I said.

"I always do," she said.

We were standing then, and Peter came up to us surreptitiously. "There is a ridiculous man here who wants to fight me," he said.

"Where?" I said.

"Yes where?" Peter said, looking round.

"He's gone to take off his glasses," someone said.

"But he doesn't wear glasses," Peter said.

"He wears them in his eyes."

"It gets more and more like Oedipus," Peter whispered. He was prowling round laughing craftily to himself.

"Why does he want to fight you?" I said.

"He says it's not good enough. I don't know what he means. He's a huge man."

"He heard you calling him a dog lifting its leg at a lamp-post," someone said; "You really can't blame him."

“I don’t,” Peter said.

“I mean you can’t blame him for getting angry.” The someone turned out to be Freddie Naylor. He looked rather angry himself.

It did not seem to be important. The gilded room was emptying as people wandered to the bar. I wanted to go on dancing with Annabelle, but the patterns of the evening had become indistinct and it was no use objecting to the inconsequence of dreams. We had come to a party and now we had to go and fight a man in the street and it all seemed the same. I did not want to think. Annabelle was unperturbed and Peter was muttering in a language that appeared to be Greek. “Do you know Greek?” I said.

“Yes,” he said.

The wooden man was standing by the door. He looked like a gander. “I would be glad if you would come along with me Freddie,” he said.

“Right you are,” Freddie said. We trooped to the door. “Perhaps this man has married his mother,” Peter said. As we went down the stairs we met a large woman who was our hostess. “Peter,” she called, “I shall want you for supper.” “I shall leave instructions with the cook,” Peter said. The hostess shrieked with laugher. “Perhaps that is his mother,” I said. “If it is,” Peter said, “she has got a bit mixed up.”

Out in the street it was dreadfully cold. “Do you know,” Peter said, “that in Africa they eat the hearts of men fallen in battle?” “I thought it was their livers,” I said. “This happens to be Oxford Square,” Freddie Naylor said. “I am glad to hear it,” Peter said. Annabelle had followed us and we were laughing and trying to keep ourselves warm and I was pleased that she was not anxious as I had feared. “This is really more like Hamlet,” I said. The hostess came out on the balcony above us and began yelling, “What are you playing? What are you up to?” and Peter shouted, “Act five scene two Mrs. Ludgrove.” “I have never heard of it,” the hostess yelled. “Watch out then Mrs. Ludgrove for they have poisoned your wine,” Peter shouted. We were laughing a great deal, but it was sad because the wooden-faced man was so serious. “When you have quite finished,” he said.

We went round the corner where we could not be seen. “I don’t see how we’re going to stop this,” I said. “Neither do I,” Peter said. “But it is so ridiculous," I said. "I know," Peter said. "And it is my fault, and I am sorry, but it is no use apologizing until afterwards, and if he wants to fight I must because I am no pacifist." "But can you box?" I said. "Oh yes," Peter said, "I can box."

The wooden man took off his jacket and handed it to Freddie, and Peter stood morosely in the flopping clothes. The man looked solid and was rolling up his sleeves. Peter was pushing his toes around on the pavement. Now I became anxious, and more than ever surprised at Annabelle. "But can he box?" I said to her. "Oh yes," she said. "He can box."

The odd thing was that he could. The man advanced upon him and Peter took his hands out of his pockets and as the man swung at him he ducked and in a flash had his hands up and was bounding up and down most professionally, snorting and making faces as boxers do. The man looked so surprised that he stopped for a moment and Peter stopped too, and then the man tried another swing and Peter took it on the shoulder and there he was bounding away again with his chin tucked down and his elbows in having hit the man hard three times in the ribs. This time the man was so surprised that he fell down. I was so surprised, too, that I could not even laugh at Peter's professional faces, which were very funny. Peter had stopped, and the man was sitting winded on the pavement, and then Peter went up to him and held out his hand. "Why," the man said, "you can box!"

"Yes," Peter said. "And I am very sorry that I said those stupid things."

"I never knew you could box," the man said. "I always thought you were a . . . "

"I know," Peter said. "And that is why it would not have been any good apologizing before."

"Well I must apologize too," the man said.

"Thank you," Peter said. He helped the man up. "You must never take anything I say seriously," he said, "because I never say any serious thing."

"Right you are," the man said. They picked up his coat and then went off side by side up the street like two unbeaten batsmen retiring in a cricket match. Freddie Naylor followed like a disgruntled bowler.

In the lamplight Annabelle looked faintly smug. We had quite forgotten the cold. "It is outrageous that Peter can box," I said.

"Why?" she said.

"I suppose he gets a lot of practice when he waltzes with you," I said.

"Don't you approve?" she said.

"Yes," I said, "but you are not the sort of people who can box." We began to walk back towards the house.

"Of course he is terribly ashamed of it," she said. "He hates beating people and he always does beat people and then he has a conscience. It would be so much nicer for him if he lost."

"What else does he do?"

"He does everything like that very well, he was always the captain of everything, I don't think it's wrong to approve of that, do you?"

"No," I said.

"Of course he's a fool to fight people, but in a way the people seem to be much happier if he does. I used to hate it once, but now I think perhaps it is the best thing for him to do. It is so much nicer for everyone else, even if he does not feel nice but ashamed himself."

"Do you mean it is a charitable act for him to pick quarrels and to punch people on the nose?"

"He doesn't pick quarrels really, you know, quarrels always happen if you get people feeling things, and the way he deals with them is at least as good as anyone else's way, and in practice even better, it seems, and in any case he only punches them on the chest. Those men at the party all started off hating him, you see, and now they will not. You will find that when we get in."

"And what do you do," I said, "when everyone starts off loving you?"

"I will box you any day of the week," she said.

"Good," I said.

"But you shouldn't say good."

"Yes, because I would beat you. And what else can you do?"

"I can run faster than you," she said.

"You can't," I said.

"I will race you to the cross-roads," she said.

"I will give you twenty yards start," I said.

"Don't be ridiculous."

"Twenty yards start or I don't race."

"I tell you I can beat you."

"I am the fastest runner in the world," I said.

She went a short distance up the road. She took off her shoes and tucked up the skirt of her dress. "Give me your shoes," I said. She threw them to me. She looked like a girl in an Edwardian bathing dress. "Right," I said; "Go!"

She ran very fast. I kept behind her for a bit and her bare feet flashed noiselessly and she did not move her arms at all. She was like a bird and her skirt was blowing loose behind her and her hair streaming back in the wind and as she flew the quick beat of her legs jerked her softly like wings. She, too, was very professional. Just short of the cross-roads I passed her as she screamed, "Damn," and made a grab at me and afterwards I felt very ill.

"Damn this dress damn," she said.

"I think I am going to be sick," I said.

"I am so furious so furious I know I could beat you without this dress."

"No," I said.

"I'll take off this dress and race you back," she said.

"Darling Annabelle," I said.

"I am not feeling sick in the slightest."

"It is you who should be pleased to have been beaten," I said.

"Yes it is different being beaten by you," she said.

"Darling Annabelle."

"I mean it is terrible with someone who . . . "

"Yes," I said.

"I will beat you some time," she said.

"You won't," I said.

"How funny that you can run too," she said.

"It is I who am pleased."

"Look, I have cut my foot."

"Darling Annabelle," I said.

Back at the party I went to find Peter. Annabelle had gone to get sticking plaster for her foot. I found Peter in the bar. He left the little group of guardsmen and came over to me. “I am the long lost brother,” he said, “the bloody old prodigal son.”

“It was copy-book stuff,” I said.

“But I felt such a fool.”

“I suppose that’s not a bad thing to feel.”

“No,” he said. “I say, are you going to be sick?”

“Yes,” I said.

“The awful thing is that they are really so nice. Why are you going to be sick?”

“I have been racing Annabelle,” I said.

“She always races people. I have got to play squash with them on Wednesday. She beats people and then they worship her and it is very bad for her really.”

“Same as you,” I said.

“Yes,” he said. “But she is such a flirt, and she has no need to be, and they feel so uncomfortable, and it is a bloody silly flirt act really. She didn’t beat you, did she?”

“No,” I said.

“Perhaps she does it as a counter-flirt act. They get such blisters. She runs very fast, you know.”

“Yes,” I said.

“I should go and be sick if I were you.” He came with me to the cloakroom. “We always seem to be together in lavatories,” he said. He leaned against the wall and this time looked rather sad. “Wouldn’t it be terrible not to be able to run?” he said.

“Yes,” I said.

“It is all nonsense, I suppose, sticking our necks out and getting them chopped off and having to go dancing round putting them on again. I don’t know why we do it except that there is nothing else to do and every now and then something happens. When you’ve lost your neck you feel better and it seems to have been worth while. She didn’t give you a start, did she?”

“I gave her twenty yards,” I said.

“That’s not bad,” he said. He sat down on a wash-basin and crossed his legs. “Every now and then something happens. I had some men in the army, once, and we were very depressed, and then we were doing river crossings and I organized a boat race and we got so excited that we went out to sea. It was a beautiful blue day and we were all singing and we paddled right out past Portland Bill and bumped the people in front, and I am sure that then something happened. We were laughing and making those sort of jokes, you know, and it was a beautiful blue day and there were seagulls that followed us with their wild unearthly cries. There was a man on the shore who was waving and waving and we got into terrible trouble. I am sure something happened. We were never depressed, not really depressed, after that. Twenty yards in how many did you give her?"

"About a hundred," I said.

"That's very good. And then there was a man at Oxford, he was my tutor, quite a nice man, really, but he used to talk to me and I was trying to tell him what I thought and why I did things, and he just looked at me with that dreadful nervous calmness that dons have, you know, and he said, 'Salvation by romps is not a credible concept,' just that, and I knew he was wrong but I couldn't tell him because he looked so sad. Are you feeling better now?"

"Yes," I said.

"I am sure he was wrong because otherwise you cannot let yourself go, and that is what salvation is, I am sure, it is only when you have gone or at least are ready to go at any moment that you can hope to know about salvation. It is like being in a car going down a hill when the brakes fail, then you have got to jump for it and unless you have been ready for that moment all your life and are good at jumping then you will not jump and you will land up in a heap at the bottom. I think that everyone starts off their life in the seat of a car and there is always a time when the brakes do fail. When you jump I do not know where you will land, but at least you will not land in the heap of old iron. There is always a precipice at the bottom, you see. I am glad that you are in love with Annabelle."

"Thank you," I said.

We went back to the party. Peter rejoined his group of guardsmen, and Annabelle was dancing with Freddie Naylor. I sat on a chair beneath a chandelier and the gilded room blinked at me. Pink and blue dresses and the old women with their powdered necks and the men slightly tufted like thistles. There was a nostalgia in the air like Christmas decorations. Fairy faces glittered above tinsel strings of lace, tasseled stars expanded into rings around the roof. Here the world was running downhill with all the elegance at its disposal. The band squeezed moisture from smoky eyes and stiff limbs jolted. Here the world came to forget and I to remember.

The car that runs downhill (the talk like tossed coins) runs and you decorate it and you hang it with bells (the counterfeit phrases that do not ring) you take out of old boxes old bangles and bells you hang on a tree. You come to admire and little bulbs mutter and sometimes the lights fuse and sometimes they don't. You do not know whether you have come to forget or to remember. Afterwards the bangles are put back into boxes and who puts them is forgotten. The car that runs downhill is always running and it is not easy to remember.

A nostalgia of trees. In a forest of firs there is always memory. The dance is an autumn to disarm the eyes. In water there is memory. The band is a deepness to deceive the ears. The trees are on the roadside where you do not stop.

When you jump you jump, but that has nothing to do with you, when you remember you remember there is something to be done. The tree on which tinsel is hung is an altar. What you do you do in memory, and when you have done it all things are possible and they are possible because you have done it. A garden of trees and a garland of tears. You come to put flowers on the altar and then the flowers of the garden will not die and in memory of the garland you can live. On the road there is the death and the suffering and the car that runs downhill and the trees have gone past you, the trees have gone past you, but still you can live. Only there is something to be done, which you can do, and then you can jump, which has nothing to do with you. You can offer your garland. At the centre of the garden is an aquarium and a tree.

"Are you asleep?" Annabelle said.

"Yes," I said.

"Will you dance with me?"

"I must go and find Marius," I said.

She came with me to the door. The streets were wet and reflected in silver. I walked to Grosvenor Square and rang the bell of the flat. There was no one there. I went out into the square and sat on the parapet.

The patterns of the day were reflected in water. It was very cold. A shape like an iceberg, with only a fraction visible. I withdrew into my clothes as into a shell. Beneath the surface the iceberg stretched and its bulk was enormous. The hospital and Marius and the hospital again. I could not see it. It was apart from me, beneath the surface, a receding opaqueness in the depths of the sea. Each time I searched for it, it disappeared and I saw only the image of my face in the waters. I waited. When I searched my face the waters broke it; when I searched inside me the cold deceived it. My clothes enclosing nothing like an empty shell.

But the touch was there and was jagged against my hands. When you look inwards you see nothing except that which you have imagined, and when you look outwards you see only a fraction of what is real. But if you put out your hand to this fragment and touch it then at least you will have the feel at your fingers, and if you put out your heart to this fragment and love it then you will have the feel of your heart. This is a rarity. You do not have the feel of your heart by keeping it within you. "Who am I?" Marius had said.

Your heart within you is what you can never feel; your heart outside you is what you know. What you are is a relationship between yourself and others. What I am is that which exists between the four of us, I thought, and thinking this I said it aloud, suddenly. The sound of my voice was like an explosion, frightening. I sat up and looked around me. There was nothing except the lights like icicles. What I am is that which exists between the four of us. The iceberg was there, in the darkness, and I could not need to see it.

I closed my eyes. There was the sensation of spaces approaching and departing, the movement of machinery like the pumping of a heart. What is required, I thought, is a body to make love bearable. It is round us, outside of us, there are no veins by which the body might live. Man is inside the beating heart and the heart sends the blood of love pumping away from him and the blood gets lost on the floors of the sea. Man is a cell in a body that does not exist. Blood is on the sea and it calms it like oil, but it is lost, always lost, and the sea dilutes it. What is required, I thought, is a bubble to make love breathable. Love is outside a man, it is not inside him, and a space is required in which he may move. If the body is impossible because the body has been betrayed then a bubble is recreated to give air to breathe. Our bodies are at the centre, they are not the whole. A bubble that might form at the bottom of the sea a small loosening bubble silvering quietly straining upwards being held down tightly straining upwards silvering beautifully breaking free and shooting upwards and then the bubble is there. "Marius," I called. "Marius!" I woke up. He was there.

He was walking along the pavement towards the entrance to the flats, and when he heard me he stopped and stood still and waited for me. I went over to him and I saw him peering at me through the darkness. "Hullo," I said. I was shivering violently with the cold. He was waiting for me. My teeth were shaking and I could not control my voice.

"Hullo," he said.

"I was looking for you earlier on."

"Yes," he said.

"I wanted to say something, but I am so damn cold."

"Let's walk," he said.

I followed him in a fever, shaking like a maniac.

"I went back to the hospital," I said.

"I know," he said. "I went there after you."

"You did?"

"Yes," he said.

"I am so damn cold."

"What is it that she wants from you? A tree?"

"And some fishes."

"Let's go and have breakfast," he said.

We went to an all-night café. It was fairly empty. The clubs had not yet closed and most of the people there were tired servicemen with nowhere to sleep. "They have very good sausages," Marius said.

"Yes. And chocolate."

"Do you often come here?"

"Sometimes."

"They are very friendly. Do you eat the chocolate with your sausages?"

"I drink the chocolate."

"Oh yes, I see."

A waitress came and took our order. It was marvelously warm.

"People do eat marmalade with bacon," Marius said.

"Do they?"

"Yes. They have a special instrument to spread it with."

"That doesn't seem necessary."

"No. It is strange how quickly time goes and yet it is static at four o'clock in the morning."

"It is when the days change and nothing ever happens in a change."

"It is very exciting," Marius said.

Our sausages came and we ate them carefully.

"All terrible things are done between breakfast and lunch," I said.

"We will go to sleep."

"When time goes so slowly."

"Some people can go to sleep at any time wherever they are. That has always seemed to me to be very dangerous."

"Generals and politicians do it, I suppose otherwise they could not bear it."

"I suppose not."

"Do you think that something happens when there is nothing happening?"

"Oh I think so," Marius said.

When we had eaten we sat for a long time drinking our chocolate.

"We have been here half an hour," I said.

"Shall we sleep? There is quite a lot of time before we can see her."

"Yes. Do you remember how during the two minutes' silence on Armistice Day one always notices the birds?"

"If you give her a tree it will be like that and then it will not be frightening."

"Come back and stay with me, there are beds in my room."

"I will," he said.

We went out into the night air where there was nothing happening, nothing happening at all, and yet there was something going on very quickly around us, the sun coming up and the sky lighting like a skin and the veins of the morning traveling static above our heads. There was an arm above the roof tops and a reach of air and the blood pumping quietly round the streets in which we walked. The world was a body and we breathed it, and we went to my room and slept till lunch time.

10

"Hullo," she said. "You can put it over there."

"It has got the most tremendous roots."

"Oh Marius, you look like a chinaman."

"I really don't know oh isn't it splendid," a nurse was saying.

"Why do I look like a chinaman?"

"With a box in each hand that is how I imagine them."

"There is water you see they are striped like silk."

"Oh mind good gracious oh very attractive."

"Where shall I put the tank, lady?" the workman said.

"Just here, please, will you put them into it quick?"

"Quick as rain, lady."

"By the window the birds will come and you will see them."

"The leaves are like fingers I will watch them grow."

"That's a rare old tree for your garden, lady."

I put the tree in its tub by the window and looked at it. It was a sad little tree, rather bent.

"And what variety would it be?" the nurse said.

"It is a fruit tree."

"A fruit tree, oh yes, they are very attractive fruit trees."

"A pond and all for your garden, lady."

"Is it heated and is there air?"

"It plugs into the wall there is a light that lights."

"There is coral and a moonstone and a block of quartz."

"Oh Marius, how lovely."

"And a lump that looks like Abraham Lincoln."

"Oh very attractive very really most unusual."

"And are there bubbles that go on and on bubbling for ever?"

"For ever, lady."

"I shall watch them," she said.

We put the sand and the stones in the bottom of the tank and there was a weed that seemed to grow as we filled it with water.

"Do not touch them," she said.

"They swim out you see you put them like this."

"There is one with a face, I can see it."

"They've all got faces, lady."

"There is one very hungry, what do I give them to eat?"

"I have a package I will give you."

"They eat oh yes certainly some food I believe."

"Do I sprinkle it on the top like seeds like snow?"

"Just sprinkle it, lady."

"They will not eat they are frightened."

"An aquarium and a fruit tree are so unusual."

"They will eat, lady."

"Can you switch on the light then the bubbles will rise?"

"Switch it on, lady."

"The bubbles I will count them they are warm I hope."

"They are warm when the light shines they think it is the sun."

We stood around while she sat up in bed and tapped at the glass with one fragile finger.

"Does that tree really have fruit and can I eat it?"

"Oh certainly, we'll see, fruit is so quenching."

"Does it matter if I eat it?"

"I do not think that it would matter if you ate it."

"They are eating now, lady, fishes always eat when you stop from watching them."

"They have eaten, then I can see their mouths."

"That's enough, lady."

"Everything has eaten, I will eat my fruit."

“Hope it makes you better, lady.”

“Oh we’ll be much better won’t we much more comfortable altogether.”

“I remember about trees once you have eaten them you go on.”

“The bubbles are like pearls.”

“I have always eaten fruit I will go on.”

“The bubbles are like eyes.”

“I will watch them.”

When the workman and the nurse had gone I stood at the end of her bed and Marius sat beside her and the fishes quivered like ghosts. “I want to thank you,” she said.

“You have thanked me.”

“Let me give you my hand.”

I walked round the edge of her bed and she lifted the hand that was like a shell and she put it in mine. “You have given me back my garden,” she said.

I looked at the fishes that were quite still as if there was no pressure on them and no time because nothing ever happened. Her hand was like coral. Only the square glass case and the light that was the sun and the bubbles that went on rising for ever and for ever.

“What are you thinking?” she said.

“I am thinking that for them there is no time.”

“Nor for me,” she said.

“They are floating and there is nothing to move them.”

“I am in this room,” she said. She looked around it. “What will you be doing in six months time?”

“The same as I do now, I suppose.”

“That does not often happen. Will you be together?”

“Perhaps we will be together.”

“I should like it if you were.”

I looked up and saw for the first time that there was a crucifix at the head of her bed.

“We shall be here,” Marius said.

“Perhaps you won’t.”

“We will have a Christmas of crystallized fruit.”

"I want to know what you will do."

Marius said, "I suppose there are still some things we can do."

I said, "Do you remember saying that you and I were dead to the world? That for us there was no future?"

"There are others," Marius said.

"You ought to be free," she said.

Marius was sitting forwards looking carefully at the fish. "You know all that nonsense about freedom," he said.

"It is not all nonsense," she said.

I was looking at the crucifix. I was sure it had not been there the day before. "Don't we have to make sacrifices?" I said.

"Sacrifices?"

"That is what you said." Marius looked at me.

"You see," she said, "whatever you do you will be children, and that is what I mean by free."

"Are we so like children?"

"I hope so, yes, it is a proper thing to be."

"Children are so cruel."

"That is nonsense, they are not, they simply have a capacity for being practical."

"They have a capacity for being hurt."

"That is quite a practical thing to have."

She saw that I was looking at the crucifix but she said nothing about it.

"Children . . . " Marius began.

"Of course you will get hurt," she said.

"I suppose so."

"I want to know what you will do when you are hurt."

Marius turned to me. "You can only do anything in the world where it concerns you. It still does sometimes."

"Often," I said.

"Children are free from responsibility like this," she said.

"Like what?" Marius said.

"That is the point of them, that by having nothing but rules they are free to make a choice."

"Rules?"

"That is where old people are so stupid, they have rules to stop you making a choice instead of to enable you to."

"Like what?" Marius said.

"Children are free to do anything."

"They are not."

"They are free from this sort of responsibility which is not practical because it is over and done with and there is nothing fresh."

"Like what?" Marius said.

"This room," she said.

I did not know what they meant. They were looking at each other and there was something disturbing between them, and I wondered if I should leave them on their own.

"When we are hurt," Marius said, "this is where we shall come to."

"No," she said.

"This is where we shall come."

"You have done something very beautiful for me, you have made my garden, but this will never be a garden for you."

Marius looked at her. She went on:

"Gardens are old things, they are where things start from, they are only a myth later, they are only for people who can live in myths."

"You . . . " Marius said.

"People who are dying can live in myths. For the rest you can do what is proper."

"You frighten me," Marius said.

I touched a leaf of the tree and dipped my finger in the water. "I must go," I said.

"Don't go just yet, you see this you have done for me, but there are other things to do for other people, I have gone back into the past because that is what I had to remember, but for others there is not a past but a present and I know it now for myself having gone to the past."

"You frighten me," Marius said.

"When you get hurt you must go forwards, I can do that now, but perhaps you will have to look backwards sometimes as I have done."

"What will we do?" Marius said.

"You will know," she said.

She looked very tired. She lay back on the pillows and rested her head, but she was not as I remembered her the first time I had come into the room, the face no longer breakable and fragile with china eyes but soft and heavy like a dying flower, the edges curling, the hands no longer a shell, a coral, but fallen petals from a yellowing rose. There is a softness in dead flowers that is terrible. As Marius looked at her I wondered if he were now frightened in the way in which once he had frightened her.

"I am going backwards," Marius said.

"For a little," she said.

The fishes pointed steadily, the leaves of the tree shone backwards, they were going with them where I could not follow them, the sand by the sea where the wind was crying. From the past I did not know what they would remember and what they would learn, but out of the sad broken unutterable tiredness of her face there was something she had to give him and something she had to do. Her eyes were like candles and I was not frightened for them. Above her head was the crucifix. "Goodbye," I said.

"Goodbye," she said. "Do not be unhappy."

"No," I said.

I went to the door. I remember the terrible softness of the fallen rose, the flame burning within the waxen ruins, the candle gutted and rearing into shapes that were wild and gentle against the altars of her face. "Thank you," she said. At the last I remember this flame that was burning that was very clear and very bright and then I left.

11

A golden evening. When the play is over you put on your coat you follow the crowd you go out into the street and then what do you do? The sun is setting on a thousand faces. When the lights went up you were caught, perhaps, there was a tear in your eye and there were no tears in other people's eyes and why were there no tears? Everything happens just once and never again. You have found your handkerchief and surreptitiously used it and there is no need to conceal your pride. In the street there are no tears and what do you do?

Standing by the cross-roads the day ran down like a tired clock, the day that was two days, the hours squeezed into one by the pressure of necessity, the effort that had lasted and that now was gone. The ticking of faces shambled to a standstill. The day in which for the first time in my life I had done something, the day which had happened and which would never happen again. Along the pavement people passed with the tired rush of those who are going nowhere and for whom tears are a luxury that they cannot afford.

Standing is a forgetting, there is nothing to do. After the play that you have loved that you have laughed that you have cried at you go back to the silence of a life that is dumb. People go past you in circles ceaselessly their mouths opening and shutting with the hunger of insects their heads nodding grotesquely in a puppet parade. There is no noise. They seize upon the crumbs that agreement offers them, the crumb of criticism, the crumb of approval, the crumb of "it is over now, there are other things to think of." From the silences of their eyes you can see them watching you, you are afraid they will get you they will make you forget. Memory is a luxury that they cannot attain. There is only poverty, the poverty of agreement. Richness is in moments, and the moments happen once and never again.

If you wish to have the sickness you say—That is a moment I shall never forget, the moment when the curtain descended and the lights went up and there were no tears in any eyes except my own. Then you are alone, very alone, and for a while you stand on the corner of a street and the evening comes down on you like a descent of birds and the cries of starlings are above your head. You watch the people and you do not hear them and the silence is a mantle to deceive your eyes. Then they cannot bear it. Agreement is that there shall be no silence and you shall never be alone and the mouths and the glances are above you this time like vultures and they get very close to you because you are dead.

When you are alone you are dead and the vultures pick at you. The mantle is torn off you and the noise comes in in waves, the insect clatter the machinery of tongues the vibrant voices that have to forget that have to make you forget that have to take you with them so that you will never remember. As I moved down the street I said that I should never be dead, that I should be alive with Annabelle or alive beneath the vultures but that I should never be dead. The machinery mocked me. But I knew that if I was to remember this was what it would mean, to be for ever with her who could know and not deceive me, which was a decision I could not make and which had nothing to do with me, or to be for ever with the vultures that would wait with naked necks in the smell of rottenness that went on and was endless. At the end of this day with the blinds coming down across what I had done I thought I could try it. I went not alone because I loved and have loved and the golden evening was inviolate about. Whatever happened I had done one thing, and I went to Annabelle so that at least I could remember.

12

"We are coming to the end of something," I said.

"Are we?"

"What are you going to do?"

"I am going to cook supper," she said. She put down the tray that she was carrying and went back into the kitchen.

"You are so serious," I said.

I sat on the edge of the table and waited for her. She had been out when I had arrived, and it was late. Peter had not come in. When I was alone with her there was no awkwardness now, but just the suggestion that what we said meant more than the words we used. "Marius stayed with me last night," I said.

"I thought he must have done."

"We were tired. Time has gone so quickly that it is difficult to remember what has happened and what has not."

"We got back very late, I wondered where you were."

"I waited by the statue. I think time will go more slowly now. When did you first meet Marius?"

"Just before I met you, a year ago."

"And has that time gone quickly? I did not really meet you then."

"I saw you, I remember I was nervous and there was something in your eyes."

"Marius and I went to the hospital to-day. I think his wife will be better now, she is happier."

"Have you done that?"

"I don't know," I said. Annabelle was carrying knives and forks going in and out of the room all the time so that the talk was disjointed.

"I remember you in the pub, we talked about musical-boxes," she said.

"Do you remember Marius saying that only individuals can begin things?"

"Is that what you mean by coming to the end of something?"

"Yes," I said. "For two weeks we have been together . . . "

"For a year," she said.

"But I . . . "

"We often thought about you, Marius said it was like being in a monastery, one is much closer to people then."

"Has Marius been in a monastery?"

"No," she said.

She was out of the room again and I wandered over to the piano where there was a large photograph of Peter and Annabelle as children with their father and their mother. Peter looked fat and portentous and Annabelle was sitting on the ground peering cautiously through her curls with her small frightened face. "I should have liked to have known you as children," I said.

"You have," she said.

"Yes." Her father and mother looked unreal as people of that generation do in photographs. He was a small man sitting bolt upright with his hands on his knees and she was draped indistinctly across the back of the chair. I knew it was not like them. "And your father and mother," I said.

"You know," she said, "we may have to go back to them soon."

"May you?" I said. This news did not hurt me as I thought all the time it should have done, because I knew there was something ending and the details were only reflections of the sadness that bathed us like light.

"Peter won't go back to Oxford," she said. "He will have to get a job and I suppose my father will get him one."

"And you?"

"I will go back too."

"And you will cook suppers for the rest of your life?"

"I suppose so," she said.

I followed her into the kitchen. She was busy with pots and pans and I squeezed out of her way between a cupboard and the door. Whatever I did not feel, I had to say it.

"I hate this ending of a year," I said.

"Do you? You see, we are not yet individuals."

"I don't want to be an individual."

"You do, I think you became an individual when you got angry with Marius, and then you have your work to do, haven't you?"

"I loathe my work," I said.

"Do you?"

"And now I am not angry with Marius, I am quite under his spell again, I want to go on as we have been going. Have you ever been angry with Marius?"

"Not yet," she said.

"So you see, it is no good."

"What is no good?"

"There is something intolerable in this, that we want to go on as we are and we cannot act as individuals."

"Why cannot you . . . "

"Because I am fond of Marius as well as in love with you," I said.

She broke some eggs into a bowl and began to whisk them vigorously. "You know," she said, "you are much more part of the world than Marius is."

"What do you mean by that?"

"I don't know. I think you are the thing that endures."

"Endures!"

"Yes. Marius is transitory, and Peter too in a way."

"How do you see the future then?"

"I would never say," she said, "not even to myself."

She tipped the bowl of eggs into a sauce pan and turned up the gas. "You make me feel like a pair of overalls," I said.

"Yes," she said, "you are."

She was rummaging in a drawer of the cupboard and I could see her laughing to herself. Squeezed behind the door I felt as if I were in a coffin. "You ought to put some milk in those eggs," I said.

"Never milk with butter."

"Let me stir the damn things then," I said.

She went back into the drawing-room and I stirred the eggs lethargically with a wooden spoon.

"I mean that you are the sort of working clothes," she said. "That is what I mean by overalls." She was speaking from the passage and I wished I could see her face. "Something that saves the stuff underneath. Without overalls you get terribly worn, and people splash you."

"Thank you," I said.

"I am too, in a way. I cook and have things ready and I don't put milk in buttered eggs, that's what I do."

"And do you have children and sow and knit and take dogs for walks in the country?"

"Perhaps. We both have things to do, to keep us going."

"I hope we get somewhere," I said.

We took the buttered eggs through to the drawing-room and ate them sitting cross-legged on the floor. I tried to imagine her in ten years time with a pack of dogs on strings. I imagined it easily. "There is not enough salt," she said.

"I am feeling unbearably sentimental," I said.

"I cannot bear sentimentality," she said.

"Then you are wrong, you are a sentimental person."

"Why?"

"Because you remember what we said in the pub, and while I was away you felt as if you were in a monastery."

"That was not meant to be sentimental."

"But it was, because sentimentality is always remembering everything and having a great regard for what is important and taking care of people."

"I thought sentimentality was going soft in the centre like Peter and chocolates."

"Peter overdoes it, but that is what I mean. Peter may one day overdo it too much, and I do not think that he will feel as if he is in a monastery."

"I did not mean that I was like those women in French novels who end up nuns."

"No, French novels are not sentimental."

"I don't think I could be a nun," she said.

She went to make coffee. When I was alone I felt impatient as if the time we had left was running out upon the floor. "I thought about you too," I shouted. And there was something that I was afraid of saying if she were not there to stop me.

"Are you sentimental because things are coming to an end?" she said.

"It is because I am that they are."

"Why?"

"It is because I have cared so much for the last week that I cannot break it by asking it to continue. I cannot ask you . . . "

"What?" she said.

"Nothing," I said.

She came back with the coffee. "Perhaps you are right about sentimentality," she said. "Things don't change all at once, people are very stupid about that, they expect them to and then they don't and they are miserable. You have to preserve the old things and they change very slowly and then what you want often happens on its own."

"So we just endure," I said.

"Yes," she said.

We drank our coffee sitting cross-legged again opposite each other as if at some ceremony. I remember her with her two hands holding her cup up to her lips and myself waiting until she should put it down. When she did I said, "And if you go away what will Marius do?"

"There is his wife," she said.

"Supposing his wife wanted him to go with you?"

She stared at me. "That is not what you have done," she said, "is it?"

"I don't know," I said.

Her eyes became frightened. She put her cup down slowly. "He wouldn't go," she said.

"He might do. When I left them she was trying to tell him something, I don't know what it was, I think she was trying to make him . . . "

"What?"

"Be an individual. I think she wanted him to be free of her because as long as he is with her he can never escape his past."

"Is that what you meant when you said that you were fond of Marius as well as . . . "

"Yes," I said.

She hung her head and pushed her finger into the carpet with the intentness of a child. "I don't think . . . " she began softly.

"But you said that things must happen slowly, that if you try to change them all at once it is disastrous."

"It is you who are changing them."

"No, I have done nothing, it is only what happens."

"You make them so complicated."

"That is what they are."

She looked up. "I don't believe that," she said.

"If they were not I would . . . "

"At the bottom there are simple things, I think they are quite simple."

"It needs a great effort to keep them simple."

"I don't think so, that is what Marius says, but he is wrong, they are quite easy."

"It needs a sacrifice."

"A sacrifice?" She looked frightened.

"Yes, that is what you would say as well as him."

"It only needs what you said, remembering everything and caring for people and keeping yourself open to what is important for others."

"So you see you are sentimental, and Marius will probably go with you."

"Supposing he is sentimental too?"

"If he is it depends on what has happened this evening with his wife."

There was a silence for a while and then she leaned forwards and said "You are wrong, you know. Why are you trying to do it?"

"If it is wrong what would you have me do?"

"I don't know," she said. She put her hand up to her face in a gesture of dismissal. "It is too complicated," she said. She stood up wearily and smoothed her hair back from her forehead. "One day we shall know it was wrong. Perhaps when Marius comes back we shall know it."

She cleared the cups and plates and left me. It was sad now I was impatient only with myself, because I did not know what should be happening. I looked at the clock and saw that it was nearly midnight. I thought suddenly that perhaps there were only a few more times that I should see her, and when I thought this it was so unbearable that I stood up and was about to follow her into the kitchen when I heard the sound of a key in the door of the flat and Peter came in. I was at least glad it was not Marius. Peter threw his coat on to the sofa, and I tried to appear at ease. I did not want to involve him in what was happening because I was ashamed of it. I did not know why. "There is something dreadful to-day," Peter said; "Like an eclipse."

"Like the end of the holidays."

"Yes." He walked through to Annabelle. "You will have to start again," he said. "I'm hungry."

"There's a letter for you on the table," Annabelle said. Her voice sounded flat and strained, and I wondered if Peter would notice it.

Peter came back. He looked at me quickly and then away. He too was trying to appear at ease. He picked up the letter. "Haven't you opened it?" he said. "I always open other people's letters, it's so friendly." I did not smile and I do not think he expected me to. He was talking to kill the silences. "It's from my father," he said. He stared at it for a second as if he did not want to open it and then as he slit the envelope with his finger he began to talk again in his over-casual voice. "On the last day of the holidays I used to do something dreadful so that I should want to escape from it." He slid the letter out from the envelope and held it folded not reading it. "Something embarrassing that I could not bear." He fiddled with the letter and I realized that it was as important to me as it was to him. "But I cannot do anything embarrassing any more," he said. He unfolded the letter. "At least I don't think so." Then he read it.

Annabelle came in from the kitchen with her knives and forks and she walked past me without looking at me. Now she would give Peter his supper and Peter would eat it and she would carry the plates backwards and forwards for the rest of her life. The rest of her life without looking at me. I wanted to scream. "There," Peter said. "Something embarrassing after all."

He handed the letter to Annabelle and she read it.

"What?" I said.

"We are going away," he said.

"I know," I said.

"Do you?" He looked at me then, but we both knew how difficult this was. He walked away and pretended to be tidying something. "In a week we will be going away," he said. "My father has fixed it."

"Yes," I said.

"And what will you do?" he said, with his hands among the flowers on the piano.

"I have got to go away too," I said.

"Oh have you?"

"Yes," I said.

Annabelle read the letter and folded it and put it back in the envelope. She still did not look at me. "I wonder what Marius will do," Peter said.

Nobody answered. Annabelle left us. Peter turned round violently and laughed. "So it is the end of the holidays," he said.

He dragged a chair towards him and sat down. "Of course we could stop it," he said. "But we won't. We can't be embarrassing any more." He flung his legs out and slumped backwards with his head on his chest. "I am resigned, quite resigned. People have always wanted me to be and now I am." He snorted. "It is terrible," he said. He was silent for a while and breathed as if he were asleep. Then "I hope to God that one day I will not be resigned any more," he said.

When Annabelle came back with her cup and saucer she stood by me and said quietly, "Where are you going?"

"Away," I said.

"I should just like to know," she said.

"I will tell you when I know myself."

"Thank you," she said. She said this almost bitterly.

I watched Peter eat his eggs and drink his coffee and we never spoke, and Annabelle came and went with the regularity of a machine. The time that I had wished to go slowly now did not move at all. The pendulum swung, Annabelle passed steadily with averted eyes, Peter chewed into the silence with the tick of clocks, but the hands on the faces that should have brought us to midnight failed and left us helpless in a dead parade. In the minutes before Marius came we lived a very long time on our own, the sadness and bitterness between us that I had tried to prevent and now could not explain. I felt as if I were at the bottom of the hill with the heap of old iron, the wheels circling ceaselessly in the dusty sun.

When Marius came we heard him on the landing, he was fumbling with the lock of the door and he could not open it, and then we heard the click of the latch as it opened and closed, and he was in the passage where we could not see him. The wheels revolved. We waited for him and he did not come in. "Marius," Peter called. He swung round in his chair and peered towards the passage. There was nothing happening. "Marius, what is this feeling like the end of the world?"

Marius moved, but still he was a shadow and still quite silent, and Peter leaned forwards with his arms on the chair. Then Annabelle came out of the kitchen and walked along until she was opposite Marius and she stood there hard and determined with her hands clasped in front of her and her head thrown back like a child that is about to ask a question that is an agony to it, and she said, "Marius, tell me, how is your wife?"

"She is dead," Marius said, coming in to where we could see him.

After that there were only fragments. I remember Marius walking to the window where he stood as he had often stood looking out into the night, and Annabelle following him and standing beside him. She hesitated only for a moment. Peter did not move at all, he was sitting turned round in his chair staring towards the passage where Marius had lingered when he had asked him his question. They remained there. I picked up my coat and put it over my arm and left them. I made sure that I would remember them and did not look back. During the second in which Annabelle had hesitated before she joined Marius by the window she had looked at me and her eyes were not frightened as they had been once, but frightened for herself and for both of us. There had been no bitterness. I hoped that Marius needed her, because if he did not it was terrible.

IV
WILDERNESS

13

Marius's wife died quietly while Marius was with her. That night I wrote two letters, one to Marius and one to Annabelle, and the next day I left for the country. My letters were very short. I thought of returning for the funeral, but I did not know when it would be. After a few days I had a letter from Peter, who said that they were on the point of leaving, and that they hoped they would see me, but it was too late then. They were going to the West Indies, to where their father had been transferred. Marius was going with them. He had some business to do with his wife's estate, Peter said. The day they left was the longest day of the summer. It lasted interminably. It seemed that the year had died with Marius's wife in the hospital.

Then they were gone. There was another day that stretched to infinity. I did not know what to do. I thought of them on my island in the blue and gold sea.

When once you have loved there is no going back on it, the world has changed and you have to take it with its differences. I had left them because I had thought it necessary to do so, but I had loved them, and my loneliness now was of a different quality to that which I had known before. There is a difference between what one has not known and what one is deprived of. Ignorance is a vacuum, but it is deprivation that is hell.

Hell is when one is conscious every minute of the deprivation of love, and aware that it is this sense of deprivation that gives one consciousness. One has the fear that once this sense has gone, one will have ceased to be a person at all. Thus one clings to loneliness, almost as a means for preservation. It is a situation such as that of the sufferer who dare not sleep because he is more frightened of the nightmare of dreams.

This sense of deprivation, also, results in a loneliness in which the world appears as mad. There is a feeling of separation from the world because the bonds of sympathy have been broken, and the world, when viewed without sympathy, is mad. The behaviour of men and women is so bewildering that it can be understood only by love, and when love has been concentrated and then has been taken away their behaviour is inexplicable. One stands upon the fringes of a twittering sea and the voices are outrageous. Then there is the hell of hatred, which is the worst hell of all.

The gyrations of men and women. In the country, where I went first, to stay with some friends to whom I had long promised a visit, the gyrations were not at once discernible. A long way away from the towns, in a different world, the beauty of it was stronger than the people who lived there. A stream ran in silver between rocks of green, and the hills like sad sentinels kept sanity under guard. Between them, with the sun cutting rocks into sculptured planes, the valleys were silent in enormous bowls. Here voices were dispelled, the silver tinkled clearly, the shepherd on the hillside called his dog with the same breath as the curlew swinging up from the stream cried above the bracken. There were no words, no speech, only notes like feathers floating on the stillness, singing over spaces like wires in the wind. Separation did not matter when the earth was wide. So long as the sun shone life was out of doors and out of the hands of people. The spaces ruled, the long green surfaces were ungovernable, and the people, gathering hay in dotted specks upon the slopes like tortoises, were quiet in their shells beneath this dominance. I remember the slow crawl of the tractor down the face of the hill, the tiny repose of figures seen from a distance across the sky.

The work ruled, and separation did not matter. Then the work was done. The hay was stacked and the corn carried and the rain came on a September evening. We stayed indoors. The outlines were lost and the spaces disappeared and the face of man became huge against a window. Then we were close to each other, and beauty was gone. The hand that had kept us spinning was swallowed into the mist, and our gyrations lurched lamely like a staggering top.

A house with the fires unlit and a dampness in the passages. Watching the faces which the light reached through the raining windows making them grey and unmanageable like liquid, it was as if the world were drowned beneath an atmosphere I could not breathe. The others could, or so it appeared;—leaning forwards, smiling, nodding, they went through the motions of communication, the proffered cup, the joke amongst the newspapers, the patting of animals, each action performed as if it were a necessity such as breathing, and with the same ease, stretching, yawning, moving the eyes, the business of communication expected, there, among the waiting rooms, and not disappointed, like a match to light a cigarette, the smoke going upwards (why did it not go down?), breathing in and out, sighing, but why were they breathing? If they stopped breathing—what?—but they would not, and if I did? Well then, so I would, for a minute, and then I would breathe again, and no one would have noticed.

A cold room with white walls, the smell of paraffin, footsteps above the ceiling, a dragging sound as if bodies were being moved, what was everybody doing? One, crossing a yard, carrying a pail, went in through a door and came out again, having fed something. From my window I watched him cautiously. I did not want to be seen. Another, on the telephone, spoke to the empty hall. On the landing the sound of brushes bumped against the banisters, the whirring refrain of a cleaner came and went in drones, an aeroplane flew above the trees lending insistence to the moment, prolonging it, so that the noise should have to cease before I moved. Time tapped past like a blind man's stick on the pavement. If I came in, I thought, I should be caught, I should be standing by a window with nothing to do. In the yard a plate was emptied into a dustbin, having fed something. A fly was lying on its back, having died of the cold. The blind man tapped along and did not get anywhere because there was nothing to see. I wondered if I should be feeding or if I should die of the cold.

On the landing there was silence. I emerged like a burglar. Creeping past some china it seemed improbable not to fall. I could rearrange the pots and hide the pieces. The banisters, if they splintered, could be stuck with glue. Myself, hearing voices, hid in an alcove. I was carefully examining some sporting prints. A horse was wedged across a hedge like a cushion. A man in a top-hat was shooting snipe. I was observed from a doorway. Good-morning. Good-morning. Breakfast was wheeled away dismembered on a stretcher.

What do people do when they are on their own? Their breathing is in communication, their atmosphere is that which they can pretend with other people; and when they are alone, then, do they breathe at all? For the atmospheres are different, this I had known, the difference between air and water, animals and fish; and if I could breathe on my own and not with other people, then why should they, who found it so easy with others, be able to breathe in solitude? Perhaps they did not. Perhaps they, like the chairs and tables of philosophers, ceased to exist when others were not conscious of them. And if their existence was spasmodic, they need not know.

When you observe someone who is alone, who does not know he is being observed, it is embarrassing. Why? Looking in through a window, sometimes, by chance, from a garden, you see something you are not expected to see. A man, pacing a room, his eyebrows raised, his hands behind his back, his head tilted—you have looked in on something that is embarrassing because it is not proper. The man, for the moment, is not a man. He is not real. He is the character on the stage, his faces are the actor's grimaces, if you were not the audience the actor would not be there. And yet he is not aware of you, he is playing the wrong part, it is as if it were you who had put him on the mad and empty stage.

A woman enters the darkened corridor in which you are standing. She does not see you. She stops awkwardly, pouting, she murmurs something. If you do not make your presence known you are being rude. Why? As you cough she will start, arrange herself, she will alter, she will be petulant in the same way as if she had been awakened from sleep. This awakening is a fact, it is the gasp of the swimmer as he dives upon the water, the moment when the breath does stop, physically, and then the breathing is different. But before, when the woman was alone, did she find the air sufficient?

She? But why not I? Is it not this that I should be saying?

I, who do not exist in water, can I say that I exist in air? It is not air that I breathe. It was I who was caught in the corridor, a phantom living with phantoms, smelling the smoke of memories and the decadence of dreams.

Have you missed breakfast? It doesn't matter. Let's get you . . . Really, it doesn't matter. At least some . . . Thank you, so much, no.

Smoke that comes in coils around the throat of solitude. It may bring tears to the eyes, illusion to the senses, but it is not breathing. In the silent house there is no existence except the phantom of Annabelle.

They are embarrassed. I know that they are embarrassed. They think that they are seeing me on my own.

It is embarrassing through the window, it is embarrassing in the corridor, it is embarrassing in the crowd when one man stands against a pillar when he will not move when he will not talk when he will not smile when introductions are no good because he would hate them. Why is it embarrassing? Would it not be more embarrassing if you were to take a person performing the functions that are expected and separate him from the crowd and watch him there, apart from his context, performing the functions that are expected? Take a man making an after-dinner speech, for instance, and put him in the desert; with his fantastic clothes his important gestures his silly words would he not be embarrassing? Producing his stories for the Sphinx would he not be peculiar? Take a hostess from her party and put her in the sea, would she not be . . . she is, in fact, often, at a marriage, for instance, in a fashionable church;—she is most disquieting. They would not be seen dead, of course: really, this is true, they would not be seen dead with their waistcoats and tiaras in the desert. But the man who lives with the sea and with the Sphinx, who sees things in these terms only, he is seen dead, yes, he is seen dead at dinner. And so he is embarrassing.

But supposing everyone at all times behaved like this, behaved as if they were in terms of the Sphinx and of the sea as if that was what they were and that was their reality, would that be embarrassing? Everyone at all times the same whether they were in the crowd or seen unexpectedly through a window or come upon in the corridor, everyone to his solitary image permanent—then there would be no speeches, no introductions, they would not be needed—you would know, you would know everything, you would have no need of others to explain that you exist. You need not die.

Everything is in terms of God, perhaps.

Someone whom you love when you see them through a window—it is not embarrassing. Not more dreadful than if you should hold their hand. Myself, I am not more embarrassing than when I am in company. I talk to myself, of course; but then I do that when I am with others. And I do not hear what I say.

Marius's serious face against the window.

They, the three of them, always acted the same as if they were alone or faced with enormities. Coming up on them in the passage they would not start, they were always amazed, so what was there to start for? And in the garden if you looked in on them it would not be improper because they would be looking out. What did Marius see?

He saw, I think, things in relation to the desert. Not even the noises, just the gestures of groups that are grotesque when put into this relationship. He was older than I, and perhaps more compassionate.

I left the house one evening and went into the town. A market town, on Saturday night, with people in the streets. I saw the groups then. The men stood quietly at every corner, the old at the back, the middle-aged in the centre, and the youths in the front. They were arranged, resolutely, as if for a photograph. They stood there for hours, with their hands in their pockets, waiting. At times it looked as if they were about to be shot.

A line of girls came up the street arm in arm through the darkness. When they passed a lamp it was surprising to see how many of them were old. They were giggling and lurching as if they were drunk. They wore short skirts and had scarves around their heads. When they passed a group of men they doubled up and screamed like peacocks.

I remember Peter telling this story. A girl asked him, "If your peacock flew into somebody else's garden and laid an egg, whose egg would it be?" "Mine," he said. "Ha ha, you silly, peacocks don't lay eggs." "But you said this one did," he said. "But they can't," she said. "Then why did you say it did?" he said. "That is the point of the joke," she said. "What joke?" he said.

Like peacocks then. A promenade of whores before their sultan. But it takes more than ten motionless men to make a sultan, and more than six raging women to make a whore. Nothing happened.

Peter did not understand. He never understood things that people did nor why they did them. He saw things emptily, in the desert, but he did not see the Sphinx. I believe that Marius did. Peter could not even find anything to ask him a riddle.

In the town, on Saturday evenings, there is an enormous advertisement, Let's go to the pictures. There is nowhere else to go.

At the pictures it is very strange, before the lights go out hundreds of people sit in rows and whistle and stamp their feet upon the floor. This is a catching habit. The men keep their caps on. Toffees are passed around and girls collapse upon each others' shoulders. Then there is darkness and everybody yells. Lovers sink downwards with closed eyes. They see nothing for the rest of the evening.

Impressions are reduced to a series of reactions. When a girl appears there is whistling again, when the funny man is spotted there is so much laughter that one never hears the jokes, when a love scene is enacted there is a dreadful upheaval like fox-hunting, and when the hero and heroine are married the audience at once gets up and leaves the cinema.

It is funny, this. In the music hall jargon of to-day the word marriage is a dirty word and the word wife is a dirty word and everyone laughs at these dirty jokes, but in the jargon of films marriage is just the end of everything and people get up and go. If ever they find out that it is not the end, then they have to come back and pretend that they have been to the lavatory.

They have a restless time anyway because they are always on the look-out for the ending—this is to show how experienced they are—and when they foresee it there is a terrible rush for the doors about three minutes before time and it is as if there was a fire in the house and everyone gets stuck in the doorway. By the time God Save the King is played they are struggling furiously and have made no headway and they are very angry at being caught by God Save the King so they pay no attention to it. It is a terrible decision for them to know what to do when they are caught by God Save the King.

It is funny also how a lot of young people cannot get through a doorway. Peter once made a study of this and he said it was because twice as many people went into a doorway as ever came out of it.

After the film there is the milk bar. After dinner there is the port.

In the houses of the rich something dreadful happens to the men when their women leave them. There is the drawing-up of chairs and the moving of glasses and then the disinterment of dirt from the death of adolescence. Moustaches, cigars, mauve dinner jackets and walnut, an elegance of candles around a warmth of silver, and the stories that creep like rats from frozen holes. What is said is unrepeatable. But if marriage is a dirty word, and wife is a dirty word, are then what are usually called dirty words clean? Words from the private school playbox, words from the dressing-room, words scratched on whitewash, words which on the tongues of boys are aged and in the mouths of men are rotten. Do they look into each other's eyes when they tell their stories? The honourable men, the barristers, the generals, the princes of the stock exchange, they write their words on plastered walls with the ink of napoleon brandy.

In the milk bars of the poor, the fish shops of the homeless, you grow up quicker. There you become a cowboy at fifteen. Your cowgirl with her great cow eyes and moue of gum. You become a gangster at twenty. But you are happier, still, really, when the women have gone.

Rich schoolboys and poor cowboys, a padded dinner jacket with facings of silk or a slouch-capped studied flounce of ties, it is all the same, all over England, black knees crossed discreetly or grey knees spread diffusely, it is all the same. Draw the chair up softly over the carpet and pierce the cigar with the golden pin at your watch-chain, snatch a stool or perch on a table and pick the cigarette delicately from the lips between forefinger and thumb and spit fastidiously with the smoke coming down through the nostrils. Play the schoolboy with your lavatory words or play the tough guy with your cinematic teaching. In a thousand milk bars all over England young would-be gangsters giving each other the brush-off and taking each other for a ride, thousands of jerking young would-be cowboys pushing each other around among the teas and cakes and pineapple sundaes quick on the draw with their coca-cola pride. And in the dining room the dirt and despair of laughter. The men of England segregated from their women in a masculine ease of corruption.

In the country there are no women. Population only increases in the cities.

In the cities there are girls. A girl is not a classification of age, a girl can be anything from twelve to fifty, a girl is someone to whom men can go in the holidays. A sister or a mother in whose lap masculinity can be repented.

I left the country. In London, among the smoke, it seemed that always I was asleep and sometimes dreaming. The remains of consciousness upon which I had lived in the country—remains held together by a view of absurdity—in the fog of solitude now lost a dimension and it was as if I were flat in a world of static deepness. This illusion, observed at first dispassionately like some assumption of geometry—that having only length and breadth I could not have existence—later became so powerful that I felt it as a fact: and sitting on a bus or stepping off a pavement I did not believe, since I lacked the depth that was necessary for solidity, that people could see me. When they did I was surprised; and I sometimes feared that I must possess some other faculty of which I was not aware, a faculty of madness such as voicing my thoughts without hearing myself speaking, and that people were being polite in not objecting to my oddity. With appearances so unmanageable it was only in dreams that there was a refuge. Life went to sleep and I cradled it.

Perhaps men are often machines, but never so much as when they are dreaming. The study of man's mechanism begins with the study of dreams, and then the question is put—Are they always sleeping? When I asked this of myself I could give myself no answer, but I should always like to believe that for a month I had been awake. A month with Annabelle which others would say was illusion, which I extolled in despair as the moment of reality. The despair, now, since I had opened my eyes for the moment, was in sensing the difference between this condition and that.

When old men say that something terrible is happening to the young people of to-day they are quite right, it is, young people are beginning to realize that they and the world are sleeping. And when this is realized the old dreams, the old attitudes, become ridiculous. Fifty years ago youth was presumed to be a time of ecstasy, and enormous words were used to describe the passion of the passing moment. Harlequin met Columbine and they danced among the fruit trees, by Mediterranean waters huge flowers were pledged like prayers. Lovers languished beneath windows, duels were fought at dawn, poets dripped with lyrics like the tears that they described. Now it is only the old that are passionate. Romance is a dead man's sickness. And the effacement of the young, like the disappearance of flies in winter, is a mystery that is observed with a scarcely anxious wonder.

And the young, wherever they are, know that they are flies and cannot do much about it. From the ceiling, upside down, the view of ancient heads is not a pattern to inspire any confidence. Like a film that is projected backwards every scene jerks horribly into ridicule,—the great lover is a great joke, success waddles quickly to failure, ambition becomes absurd with the regress to nonentity. Even the artist, attempting to see things clearly, finds that he has to make an enigma of himself, to laugh at himself, to contradict himself, in order that he may pay his respects, as it were, to ridicule. And amongst the graying heads themselves there is an air of pathos about existence. At any moment the world may cease, or at least become so disintegrated that the processes of normality will not apply. Illusion is out of control: assurance is abandoned. For the first time for centuries Europe is adopting the doctrine that in words it has accepted. The world is lost; but what is saved is not apparent.

This is the age of the man without passions, the man without poetry, the man without a past. Tradition is poetry, the myth is poetry, and now the myth and traditions are dead. The powers of the subconscious that have pulled the strings of the world for thousands of years, the power of passions, they now do not apply. Oedipus is irrelevant: Hamlet is irrelevant. In the age of psychoanalysis for the first time psychoanalysis is nonsense. It explains the past but it has nothing to do with the present. The end of the world is the end of the dark powers of humanity. The past is meaningless. Now for the first time man is faced with eternity and with nothing else.

The tears of the lyricists are dry; the shouts of the propagandists are empty. The words of progress, words with capital letters, have become more ridiculous than any because their sense is quite consciously nonsense. The world of the politicians has effaced itself even beyond ridicule, it has joked itself towards horror like the clown that becomes obscene in despair of failure. A Capital Letter may be put anywhere, may stand for anything. Freedom can mean Slavery, Peace stands for War, Democracy is inseparable from Intolerance. There is no laughter left for this absurdity. Big words are dirty, the car is running downhill, the smallness of the situation is in each man's chance of survival. And his chance, as Peter had said, depends for nothing upon time or events or circumstances, but merely upon his ability to jump.

Passive, lonely, it is only a Sphinx because it is blind that can smile at a desert. The Sphinx does not dream because it knows. But for others there are still eyes for the sun to weary, mouths to breathe dust, ears to ache in the wind. Impotent among the sunsets a man receives the impressions that his machinery gives him—snapshots along the pavement, sound-effects at night, the touch of dull sensations like a pattern stamped on wax. Instead of ecstasy there is a perspective of rottenness: Columbine is a harlot with grease-paint in the rain, Harlequin holds a lily and grins and strokes its stem. They are the same people: it is the viewpoint that has changed. A machine can only record what is inanimate and deathly. And if at the centre there is still a spark of life, a spark of humanity, it is only in fantasy that this flame creates. The light that the fire engenders is sometimes fond and sometimes pathetic and sometimes filthy, but always it is pointless and often touched with shame.

In the city the machinery that possessed me received its impressions and mixed its dreams and I observed my fire dying with a vague despair. The shadows it cast were the company I lived with, shapes in the gutter like the temptation of trees. When I went to eat there would be a girl at the counter before me, a girl with long hair and a fox-face and a memory of apples. I watched her. In the crowds at night there would be many; fairy feet beneath the palms of candelabra, tails that brushed against the undergrowth of knees, a hunt of hounds in the woods of degradation. If I spoke my breath would destroy the dying candle, shadows were better than the darkness of night. I did not speak. Music appeared to comfort the silence, and in the circling of leaves the wind was dispelled. Serpents jerked upon the dance floor, branches of arms were supported in smoke, the dark garden wept. Then one evening in a weary promenade I saw the bald men who were the same as I and I was one of them. Our noses were pressed against desire like prisoners. That is what I could not bear, being one of them. A hound with its tongue out, silent because it was strangled. After that I did not go out any more.

Often I dreamed about Annabelle.

Living in one room, in a cage, like a monkey, the faces outside that I cannot bear to see, that must not see me, there are no minutes to the days and it is the nights that are terrible. Love is a cage in which a monkey crouches and there is nothing human in the vision outwards nor in the vision inwards, there is nothing but waiting for what will never arrive. Love is this in which I had never believed, of which I had acted in defiance—a condition of failure and the absence of life. When love is returned it is not love, it is living, and when love is real it is the desire to die. This love is worship and you do not get what you worship, if you get what you worship your life will cease. There were times when I thought that if I had possessed Annabelle, had held her even, if I had come so close as to touch her then something so dreadful would have happened that I could not have borne it. In all our days together I did not remember having touched her except once when we had danced. In dancing touching is unreal, it is not hearts that you touch. If our hearts had touched we should have died.

A room at night with life nowhere near to me. Around me the objects that are close are waiting in the shapes of people that should use them, chairs that are never sat in, beds that are never lain in, wood and stuffing that will always remain. If I sit I do not sit because for hour after hour it is not I who forget myself, chairs and tables are more real than my mind. If I should recreate Annabelle in words I do not know what I should say except that I tried to love her without desire and without covetousness and without jealousy and that now I find I am without myself. I should say that it would have been possible if she had stayed close to me, but sacrifices are useless if the idol is away. There is nothing that I want. If she came into my room I do not suppose that it would please me, I have no eyes that would see her nor any heart to touch. There is a corner of the ceiling that might speak to me. That is more real to me, containing more hope.

And then before death the flame that is dying cries for a minute and I say I will do something I will do anything I will make the last use of this will that is left to me, I will go out into the street and I will walk until I have done something and then it will be done. I will choose to do this and there is nothing easier to do and if I don't I shall go mad. I get up from the chair in which I have become as dust and I walk to the door through the tomb of centuries and on the stairs I have to become savage so that the violation will be done. I step down pitifully knowing that this is pitiful, treading as if in fury past the objects that deride me and on the threshold of the sun I must stop to decide. I stop on the pavement with the street on either side of me, a direction stretching to the right and to the left and a road to cross with railings in front of me. I can go this way or that and it is I who must choose and then I know that I am mad. I cannot choose. There is nothing I desire.

There is a donkey, theoretically, who starves to death when he is placed between two bundles of hay which are equidistant from him. He has no means of deciding which way to turn. Now there was no hay, no hay in the world, and the effect was the same. The donkey could not move, I could not move, and I was the donkey.

There was nothing I desired. I stood on the edge of the street in which there was nothing, between the ends of perspective at which nothing belonged, and it was no use thinking, This or that will lead me to intention, and no use turning my head in hope. I knew I was the donkey. As a lunatic I waited while the emptiness of the world drained me and drop by drop I was emptied too. Now I am mad, I thought; I am finally in Hell. I stood in the sunlight while no one looked at me and nothing was part of me and I did not belong. It is no use trying, I thought. It is no use waiting even for the police to come and arrest me and to lead me away. There is not really enough of me for that.

V
FUGITIVES

14

It was another year before I saw them again. They wrote to me, once or twice, without saying much. Peter was working in an office, Annabelle was with her mother, Marius was not mentioned. In their letters there was a suggestion that they were as listless as I. Yet I did not believe this, I could not imagine them failing. Then at Christmas I had a postcard saying that they might soon be returning to England. For a while I revived, my dreams became a possibility. But they did not come. Time went slowly again; the winter dragged. At times I wondered what the year would have done to them, if it would have changed them so that when they returned we would still be apart. It seemed that this was what we had intended—that we should all change, perhaps—and it would surely only be I who had gone backwards into futility. When I thought this I was frightened that their return might be worse than their absence. Yet I hoped for them, always, as my only means of awakening from nightmare. And when they did return it was not as I had feared. Things had changed, but from the outside, not from within. Perhaps it was just that we were all a year older. One makes certain contacts with oldness in a year, even if what is contacted still tries to remain the same.

I felt I myself had grown older. There was still, however, something of which to be afraid.

On the first day of spring there was a procession going down the road with its brass bands its soldiers and its children with their tiny toy flags. The visit of some foreign royalty or the commemoration of a dead event, I forget what it was, but the people were there waving their sleeves and taking their hats off just in case (a funeral perhaps or something to do with the Cenotaph?); the horses trotted in trappings of silver with sad sightless men on top of them and the band thumping out the heavy blaring music that goes on and on in circles ceaselessly like the revolutions of the word or the roll of the universe, a line coming up the street swinging in step and the people cheering as they always cheer at the beginning of war or at the symbol of death because war is deliverance and what they want is a holiday. The symbol of death on a bright spring day and a child upon the pavement. I saw Peter on the other side of the road and I waved at him.

Everyone was waving. I jumped up and down and was doing no more than paying my exaggerated respects to the carriage which, approaching from the direction of Trafalgar Square, contained two bowing personages who acknowledged my efforts. Peter's fair head arose like a sunflower above the opposite border of bodies, but he was not as he had been once, the child leaning forwards flipping his pennies to the circus, he was older and tired as if he had watched a circus each night of his life until it had betrayed him. "Peter!" I yelled. He stood as if he were waiting to remove the debris. The pageant passed. He was like a shifter of cages who works in the dust.

His eyes did not see. I knew this look of eyes that did not see, I had stood so often myself with my head turned upon an imaginary shoulder, my own yet not my own because I was so distant from it, that it might have been I who was standing there on the opposite side of the road with my head drawn down beneath a waterfall of dreams. His ears did not hear. I did not believe that he could be sadder than I, having given up hope of the returning spring. Yet I was afraid of it. I wished I could throw something at him through the spray of sunlight.

There were horses trotting. I had seen them before, with Marius, in the running of crowds. Then a brick had been thrown through the stillness. "Peter!" I yelled.

Hearing only himself, or what he was thinking, with the band between us, he did no more than lean forwards into the sun so that the shadows came down over him like Marius again. Was then Marius now the bright-eyed angel? Peter having taken upon himself the sadness of the earth.

The carriage passed. Peter walked away. I would lose him on the barriers of interminable soldiers. I could not bear that my hope should go so suddenly.

I ran down a subway. There the crowd was swerving, thick, a child leaned steadily against my knees. I stepped over it, pushed, kicked against an ankle, they all turned behind me in affected concern. I fled, dodging, up some steps marked down. In the street there was dispersal. I ran to Trafalgar Square and found Peter beneath a fountain.

"You're back," I said. "I didn't know."

When he saw me he looked to each side of him as if he were expecting someone else. I thought, Perhaps he has been with people so long that he doesn't understand his loneliness. "Didn't you?'" he said. "No, we didn't know where you were."

"I saw you when the band went by. I thought I had lost you."

"Those damn bands," he said. "They should only play at funerals."

"I knocked a child over in the subway. I thought you had gone."

"I hadn't gone far," he said.

He was leaning against the edge of the fountain with the water coming down behind him in a curtain. He screwed up his eyes as if the spray was in his face. "What have you been doing?" he said.

"Nothing important," I said.

"No," he said. "Nothing important." It was as if he were leaning into the wind with the salt sea hurting him.

"And you?" I said.

"Well," he said, "there really isn't anything to do, is there?" People were beginning to look at him as if he were ill.

"Shall we go somewhere?" I said.

"Yes," he said.

We crossed the road and passed beneath an arch that hung in forgotten triumph. In the Mall the trees narrowed into the distance. "When did you get back?" I said.

"The other day," he said. A long straight road carrying cars to a palace. A world of Cinderellas with the fairies dead. "We didn't know where you were," he repeated.

"Nowhere that I could not have found you."

"There is nothing to find," he said.

We walked on. A ruined terrace beneath a ruined colonnade. In the park thin grass was brushed up over baldness, the trees shed palely the pretence of the sun. "There is nothing to find?"

"Up this road go savages to the sack of Rome," Peter said.

We walked into the park. Lovers sat on the grass in couples. It was as if we were seeing ourselves already from memory. "Can you tell me a thing worth doing?" he said.

"Not if you think that is a question worth asking," I said.

"Don't you?"

"Yes," I said.

"Damn them for making me hate them."

"Who?"

"The beautiful people who lie on the grass," he said.

A man lay with his girl's head on his shoulder. Another leant with hair against his throat. "That is your answer," I said. "Is that why you hate them?"

"Yes," he said.

"Then it is you who are the savage at the sack of Rome."

I stopped by a tree. I watched a leaf-bud drooping before me. The air contained it like rain. I thought, At this moment I know it is all over, that Peter never again will recognize the spring: I wonder how long it will take me to believe this.

"I was told," Peter said, "to go abroad and gather flowers. These are instructions which are supposed to be profitable to a young man. It is presumed to be an encouraging metaphor. You see people practicing it in the bluebell woods in summer."

"Didn't you work?" I said.

"I sat in an office and circulated papers. Is that work? The papers enabled others to move upon the bluebells. Whatever it was, there was a great destruction in the woods."

"Damn the woods. What did the work do to you?"

"I sat in a room like an electric cooker. There were a lot of figures: the figures did not mean anything, they were just on paper. Nothing meant anything. There was nothing but paper. We had enormous paper assets and not a penny to spend. What is the meaning of assets if you sit in a cooker? We bought and sold stuff that didn't exist, we transferred money that didn't exist to people who didn't exist, the non-existent people spent the non-existent money on non-existent goods. The awful thing was that there weren't even any bluebells. I couldn't even get angry. I just cooked. I have now officially been eaten."

"Why then did you try it, you knew . . . "

"What else was there for me to try?"

"I don't know."

"Should I have stood at street corners and made my complaint to the chariots? Would they have listened?"

"Then be a doctor or a teacher or make something with your hands."

"Can you see me as a doctor or a teacher?"

"No," I said.

"And there is nothing that I can make."

"Lie on the grass, then. For God's sake lie on the grass."

"There was a girl called William. They all have boys' names now. I could not speak to her."

"Did you have to speak?"

"Yes, I had to speak. Any ass can like a William without speaking."

"And couldn't you admit for once that you are an ass?"

"Could you?" he said.

We walked again. It was sad that he was playing the part that I wanted to play and was beating me. I wondered what I should have said to myself, but I knew that he was different. He was, I realized, even sadder than I.

"Besides," he said, "William was a friend of Annabelle's."

I was angry that he was different. "Is it true then that you have to live on incest?" I said.

He stopped. "What?" he said.

"This mumbo-jumbo of incest, this Hamlet rubbish, are you really the savage that should have to be kept from the smell of Annabelle?"

"Damn you," he said, "don't you love her?"

"I am not her brother."

"God damn you to hell," he said.

We moved on. I remembered how I had been angry once before with Marius. And then I had been happy. But now I did not know what I could say to someone with not even hope.

"Have you then gone over to the side of the old?" he said.

"Hamlet was old. He was twenty-six."

"I thought he was seventeen."

"No you see, it is you who are on the wrong side. It is the old who are ditched by their own imaginations."

"But they do not know it and I do."

"They are the very old. They are the dead."

"You don't know how right you are about Hamlet."

"Why?"

"You will see," he said. For the first time he smiled.

Walking and stopping in jerks we reached the palace. A flag licked limply against the sky. I said, "I know that one has got to do something or one goes mad."

"That does not matter, one has to do the right thing."

"The choice should not be difficult."

"It is. Doing the wrong thing sends one mad too, and then it is worse, because then, as you say, one is dead. It is not simply a matter of application."

"Then choose, choose and try it. You can choose for the whole of your life."

"I do not believe you can."

"These are old questions, anyway, why did you ask them now?"

"Because now we are old too, didn't you say so?"

"I meant that we should be younger," I said.

We watched a man sweeping up the gravel. He moved precariously like a toy that is running down. "They are the questions that saints ask," Peter said.

"The questions that saints answer."

"They ask them first. The most developed form of extrovert is the thug."

"Is Marius back?" I said.

"Introspection deals with conscience. Conscience is life. Extroversion is the denial of conscience."

"Or the fulfillment of it."

"I don't know whether Marius is back. You have to cultivate your conscience. Yes, after all, I believe Marius is back."

"And then you have to grow something when your conscience is cultivated. Cultivation is a means and not an end."

"Yes, yes, but do not deny the means."

"I am afraid I have not been able to," I said.

Peter then turned and for the second time he smiled. "And now you must come and see Annabelle," he said.

"How is she?" I said.

"Old," he said. He shrugged his shoulders. "Older and older. As old as Hamlet's mother." He laughed and walked into the middle of the road and waved for a taxi.

There was something wicked about him. He seemed, in a way, to have suddenly turned into one of those sinister men in foreign cities who take young men round the brothels. It was as if he was eager for ruin like a general haranguing troops before an attack.

As we climbed into the taxi I said, "What has happened?"

"Nothing," he said. "Nothing ever happens." We drove up Constitution Hill past the crocuses. The sun was warm. I might have been angry with him, but I preferred him sinister to hopeless. "They want to have me psychoanalysed," he said. He said this almost with relish.

"Who are 'they'?" I said.

"My father," he said.

"That is nothing new either."

"You will see my father."

"Fathers always want to have their children psychoanalysed. They like hearing about themselves." This was a silly remark, I thought.

"They want Annabelle to see a doctor, too," he said.

"Why?"

He laughed again that desperate laugh of a child at a tragedy. I do not know why I was not afraid. Perhaps anything was more endurable than Annabelle being well and apart from me.

Revisiting a scene that in the past has meant much to you plays tricks with time and is as unnerving as ghosts. Driving to Grosvenor Square through the angry traffic I had the sensation that all the scenes that had been enacted there had happened twice, that I was living in a circle of endless repetitions and it was my folly not to break the circle with the knowledge that my memory gave me. But my memory played me false I felt;—I did not know how many times I had made this journey in the taxi or how often I had met and renounced Annabelle—it was only after the event that the sense of duplicity became apparent. All I knew was that that evening I should feel that I had done something twice, and that at the second time of doing I should have remembered the first.

I thought: Perhaps there is a life as it is intended as well as a life as it happens, and it is only in memory that one can know if they are the same.

The taxi stopped. Flowers, scent, the wealth of carpets. We squeezed into the lift like an upright coffin. I thought: If the scene that is about to happen is already in my memory should I not feel more sad or more excited rather than wishing to escape? The lift carried us.

Peter opened the door. I followed him. There was a small man sitting on top of a step-ladder. "This is my father," Peter said.

"How do you do," the man said. "I am sorry I cannot get down. This machine folds up on me like a mousetrap."

"How do you do," I said.

"I am trying to remove these curtains. If you would kindly hold on to the ladder I should feel more secure."

"Yes," I said.

Peter had gone. Annabelle was not there. If this has ever happened to me before, I thought, I am sure I should remember. I clung to the ladder.

"Spring cleaning is a ritual to which I am addicted. My wife and daughter are not. My wife is three thousand miles away. My daughter is making tea. Will you stay to tea?"

"Thank you," I said.

"I find that now it is not the custom to invite people to tea. My children are consistently rude. Peter, for instance, has not mentioned tea?"

"No," I said.

"In my day it was natural to mention tea. It appears that now it is taken as an insult. People imagine that one is accusing them of greed. I fear that soon one will not be able to offer a bed to a visitor without it being taken as an improper remark."

"Yes," I said.

"I don't know how people can think of what to say without manners. I am supposed to be a very rude man, but I am not, I simply can't think of what to say. Now you, I can see, have good manners. Would you be good enough to hand me the scissors?"

"Yes," I said.

"Thank you. It is the same with spring cleaning. People despise it now. And soon they will despise eating, and sleeping, and breathing, and then they will die. They simply won't think it worth while."

"No," I said.

"You are a young man of great equanimity. The prospect does not disturb you?"

"No," I said.

"I find that most remarkable. I, I fear, was upset even by these curtains. My daughter says she never drew them because she liked looking at the night. I myself can never find anything to see in the night. It appears to me to be quite dark."

I began to laugh. He descended the ladder. He had pale smoky eyes and hair that was brushed with great precision. A small, dapper man with a face like a nut. He folded the curtain and placed it on a chair. "Annabelle," he called, "your friend is laughing at me."

"Tea is nearly ready," replied Annabelle from the kitchen.

I wanted to go and see her, but I did not know what to do. Pale eyes watched me courteously. This was something that could never have happened to me before, even the room was not the same when he was in it. I had the impression that he did not want to be in it, that he had talked to excuse his presence and make light of the change he had wrought. Annabelle remained in the kitchen. He took a cigarette and fitted it into a holder and began talking again. He spoke of London in the spring. I could not hear him. Annabelle was in the kitchen. If he stopped talking I felt that I should die. Stop sleeping stop breathing and die. His voice was necessary to me and he knew it.

When Annabelle came in from the kitchen she was carrying a tray in front of her and I did not see. "Hullo," she said. She put the tray down with her back to me and I still did not see. Then she turned round and for a moment I did not think that it was her at all, and then I saw that she was going to have a child.

"Hullo," I said.

Her father was saying, "The dreadful thing about living in a tropical climate is that one cannot believe in the seasons. Returning to England is a return to nature. Elsewhere climate is geography."

She looked at me calmly. I was sure she did not mind. It was I who turned my eyes away because I was so glad to see her.

Peter came in and we sat down to tea. Peter did not speak. Men in foreign cities come no farther than the door.

I said, "But living with the seasons makes people callous, don't you think, in the country one is of no importance until one has been destroyed by a bicycle or a pig, and then one is only a joke that holds its own for a moment with the seriousness of vegetables."

He said, "But I like vegetables, I like them much better than people, I know exactly what to do with them and I don't know what to do with people at all."

We talked like this. We talked for a quarter of an hour. He did it naturally, I think, for he was an expert talker: and I followed him better than

I could normally have done because I needed this flow of nonsense to conceal an emotion that I did not understand. We sat in a small square around the tea-table, the four of us, while Peter's scowl deepened as our chatter increased ("You can't really love vegetables." "Indeed I can, yes, the aubergines at Toulon those I really love.") and Annabelle sat back holding her saucer in front of her as if waiting for birds to perch on it from the sky. I do not remember looking at her but I know exactly how she seemed, calmly and monumentally waiting for some great joke to burst about our heads that would confound us, to be sure, but never her, because she had heard the joke, and knew it, and would be pleased only to notice the reactions of our eyes. And for me, too, the emotion was one of laughter: for her sake I would enjoy the joke, for her sake I would smile. It was she, after all, who was having the child: and if she was pleased to be benign about it with her saucer held out to receive pennies or crumbs, I swore that it would not be me who would pass her by without giving what I had.

"If you loved food, really, long enough, you would turn into a vegetable yourself."

Her composure, in profile, was that of a shuttered house on a burning day, the lids of her eyes heavy with a suggestion of sleep, her breathing like the heat of a lazy mimosa. Around her was an air of preternatural stillness like the echoless calm that precedes a thunderstorm. She awaited our laughter with the tranquility of flowers: and after the storm had passed, I thought, there she would be with the rain untouched on her lashes.

"I have noticed, certainly, a tendency among gourmets to resemble their favourite dish. There is an earl, for instance, who is probably *bouchées à la reine*."

Being near her, keeping the nonsense moving, I felt myself, or what I hoped to be myself, return to inhabit the body it had left. This was a sensation similar to that of a limb that has gone to sleep, the removal of the pressure that had stopped the blood from flowing and then the slow creeping pain of renewed belonging and the pleasure of waiting till the limb was whole. While feeling encroaches there is a terror of moving, a concentration or stillness till the blood is there. I waited cautiously while old love and old joy crept through me and then it was there, suddenly, Annabelle was close to me and was impervious to damage, and I laughed, hugely, while the table rocked and a spoon fell abruptly on the floor.

Peter got up and left the room. I laughed with the tears coming into my eyes and my lungs aching until I choked upon a crumb and lost my breath. Annabelle gazed at me. Her father, with mock concern, removed his tea-cup from the table. I turned aside and buried my face in a handkerchief and Annabelle came quietly and patted my back. Then it was over. I wiped my eyes and apologized. "I trust it was something other than my wit," her father said, "to have so alarmed you."

"To-morrow," I said to Annabelle, "will you have tea with me?"

"I have to do the cooking," she said, "but I will walk with you in the park."

"Annabelle is a tough nut," her father said, "A very tough nut."

"Do you still do the cooking?" I said. "Do you sow and knit and take dogs for walks?"

"And have children," she said, beginning to pile the crockery.

I left her soon. I did not want to stay. We had said what was required and I made my excuses. Her father came with me to the lift. "Perhaps I can drop you somewhere," he said. "I have an appointment myself."

"Thank you," I said.

We sat in a very small car. I felt once more that I had work to do. He drove fast smoking a cigarette in his holder. "How do you think Peter is looking?" he said.

"Not very well," I said.

"No." He stopped at some traffic lights. We sat staring in front of us, a small impassive man in a Foreign Office hat and I who admired him. "He seems to be suffering from a disease that is quite common nowadays," he said; "A lack of purpose."

"Yes," I said.

"And a very understandable one."

"Do you think so?"

"I hope I understand. I know that if I were a young man now I should find it difficult to know what to do."

"What would you try to do?"

"The same as before, probably. But that is no good for Peter."

"No," I said. The traffic lights changed and we proceeded sharply.

"I think that in many ways it is my fault," he said. "I tried to bring up my children on the theory that it is best for them to be left alone."

"Surely you were right," I said.

"Was I? I don't know. When you reach my age you will realize that it is a highly dangerous position to be left alone."

"But it is like free will, you have got to risk it."

"Well," he said. We shot across Bond Street. The road was thick with American limousines. "About free will, you know, I have a suspicion that we deceive ourselves."

"There are instructions?"

"More than that. I feel that perhaps some canvassing goes on behind the scenes. String-pulling. Fiddling. To be a good father one must be as crafty as the devil."

"I don't think that's possible," I said.

He turned to me so that his cigarette-holder jutted straight towards my nose. "Tell me," he said, "are you in the habit of despising the older generation?"

I laughed foolishly. "That was a bad habit," I said.

"Ah!" he said. We brushed remorselessly through a curtain of pedestrians. "A habit that goes with the complaint. And you believe in freedom. Freedom from conventions, controls, and the claims of parental authority."

"Yes," I said.

"And the claims of love?"

"The claims," I said, "yes."

"Rubbish!" he said. We sped down Regent Street. "I don't believe you for a minute." I laughed again. "But I know that that is what Peter believes," he said.

He pulled up near Piccadilly Circus. "Look here," he said, "are you doing anything for half an hour?"

"No," I said.

"Then would you like to have a drink at my club? It is only just across the road."

"I should like it very much," I said.

"Right," he said. We swerved out from the pavement and a bus shrieked to a standstill. "You see how crafty I am. I have no appointment." We dodged the cursing traffic. "Another intolerable deceit of the older generation. But then, of course, you did not have an appointment either."

In the club there was a room like a railway station. We sat in ageless leather chairs. "It is true," he said, "that this place is rather appalling. Is that why you despise us?"

"I don't," I said.

"That's cheating." He nodded as an old man passed him. "I gather you think us mad." The old man came up to him and they whispered at each other fiercely. Their heads pecked strangely like puppet birds. When they had finished he said, "It is interesting talking to you. Peter won't talk."

"I don't think you're mad," I said.

"That is because you are older than Peter, then. When you are older still you will realize why we act like we do. Not all of us, of course. But you will see that it is difficult to do any better."

"Do you despise us then?"

"Oh no. I only look on you with slight alarm. It seems to me that you are obsessed with the Garden of Eden. You insist on trying to recreate it and at the same time insist on making the original mistakes. I do find that alarming. But despicable, no."

"Can we help making the original mistake?"

"I don't think you can. I think it goes inevitably with Gardens of Eden."

"Then what should we do?"

"I think, since we are talking in these terms, that you should read your bible. Isn't it something about getting it within you? You mustn't despise the bible, you know, although it may strike you as peculiar."

"It does," I said.

"Yes, but still, you must translate it. It is, after all, not a text-book. You have to learn the language before you can understand what it means. The trouble with Peter is that he either translates it into someone else's terms or else he despises it. He will not trouble to learn the language."

"It is very difficult to have faith," I said.

"Why yes, of course."

"You agree then?"

"If you say so. If you don't want it."

"But that's what Peter wants."

"And he can't get it. So that's that."

"He thinks that you want to have him psychoanalysed," I said.

"Does he? That was a chance remark of his mother's, which resulted in a slight misunderstanding. It is no good being psychoanalysed, either, unless one wants to be."

There was a silence for a while. I began to imagine what he wanted. "In fact," I said, "in order to get results, someone has to be as crafty as the devil."

"As many people as possible," he said.

"I don't trust that," I said. "Not unless the people are very sure of what they are doing."

"There can be, so to speak, limited objectives. It can do no harm, I am sure, to act simply upon what of course must be a genuine regard."

"A regard for Peter?"

"Yes. And I know for certain that he has a regard for you."

"Has he?"

"Yes. And he is not lavish with his respect. There are few people, I feel, who can influence him."

"There was . . . " I began.

"There was someone whom he respected? Yes, I believe there was, and now there is no longer. You will have noticed, perhaps, that that is part of the trouble."

I had noticed. I remembered Marius in the square with Peter running beside him, a moonlight night with emotion gone wrong, Marius as Mephistopheles and Peter as Faust. It had been a holiday beneath the statue that we had none of us understood. And now there was retribution. "I had noticed that," I said.

"You see," he said, "there is something in this century that is inimical to children. Peter is still a child. We have talked about the chasm between generations, but it is really not that, it is simply a difference in ages. My generation were children once, at the beginning of the century, and it is interesting to remember us. We were mostly killed in the war. There was an obsession with death when I was young just as now there is an obsession with futility. Then it was active and now it is passive; that is the only difference. We all of us arrive at that age when destruction becomes a mania of the soul—the age when we cease against our will to be children.

"Have you ever read the letters of young men at the beginning of the first world war? They are extraordinary reading. I mean the young men who, like myself and Peter, were brought up with every material advantage. I do not speak for those whose childhood was a material struggle, for their problems were different. My generation, the generation of Edwardian children being brought up in Edwardian luxury, came to an age at which they wanted to die. They said so, in their letters. They were children, and they did not know how to grow up, so they went to war to absolve themselves from the responsibility. There they found what they wanted. They said so. The war was a release, a fulfillment of childish continuities. They lived as children and they died as children, and I think they were glad."

"It was not the same in this war," I said.

"No, but that was because this war was not a children's business. One gets, as it were, wise to war's futility. We did, of course, after a few months in the trenches. But you were older than we, you knew it all before, you could find no release in sacrifice because you knew that it was sacrifice for nothing. We did not. And now you are alive, but you still don't know what to do about it. It is funny how there were fewer deaths in this war probably because there were fewer desires for it."

"Yes," I said.

"Peter, of course, is different. Peter had no war. He did not have the opportunity for sacrifice. But the situation is there. He has reached an age at which he requires an opportunity to fulfill himself, and he does not find it. He was an extraordinary child, and the memory of that does not help him. He was brought up in the old style, and life ran kindly for him. We spent much of our time in foreign countries, you know, where English children are, so to speak, at a premium. And then he was at school. He was very successful at school. And then he was fond of Annabelle. I think he was quite unusually fond of Annabelle. They never fought, or quarreled, as brothers and sisters do. They used to guard each other carefully like ancient maiden ladies. There were times, indeed, when their regard for each other almost worried me. They became quite solemn and detached in their affection."

"Yes," I said.

"Once, you see, the world was not inimical to children. Once there was continuity between the expectation of a child and the expectation of an adult. The pattern was set, and the child advanced in it smoothly. Now the pattern is broken and the grown-up child is lost. This is a direct result of the freedom which children nowadays are given. This freedom is not right unless the child can build something out of it."

"No," I said.

"So, you see, this is a time of testing. We have agreed that children should not translate things into their parents' terms, and this I have endeavoured to put into practice. Now we have to see whether our theories are justified. For Peter it is a time when childhood ceases. The old life dies and the new life begins. He has to find his own translation. I think it is only right that we should help the death to be as comfortable as possible."

"But with no bluff, no craftiness—that is always recognized on a death-bed. We must face what is real."

"If you will allow me to say so, I think that this might be taken as a definition of the difference between the old and the young—that the young are realists on the surface and not underneath, and the old are most likely the opposite. Reality, you see, is not solely concerned with behaviour. In manners, words, and affections the young endeavour to be the most ardent realists, but they are not often wise enough to be realists at heart. The aim of a realist is to come to terms with his situation, and to the successful achievement of this manners are a means and not an end. The charge of hypocrisy that is so often leveled against the old is of no validity unless one knows what is in each man's heart. There are certain intentions, and certain failures, and the behaviour that arises from them. But it is in intention that the old are the realists."

"And the intention is to come to terms?"

"In the best possible way, with the way of each person different. There can be no other realistic intention. You will perhaps know the futility of refusing terms and fighting."

"Yes," I said.

"So that, with Peter, we must be realists, certainly, but realists primarily in aim. We must help him to come to terms in the best possible way. As to what that way is, your guess is as good as mine. Also, I am sure, will be your manners. I trust that you will not find mine too frivolously indirect."

"Nor mine too earnest," I said.

"The old, you see, have their little tricks of appeasement. I do not think they are wrong. It is the intentions that matter."

"Not the results?"

"I have said that there are failures. I would go so far as to say that there are too many failures. But that should not prevent one from trying."

"No," I said.

We lay back in our chairs. For a railway station the room was unusually quiet. Rubber-soled porters crept by with muffled trays. I felt enormously flattered. With me, perhaps, had he been insincere? A tactical manoeuvre to enroll my support? It did not matter. I believed him. "I will do what I can," I said.

"Thank you. And now, if you will excuse me, I really must go. Perhaps, in fact, I had an appointment all the time!" He did his wicked smile at me through a pillar of smoke.

I followed him. Going down the steps he laid his hand on my arm. "Also," he said, "there is Annabelle. But you will know what to do about that." Then he walked on ahead of me.

In his tiny car he looked like an ancient carved idol. He wound down the window. "I hope I see you again," he said.

"I hope so," I said.

"I have to go to Paris to-morrow, but perhaps after that."

"Yes," I said.

"I used to know your father," he said. "In fact we were very good friends. Good-bye."

"Good-bye," I said.

He drove off rapidly through the taxis like a dog splitting a flock of sheep. I watched him whizz round the corner. I stood on the pavement and wondered if he had been talking all the time about Annabelle, but I did not think he had.

I rang up Peter. "Do you know where Marius is?" I said.

"Where are you speaking from?"

"From Pall Mall."

"Have you been with my father?"

"Yes."

"My father would charm the leg off a horse," Peter said.

"Do you know where Marius is?"

"What have you been talking about?"

"About you, of course. And Marius?"

There was a silence for a few seconds, then, "I believe he is staying with your friend Alice," Peter said.

"Oh." I thought about this. "Will you be in this evening?" I said.

"I expect so."

"Perhaps we might meet sometime afterwards."

"After what?"

"Anyway, I'll ring you up."

"Yes do. Do let's meet."

"All right then." I rang off.

I went round to Alice's house. She stood defensively in the doorway like a chucker-out. "Oh it's you," she said. "Fancy seeing you."

"I wondered if Marius was here," I said.

"How rude," she said. "No, he's out."

"Can I come in then?"

"Have you got any cigarettes?"

"Yes," I said.

"Then you can come in." She held the door open and I went through.

"I'm in a mess," I said.

"For God's sake don't start talking about yourself again," she said.

"All right. All right," I said. "How's Marius?"

"He's a bore, but I don't see much of him. Why can't he stay at Grosvenor Square?"

"Annabelle is having a child," I said. "Didn't you know?"

"No," she said. "Is she? Can't I have a cigarette?"

I gave her one. "You don't seem very surprised," I said.

"I don't think anything that goes on between you and your friends would surprise me," she said.

"It's not my child."

"Whose is it then?"

"I supposed it was Marius's."

"Oh," she said.

"I can't see why they aren't together, can you?"

"No," she said.

"I mean, why doesn't he marry her?"

"Good heavens, why do people not marry each other?"

"But they must want to."

"Must they? God knows I shouldn't want to marry Marius."

"But she must want to. I suppose it is Marius who won't."

"The way you think you understand people!" she said.

I sat down. The room was hot and oppressive. I felt faintly pathetic like a private detective. "I suppose you want me to leave you my cigarettes and go," I said.

"Darling, you know how I love seeing you. Tell me what you have been doing lately."

"Nothing," I said. "I've finished my book."

"I'm sure it's dreadful."

"Yes. Do you know when Marius will be in?"

"No," she said. "And why make such a fuss about Marius? You're not going to ask him why he doesn't marry Annabelle, are you?"

"I might," I said.

"Oh how dreadful," she said. "How perfectly dreadful. Please don't do it in my house, that's all. You can do it anywhere else."

When Marius came in I saw at once that he seemed younger. He had always been theatrical, but now he made his entrance with some of the awkwardness of inexperience, his movement from the door to the chair being performed self-consciously as if he were watching himself from the audience. Once he had acted as if there were no one present to him except himself. Now there were others. It was strange that I was not more glad to see him.

"I'm going to my bedroom," Alice said. "I can't bear to hear your conversation."

Marius sat in the chair and smiled his half-smile into the carpet. Then he pulled a packet of cigarettes out of his pocket and took an enormous time to open them. "How did you know I was here?" he said.

"Peter told me."

"Yes," he said. He searched for matches. "I didn't know where you were," he added.

"No," I said. "That's what everyone says."

Once, I remembered, what Marius had acted had been the same as what he felt. Now I had the impression that it was not. But that, surely, was what happened when one grew old? For Marius, then, growing younger, was this situation merely one about which he felt nothing? I found this difficult to believe.

"How did you think Peter was?"

"Not very well."

"No. I'm thinking of going away," he said.

"Away? You've only just got back."

"I've got nothing to do here."

"Haven't you?"

"No."

"Then why did you come back?"

"Oh I don't know," he said.

So here we were, I thought, back in the shop window where what is displayed has nothing to do with what is underneath, where the little packets are sham and the meanings, like Peter's figures, non-existent. The only oddity was that in Marius's window, as in those of the more exclusive establishments, there did not even seem to be anything on show. No feelings and nothing on show. It was at least logical.

"Where will you go?" I said.

"Back home," he said. I had not heard him use the word "home" before. "There are things to be done there," he said.

"And what will Peter do?" I found myself talking of Peter instead of Annabelle in the way that everyone did.

"I believe his father is trying to get him a job in Paris."

"Will Peter take it?"

"I hope he will."

"Do you know his father then?"

"Oh yes. I stayed with them, you know, for quite a time. He is a very remarkable man, his father. Very remarkable indeed. I was doing some work for him out there."

"What sort of work?"

"Various things," Marius said.

There was nothing else to say. I stood up to go. I was angry, but this time it was with a quite dispassionate annoyance, a desire to get away into an atmosphere that was whole. Marius watched me and then asked me, more from politeness than anxiety, I thought, if I would have lunch with him the next day. I thanked him. Politeness was better than nothing. I walked along to say good-bye to Alice and I found her lying on her bed in the shaded light. "I told you you would be in a mess if you went with Marius," she said. She was looking very tired and the light made hollows in her face as it lay on the pillow. "Are you in a mess?" I said. "No," she said. The room smelt of smoke and the curtains were heavy against the window. I thought of how Marius had once said that

Alice did not have an effect on people and now he did not have an effect on people either. "I don't mind being in a mess," I said. I left her my cigarettes and went.

15

I met Peter in the square. I was glad to see him. "I'm sorry I can't ask you in," he said. "The place is full of priests."

"Priests?" I said.

"Substantially there is only one, I suppose, but he is like one of those jelly-fish that are composed of a million minor orgasms."

"Organisms," I said.

"Yes, organisms. He knows all about cricketers and actresses. He is that sort of priest."

"Come back to my room," I said. "I can make some supper."

"Anywhere," Peter said. "Anywhere for God's sake that is not holy."

We sat on a bus. I felt again like a private detective. It was as if Peter were my witness from whom I had to extort the truth before he was killed. "Start from the beginning," I said. "Is that Marius's child?"

"I suppose so," Peter said.

"I was beginning to wonder even about that."

"Yes," Peter said.

"So what's wrong with Marius? Why's he going away?"

"There's nothing else for him to do."

"Doesn't he want to stay with Annabelle?"

"Yes," Peter said.

"Then what's wrong?"

"Annabelle says it's no good," Peter said.

We sat together handcuffed by what we did not understand, and I could think of nothing except the fatuity of my questions. "What happened when you were abroad?" I said.

"We were with each other for a time," he said. "My father was sent to the West Indies, you know, so that we were there with Marius. We were moving in and Marius was round about the house and it was all right then. Annabelle was all right. Then I went away to do this ridiculous job and by the time we were due to come home it was all wrong. Nobody was saying anything and Marius just followed us hoping for the best. And now here we are. Why the devil did she start a child if she didn't want to stick with him?"

"I don't know," I said.

"So he's got to go away and the whole bloody thing's breaking up. I could kill her."

"Yes," I said.

"And now what's she going to do? What's she going to do with the baby? No one seems to be interested in that. All they do is call her a tough nut. They seem to be more interested in me."

"They can talk about you," I said.

"Why can't they talk about her? It's going to be very awkward for my father and mother if Annabelle has a child. They can't very well cart her around with them. Yet everyone treats her as if she'd done something marvelous and me as if I'd been certified insane."

"You know this psychoanalysis stuff is nonsense," I said. "Why keep on bringing it in?"

"You don't know it," he said. "You don't know it at all. My father could charm the hindquarters off an ox."

We went up to my room. Its ugliness hit us. "Oh dear," Peter said. I lit the gas fire and cleared some clothes off a chair. Peter was examining the writing-desk that turned into a washstand. The walls were the colour of the inside of a trunk. "Why do you live here?" he said. "I don't mind it," I said. I found myself being almost proud of its ugliness, proud of the condition of poverty which was the disease of the post-war world. I found a bottle of beer among my boots.

"I wondered," Peter said. "It is funny how none of us know anything about you. Perhaps this is the hold that you have over us, that you live in a place like this."

"I only live here because I choose to."

"Why?"

"A reaction, probably. Reactions are necessary. I think it is the way to live."

"In order to be free?"

"Free from the opposite."

"It is this freedom that is crazy," Peter said.

We drank our beer. The gas fire popped, gave out, was revived by a shilling. "What is it that is crazy?" I said.

"That we are no better off. When Marius's wife was alive, do you remember, we were all right, we were fond of each other, Marius and Annabelle were in love. Now she is dead and they are not. We none of us are. The world has become a place in which there is no love. Why did you laugh with my father at tea?"

"Because I don't think that's true."

"When Marius's wife died she gave Annabelle and Marius freedom. Look what they have done with it."

"I don't know what they have done with it. You said that they were happy abroad."

"I said that they were all right because I thought that they should marry. That was what I meant. But I do not think that they were happy. I do not think that any of us have been happy together since we last saw you. Does that make you glad?"

"Yes," I said.

"Why did you walk out that night?"

"I don't know. I thought it was the thing to do."

"It doesn't seem that it was."

"Perhaps Marius's wife was the cause of it. Perhaps she was more important than all of us so that while she was alive we were all right. Then she died and we were free from importance and it was not all right. Even when we did not know her we felt that there was something beyond us that made the rest possible. Now there is nothing of importance and that is the despair."

"So you walked out?"

"I walked out because I thought there were other things of importance. There were to me."

"And are there still?"

"Yes, that is why I laughed at tea. I did not know that there would not be anything of importance to you."

"There should have been," he said. "Why don't you marry Annabelle?"

"Annabelle is happy," I said. "Do you know why?"

"It is those priests," he said. "Those bloody damn priests. It is they who have ruined us." This was the saddest answer I have ever had, and at the time I had to take it as true.

I turned away from him. I lit the gas ring and put fat in the frying pan and watched the liquid spread. I thought of Annabelle cooking and knitting and having children and Peter's priests like great black spiders to entwine her. "Who is this priest?" I said.

"You will see him. He is what is important now. He is called Father Jack Manners. Isn't that a silly name for a priest?"

"Yes," I said.

"They all have names like that. It is like the girls who are called William. They have to present themselves as the opposite of what they are supposed to be. Why do they do it? I don't understand. I should have thought that a priest was the one person who shouldn't."

"Perhaps they have to present themselves strangely in order to get what they want . . . "

"But do they get it? Surely, that is the greatest fallacy in the world, that you can hope to get what you want by pretending something different. You can see the results of it all around you. I like people to say what they are thinking, I believe it is necessary to say what you think in order to get what you want, and surely it is the business of a priest to think of something other than Wisdens or the Tatler."

"But it is what he does, the effect he has, rather than what he says . . . " I was trying to remember all that Peter's father had told me and was failing.

"Admittedly he is not like one of those monks of the middle ages. Have you read Boccaccio? It is interesting, that. I don't know how true it all was, that world of lecherous monks, but at least it was the fashion to make up stories about them. And stories, if they are good ones, have at the worst a superficial resemblance to facts. It was the fashion then to be lecherous, and the priest was taken as the fashionable man par excellence. Now it is the fashion to be in with the latest gossip, and priests are there at the head of the field again. Talk is the big thing now, and by talk you can judge people. I tell you, this man knows what's going to win the National and what names will appear in the engagement column of the Times. That's what he talks about. The one thing he doesn't talk about is the difference between right and wrong."

"Have you asked him why he doesn't?"

"No, I don't think I could bear to."

"I shall ask him," I said.

Peter smiled. I was no good as a detective. I should always, I thought, sympathize with the suspect. A person's reasons for choosing to be what he was were more convincing than the judgments of others upon what he had chosen. The motives I should like to question were those of the police.

"Do you know this religious racket?" Peter said.

"No," I said.

"I tell you, there is in it no question of right and wrong. It is a matter of good form and bad form, and whether you can keep a smile on your face like a bloody Aunt Sally."

"How did you get into it?" I said.

"It's my mother's racket. Mothers always have a racket, and the Church is hers. So I'm an Aunt Sally whether I like it or not."

"She's not a Catholic, is she?"

"Yes, she is. That's one of their tricks. She's a Catholic but she isn't a Roman Catholic. It's a very clever trick. They get you feeling a fool before you've begun."

"Yes," I said.

"All part of the racket. No one knows anything about it, you see. And they never tell anyone so you go on not knowing. They talk and talk and make you feel a fool and you don't know what the devil they're up to. I doubt if they know what they're up to themselves. I'm sure my mother doesn't. She doesn't know the difference between a Baptist and a bishop.

But she's put her money on God because she thinks his shares are rising. He pays out the interest of making her feel on top of everyone else. She's in the know, she's on to a good thing, she's got that damned satisfaction of having jumped the market. And she never explains it. Why doesn't she explain it? Why else except that to make a bit for herself she has to keep others in the dark?"

"She doesn't try to convert you?"

"They never try to convert you. It's like some club, some damned secret society, you have to come begging and knocking before they let you in. And yet they say it is a matter of life and death to you, a matter of eternal heaven or eternal hell. Why don't they try to convert you? They are supposed to be charitable. You have to get the right knock or the door won't open, you have to pull the right strings or your name will not be proposed. The knock and strings are there, I admit. But they have bloody funny ideas in the way of advertisement."

"But you said you were an Aunt Sally . . . "

"I am an Aunt Sally because although they don't try to convert you by stating their case, they do everything to demoralize you from having a case of your own. It's like having a disease in the family, or drunkenness—their eye is on the bottle and the bottle fills the room. You can't escape from it. There is a smell of it in the corridors, if you went into the jungle you would hear it on our trail. And now everyone is talking it up, everyone muscling in on the racket. I tell you my family is a nightmare. I believe if I went to the North Pole I should find a bloody monk on top of it like Simon Stylites."

"How did it begin?"

"I tell you how my mother began it. I don't believe my father cares a damn, but he says he does. She got the priests hopping around—they are the most frightful snobs, you know—and then Marius got wind of it . . . "

"Marius?"

"Yes, didn't you know? Marius got wind and made a nice little investment and had a nice little sinful affair with Annabelle all at the same time—that's funny, isn't it, that's really bloody funny—and then Annabelle . . . "

"Annabelle?"

"Oh yes, of course, God almighty, Annabelle was their darling and she went to bed with Marius, doesn't that make you laugh?"

"No," I said.

"They all took it up, they all made lovely big jokes about it—that's another of their tricks, you know—all being beautifully irreverent and jolly, and darling Father Jack mopping up the cocktails and Marius floating round as if he'd seen a vision and Annabelle getting bigger and bigger as she knelt in Church;—Oh Jesus Christ oh bloody Jesus Christ if it doesn't make you laugh then isn't it too much to make you cry?"

"Begin again," I said. "Begin again about Annabelle."

"I tell you Marius began it. Marius's wife died and Marius got religion. Did she do it for him? Do you know? It doesn't matter. Marius came to my mother and she took him under her wing and they got their tame priests with leads around their necks. Tame priests wear dog-collars, did you know? Then Annabelle. Annabelle always had it, you remember how she talked, but she did not have it like this. Now she does not talk. And I will tell you why she now has it like this, because Marius gave her the baby and that's a mess for anyone to be in and this is her way for getting out of it."

"I don't believe that," I said.

"You don't know it, you don't know it at all, I tell you this is the racket which has ruined us and the world. When my father got hold of you this evening what did he say to you? I know what he said, he said that I was in a muddle and you must all pull on the bloody old rope to get me out of it. Did he say anything about Annabelle? Did he say anything about Marius? No. And now who do you think is in the muddle. I who have never changed my creed for one instant and who have done my best to live by what I believe and who admit my failures according to what is left of my conscience, or Marius who sins and Annabelle who blinds herself and my father who will say what he said to you without having the honesty to say it to me and Father Jack Manners who puts his blessing on the assembly and bluffs them all into thinking that they are acting in the name of God? Who is in the muddle?"

"I don't know," I said.

"Then tell me this, when you saw Marius this evening, did he appear to you to be alive or dead?"

"Dead," I said.

"Well then, there you are, thank you, thank you very much, so long as someone agrees about something it is not so very terrible."

He sat back. The food had gone cold, the sausages congealed, there was a feeling in the room as if devils were close to us. "But now," I said, "now, with Annabelle, in the flat, with that priest, what is he doing there?"

"She asked him. He had to be in London and she asked him to stay. She is hooked, collared, you see, and they lap each other up like saucers of milk. They lick together round the rims of plates. But it is for me he is there. He is a good solid base for the tug of war. Is it presumptuous to say this? You will see what I mean. I am just so sorry for everybody."

"And Annabelle . . . " I said.

"You must see," he said. "You must come to breakfast and hear him talk. Annabelle? I don't know about Annabelle. Marius was alive and now he is dead. I don't know about Annabelle. It is quite an education to hear him talk at breakfast. He is one of those people who say how dreadful breakfast is, how it should be suffered in silence, and then talk for two hours. The priest, I mean. I can't think about Annabelle. You must watch her while she listens to him. May I stop here the night? Thank you. I'm very tired. I can't bear to go back in case there is someone sitting up for me. I love Annabelle. Sitting up like a Nanny with a cup of tea. It is kind of you to let me stay. A bloody old nanny goat bleating in his sleep. I love Annabelle. You will see what I mean."

"Yes," I said. I went to bed that night believing in Peter.

In the night I found myself awake. I thought, as I had done once before—Time does not have to go so quickly as this.

I lay in the darkness. More had happened in nine hours than in a winter. I had woken, and the world was running again, and it was not myself who had changed.

I waited for the morning. Two things surprised me: one, that what had changed us had come from outside; the other, that I felt myself in a position to control it. I had not expected either of these during my dreams of the winter.

I thought—I might have been changed if this had come to me in my loneliness: Annabelle and Marius were more lonely than I: it is strange that they should have been lonely. Peter is fighting it. I can fight something which comes from outside.

I can fight it because I am awake again. In the morning time will run and I will run to keep up with it. I am awake because during the winter I was at least impervious. Now I can run more quickly than time. I can give to them, and help them, because the only change in myself is this being in control again. If priests have given me this strength by weakening the others, for this alone I can be grateful to them.

I enjoyed this illusion, of being in control again.

16

Father Jack Manners, at breakfast, said:—

"Good-morning, Peter, good-morning, how do you do, well and what has Annabelle got for us this morning? she has the most magnificent black market in eggs, you know, really magnificent, for what we are about to receive may the Lord make us truly thankful, I don't know where we would be without the black market, do you? do I think the black market is wrong? no I must honestly say that I don't, I am afraid that eggs are one of my weaknesses, I remember once when I was asked to say grace in Sussex the old parlourmaid an admirable woman said 'You should thank Mr. Goldberg, Father, not the Lord,' and so I said that I would, and I did, yes, Annabelle, I know that that is a very old joke but I am a very old man and I like old jokes, Mr. Goldberg? no, I don't know anything wrong about Mr. Goldberg, do you? oh dear, what a cross-examination at breakfast, I am afraid I am not at my best at breakfast, you should learn about the difference between morality and religion, is there a difference? yes, most certainly there is a difference I should say that there is all the difference in the world, or rather of the world, I remember a story told by Prebendary Dodds, he had just smacked his young nephew for some minor offence and a good woman asked him how he came to reconcile his action with his religious belief, and he said 'Madam I am more concerned with coming to a reconciliation with my nephew,' yes Annabelle, yes, I know that it is not quite the point, but you don't know the good Prebendary, he is a very small man, very small indeed, at least three inches shorter than his nephew, so that it really was a problem, a problem indeed, I remember him as a young man doing missionary work in Lancashire, and a weaver of considerable size slammed the door in his face, and Prebendary Dodds couldn't move away because his overcoat was caught in the door, so he knocked again and the weaver who had probably had too much to drink came rushing out and tripped clean over Prebendary Dodds and knocked himself out on the pavement; what? but religion is concerned with facts, you see, it is simply concerned with facts, while morality, surely, is not; I remember when I was traveling in a train during the war and a young lady started talking to me, it was interesting how people started talking at that time, and this young lady said, 'Of course I myself am not a very religious person,' and I said, 'Neither, if it comes to that, am I,' and she was very surprised but what she had intended to say, of course, was, 'I am not a very moral person,' and I am sure I do not know what I should have answered to that; I was too old, I fear, for it to have interested me greatly; but this is the point, you see, all right, Annabelle all right, that that young lady, although I am sure she would have been most startled to hear it, was a puritan, yes a puritan, she had got religion muddled with morality and that is what puritans do, all the time, and I am afraid that puritans have been responsible for the most dreadful amount of muddled thinking about religion, a really dreadful amount, you find their influence everywhere, in the most unexpected places, at the breakfast table, even, forgive me, but you must believe me when I say that they see the position quite wrongly, that they have done the most unaccountable amount of harm, that morality must on no account be muddled with religion; and now, Annabelle, thank you very much for the most delicious meal, I trust my lecturing has not disturbed your enjoyment of it, I myself find talking most distracting in the morning, there is a lot to be said for the monastic rule of silence at such hours, especially if you are a sufferer from indigestion, as I am, and now, if we have finished, Benedicite Deo."

I walked in the park with Annabelle. She said;—

"I can't answer questions. What happened last year happened as it did and now we are past it. We were together once and then we went apart, to be individuals, didn't you say? and we found that we were not individuals, that it is impossible to be an individual, isn't that what you found? I was unhappy, yes, did Peter say I was happy? then he is a fool, I wasn't, were you? No, we were alone, I couldn't bear it, and then Marius was there, and it didn't work out like that, so we stopped it. You have got to have faith, do you know what that means? you have got to have faith in order not to be an individual, or to become an individual, it's the same, and that is all I have done. You either have to have something which you wish very clearly to do, or else you have to have a faith which will tell you very clearly what to do. I did not marry Marius because that was the wrong thing to do, because marriage is not simply a matter of love or admiration or convenience, it is not even a matter of making the best of a situation that is irrevocable which is at least a stronger argument for it than admiration or love. It is something that one has to be dedicated to and Marius will never be dedicated to marriage again, and neither will I, I think, because I am past that now. The chance for these things happens just once and never again. And now I say what we must have is faith, that we have got beyond the stage when love like the love of children arises spontaneously without a faith and is held there by an instinct that is unconscious, that now we are all too conscious and nothing on our own is spontaneous any more, and for love to be held and maintained it needs a faith to keep it there. That is the only answer that I can give."

"And have you got this faith?"

"No," she said.

"Then why . . . ?" but the question ceased, hopeless, like a dream that is lost in waking memory.

"Because I am confronted by it," she said. "Because I want to have it. Because I like people who have got it."

"Yes," I said.

The dream, caught in glimpses, was of Marius's wife, in the hospital, in that tomb of unbearable summer, sitting up in bed and saying all the things that Annabelle was saying. Love as a triangle, with faith as the further corner: love in the presence of someone else, the eternal lover, God. I remembered the crucifix above her bed, the crucifix that Marius must have brought her. It was she who had converted Marius, who had told him that he was wrong, that it was only through the Church that he could find the love that he wanted. Just as he had once frightened her to death by his loneliness, so had she then frightened him to faith by the act of her dying.

"I know all this," I said. "I remember it so well."

"Do you?" she said.

And the waking memory was of Annabelle a year ago also saying the same things as she was saying now. But then she had said them as if they meant something, and now as if they did not. There was fear, too, with her. A fear of loneliness to death and a faith that denied the dying. I wondered if her calmness of yesterday was only the calmness of successful denial. I could find out.

"I remember all this going on and on just the same," I said, "a year ago as it is now, we said the same things, acted not for ourselves but for others, loved not for ourselves but for others, why do you try to make out that then we were selfish children?"

"Because then it was spontaneous and now it is not, when we went away we found that it failed, it was then that we had to find something different."

"Or to come back."

"No, not to come back, you can never come back, you never have the choice again."

"You can always come back."

"That is not true," she said wildly.

I walked beside her. I had never felt so dead or so destructive as on that grey carved day with the trees like rusty iron and the mud rolled smooth as marble. I felt that I was betraying more than the things that I had said to her father, and all in the name of a belief that I would not myself have dared to call a faith. "So what you have found is Father Jack," I said.

"I am sorry about Father Jack," she said.

"Why are you sorry?"

"I am afraid he talks rather a lot, I didn't know if you'd like him."

"Does it matter if I like him?"

"Yes, of course."

"Then I like him," I said.

She raised a hand to her forehead. She said miserably, "That is what we need, you see, a truth that is definite, that will tell us what to do."

"That tells Peter he mustn't be a puritan?"

"Yes, I think that is true."

"Supposing Peter were not a puritan, do you know what he would be?"

"I think . . . "

"He would be a smooth lecherous man fumbling girls in the back of taxis, is that what you want?"

"He would not, that is not the point, the point is that Peter only hates and he should love."

"Then why is that not mentioned? He does love, anyway, that is why it is not mentioned. He loves in such a way as makes you uncomfortable. He is not a puritan, he is a moralist. A puritan is someone who gets his moralizing wrong, and supposing Peter gets his right?"

"He doesn't!"

"Why? Because Father Jack says so? Father Jack who would prefer to turn him into a lecher and who has turned you into someone who has not changed their belief or faith one atom but is now merely miserable and uncertain about it?"

"I am not, I am certain, I had no conception of it before, and why do you say I am miserable?"

"Because you look it."

"At tea, yesterday, was I miserable?"

"No."

"Then it is only you . . . "

"Only I who have made you miserable? Is that true?"

She made no answer. I could see her hand trembling against the edge of her coat. All she said was, "Anyway, you said you liked Father Jack."

"I will explain. I like him at breakfast. I like him when I am not thinking about him. My instinct is to enjoy being with him and to escape from Peter, but when I think about him the feeling changes. And for this reason, that Father Jack doesn't like a person who thinks."

"Doesn't he?"

"Tell me if I am wrong. The Christian ideal is a person who believes and who functions, it is not a person who thinks. Thinking is danger: curiosity is the devil. It says so, and I can see it, I can see it in Christian people. Why do you worry so much about Peter? Why do you worry more about him than about someone who sins in a state of believing? Because to you the only real sin is the sin of thought, and the sins of action don't matter. And to me it is the other way round. Peter's only sin is that he puts everything into question. He is lucky if he has no other."

"It is the one thing . . . "

"It is the one thing that you hate, I know. It is what you call being egocentric. But everyone is egocentric, it is a condition of being human. If you take it to stand for anything more than this then the word is meaningless."

"It isn't," she said. "Don't you trust your instinct? Your instinct is love, and being egocentric is when there is no love."

"You do not answer me. You never answer me. Peter makes the same complaint, that there is no love. It is a failure for which you are as much responsible as he. In fact you are more responsible, because you claim the means of love. Your words are meaningless if there is this failure. Your religion is meaningless if there is this failure. I am no puritan, I do not know what is right, but I say this, that what is wrong is that which contradicts itself. And I say that this is a contradiction, that you condemn a person for being egocentric when everybody is egocentric, that you do not judge actions when it is only actions that are judgeable, and this most of all, this failure is a contradiction. You claim to have found the means of salvation and now, as a result of it, there is less love than there was before. There is now no love between you and Peter, there is no love between you and Marius, there is no love between you and . . . " I stopped, on the brink of some great evil; "Why were you happy at tea?" I asked her.

There still was no answer. She was talking almost before the question was put, saying, "It is Peter's fault, Peter only hates, moralizing always turns to hate when there is no faith to guide it. Oh can't you see, can't you see this, that we talk and talk and talk and never do anything, that love is a performance and not a feeling, that all the time last year we were judging things by ourselves as if we were so important and we were not important, not at all, and that was why things went wrong, it was then they went wrong, I told you, didn't I tell you? and now we are trying to live as if we were not important, quite simply, as if we just had a duty..."

"We?"

"Yes, we, why are you looking at me?"

"Why are you crying?"

"Because you are so bloody, you will think of nothing but yourself, you will not admit this, that love is a performance..."

"That is what I have always admitted."

"You have? Then why do you hate me?"

"Can I ask you to marry me?" I said.

"Oh damn you," she said, "damn you," and she ran away across the grass.

I could see Peter approaching. He came through the trees like a weary lion. "Listen," he said, "listen, there is nothing to be done." Annabelle went fluttering like his wounded prey. "I tell you it is no use talking, I have done all the talking, they have all gone mad." She slowed down, walked, went steadily away from us. "There is no truth any more, they are different people, there is no means of approaching them." She turned, disappeared, and the morning died. In its grave I listened to Peter. "Their words mean different things, their faces mean different things, it is no use fighting them. You can't fight them, it is like fighting Medusa, out of every head you cut off two new ones grow in its place. They have an answer to everything, an excuse for everything, they have different memories about what has happened. They make their own truth, they make their own history, they are lunatics in their certainty. If you charge them with their failures they say that they are human, if you question their claims they say that that they are gods. There is nothing to be done, I tell you, it is either they who are mad or we are. Come back and have lunch with us and you will see again what I mean. Either they are mad or we are. You have got to face this, come back and have lunch, I have got to know if I am mad. Doesn't it interest you that you may be a lunatic? You can't have lunch? No? Then where are you going?"

"I don't know," I said. I was going to have lunch with Marius, but it already seemed that I might be a lunatic.

In the restaurant I found Marius sitting with an enormous negro, who as I approached arose as if to go. "Excuse me," he said. "Excuse me." He was bowing politely in several directions. He was dressed quite simply in ordinary clothes, but as he turned I saw by his collar that he was a priest. This vision, after the funeral morning, appeared so ludicrous that I wanted to laugh. It was as if there had suddenly sprung up in the world a geometrical progression of clergymen—a multiplicity which, like some nightmare mathematical problem, might lead me to infinity before I knew where I was. I walked carefully, as if on tombstones. "Hullo," Marius said. The enormous man was swaying round the back of his chair, a graceful elephant like in a Disney cartoon, an elephant that dances and floats on its toes. "I shall now leave you," he said. "I shall leave at once."

"Don't go," Marius said. "Why don't you stay and have lunch with us?"

"I fear I am intruding."

"Of course not, no, do sit down." Marius introduced him to me as Mr. Palmerston.

Because I wanted to laugh, and was afraid that if I did he would think I was laughing at him, I did my best to like him. I remember it starting like this, that I was sorry he might misunderstand me.

He sat down and spread his hands on his knees. "You must forgive me," he said. "I happened to meet our friend Marius on the sidewalk, and he prevailed upon me to come and sit with him. Naturally I was honoured." He spoke meticulously, with a faintly foreign intonation.

"I am very glad," I said.

"I knew our friend when he was a child." He leaned towards me. "I was intended to be his teacher, and I discovered that it was he who was teaching me." He raised one eyebrow so that his forehead furrowed into a thousand tiny wrinkles.

"What did he teach?" I said.

"Life," Mr. Palmerston said. "Life!" He began to sweat, and his face was like the night sky with a moon reflected on his cheek-bone. "I was very ignorant," he said.

Marius ordered lunch with a professional assurance.

"And now he is coming back to teach us again," Mr. Palmerston said. "I am very glad. In my country he is a much needed man, a very much needed man indeed."

"What do you do?" I said to Marius.

Mr. Palmerston waited for him to reply and then answered for him. "He does everything," he said. "Everything. He is the goose that lays the golden egg." He smiled dazzlingly and then leaned towards Marius. "I intend nothing personal," he said. His concern was enormous, as if he were going to cry.

"Nothing," Marius said.

"Oh he is a great benefactor. Great indeed. He gave me a kitchen for my church." Mr. Palmerston began to mop his face with a crimson handkerchief. "And a great deal besides. For my school, and for my poor people who do not trust. There is so much to be done." I could not understand why he was sweating when he must have been accustomed to the heat. It was as if he were being roasted. "It is quite frightening," he said.

"It is for you it is frightening," Marius said.

"No, I do no more than follow my nose. And if I sneeze, I am a priest, and I have my handkerchief." He waved it comically in front of his face. "It is for you I am afraid, if you catch cold." Tears came into his eyes so that he could dab at them with his sleeve.

"Don't worry," Marius said.

"Worry?" He said. "Of course I worry. See!" He held out above the tablecloth a hand that was trembling.

We watched his heavy, heavy hand with the backs of the fingers knobby like wood and then he turned it over so that we were looking at his palm. It was pink as if it had been scraped and bleeding. "Tell me," he said, "do you go to Church?"

At first I did not realize that he was talking to me, and then I said "No."

"Oh I am sorry," he said. "I am so terribly sorry." He turned his huge agonized face towards me so that it was like a dark pool in which my own was drowning.

"You are the only clergyman who has ever asked me that," I said.

"Oh," he said. "Oh, I see."

He sat there with a crimson handkerchief against his heart like the corner of a sunset. He stared at me. "You have wanted to be asked?"

"I have expected it."

"How extraordinary," he said. "How extraordinary indeed."

"Isn't it a serious question?"

"Certainly it is serious."

"Then why is it that in this country no one asks it?"

He looked at the plate of food that had been placed in front of him and he pushed it a few inches away on his tablecloth and he turned his glass upside down beside it. "You say that in this country it is not serious? Not serious enough? What is it that is not serious?"

"The people who go to church and the people who do not are part of the same thing. They like having enemies. The people who talk about love do not love, and those people who talk about hell do not dissuade their neighbours from going there. The people who are supposed to intercede on behalf of the world have something to do when the world is going to damnation."

"Intercession! You are not talking about intercession!"

"About action, then, if intercession is useless."

"And if it isn't!"

"You can see that it is."

"Oh!" Mr. Palmerston said.

He closed his eyes and his lips were moving as if he were talking to himself. He sat down with his hands folded like an enormous Buddha. Then his whisper became audible. "I have never before heard it called not serious. Never before in the world." He opened his eyes so that the pool rippled across its surface. "So you would judge us then?"

"I judge nothing, I say that you fail."

"You can say that about no one!"

"I will say it about myself and when others do not say it I will wait for them."

"We say it every day of our lives!"

"Then why are you not more miserable? I tell you that you should be miserable, misery is your prerogative, and yet misery is the one thing you despise. If you despised your failures you would be more serious."

"You put everything upside down, it is the opposite that has always been said . . . "

"And it is the opposite that you have always known was not true. Once the world attacked you from behind, it attacked you because you made a virtue of poverty and simplicity and that was what you knew how to answer. Now the world has gone past you and you are still looking backwards to present yourselves as worldly to a world that is not there, now the world looks back on you and calls you frivolous because your back is turned to it and your back is all it sees. If you turned then you would not be able to be so glib, you would not be able each day to forget your responsibility in the joke of being subtle and disarming. The world has gone away from you because you have forgotten your responsibility to it, you may not have forgotten your responsibility to God but you have forgotten your responsibility to your neighbour. And if you remembered you would not smile!"

Mr. Palmerston pushed his chair back from the table with a screeching sound on the floor like an animal, and then he lumbered forwards onto his hands so that I thought he was ill. Then he went down on his knees and I saw he was praying. In the middle of the restaurant he knelt while the talking like the ceasing of canaries drained away and in the silence he was motionless like a dying bull. Marius and I looked away from him and nobody moved and then he struggled to his feet with a huge motion like a camel and he swayed towards the door through the awkward eyes and went through it and was gone. I sat for a few moments but Marius did not say anything so I left my food and followed him. I could not see him in the street.

Marius had come out after me. "Don't worry," he said.

"Worry?" I felt sure I was mad. It was extraordinary how Mr. Palmerston had disappeared so quickly.

"There is nothing to worry about."

"Of course there is nothing to worry about!" I was furious that he should know how much it meant to me.

"I'm sorry," he said.

We began to walk aimlessly away from the restaurant. "Have you paid the bill?" I said.

We walked again. The afternoon was running like a defeated army. I could not imagine why I had felt so confident in the night.

"You find all this odd?" he said.

"Yes," I said. Annabelle and Mr. Palmerston had run, but it was I who had been defeated. Marius maddened me.

"It is of no significance," he said.

"What isn't?"

"Mr. Palmerston. He does things like that. I thought it might seem peculiar."

"Not a bit."

"Good. He is emotional, you see, not like an Englishman. I expect he has gone to pray for you."

"To pray for me."

"Probably. You talked about intercession."

"This is crazy," I said. Then, remembering Annabelle and Father Manners, "You talk of Mr. Palmerston as if you were ashamed of him."

"Do I?" He seemed surprised.

"Yes. Why don't you want me to worry?"

"Because it does no good."

"What do you mean by good?"

"There are others who do the worrying," he said.

"Do you realize that everything you say seems insane?" I said.

"Probably. I am not good at talking."

"What are you good at?"

"Not much," he said, smiling.

I remembered the time before when I had attacked him. Then we had been passionate and something had come of it. Now we did not seem to be hearing each other at all. Marius was full of a cheery humility that made communication impossible. He was like a knowledgeable schoolmaster trying to pretend to be as stupid as his pupil.

"What do you mean by the others who do the worrying?" I said.

"I mean it's no good being anxious about oneself."

"I'm not, I'm anxious about you."

"Thank you."

I wanted to say, "You're welcome," but I thought he might take it seriously. Instead I asked, "Do you know how much you have changed?"

"I expect so."

"Do you remember saying that the church was no good?"

"Yes."

"And now?"

"I didn't know anything about it then."

"So everything that you said last year you would now deny?"

"No, I have just gone on from there, the seed grows slowly, and is often not discerned."

"The seed that others are anxious about?"

"Yes," he said. He seemed pleased.

"Now you're like a gardening advertisement," I said.

He still smiled. "We always talked in images," he said.

"Did we?" I thought, suddenly, how awful we must have sounded. Then I remembered that to Annabelle, only an hour ago, I had argued that we had said the same things then as we were saying now. This was true of Marius, too. It was I who was contradicting myself. "I know that I am crazy too," I said.

"That's all right."

"It's not what you say that I don't understand, it's the way that you say it."

"What way?" He again seemed surprised.

"So complacent. If you don't worry about yourself how do you ever get anywhere?"

"By doing things. By worrying about others."

"By being crafty?" I remembered Annabelle's father.

"It is as if there was a war on. When you know there is a war you naturally act differently from the way you would act if you didn't. It is useless worrying about yourself in a war."

"What is this war?"

"What we have always talked about. What we have always fought in, too, I think, except that once I didn't know what we were fighting. Now I do and I see things in terms of it. Perhaps that is why I sound odd."

"Yes. Soldiers never know why they are fighting."

"Don't they?"

"They treat everyone as if they were already dead."

"Perhaps they do." His eyes flashed at me.

"As if they were dead themselves," I said.

We had by this time reached the door of Alice's house. On the steps he stopped, as if he had remembered something. He still had the knowledgeable look on his face. "I forgot," he said. "Annabelle is with Alice this afternoon."

"Annabelle?" I said. I wondered if he would not go in because I was there. I felt that he was even capable of knowing what had happened between Annabelle and me that morning. Then I remembered what had happened between her and him. "What is Annabelle doing with Alice?" I said.

"What? Just seeing her. I don't think I should go in at the moment, perhaps."

"All right," I said. We walked away again. I was beyond even being surprised at his calmness about Annabelle, although I felt, with a shock, that there was something uncanny about it.

"I wonder if you would be very kind and do something for me," he said.

"Of course." He seemed embarrassed, and I thought he was going to ask me something about Annabelle.

"I wonder if you would very kindly put me up in your room for a short while until I go home. I remember staying with you before, and I will only be sleeping there."

"Of course," I said. "You are leaving Alice's?"

"Yes, I think so." I did not ask why. It seemed extraordinary that he should not then have preferred to go to a hotel. "That is really very kind of you," he said.

We stopped. I felt that I should leave him, but there was an awkwardness that held us. "You are going away soon?" I said.

"Yes. I saw in the papers to-day that there has been trouble in my island."

"Trouble?"

"Rioting. I must get back for it."

"Will we ever see you again?"

"I hope so," he said.

"You all seem to be intent on killing yourselves."

"Didn't we say a long time ago that we were already dead?" he said, flashing his eyes again at me.

I said good-bye to him. As I turned to go he stopped me; and then, almost formally, with great embarrassment again, he said, "I must thank you for what you did for my wife before she died, you cannot know how much it meant to us, I am sorry I have not said this before to you, but I want to thank you now and tell you how important I think it was. Perhaps I have to thank you for many things."

"No," I said. "No." I found myself as embarrassed as he.

"That is why I tell you not to worry," he said.

He turned to go. I did not understand him, I did not know why I should not worry, but I was filled with such a peculiar remorse that I found myself running after him, saying, "Marius, tell me, am I a lunatic?"

"No," he said, "surely, I don't think so at all."

When I got back to my room I found a message from Peter asking me to ring him up. I did so. He was out.

I sat on the edge of the bed. I thought: It would have been easier if Marius had said I was mad.

All confidence had gone. I could not remember it. Marius had talked about a war, and if there was war then I was a refugee and not a participant. I was lost, bewildered—a man wandering up a road with his belongings left behind him.

The road was crawling as if with ghosts. The armies went past, heedless, in a different direction. What war? The war between good and evil, light and darkness—was there really a world of which I knew nothing? A world in which a war was being fought by people to whom it was the only reality, who marched and acted and who in the intervals could afford to be frivolous because frivolity is part of war, the jokes of serious people are part of their armoury. If the war was true, the world of which I knew nothing, then I could forgive them their jokes. But I was still a fugitive, in the wrong direction.

I rang up Peter again. This time he answered. As I listened to his voice the road thickened until it was difficult to keep up on the surface.

"I had to tell you," he said, "it was really most extraordinary. I have been talking to Father Jack, you know, like you suggested, we went on from where we left off at breakfast, and he says he absolutely agrees with me, agrees with me entirely, that it's all right for me to be as I am, to go on as I am, don't you think that's odd? I said that faith seemed nonsense to me, all the contradictions and so on, and he said, yes, of course, to some people it does; and I said Is that all right then? And he said Yes, indeed it is; and then I said about just sticking to right and wrong, and my conscience, or whatever it is, and he said, Good, that's perfect, and gave me a pat on the back. Don't you think that's odd?"

"He told you not to worry?" I said.

"Yes, exactly, he is really a most sensible man, he understood me directly, he has an extraordinary faculty for knowing what I mean, which is more than most people do. Isn't it funny? Perhaps his racket's all right after all, perhaps it's all quite proper. These priests are really far less bigoted than one thinks."

"Did he talk about a war?"

"What war?"

"Nothing. Marius talks about a war."

"Oh that, yes, that's all about the spirit, it is very complicated, I don't understand a word."

"What spirit?"

"But that doesn't matter either, you see, because everyone's got this spirit, apparently, even me—isn't it funny?—and we battle like anything."

"How the devil can one battle without being in an army?"

"But that's just it, one fights the devil, people do it in different ways, Father Jack says so, his way is not better than anyone else's."

"He said that?"

"Yes."

"I don't believe it."

"He did, so that makes his racket just an ordinary one, like any of the others."

"I think he's mad."

"Why? It makes it all right for you and me."

"I don't want it to be all right."

"You can't have it both ways. What's wrong with it?"

"I don't believe a word that any of them say."

"It seems all right to me. And it's one in the eye for Annabelle."

"Why?"

"She won't like it at all."

"It was better when they thought us crazy."

"I'm quite happy," he said. I rang off.

I went back to my bed. I was in the ditch now, with the ghosts of the road on top of me. If everything was in terms of war then all was fair in terms of the war, and they were capable of anything. Truth became propaganda, love became defence-work, actions might be camouflage or bluff. Looking back on the afternoon it seemed that Marius might have meant anything by asking if he could stay with me, Annabelle might have meant anything by visiting Alice, Father Manners might have meant anything by talking to Peter. My suspicions rose in a body until

I was suffocated by what I did not understand. I found that I had even lost the power of introspection, since I was as suspicious of myself as of others. Nothing was real—the chairs and tables might be phantoms—the world was haunted by a world that was not there. This haunting, this intrusion of what was deathly, was worse than the loneliness that I had known before. Now I felt the necessity for company like someone who has been frightened. It was with an enormous relief that I remembered Marius was coming to stay with me. Perhaps that was why he was coming. Questions were futile.

But there was the whole of the evening in front of me. Alone it was not bearable. Aloneness is insufferable in a world of ghosts. I went out into the street, and walked, rapidly. I found myself going towards Alice's house. I thought that there I might find Annabelle, or if I did not I would at least find with Alice a world which was familiar to me.

I found Annabelle climbing into a taxi and I ran up and held the door open while she sat inside looking frightened. I must have appeared rather mad. I stood in the gutter in the flickering light and spoke to her. "Tell me," I said, "what you said to me this morning, what you said about faith, did you believe it to be true?"

"What?" she said. I repeated the question. The taxi-man was motionless, like a statue. I wanted to giggle. "Of course it is true," she said.

"Is it true in the way that a person who thinks it untrue is wrong?"

"Of course he is wrong," she said.

"And is there nothing else but this faith that can make a person true at all?"

"Nothing," she said.

"And it is something to worry about?"

"Of course it is something to worry about."

"Thank you," I said. "Thank you." I stepped away.

"Don't go," she said. "Please don't go."

"There is one more thing," I said. "Does Father Manners like Peter?"

"Like him? No, I don't suppose he does. Why?"

"Does he like me?"

"I don't know, I don't know." But I could see the truth in her eyes. The truth for all of them. "Stay," she said, "stay, where are you going?"

"You will find out," I said. I laughed. I was quite mad then. "You will find out when it catches up on you." I did not know what I was saying.

"Come here," she said, but I slammed the door, and waved to the taxi-man. He drove off and I ran up the steps into the house.

Inside I waited. Alice was not in the ground floor rooms. For a moment I considered killing myself. As I climbed the stairs I looked down towards the basement and felt rather sick. I had the sensation again that something was going to happen that had happened before. I waited on the landing. Something was going to happen and then I would remember it. The sound of the taxi door when I had slammed it against Annabelle had been like the thud of an axe. Heads were falling, the world of death was intruding, it did not seem that I was responsible for the future or the past.

Alice was lying on her bed in her dressing-gown. It was as if she had not moved since I had left her the day before. The room was scented like a velvet box. Time had stopped, we were into another dimension, our existence was not that of the people we might have remembered ourselves to be. I stood in the doorway and watched her. I wondered if she had been taking drugs. The light was muffled by stained-glass curtains, shedding pools of violet above her head. "Oh darling," she said.

I went in and sat on the bed. Ghosts, there were nothing but ghosts. The air was thick with them. "Oh darling," she said.

"Dear darling, darling, talk, yes, will you? Will you sit with me, here it is so terrible, it is the nights that are terrible, what is there to do? I close my eyes and then there is a lurching like a ship, something goes over on to its side and I cannot straighten it, it is like a ship that someone invented which had its inside hung on hinges so that it was supposed not to roll, and when they got it out on to the sea it rolled twice as much, it rolled even when the sea was quite calm, it must have been terrible. Once when I was young my inside was hung on hinges and I tried to kill myself, I rolled little pills out of a bottle and they formed up in a line and they looked at me like cat's eyes in the darkness, and as I ate them one by one I could feel them in my throat like fingers and they strangled me before I could die. I lurched and I could not keep myself upright, so they could not go down. Dear darling, darling, it is better not to have an inside that swings on hinges and then you roll only when the sea rolls and you do not roll when the sea is calm.

"I am so much in love, it is the heights that are terrible. Dear darling, darling, have you ever been in love? I do not think you have, perhaps you have found the secret of the ship that does not roll, you are so calm, you are the only person I have ever known who is so calm. You can probe about inwards and inwards and you do not feel sick, you do not . . . I should like to shake you, I should like to upset you just for once so that you know what it is like, what love is like, you would have pity. I was married once to a man who came and cried each time he was unfaithful, and I hurt him so much that I thought I should kill myself. And then there were men who were not men at all but statues quite hollow who were cast in bronze and they had no inside, no inside to roll, and nothing to feel, and they were terrible to love. I do not think that anyone with an inside is so calm, so calm, but you are, and will you stay, will you stay with me then, will you give up for a little, oh darling what are you thinking of?

"Everything is so old, there is nothing to do about it. All this goes on and on and there is nothing left in the world to worry about. If you would just stay with me you would know and then you would stop probing inwards and inwards and then you would pity. There is nothing that is wrong until you know that everything is wrong, and until you have done something you will never know. Until you have done something wrong you will never have to forgive yourself, and until then you are not human. Until now you are not human, dear darling, darling, and afterwards you will know what humanity is and how it suffers, and when you hate yourself it will be good for you and then you will see. You will see everything in your life and how terrible it is and then you will have to forgive yourself. You will give up and you will be frightened and then you will be human."

As I lay beside her on the bed I did not move and I did not answer, so she raised herself up on her elbow and leaned across me with one arm stretched on the far side of me to take her weight and I could see her ribs where she breathed, and as she bent down to kiss me I could feel her pressure on my chest like the weight of two soft hands. I put my arms around her and held her and I thought of Annabelle and Marius and how I did not care any more. She moved her body and I could feel nothing but the heaviness of her and the dryness of her mouth and I held her so that she might feel something better. I put my arms beneath her dressing-gown and stroked her, and I did not think it was myself who was lying. Then she lifted her head and pushed her hair back with her hand and she said, "Don't you love me darling?" and I said, "Yes," and she went on looking at me with her sick enormous eyes, he dressing-gown was away from her front and from her shoulders and she tried to close it and then she said "It is Marius that I love." "It doesn't matter," I said. I tried to hold her again in my arms but she pushed herself away from me and sat up on the edge of the bed and I thought she was crying. She was searching under the pillow for what I thought was a handkerchief, but it was for a cigarette which she found and I watched her light it. "You'd better go now," she said. The room seemed to hold me like a bath that has gone cold, and I did not want to get out of it. "Go on," she said.

17

Marius came to stay with me. In the mornings he went out early to do the business that still detained him in England, and I had the room to myself in which to work. In the afternoons I usually saw Alice. We sometimes had tea together.

One day when Marius was out Father Jack came to see me. He was an old man, but he climbed the stairs rapidly talking all the time and his small wrinkled face showed no sign of fatigue. He sat down and he did not notice the room at all, it might have been beautiful to him. He said:

"The trouble is that you do not understand the position, you do not understand it at all, you look upon the Church as a team of hospitable cricketers, a home for stray sufferers, an army of thin crusaders doing battle against the flesh. You see some special significance in the numbers that this army contains, in the individual behaviour of some of its members, in the errors that they may make. You talk of this significance as if it affected the function that is proper to an army. It does not. An army has its function no matter what its numbers and its mistakes. You imagine that we are engaged upon some game of tip-and-run with immorality, that we have charms to dispense with pain, that we are fighting for the truth and are concerned about our chances of victory. We are not. What you must realize is this, and this is everything, that whatever war we are fighting it is not one of which the issue is still in doubt. We are not marching towards truth because the truth has been given to us. We do not struggle for victory because the victory has already been won. We know the truth. We enjoy the victory. Our function now, if you like to use these metaphors, is that of a triumphant army in occupation of the world.

"You do not know these things because as a child you did not listen or else you were not taught. The world is full of people who have received no instruction or who have ignored it, and who do not know what Christianity is about. Many of these are settled firmly in a way of life that seems satisfactory to them, and when instruction is offered it is most often incapable of being heard. Others are not settled and are interested in instruction, but their condition of bewilderment is seldom one which can advantageously be used. A man must come to his own conclusions, he must not be persuaded by the rhetoric of a priest. There are practical considerations in this, as well as ethical ones. A conversion against a man's conscience is not a true conversion, and the results of it are dangerous for everyone concerned. A priest is dealing normally with practising Christians, and his function is one of service to the Christian Church. Instruction is given to children because that is the time for instruction; ministration is given to adults in the pattern of what they believe. It is true that now, in the conditions around us, the pattern is upset and the world is not normal. These are conditions which are unfortunate but which do not affect the position of the Church. Its function remains the same.

"This function you can learn to understand and practise or you need not learn to understand. That is up to you. It is quite a simple function, of love and worship, which begins with the sacraments and extends to the whole of life. You can learn it if you wish. I hope you do. But what I would say to you is this, that it is what a man believes that is important. I would rather a man lived faithfully by what he believes than attempted to persuade himself of what he does not. A synthesis of persuasion is useless: an antithesis of truth is not. This is perhaps what you will recognize. There is something of the truth in every man, however contradictory expressions of it may appear. It is this truth that can be respected: I should say more than this,—it can be loved. The claim that the Church makes, you see, is a very large one after all;—it claims that if every man will observe and honour the truth that is in him, then there is not much more that need be done. The Church, as it were, is doing the rest. It is working for the world in the only way possible for it. There is a good deal of confidence in this, and certainty. This is what you will learn to understand. Do I make myself clear?"

Marius came back in the evenings and he looked at me with eyes that curiously had no depth. It was difficult to talk to him. He said:

"Yes, I know Father Jack, he is a good man, a very good man, he is what they call their West End turn, does that shock you? I know what you mean, I didn't think he would help you, but don't let anything shock you until you know what it is about. Then you will see that he is a very good man, and not a spider—didn't he say so?—not a spider to entwine you. I do not think that he is the person for you to talk to, however, and I? no, of course not, I am not the person, but you know where you can go.

"In one way at least I think I am like Father Jack. The life of everyone is like a circle and at one stage you stand on the circumference looking inwards and you search for the centre and the centre is not there. Then you find it and you turn outwards because the centre is established and you don't have to search for it any more. You stand on the circumference looking outwards and outwardly your life becomes quite a passionless business, to do what ought to be done, and in the centre because it is established the passion is not seen. Passion is not often discernible in a thing that does not move. Passion in sculpture needs a specialist's eye to observe it. If you have not these eyes then you think it is dead. And it is not easy for some to turn inwards again.

"Perhaps I am dead, I say this for the last time, for the last time I go back into the centre, I do not think I am dead. But whatever has happened in me is established and I do not feel those things anymore. I am sorry about Annabelle, you do not know how sorry I am, but being in love is not necessarily a condition of marriage, she knew this better than I did, but we did not know it at the time. Marriage is when you find each other at the centre, and we could not pretend for us this was true. I could not give this to her and I cannot give what you want to you, because there are only certain things within my capacity. These I will try to do, and the rest leave to others. There is much for which I shall have to ask to be forgiven, as you must know.

"Perhaps there are only certain things in Father Jack's capacity, too. Perhaps he feels that reality is what it ought to be, and that it is unreality when it is not. He distinguished between what is becoming and what is. This is what you must do. There are others to whom you can talk. I think that you understand this, I think you know what I mean by being passionless and turned outwards and waiting. I think that when you have found your centre there will be a great deal for you to do. When I left Alice's house she said a strange thing to me, she said that you could not corrupt other people even though you tried to. Perhaps this is true. She meant that you did something else to them. I think that you will go further than I have done because you have the ability, and I have had to wipe out so much that I sometimes think that there is not much left of me anyway. I am not a Christian, not really a Christian. There are just certain things that I have to do each day and I have to have a standard by which to do them. When you have no emotions you have to have reasons. My marriage died. But one day you will go into the centre and the emotion that has taken you there will be a living one and then when you are turned outwards your life will be joy. It will be something, this, in the despair of the world, to know the vanity of it. The remedy for despair lies in possessing the means for action; and the means, at the centre, is what you will find."

Mr. Palmerston was staying in a small bare room in Notting Hill. At night he wore a skull-cap made of wool. He sat leaning backwards with his hands between his knees. He said:

"I cannot teach you, teaching is not relevant to you, what is it that you believe? Teaching is only for those who believe already. You believe in nothing? My friend if you believe in nothing then death is the end of life and life is nothing and that is not possible, that life is not possible, because you know about this life, you have eyes to see this life, you know the evil of it. Man is evil my friend you know he is evil, I am not here to talk about sin, I tell you, you know about sin there is no need of me to talk about it. Sin is humanity and I tell you that it is impossible for humanity not to sin, that is the pill that you have to swallow, again and again you have to tell yourself things, that it is impossible for humanity not to sin. And therefore there is one thing and one thing alone that humanity can do, and that is to plead for the absolution from this sin and to remember the triumph that is the justification of its plea, the triumph of a life that did not sin and yet which died in the way that sinners die to make a triumph for them. Upon one day and between the hours of darkness and light there was given to this world its salvation and its redemption. It has been given no other.

"You say that you want no salvation, that you need no redemption, that you will take the responsibility for what you have done and you will live out each day of your life in misery for it. And I say to what end do you do this, to what end do you desire this misery? You do not desire misery for the sake of misery, you cannot, you desire misery so that truth may come in its place. And I say that this is the most foolish dream of the world, it is the dream of the mad dog barking for the moon, because you have no hope for it, no hope at all, because the mad dog cannot fly and you are human. If you wish to make yourself sufficient for your responsibilities that is an aim as wild as the moon and you will miss it, you will fail, you will end up in delusion and that is the greatest sin of all. You will think you have reached the moon because you will have stared at it so long that it will have blinded you, the image that you will hold in your arms will be the deception of your eyes. It is you who have talked of failure and I tell you that this is the most terrible failure of all because it is deliberate, it is the deliberate will to failure arising out of pride. It is the sin that we call unforgivable, and this is why we call it unforgivable, because it can only be committed by those who have seen the moon and who have had an opportunity to worship it and who in its light have decided to deride it. In envy they bark at it and in hatred they blind their eyes. If for one moment you will look into yourself with the eyes that you turn upon others you will see this, you will see this choice, the choice between humble worship and the mad and bloody hound. You still have eyes left, then do this for me, look into yourself as you look into the world and then dare to say that you can tell what is your truth and what are your responsibilities, dare to say that you can bear them, dare to say that you are so much less mad than the world is that you can bring light to it! Remember, you are responsible for everything! Look now and tell me what it is you see that is so powerful!

"And if you look and truly say as you are saying now that you can do nothing, that alone you can do nothing, then there is still something that you can do. Alone you are mad and useless as are dogs that chase their tails around the gutter, but you have a choice, you have a choice which even a dog has, you can do what you are told. And for you who know your uselessness, who in your own words for a year have lived in madness is this not a possible thing to do and even a necessary one, to give yourself up to that which can bear what you will never be able to bear, which can do within you what alone you will never be able to do, which can give you the moon when you do not even desire it? When you come upon beauty you have not asked for beauty and yet beauty is there, and when you see it it possesses you and what is beautiful is this, that you have given yourself up to it, that you are yourself no longer, that there is within you a gift that is greater. In all beauty there is something within you and something outside of you and something which exists between you and the world. In all love there is this threefold existence, the giving and the receiving and the gift itself. This existence is God. What you give to God is given back to you and this gift is a greatness beyond compare. That to which you have given is given within you and the gift is a fulfillment of freedom and love. This is what love is, and this is what freedom is, and this is God. But God has given already, and it is for you to receive Him. To receive Him you have to give yourself and this is the choice. You can live as a madman chained to his lunacy or as an angel free in the service of love. You have no freedom now except this choice.

"You have no freedom. You have said that you are a machine. You cannot talk about your failures or successes because you are living as a machine and not as a man. Only a man has freedom, who has chosen love. Until you have made your choice this futility will continue, you will never know what happens and what there is to be done. And for us who have chosen, who have attempted to make the choice, do not talk to us about our failures or successes because failures may be triumphs and it is not for you to say. Nor is it for you to presume that we should live our lives in misery; when here, now, there is a joy such as you have never dreamed of, once and for all and always there is this joy that was given at the moment of time, the greatest triumph in history that is the whole of history, the point of triumph of eternity. And when there is this triumph and this justification and this redemption it is not for us to be miserable, it is for us to do our duty to our neighbour, yes, but this duty is not what you would make it out to be, the comfort of sickness by pretending there is no health;—it is simply the living of lives in the light of this triumph and saying over and over again in every corner of the earth that there is this triumph and there is this light and that all a man must do is to lift up his eyes in humility to it. This is what we do. Man does not require comfort, he only partly requires aid, what he requires is absolution. Sin exists and man lives in sin, there is no real aid other than this absolution. This is what we work for. And when you have realized this and have lifted up your eyes to the light of this absolution then and only then will you realize what this world is and what is the perfection of it. You will realize then that everything in the world is beautiful, that every horror and every terror and every pain in every corner of the world is beautiful, that it is beautiful because it is known by God, because God himself has suffered it, and then you will understand. You will understand everything, you will understand even this,—that when the lion eats the heart of the deer, yes, that is beautiful; that when the hangman puts the noose around the neck of his innocent victim and the floor drops and the tongue comes out and the neck screams as it is torn from the shoulders, yes, that is beautiful. You will realize that even the hangman is beautiful. Think of this when you talk about misery. Then you will know the meaning of that moment in eternity."

In all these evenings—Mr. Palmerston's huge face with the moon upon its cheek-bone, the cold room listening, the dampness of walls outside which there is the darkness waiting like water round a ship—there is nothing that I can do, I cannot do as he asks me, there is no I to do it when the centre is not there. I see the savagery of eyes that are kind and terrible, the sad night face that weeps and weeps, the collar like a horizon between dark and dark, the cold moon running as if with oil at some last benediction. I hear the voice beautifully modulated and controlled beginning and going on in one key always from creation to birth to death to deliverance and it all goes past me in a wild thin stream and I am left again in silence when the sound has gone. It is like an autumn night in the long lost grass when you stand and hear the sound of swans' wings above you, a stream of swan-water flying whirring round the world and it gets very close to you, very close to your heart, and yet when it has gone you are still alone and loveless, although the earth is circled the mystery is apart. Whatever was happening to me happened in the spaces outside, and was not within me.

With Marius, too, in the mornings, it was as if my consciousness were more with him than with myself. He did not make things difficult. In talking to him there was always the feeling that he had ceased to be the person I had known before, that instead of being able to impose his will by subtlety he was now more concerned with the simplicity of making his will seem absent; but that it was possible, nevertheless, to understand that he was the same and to see the course of his change. Once he had dealt with life like a juggler; and now, with the suddenness of a child, he had given up his toys and was letting life do the juggling for him. In this condition, somehow his character was stronger. All the things that he had said a year ago were still part of him, yet by ceasing to impose them he made their presence more felt. He said that his marriage had died, and I wondered if what he had believed had died too; but it hadn't and neither had his marriage—what he said was not true. It was rather his selfishness that had died. He had searched for his centre by heightening his power and he found it only when his power had failed. In this sense, really, his marriage lived.

That I felt myself nothing when in his presence was part of this, inevitably,—what there had been between us a year ago was a juggling game of power and now the desire for power had gone. There was the possibility of something being put in its place, but not the fact of it:—a game that was played beyond us, in which our desires did not create the rules but rather had to be subordinated to them. I was conscious of this possibility as one is conscious of a truth that is at the moment beyond one's comprehension; but it was not Marius, as he had said, who could give me understanding. At times I felt so much less than him that if he had been selfish it would have been awkward, but as it happened he did not seem to notice the disparity in our states. He kept me amused, and I listened to him. He was never sad. It is always this that I remember, that he was productive of happiness. Whatever he said about himself was not true of what he gave. On the surface we lived with each other irrelevantly, with myself as looker-on, but there was always something relevant in what I saw of myself in Marius.

One day I went to Church. I did this only in order to see if there was anything I had forgotten. I went indifferently and yet warily, as if I were having some joke within myself. I was surprised to see how much I remembered. There were memories of schools, of the smell of stale clothing, of the incongruous backs of necks. I became lulled in the old inertness which was broken only by the recurrent pain of kneeling. I found that I could do what I was supposed to do, that there was nothing I had forgotten. I sang descants to the hymns, got the timing of the psalms right, went through the words of the confession. And then, as always, my thoughts wandered away from what was going on around me. This always happens when nothing seems to be going on at all.

The words wander, music wanders, why should thoughts keep still? It is not of myself I should be thinking. Words and music drone without form and without ability, they are like the noises of birds, and should I notice birds? The building is not ugly. But the people, here, is it true that no one beautiful ever goes to Church? They are supposed to be beautiful. They whisper and do not care for each other, and yet I must hope they are beautiful. Can beautiful people kneel and say that they are ugly? If they are beautiful, do they need to go to Church? Church is for nothingness in the memory of schools.

The words are words and they do not mean much to me. A stream without sound no closer than the door. And yet there is something else I should think of. On the altar there is something that is never not beautiful, a body in silver shod with candles of light. There is sacrilege done each day in church, but not to the altar. Why is not sacrilege done more often? For one who believes in nothing it should be possible to think of it. A piece of smashed silver and a crumb on the carpet: a falling body spilling its blood against the stone. And yet it is not possible. These are trifles, explainable by custom, and yet they frighten me. Would it even be possible to sneer at a priest?

I cannot even say to Mr. Palmerston that all this means nothing to me. I cannot say that everything cancels out and has its opposite, that beauty is cancelled by ugliness, hope by despair, Christ by humanity. I cannot say that I have been to Church and that is one world and soon I shall be walking in the street and that is another world, and that it is absurd to join them because there is nothing in between. There are bits of people that live in one world and people who live in the other. I cannot say this to him because it would frighten me. And are the bits really any less of machinery? I have watched them and would not like to believe this. I cannot say to Mr. Palmerston—I have heard you and thought about it and I do not care a damn.

I left the church. I walked in my world which was not a world and I had my jokes which were, at most, jokes against myself. I had forgotten that my world was not a world. I came to a cross-roads where traffic was passing, and I waited for the lights to change so that I might cross. It was then that I was reminded. I watched a small car approaching and as it drew near me I knew that it was familiar although I did not know whose it was, and even after I had seen the occupants who were Annabelle and her father the recognition of them did not strike me, and it was only after they had been drawn up beside me for an instant that I knew who they were. They sat side by side staring rigidly in front of them, and as I stepped forwards in response to my surprise they did not move and did not look at me, and so I stopped, I thought they must have seen me, I thought they must be ignoring me because they did not wish to speak. I remembered then that this would be possible. I stood stupidly not being able to go forwards or back while people pushed past me and I did not know what to do, I wished only that they might not be made to do something that would hurt me. I pretended that I had not seen them, I waited terribly while the seconds dragged like hours and then I moved to the back of the car because I could not bear it. When the lights changed again the car went away and I found myself trembling. Then I did not think that they could have seen me, I did not believe it, but I did not know. I only knew that it was true that I had imagined it.

So, beginning to walk again, I knew what was terrible. It was I who had asked for this and now I had got it. No one else could have told me but her, and what she has told me is this sickness of it. Sickness of a world that is nothing, that kills what it loves, that on a grey carved day once made her cry, that in brutality betrayed itself. There is no love that I would not kill that was the means of life to me, no madness that I would not allow in the name of sanity. O fool, fool, there was a love that was given to you, a love that you would not give to, you ugly damned fool to pretend you do not care. Walking dead and unbearable this is what you cannot bear, you can bear any folly except your own. For your own there is no mercy when it is you who must suffer it, judgment is insufferable when it is you who must judge. I have played with the world and lost it: it is what we should have made ourselves. O Annabelle, Annabelle, you are the only person I shall love. I will ask you, once, and there will be no pride in it. Without it this time it will be I who will cry.

I thought there was time.

VI
CHILDREN AGAIN

18

Annabelle looked sad in the rain. "I did not know if you'd come," I said. Her hair was dripping like seaweed around the white face of a stone. I wondered if she were ill. "You must come in," I said.

"I got your letter." She went up the stairs ahead of me. In my room I had put flowers and some candles against the wall. She sat on the bed with her feet turned inwards as if her ankles were broken. She did not take off her coat.

"Why don't you lie down?" I said. And then, because she did not answer me, "Perhaps you are ill?"

She lay back on the bed. She said, "If I walked now in the streets I could get rid of this child."

I was lighting the candles. The flames burnt with a vacancy at the centre like a soul. "Is that what you want?" I said.

"I am ill," she said. "Will you walk with me until it happens?" She spoke to the ceiling where the plaster crumbled. "That is what I meant," she said.

"That is not what you want," I said.

"I cannot go through with it, for months I have pretended, I have thought . . . but I hate it so much, there is this terrible hate, and that is what makes it impossible. There is a failure too that I cannot bear."

I sat at the far side of the room so that I should not touch her. "Why do you feel this now?" I said.

"Because what I have lived with is a lie. What I have believed is a lie. It was not you who were the devil to tell me. You were a devil once. Why did you not ask me to marry you?"

"When?"

"That night ten months ago when you left me. Why did you leave me?"

"I will marry you now."

"I will not marry you with Marius's child. If I die I will not marry you with that to remind me. Marius is a devil."

"You are ill, you must stay here . . . "

"I will not marry you now. I will walk in the streets until it is dead and even then I will not marry you. What devil were you to come into our lives and to tell us everything and to leave us? In order that you might return when it was too late and tell us again? Everything I have believed in is a lie. Thank you for telling me that."

"What is this lie?"

"There is no forgiveness. In their hearts there is no forgiveness. Why do they come fawning round us to talk about it? They do not say what is in their hearts, if they have any hearts, which I do not know if they have. They have charms which they wear on their sleeves like bracelets and inside there is a terrible condemnation or at best a pity that is as cold as ice. Should it not be the other way round, that they wear their ferocity on their sleeves and inside there should be a heart that loves? I cannot forgive what they have done to Peter."

"What have they done to Peter?"

"They have charmed him and yet they condemn him. Has he told you that they have charmed him? He is now full of some dreadful pride with which he can . . . scorn me." She broke off. "Is that then all it is?"

"What?"

"That I am resentful because Peter has been given the means to scorn me? Oh God, there are motives that are unfathomable."

"Perhaps Peter has misunderstood . . . "

"Then it is their responsibility. It is for them to explain to him. He thinks they approve of him, and I know, I know what they think. And if it is all charm on the surface and that is what they think of him, then what do they think of me?"

"They love you."

"They love you and yet they think you dreadful. They call it love. I loved Marius once and that is what I call love. I loved him when he was something, when he was a person, and I am not sorry about the love. I am not sorry about what happened between us. But then he became nothing, and I was nothing too, and so I would not marry him. It was I who would not marry him. When we were both something I would have done, I loved him, I loved this child as it might have grown up with us, and then all life became a dead flat sham with no love no joy and no reality, just yellow smiling faces with nothing underneath. That is what they do to you, they have done it to all of us, they turn into waxworks what they cannot destroy. Have they done it to you?"

I did not answer.

"I will marry no one. I will give myself to nothing to be pitied and condemned. And if they think this about Peter whose sin is so small . . . "

"It is the greatest."

"Mine is greater. I have got this child. Why do you say that about Peter, and what is this love that smiles on the surface and does not say what is in the heart?"

"What is in the heart is on the surface and it is only in the mind that there is condemnation and pity."

"I tell you that they have lied to Peter, whether they have lied to him with their hearts or with their minds doesn't matter, they have lied to him and when he discovers this lie what will he do? I tell you he will kill himself."

"He will not kill himself."

"He will, he has used this lie to scorn me, and I have given him this lie, that is why he will kill himself. In all his life up to now he has never scorned me, I could have stopped him before but now I cannot stop him. He is a person who would kill himself for anything, he would kill himself out of despair or out of happiness or out of love or out of hate, he would kill himself because he knows it is the one thing that is irrevocable, because it is the biggest thing he could do and it is the big things that he is involved in. He is the one person in the world who lives always in big things, he is the one person who lives as the moralists tell us to live, as if each action is irrevocable, he is the one person who would kill himself to hell if he thought he deserved it. That is why he is so much greater than anyone, so much more than anyone, why he is so much beyond them, because he does not ask for redemption, he does not desire it, he asks only that he shall be judged for what he has done and that the judgment shall be irrevocable. That is why he will kill himself when he has reached a judgment on himself, because that will be irrevocable."

"This is nonsense, Annabelle, this is not true . . . "

"You have said that his sin is the greatest, they have charmed you too. All right, you have come to know what I meant that day in the park, and what you know is this, that the great sin is to imagine yourself a god by denying God, and this is what Peter has done all his life. And this is what I have loved him for. This is what I am doing now myself and so long as he loved me I could have stopped him because there were two of us, but now there is only one because they have taught him to scorn me. He thinks I have betrayed him and when he finds out their lie he will kill himself. He will kill himself as an act of a god that makes amends to me. Am I mad then?"

"Yes," I said.

"That is what gods do, isn't it? They kill themselves to make amends to those who have suffered for them? Don't they? Isn't that what God did and isn't that what is taken as a sign of a god? Peter will kill himself and they will have made him because it will be they who have betrayed us."

"There is no betrayal," I said.

"There is the betrayal of charming him deceitfully. It is my own fault because I made it possible for them, because they have done it to me, because they have made us condemn each other. He is mad now, have you seen him? It is my own fault that he is scorning me. They have given him a pride that he never had before, a pride to be righteous. He excuses himself anything because he thinks he is superior to me. But I love him, I know that I love him, I love him because he has a heart and because he lives on the edge of the sky and has made himself great enough to stand there. If he kills himself I shall love him more and I shall hate everyone else, I shall hate them for ever, I shall hate these priests with the flat sham manners and I shall hate Marius. Marius is a person who has been charmed to death already, who has no heart and desires no soul no existence who is a hard flat cipher against the walls of other men's eyes, who has destroyed himself so that he is a dust that can settle in heaven. I hate Marius. I loved him when he needed me and now he needs nothing and I hate him. If Peter kills himself I shall hate God."

"You are talking about people, you are not talking about God."

"I will kill Marius's child because it has grown into all I have hated, and because Peter will then have reasons for scorning me. I will kill myself so that he will have reasons for pitying me. If I could save Peter I would kill God."

"You do not know about God!"

She sat up on the bed and it was as if she were trying to prevent something from strangling her. "So they have got you too?" she said.

"Annabelle . . . "

"You do not love me, you are dead!" she shouted.

I stood up to go over to her and as I moved she shouted, "Get away from me, get away," and she struggled from the bed and began to run to the door. I caught her round the shoulders and held her as she fought to get past me; she screamed and clawed at me with the nails of her fingers. I got in between her and the door and tried to push her back towards the bed but she screamed again with a dreadful choked cry in her throat and I hit her across the face with the back of my hand and then her head fell forwards and she began to cry. I took her to the bed and she lay down with her back to me, and as she cried I could see her nails tearing scratches in her face and hair coming out in her hands where she pulled it. The crying came and went in gasps and it seemed to possess her body terribly as if there were a devil in it. I waited until she was quiet.

I rang up Peter.

"Annabelle is ill," I said. "She is staying here the night."

"What's wrong with her?"

"She is ill, it is to do with the child."

"Isn't that what she wants?"

"No."

"She gets it either way, I suppose, according to Father Jack."

"Is Father Jack there?"

"He's away."

"Do you know where I can find him?"

"He's on a train."

"Peter, do you know what he has said to Annabelle?"

"He said she wasn't quite sorry enough, if you ask me."

"Sorry for what?"

"For having a child with Marius and not marrying him."

"Why should he say that?"

"Well she isn't sorry, is she? Perhaps she went to tell him about it."

"To confess?"

"That is what they do, isn't it, when they want to be good little girls again?"

"And he said . . . "

"How the devil do I know what he said, I don't even know if she went, but whatever he said she didn't like it."

"Peter . . . "

"Is she really ill?"

"No. Peter, have you ever confessed?"

"I? What have I got to confess?"

"Nothing," I said.

I waited for Marius's step on the stairs and when I heard it I went to warn him. In the darkness of the landing we whispered. "Has she seen a doctor?" he said.

"It is not necessary."

"Of course I will go away. That is no trouble. Can I do anything for you in the morning?"

"Do you want to see her?"

"Should I?"

"Perhaps not. I should be glad if you would telephone."

"Of course."

We waited.

"Marius, what is the point of confession?"

"The point? So that one may receive absolution."

"And if one does not?"

"What?"

"If it is refused?"

"It is only refused when there is no repentance."

"I see."

We waited again.

"Where will you sleep?" I said.

"Anywhere," he said.

"Marius, does Father Jack approve of Peter?"

"Approve of him? I suppose not."

"Someone should tell him."

"Why?"

"I remember it being important."

"Do you?" He looked at me. "All right," he said.

"Good-night," I said.

When I awoke it was still dark and I did not know where I was. I had the impression that my bed was placed in such a position as made the rest of the room impossible. I struggled to get my bearings,—the door on the left, the window, the table . . . it was as if the surroundings of my life had become unrecognizable to me, even the furniture assuming a temporal disguise. I sat up. Then everything clicked into place. But I was left with the feeling that I was a foreigner in a country that was new to me.

I knew that Annabelle was awake. This was a realization that came strangely.

"Annabelle?"

"Yes?"

"Have you slept?"

"Yes."

"Shall I put the light on?"

"No."

It was extraordinary to be so close to her and not to know what she was thinking. She said: "Was Marius staying with you?"

"Yes."

"And you have sent him away?"

"Yes."

"It is dreadful how trivial all this is," she said.

I tried to see her in the darkness. "I mean," she went on, "that we are the most trivial people in the world, we do nothing, we achieve nothing, we work for nothing, we have no place in any society, we are useless, yet still we think that our trivialities are important. Isn't that ridiculous?"

"I do not think that they are trivialities."

"They seem to me to be. Did I talk a lot of nonsense?"

"Yes."

"And contradict myself?"

"Yes."

"Do you think it is true about the devil?"

"I don't know," I said.

"It must be when someone starts turning everything upside down. I hope Marius did not mind being sent away."

"Of course not."

"I really do feel ill, you know. I didn't mean it about you and Marius. Perhaps one does have to have something given to stop the devil getting in. Otherwise one doesn't know whether he's in or out. He may be in now for all I know."

"I don't think he is."

"He may be. They say you know where he is if you go on long enough. But then one only thinks one knows."

"It's better to think one knows than know one doesn't."

"It is? Only because not to know is unbearable."

"Then that is a good reason to think one does, especially if it is true that for us there is only one way of thinking it."

"And is it true?"

"It is beginning to look like it," I said.

We lay in the darkness and I began to imagine I could see her. She said: "But look at our lives, that is what I mean by triviality, we live in a tiny circle on the edge of idleness, we have never come close to touching any of the passions that move those who have to struggle, we have nothing to do with war or peace or justice or enslavement, we are in a backwater drifting like leaves towards death."

"I do not think so."

"I should like to go into the real world and do something passionate."

"There is only one real world."

"It is not ours."

"It is what we have a chance of."

I spoke not knowing at all whether or not it was true. "Reality is a condition, it is not a matter of where you start from or what means you use to achieve it, we have as much chance as any one else of our generation, no less and no more. You think that we are useless because with us the issues are all on the surface, we live surrounded by questions and failures, and this makes us very unpleasant and perhaps very dull, but it doesn't make us trivial. It will only do so if it continues."

"Supposing it does?"

"It won't."

"Will the world then be real?"

"It might be. It either will or it won't. We shall think it."

"And what will be the difference?"

"If it is we shall be true to something outside of us, and if it is not we shall think we are being true to ourselves. In either case the world of events will be secondary. Most of the world lives in shadows, as we have done, and it does not matter much which way the shadows fall."

"It matters to the plants that die beneath the shadows."

"You cannot move the shadows. And you cannot move the sun. All you can do is move the objects that cast shadows upon the ground. To do this you have to know the objects. You have to have eyes."

"And hands."

"Then you will have hands."

"And is it only ourselves that cast the shadows and not ourselves that can move us? Is it you who are now trying to convert me?"

"If you like."

"Why do you do this?"

"For my sake, not for yours."

"Something is going to happen," she said.

We lay a long way apart from each other and nothing happened.

"What I mean is this," I continued, "that we ourselves are of no value, no value at all, it is only by fitting into reality that we become of value. We cannot tell when we have done this by examining our motives, we can only tell when we have fitted by a realization that comes from outside. Then we shall not have been true to ourselves but to our not-selves. Being true to oneself is the saddest behaviour in the world."

"We shall always cast shadows until we are one with the sun."

"Then we shall become one with the sun."

"We shall be nothing."

"No, I think we should be something."

"Why?"

"Because to think of it now is so frightening," I said.

"Something is going to happen," she said again.

I began to shiver although I was not cold.

"Do you know what are the two most frightening things in the world?" I said. "To hear a confession and to be praised."

"Is that harder than to confess and praise?"

"Yes," I said. I felt rather sick. I began, "It is I who have betrayed you because I have loved you and have not been true to it."

"No," she said.

"Once we lived in a garden and love was something we did not have to think about. Then we thought about it and it was myself who made this happen. It was I who took upon myself the appearance of decision and who tried to decide what love should be. Then we were out of the garden and I tried to recreate the garden and I created a wilderness."

"It was not your fault," she said.

"In the wilderness we betrayed each other. It was my betrayal. I thought once that it was I who was true because I remembered the garden and would not come to terms with the wilderness, but this was only my conceit. I am the betrayer of my own remembrances. It is I who caused destruction because I thought the world could be trodden by a man with only memory. I betrayed even the memory and that is how I know that I am wrong."

"It was not yourself," she said.

"If it was not I was not even true to it. What happens is caused by the man whom it happens to. I am both the cause and the disaster. When we knew that we were in the wilderness it was I who undertook to come to terms with it and who still walked boldly as if the terms were of my own arranging. This is the sin of it. If Peter or you had died it would have been I who had killed you."

"You are the one who has always been true," she said.

"I am not, Annabelle, because I had made myself a victim. All that I have given you is the guilt for what has happened, and the guilt is mine, for having caused it. Listen, I have loved you and have done nothing for you, this is what is most terrible. It is I who have set up false idols to whom I did not give but from whom I take, and having done this I find myself with nothing. My gifts have been nothing but monuments to my pride and when I got nothing back I would have hurt you. You were closest to me, who had got things back. This is what I have got to tell you, that you must have no trust in me because I have never been trustworthy, that I would have sacrificed you jealously on the altars of my monuments. I have been true to myself but never to you, and this is what matters. You are that part of me to which I should have been true, and it is my failure that is the disaster. I tried to save myself and have lost you. I only realize now that it is myself that is lost because it is only you who could have been the whole of me. And all I ask now is that it is you who shall be saved because that is my love for you. The rest of me is deadly and I pray it may go to extinction."

"It will not," she said, "because it has been true for others."

"Annabelle, Annabelle, nothing of me is true, nothing is not wicked, there is nothing good I have done in the whole of my life and no evil I have not attempted. I must tell you this and you must believe me. Nothing will be saved unless you believe me. In a moment I shall not believe it myself, but at the moment I believe it. You must help me to believe it because a moment is not enough. You must believe that you cannot trust me."

Pray God, I thought, that I have said this truly.

"You are the best and most generous person in the world," she said.

Pray God, dear God, that I meant it. Pray God that it was not a lie.

"You are the only person who is true, who has had something not yourself to be true to, who does not cast shadows."

Pray God that I believe it.

"You are one with the sun," she said.

"Annabelle!"

The shivering that was in my body had gone into the room and I sat up saying "You must not say that Annabelle for God's sake that is not what you must say," and there was a violence in the room like a wind and I wanted to die. I had never been frightened till then and then I was frightened and I got out of bed against the wall so that I could die there. It was an impact against the mind like an agony of the body and I did not know what to do, I did not know what to do against it, I wanted to die. Everything was going out of me into the room and the black walls were breathing and there was a strain in the darkness like the sweat of stars. It was as if I were at that moment conscious of all that had happened in the whole of time, of all that was happening, each instant spread to enormity and exploding before my eyes. The room could not hold it, I could not hold it, I was fighting against the sky. I found myself kneeling beside the wall and there was no noise, no noise at all, just my life projected fighting into the heat of eternity, the world created and ended, an atom of the night. Then there were words going through my head which I had forgotten and which I thought I had remembered, forgotten words running like oil on a scorched machine. The fear stopped. I found that I was praying. In the calmness I knew that I had lied and that now I was not lying. My head was close to Annabelle's shoulder.

"It happened," she said.

"Did it happen to you?"

"Yes," she said. Her body where I held it was wet with sweat. "I am afraid I could not move," she said.

"It did not need to happen to you."

"It did," she said.

"You know what you mean and what you don't mean."

"I do not," she said.

"That is the hardest thing."

"Don't you begin," she said. She tried to laugh. "I haven't meant much this evening." She laughed again. "Until now, at least, and I don't have to say anything now, do I?"

"No," I said. "Not now. Not now it has happened to both of us. That is all that will matter to us always."

19

In the morning I went out before she was awake. The sun was like water. I shopped among the fruit stalls and bought bread that was warm. The streets were glistening as if they had been washed. I walked with my arms full of parcels and a grapefruit like a globe. I remembered Marius's story about the grapefruits, how he had caught them as they fell from a very great height. I threw mine up in the air and it spun like the sun and I caught it. There were wrinkles on its skin like mountains.

Annabelle had woken. I made her stay in bed while I brought her what she needed. We cut the grapefruit and ate it and drank milk in bowls. She had tied her hair into a knot at the back of her head, and her face was transparent like spider's-silk on roses. The sunlight shone in a shaft across the room and it was like a skin beneath which fluttered the veins of our temples. I had a machine which made coffee, sending small airy bubbles bursting softly against a dome. It was made of silver, with a flame at its base, and Annabelle said it was like a thurible. I did not know what a thurible was. It smelt of nuts. When we had finished she sat with her arms around her legs and I watched her. Below us in the street there were two men in top-hats with a guitar and a trumpet, and they played sad jazz music that rang against the stones. I leaned on the edge of the window and Annabelle watched me.

When Marius rang up he said that he had met Peter and had talked with him. He thought that I should go to Grosvenor Square because something was happening. I told this to Annabelle and it was she who insisted on going with me. When we were ready we went out and the two sad men were still playing on the corner. One of them took off his hat and held it out to us and then bowed to us gravely. We did not go to Grosvenor Square until the evening because there seemed so much to be done.

Peter stood in the middle of the room holding a tennis racquet. "Are you better?" he said.

"Much better," Annabelle said.

He looked at her slily and then twirled the tennis racquet around in his hand. "I'm sorry I couldn't produce Father Jack for you," he said.

"I didn't want him."

"I thought you did," he said.

"No."

I wished that Annabelle had not come. I was afraid that she was still more ill than she admitted. Our day had gone quickly and I did not believe that there was any need to worry about Peter. In fact I found it difficult to care about Peter at all. He was swishing at the flowers with his racquet.

"I saw Marius this morning," he said.

"Did you?"

"I met him in the street. Does he know Father Jack well?"

"Quite well."

"He is coming round this evening to say good-bye. He should be here soon. He is going away to-morrow. Father Jack will be back too. It will be quite a party."

"Peter, do be careful with that racquet."

"Racquet!" He knocked the top off a daffodil. "Father Jack is a hypocrite," he said.

"Is that what Marius told you?"

"Marius said Father Jack doesn't like me at all. That is very wrong of him, you know." He said this in a off-hand way that was almost arch. "Silly of him to think that and not to tell me."

"What didn't he tell you?"

"I had a talk with him, do you remember, that day after breakfast, and I thought I'd be nice to him as he is after all an awful bore, so I said what I thought quite pleasantly and he simply lapped it up, at least he said he did, and he told me to go ahead, it was all right by him, so he's a liar. I suppose they have to be nice to you if you're nice to them."

"I suppose they do," Annabelle said.

"Well they shouldn't. He's an old hypocrite. A silly old gardener leading fools up the garden path."

"Did Marius say he was leading you up the garden path?"

"He used absurd language. That was what he meant. 'Knowing well that there would be thistles on the way,' Marius has become like a guidebook, one can simply hear the capital letters. As if fools cared!"

The room was hot. I felt that Peter's indignation was enormously trivial. He was trying to hit the broken head of the daffodil through the open window.

"Are you going to play tennis?" Annabelle said.

"Definitely."

"Who with?"

"Father Jack," Peter said.

I think it was the day that Annabelle and I had spent together that left us unprepared for the scene in the evening. Emotion is never trivial to the person who feels it. I should have known this. But we forgot it, and did not know that Peter was desperate. We did not manage the scene well.

"When is Marius coming?" Annabelle said.

"Soon. I didn't know you'd be here. I hope you don't mind."

"Of course I don't mind."

"I suppose it will be nice for you to say good-bye to him."

"Peter!"

"Yes?"

"Nothing." She suddenly looked very ill as she had done the evening before.

"I mean, you probably won't see him again. What does Father Jack think of that?"

"I expect he thinks it's dreadful."

"For a man who has lived with us for a month, who has eaten our food and been waited on by you, he seems to have rather a low opinion of us."

"He loves us," Annabelle said.

"I hope he doesn't love you like Marius did," Peter said. "Or perhaps that would be a good way to get rid of him."

"Oh Peter, please."

"Sorry," Peter said. "Sorry. Let's ask him what he thinks of Marius. Perhaps he loves him too."

It was I, standing by the window, who saw Father Jack arrive. He was a tiny black figure crossing the road with a suitcase. I nodded to Annabelle, and she went out of the room. "Where's she gone?" Peter said.

"Father Jack has arrived."

"Damn her," he said. He started for the door.

"He's coming up," I said.

"Has she gone to warn him to bring some thistles for the fool?"

"She's gone to tell him something about herself, nothing about you."

"To say she's sorry?"

"Yes."

"How miserable. How bloody miserable!" He threw his tennis racquet onto a chair and then picked it up again. "How damnable of him to demand it!"

When Father Jack arrived his face was wrinkled in smiles and he began talking at once. Peter went to take his suitcase with an affectation of politeness and it was then that I began to be as worried as Annabelle was. "Have a drink, Father," Peter said.

"I think I will, thank you, I have a throat like parchment."

"A good big one, there, that will be nice for you."

"Aren't you drinking, Peter?"

"No, I've given it up, I suppose that is dreadfully immoral of me."

"Indeed, I hope not, I should not like to think so."

"I hear that you think us all quite dreadful, Father."

"Indeed I do not think that you are dreadful."

"Myself, at any rate, you think I am most wrong."

"There is no one, I suppose, who is not most wrong."

"Can't you do anything about it, Father, or would you like another drink?"

"I do not think I will have another drink, thank you."

"Perhaps a little omelette which Annabelle will cook for you?"

"Thank you, no."

"I am afraid we have nothing else to offer you. What can you do for people who are most wrong?"

"You must remember, I think, that one is wrong oneself."

"Really? And is that an excuse for not doing anything?"

"Certainly it is not an excuse."

"So?"

"But what are you asking me, Peter?"

"I am asking you what you do when the world is going to hell."

"The world is not going to hell. It is individuals who may go to hell."

"Then do you tell them the truth of this?"

"One is not in a position to say who will or who will not go to hell."

"Do you tell them the truth?"

"The truth as you endeavour to see it."

"Or do you endeavour to assert your superiority over them by every trick at your command?"

"You do not."

"Then, again, what do you do for them?"

"I can tell them what to do but I cannot make them do it."

"You lead the old horses to water but you cannot push them in?"

"People are not horses."

"No, of course not, they are much wickeder than horses. So you drag them to the water and pour a bucketful over their heads. Is that what you do to help them?"

"It is something that may help them."

"And if after the ceremony they commit all the crimes that human wickedness can imagine, you do not take this as an adverse reflection upon the ceremony but merely as an illustration that men are wickeder than horses?"

"There is no question of horses."

"Have you ever known a horse that is so bestial as a Christian? All right, there is no question of horses, there is the question of the man to whom evil happens because he has no faith in eternity and the man who causes evil in the name of God."

"They may both be punished."

"And when there is an institution that does evil in the name of God, that for centuries has been responsible for more killing, starving, imprisoning, and torturing than any other institution in history, do you not take this responsibility as a reflection upon the institution or do you happily look forward to a further riot of punishment in the light of which these earthly crimes might indeed appear beautiful?"

"Peter!" Annabelle said.

"And when you call out to this God your Father to spare you from this punishment, do you not consider it pathetic that this cry should be made to the one who has created you, who is supposed to love you, whose nature is said to be forgiveness? Pathetic that you should be expected to crawl on your knees to this Father, this so-called father, who loves you but would have you groveling before he deigns to listen to you, let alone give his blessing to you? Pathetic that you should use such a word as father to describe such an image of malevolence? Is there any earthly father who would not weep to see you crawl?"

"Peter!"

"Has he not created you and created you thus? Is it for him too to create hell for you? Those whom he has created wicked, does he not know them to be wicked and is not hell where he has desired them? And is not this creation to hell the deed of a devil? And you, you who follow him, is not that why you regard the desperation of the world with such equanimity, why you drink your drinks and laugh your laughs and make such light of agonies, why you smile as you lie and continue to sin excusing murder and every atrocity? There is no destruction that has not had the blessing of the church upon it, no false blessing that has not had a fictitious devil to excuse it. Why do you bless hatred and search for excuses in the name of a creed that condemns hatred and has no cover for excuses? Why do you lie and sin and allow all villainy if it is not power that you desire instead of truth? There is no truth to you, there is only power. Why do you behave as devils when you say that you are fighting the devil? Why else except that there is no devil but that which you call your God!"

Annabelle began to cry.

"A pathetic God and a pathetic devil whom you crawl to love on your knees like cats, who bids you love your neighbour with the strangulation of frogs—on top of him, always, superior to him, scorning him—soft frogs squatting on top of the world's monstrosities. For two thousand years you have ministered to the world, have had your power over it, have done what you wanted to it; you have assisted at the birth of every generation and seen them reborn into Christ; every generation has worshipped you, followed you, and this is what you have got—frog spawn, frog spawn, a nasty mess in the mud-heap with a tadpole as Holy Ghost!"

There was a silence for a while and then Peter said in a voice which by this time he made no effort to prevent from shaking: "Or would it be more charitable just to think you mad?"

Father Jack replied, calmly, "Peter, you must realize this, that either you believe in the God of Love or else you will think for ever that the world is mad."

"Then I think it mad."

"You must realize also that it is not possible to live in a madhouse. It is not possible to remain a human being if you believe that the world is a madhouse."

"I believe it a madhouse!"

"Then you better get out of it quick."

I do not know if this was said in anger. Father Jack's old wrinkled face betrayed no anger. But Annabelle looked at him through her tears and

I wished he had not said it, and then I thought that perhaps it was said on purpose because Peter at that moment would have done anything rather than obey Father Jack's instructions. But we none of us guessed the speed of Peter's reaction.

The reaction from pride. The last refuge of pride. I should have guessed it.

Marius arrived. There was something unbearable in his coming. He looked at us all quickly and then went straight to Annabelle. He was embarrassed like a child that is introduced to strangers. For a long time they had not seen each other and now they were saying good-bye. Father Jack joined them. Annabelle was smiling and Marius had lowered his head. They stood there. It was as if they might join hands and remain.

And for Peter, I thought, it was his best friend who was saying good-bye to the sister whom he had seduced and was leaving with his child. And the priest to bless them. As I watched him this was what I imagined.

They ignored Peter. As if in defiance to him they stood in their circle with their backs to him and denied him. What was between them was very evident, like the holding of hands. I did not know what this would mean to Peter. When I looked at him again I thought it was only his position in the room that made him seem so lonely.

When Marius had said what he had come to say he moved as if to go. Then he saw Peter. "Good-bye," he said. We were separated from Peter by enormous distances. It might have been true that we did not care about him. "You are not going?" Peter said. "Yes," Marius said.

Annabelle had sat down; and now, as if the spring of her energy had broken, the white face of the stone had returned and she looked as if she were dying. Her hand clutched the arm of the chair and her body was twisted.

"Don't go," Peter said. "Please don't go."

Because of Annabelle again we ignored him. We moved towards her, and in a last violence of effort she said, "Marius, remember everything, and now you must go."

"Annabelle," Peter said, coming across the room.

She snatched herself away from him. "Go, go, for God's sake go," she said. And it was Peter who went.

From the middle of the room where he had stood alone and in loneliness had denied us and in loneliness been denied he went out softly so that we still did not notice him. Then as we caught Annabelle falling forwards in her chair she put out her hand to me and drew my head down to her own and whispered, "Peter, now," and I understood and I left her still falling forwards as if she were dying.

20

Peter was not on the landing. He is going to kill himself. He was not in the lift because the light in the panel was stationary at the bottom. He is going to kill himself to make amends and Annabelle is dying. I ran down the stairs in an unending spiral. You do not kill through scorn or hatred or even despair, you kill because something has happened that has killed you already. I stopped and listened and could hear no footsteps. You kill because you are lonely and your love has denied you. I saw the huge well of the staircase and a stone floor at the bottom. Annabelle loves Marius she will always love Marius it is Peter whom for one moment she has ceased to love. Still no footsteps and a stone floor at the bottom. Peter is standing upon the staircase and looking at the bottom.

I began to run down again. He is alone with everything that he has loved denied to him, everything he has lived for destroyed by his loneliness. He is alone knowing that love is a lie and that life is too much for him. There is only pride left to him and only one thing pride can do. Existence is nothing when there is only pride, and he can only make an end of it. It is I who have known this feeling. And then I was at the bottom of the staircase among the graves of the basement and I knew that Peter could not have been in front of me because all the way down I had seen the bottom. I must do this I must do this one thing because Annabelle would have done it and now she has asked me. I must do it because we ignored him and it was my fault that he was denied. I must do this thing if I never do anything else in my life. And then I thought he has gone to the roof.

I was running again. Upon the roof the sun was white like dead stone faces. Peter sat on the parapet with his legs over the edge. He had put his tennis racquet on the wall beside him and on top of it a tennis ball. He saw me. I felt very tired. I thought he is like a child, this has got to be something extraordinary.

Across the enormous spaces of grey concrete a life such as everyone's on the edge of the sky. A life to be saved or to go to damnation. Twenty yards of dust and eternity to span it. If I approach him, I thought, he will have no alternative.

Words, Marius's words, I remembered. "Everybody wants to love their neighbours, of course they do, but they can't. They don't know how to set about it."

He is a child, I thought. I cannot approach him and I cannot leave him. He would then have to jump, to create his eternity. His car is running downhill. And he is facing the wrong way, that is what I have got to tell him, that he is facing the wrong way. I have got to give him eternity. When you jump you do not jump to damnation, that is worse than wreckage, more deathly than the iron in the rusty sun. It is ironical, I thought, that he should have used the word jump. All his life he has been ready for this and now he thinks that he has come to it. He has not, and it is I who have always known this, that if you make your own moments you are facing the wrong way and when you jump facing rightly it has nothing to do with you. It is to do with those who are concerned about you. "It must be something new," I remembered.

I walked keeping my distance from him and I sat on the parapet at the far corner of the roof. Twenty yards of stonework and the precipice at our feet. I will sit here, I thought, until I have destroyed those spaces. In eternity all spaces are destroyed.

London lay at our feet like the world. A pale grey evening upon the heights of the wilderness. There was an old temptation;—to cast yourself down, to be picked up, to prove that you were a God. And now;—to cast yourself down, never to be picked up, to prove that you are a devil. This is a new temptation.

The people of London like ants on a mound of dust. O world, world, flat round shapeless shape, be loved or not loved but do not ask for everything. Suffer us to have the illusion that we are beyond you. Perhaps after all we can fly.

Peter did not do anything. He was looking at his toes in the evening sun.

O God, God, to destroy those spaces you must destroy time. Let us go back and begin again and then this will not have happened. This is what you have promised, what you have told us is possible. It is only that I must remember, and there is something I must do.

I thought:—Perhaps we must all become again as children. Was it not this that we were told?

A sky of violet and an earth of grey and ourselves in between them. Once we were part of them, we spread veins to enclose us, around us and the universe there was a body that was whole. There is nothing new, it is just what is old that has been forgotten. You can always go back, that is what I have known is true, when the car is running downhill there are always trees on the roadside. The trees are all the same, it is only one tree that is needed. We have looked for something permanent, but a moment will do. A tree is eternity. There would be moments if I could remember them. I remembered an evening with the square huge and moonlit when a statue stood folded like the wings of a bird.

Looking downwards, to the ground, I saw Marius step out of the entrance to the building and walk sedately into the middle of the road. He gazed on either side of him and circled slowly like a weathercock. I dared make no sound. He was a tiny figure distorted by the distance. Then he stood still, facing the building, and looked up, and saw us.

We were the three corners of a triangle. I had an extraordinary desire to jump myself. Marius stood with the traffic running past him. I wanted to jump so that there would be communication between the sky and the world. The white light waited. Then Marius raised his arms and shouted, "Peter, Peter, there are always shooting stars!"

His voice came to us clearly as an echo from stone. There were so many memories. Salvation, I thought, and the catching of grapefruits. "Throw him your tennis ball," I said.

For a while Peter made no move. The spaces were between us. Then he picked up the ball in one hand and the racquet in the other and he threw the ball up into the air and lashed at it with the racquet and the ball shot away into the sky like a star. "He will never catch it," he said.

"He will," I said.

Marius began to run. I had never seen him run before. He ran fast and steadily through the raging traffic with a car hooting and skidding at him his long legs wandering a bicyclist lurching and a crowd turned to watch. By the side of the road he stopped, beneath a tree. There he stood while the ball fell for millions and millions of years and then he leaned backwards with his hands clasped in front of him and the ball bounced against a branch of the tree and he caught it as if he were making love.

"There!" I said.

Marius held the ball up so that it was whiter than the evening. There were no more spaces. Then he put the ball in his pocket, turned, and walked away from us. We watched him grow smaller and smaller until he disappeared behind the trees. It was the last time that I saw him in England.

"Romps!" Peter said. "They are still a credible concept." He had stuck his feet out straight in front of him and was smiling at his knees. "But I am facing the wrong way," he said. He swung his legs over the parapet and waited there, still smiling. Then he stood up and walked across the roof. He did not look at me. I saw him go through the door and down the steps into the building. He never saw Marius again. I looked down from my height upon the old iron of the world and felt tired. I remembered Annabelle.

21

On the landing I met Alice. "You?" I said. "Marius telephoned me," she said. Father Jack opened the door to us and she went through with the furious assurance of a professional. Father Jack was making enquiring faces so I told him, "She is a nurse."

Peter was not there. Alice had gone through to the bedroom. We could hear her talking to Annabelle. When she came back Father Jack said, "Can I be of any assistance, nurse?"

"I'm not a nurse," Alice said.

She rang up for a doctor. She took everything into her hands. She appeared to be in a rage that made all other efforts seem trivial. I knew that at the moment there was nothing more to be done about Annabelle.

"Can I help, Alice?"

"By keeping out of the way," she said.

I could not bear to stay with Father Jack. In his presence I felt an irritation that drowned even my anxiety about Annabelle. I went out into the street to recover my anxiety.

Once before I had stood on the steps of a doorway and there had been nowhere I had wanted to go. Then I had gone nowhere. Now, in the same situation, I chose to go to the right, and went.

The rage that was in Alice seemed to have entered into me. I found, with surprise, that I did not recover my anxiety. I continued to be irritated by the image of Father Jack, by thoughts of the scene in which I had just taken part, by memories of absurdity that seemed to stretch through the whole of my life. I felt as if I dragged behind me a string of tin cans that clattered against my ankles;—cans of falseness and sentimentality and the dregs of everything trivial. There were also, on another string, a trail of responsibilities—the pain of Annabelle, the insanity of Peter, the waste which was myself. It was this that was uppermost, the knowledge of waste. And yet I felt no emotion about it except a determination that it should stop. I jerked savagely at my memory so that the tin cans rattled.

Passing on the corner an old man selling evening papers I saw upon his placard the latest reminder of disaster. I bought a paper and read it as I walked. There was the inevitable news of misery and madness and the fiddling of politicians in the face of death. I found with less surprise that this did not worry me either. I stopped, so that the cans should not divert me, and tried to think what was happening.

Annabelle was ill and I did not worry. The world was dying and I did not worry. What would happen would happen anyway. What would happen had happened already. This was not important. What was important was the condition in which I would see what would happen anyway. What was important was what I did. I walked again and my tin cans rattled and I cursed them. I stopped.

Nothing mattered. Once we had had the fact of freedom without searching for the illusion of it, and then we had found the illusion and lost the fact. Now we had neither fact nor illusion. We had lost all powers. We simply had, at every moment, a choice. A choice that was given, to the right or to the left, like in a maze. We were at the centre, and the object was to get out. The maze was there, mankind was there, there was no question of freedom. One walked, and there were a million junctions, and every time one must choose. One did not know if one chose right or wrong, if one went outwards or inwards, it was only true that one went. Freedom was choosing right and death was choosing wrong, but one did not know until the end where one had gone. So it did not matter. Where one goes one would have gone anyway. I walked, and my tin cans tripped me, and I laughed.

Moving thus, alternately walking and stopping, laughing and cursing, in the manner of a man with his feet in a sack, I found myself at the entrance to a large hotel. I went in, so that I could rest, and I observed the world that I hated. Upon the walls and the chairs the upholstery bulged with the fatness of fruit gone rotten in a warehouse; and the people, taking their cue from the decorations, paraded faces like wax apples, clothes like banana skins, buttons and brooches like cloves in a suet pudding. Old men were like slugs, young tufts like caterpillars, and the dried hobbled women like sticks of liquorice. I sat down and watched them. I thought, These are the godless people I have to love, the ugly people who are beautiful. And then I remembered my own trail of garbage, my feet in the sack.

I thought—It is easy to love the horror and the suffering, it is easy to think beautiful the child with cancer and the hangman's rope, but it is not easy to adore this rottenness. This smell has nothing to do with eternity.

Eternity. If life is a maze and time is a moving staircase then you can run against the moving staircase, that is the easiest thing in the world, you can go back, you can begin again, you can undo what you have done, every action of the present can wipe out consequences of the past and once the consequences have gone then the actions of the past do not exist. You can absolve wrong choices, creating your own absolutions. I am responsible for everything that I have done in the whole of my life, I am responsible for the causes of what I have done and the consequences, I am responsible for the death of Marius's wife, for the loneliness of Peter, for the pain of Annabelle. If what I have done has been in honour of this responsibility—if the pain is lessened, the loneliness gone, the death made beautiful—then I have created my own absolution. But I have not. The past is around my ankles, my feet in the sack. Whatever I have done my feet are still hobbled. What is time?

I am responsible for not only what has affected me, I am responsible for everything that has happened in every part of the world for ever. Whatever I have done this is what I cannot alter. Whatever I do I cannot move. The maze is around me and I cannot move. What is time?

It is necessary that I move. It is necessary that I get rid of this garbage. It is necessary that I love. And then I thought, What have Annabelle and I to do with time?

What if Annabelle should die?

Thus, in the hall of the great hotel, among the perfumes and the cigars and the odourless flowers, I answered the question. It was necessary that Annabelle should live. If Annabelle died in the night, of her illness, it was still necessary that she should live. The first time that I saw her two years ago, when I talked with her and gave her up, when I held her last night and was terrified, it was absolutely necessary that these moments should live. And they did, that was what love meant, it was irrefutable. Annabelle would live because that is what love meant, and time was eternity.

And if time is eternity then you cannot go back, you cannot undo what you have done, your mistakes are always with you. You can only move by asking for an absolution which is beyond you. Eternity is beyond you, and this is what makes nothing matter and then when you have realized this, it makes everything matter. This is not a paradox. Things are on different planes, the part and the whole, what becomes and what is completed, the maze as you see it from within and the maze as it exists from without. The part on its own does not matter because it is helpless. The whole on its own does not matter because it is finished. What does matter is the relationship between the part and the whole. What is important is what you do in relation to the whole. And this relationship is possible because eternity exists, there is the possibility of apprehending it because what is becoming is part of it. There is to every man, either in the sky or in the heart, or somewhere between them, a reflection of the whole. There is a periscope to eternity. It is possible to outwit the helplessness of the part, to achieve the whole by mirrors. The mirrors have been given.

And then, beginning to walk, you find you can walk freely. When love is honoured there is absolution, when nothing seems to matter it is possible to decide what matters, when there is a glimpse of eternity there is guidance through the maze. At once, in a double stroke, the past is cut loose and a thread is given to the future. You walk, thus, leaving the refuse behind you: you go, step by step, and there are stars to guide you. The stars are there, as light, between the world and eternity. With mirrors you can see them, above the dark walls of the maze. There is everything to be done and all life is a learning: the mirrors of the heart have to be focused to the sky. There are instructions for this, to be read most carefully. I will read them. But now, at the centre, at the beginning, I can walk. Aware of the end, the outside, a step can be taken. It is love that has turned me, the beginning and the end. There are things to be done. And finally, in the hotel, among the scented wreaths dissimulating corpses, I looked round, curiously, for the last time, and thought—All right you goats, be Gods and Goddesses.

I rang up Alice. "How is she?" I said.

"You keep away," Alice said.

"I know," I said.

"It was bad enough with that blasted priest."

"I know," I said. "I'm sorry. But how is Annabelle?"

"I don't know," Alice said. "Is her father in Paris?"

"Yes."

"And her mother?"

"Her mother is away."

"Has she got any relations beside that blasted brother?"

"I don't know," I said. "Does she want relations?"

"No," Alice said. "No, she doesn't."

"Thank you, Alice. I really want to thank you."

"She's all right," Alice said. "She's sure to be all right. You ring up again in the morning."

"Thank you," I said. "Alice, you have been right all the time."

"In the morning," Alice said.

Around the grass of the square there had been erected a small wire fence to discourage trespassers. I stepped over it and took my seat beneath the statue. This was a familiar place, as well as being one from which I could intercept Peter. I looked up and saw a light in the window which I thought was Annabelle's. I prepared for the night.

It was now quite dark. I hummed a tune. It was funny, I thought, this finding oneself at the centre. The night made a noise as if the world were humming. It was funny the way things returned to their beginnings just as I had returned to sit beneath the statue. A drunk man passed: we exchanged salutations. There was no regret, since excursions could not be avoided, and everything happened over and over again. It was possible, I believed, that everything could be dealt with better each time it arrived.

At some period of the night I had a sudden vivid memory of Marius's wife. I was thinking of the last time I saw her in hospital and was trying to remember the things she said. There was something that eluded me, and the harder I thought of it the further away it got. Then it seemed that she was very close to me herself and was trying to tell it to me. In the silence I became startled and spoke to her out loud. I must have been half asleep because the noise of my cry woke me, and then it seemed that I had been speaking to Annabelle. I wanted very much that I could take upon myself what Annabelle was suffering, that I could get close to her. I thought that if I tried hard enough I might be able to. It was necessary and possible that I should. And then I knew that what had been suggested to me was not what Marius's wife had said, but merely that I should try this about Annabelle. I tried to carry her sadness.

And then, in the night that had become the universe, it was as if this were the purpose and the justification of everything. The world was one, suffering was indivisible, what was carried by one took the burden from another. Whatever would happen in the rest of our lives—if Annabelle should die, if I should fail her—still there was this oneness by which the whole might be revived. In all time all people were responsible for one another. These were the ghosts that I remembered, the ghosts that had to be laid. Whatever would happen, however agonized the future, there was always this communion by which meaning was given over. After this night, I thought, when we go out into the morning, we will know this, and remember this, and nothing will not be worth while. Love is its own justification, and so is suffering. We can all go into eternity and die there for ever. It still will not matter. What matters is the whole, for which we will have died. In the early morning a policeman came to turn me out of the garden and I talked to him and he went away.

22

Peter came when it was light. He stood beside me, tired, requiring information. "How is Annabelle?" he said.

"She is all right," I said. "I am going to ring up soon."

"I must see her."

"Wait till I telephone."

"I'm going to Paris to-day."

"I will be telephoning soon."

The sun had not yet warmed us. We were dry, brittle, with the weight of consciousness heavy like sand. Peter was blinking his screwed-up eyes and my body was stiff so that if I moved I thought I would break it. We were both like men hung from parachutes above a desert. We waited.

"How do you know she's all right?" Peter said.

"Alice is with her. And a doctor."

"A doctor?"

"Yes."

"Why a doctor?"

"Of course there is a doctor. Wait till I ring up."

"Yes," Peter said.

As the heat started it seemed to rise from the stones like a mist. There was a gradual melting of stiffness and time began to tick like water dripping from a cracked pipe after a thaw. Peter stirred uneasily.

"I must go in," he said. "I must see her."

"I will ring up," I said.

"I am going to Paris to join my father. I won't be back for some time."

"Wait," I said.

There was a call-box on the corner. Walking was a mechanical business like exercises. As I moved the heat was ruffled and I shivered. Alice's flat undeviating voice answered me.

"How is she?" I said.

"She's all right," Alice said.

"Good," I said. I didn't know how to put it. "And the child?" I said.

"There is no child," Alice said.

"Oh." It was extraordinary how the sun still shone and the traffic moved and the news had made no difference. I watched a fly which lay on its back on the ledge of the window faintly moving its legs against the light. "I don't know about these things," I said. "How bad are they and how bad was she?"

"She was all right," Alice said. "They can be bad but it didn't happen too bad to her." The fly was waving its tentacles in death.

"Can I come round?"

"Yes," Alice said.

"Peter is here too."

"He can't come."

"Why not? Why not if I can?"

No answer from Alice.

"He's going away to-day. He won't be coming back."

No answer.

"He's all right now," I said. "He'll only stay a minute."

"All right," Alice said.

I went back to Peter. "She's not bad," I said. "Would you like to see her?"

"Yes," Peter said.

We went in and walked to the lift. It was as if there were a lot of people watching us. On the landing Alice opened the door to us and Peter said, "Thank you," and then he went quickly along the passage. Alice was staring at me with her hard tired eyes.

"Well," she said, "there you are, it's over, and are you now going to grow up?"

Peter had opened the door of Annabelle's room and I could see the corner of her bed beyond him. He went up to it soundlessly like a man going to fetch something and then he went down on his knees and knelt by the side of the bed and put out his hand across the covering. I did not hear either of them speaking. His hand was towards her where I could not see and his face was turned to the ground so that he was not looking at her. There was only his arm, stretched out, like a branch; and she, somewhere distant, touching it. They remained there. Then he rose with a quick single movement from his knees as if a wind had lifted him and he came out of the room quite soundlessly still and went into his own room next to hers. Her door remained open, a straight continuation of the passage leading to a mirror which reflected the passage straight back again to where I stood, and there was just the one straight line with myself at either end of it and Annabelle in between. I could hear Peter in his room moving ceaselessly and precisely like a tiger in its cage, and as I stared at myself along the passage I was a dangling figure at one end and a small darker replica at the other, myself seeing myself not from either end but both and from the middle where Annabelle lay beyond the one blind corner of the bed. Then Peter emerged carrying an enormous suitcase into which he had packaged all his belongings for a month, and he came up the passage momentarily blocking the view, moving still precise and still ceaseless and he went past me and past Alice and then stopped at the door. "Thank you," he said. "Thank you." Then he went out. And the passage remained.

"There," Alice said, "there now, and have you finished?'

I walked along the passage. In the room I met myself. Annabelle was crying. She was veiled with her tears like a moon. "Annabelle," I said.

The windows were stained with curtains. A blue light dripped down from the morning, the room was blue with light like water, the water flickered, and we were beneath the water, swimming. I thought, When I am with her I shall always think of the sea. "Annabelle," I said.

"Yes?" she said.

"I am so sorry," I said.

"I have lost the only thing that I shall ever love," she said.

In the sea we should have been made silver. I should have liked to have rested there.

"I know," I said.

VII
ETERNITY

23

It was at a political meeting that they killed Marius. We were there when it happened. We had gone out to the West Indies, to stay with Annabelle's father, and Marius was shot. He had been mixed up in a strike of the sugar-cane workers, and when he died the strike was broken and everything went on as before. He would not have been surprised.

Annabelle had said she wanted to die, but she didn't. She got well slowly although she cried much of the time. We went to the sun to try to get her laughing. It was very hot, and we lay in bed with a fan whirring continually.

On the way out we saw Peter in Paris. There was a strike there, too, of transport workers, and we had to walk from the station. People were standing about on the corners of the streets and occasionally they ran out into the road to try to stop a car which went past them. There were a lot of soldiers being carried around in American trucks and the traffic had to stop for them. The people watched the trucks go past and then they began running out into the road again.

Peter was sitting in the hall of a big hotel, drinking whiskey. He tried to pretend that he was glad to see us. He had big rings under his eyes and he kept on looking round the hall of the hotel as if he were about to be arrested. A girl came to join him and she carried a big bag like a drum and her earrings clashed like cymbals when she turned her head. I tried to think where I had seen her before, and then I remembered. When Peter was with her he was rather like a dog.

We had dinner, the four of us, and the girl kept talking in a hard hysterical voice using strange slang phrases that required no answer. Peter echoed them for conversation and called her darling and laughed very quickly whenever she stopped. When he looked at her his eyes were watery, but he never looked at Annabelle or me. The waiters treated him with great respect and the girl made eyes at them to impress us. The restaurant was full of old men having dinner with younger men and their faces were artificial as if held together with spirit gum. In front of them were a lot of little bottles and plates like those on a dressing table, and hands fluttered over them as if they were choosing jewels. The young men sat very straight and obedient and sometimes the old men helped them to wine.

Later in a café we came across more of Peter's friends. It was a small airless place like the crypt of a church and we drank brandy that tasted of syrup. There was a man playing a guitar and the girls chattered so much that he could not be heard. Peter was enjoying himself and repeated everything that was said and a girl came and sat on his knee. At midnight there was a cabaret in which a very old woman appeared in a bathing dress. She sang dirty songs and did a dance holding a carrot. Everyone clapped and cheered and Peter kissed the girl with the earrings. For a while he seemed happy and talked louder than anyone else, and then he became drunk and did not talk anymore. We took him back in a taxi and his face looked dead.

I helped him to bed in his small ornate room and he lay face downwards in his pyjamas. I thought he was asleep and was about to leave him when he put out his hand and said, "Don't go," and held me. The room was very hot and was padded with black silk like the inside of a coffin. Peter had covered his face with a pillow and he pulled at it and said, "Oh God, God," several times out loud. Then he sat up in bed and lit a cigarette and smoked it with the ash crumbling off onto the sheets. "What day is it to-morrow?" he said. "Sunday," I said.

Peter had got a job with a newspaper and he had been doing it for two months when we saw him. He had not come back to England when Annabelle and I were married. We had heard news of him from time to time and it was always suggested that he was being a great success. The opinion was that he had settled down, had grown up, had got over an awkward stage in his career. As I watched him sitting in the bed he somehow reminded me of Alice. His hand holding the cigarette drooped and burned a hole in the blanket. When I left him he asked me to tell the concierge to wake him early in time for church.

We were with him for one more day and we saw him being successful. He spent the afternoon in the bar of the big hotel with two blonde Italian girls who looked like madonnas. They sat on either side of him and he appeared very small between them. There were a lot of pansy men at the bar who seemed to be keeping clear of him, and Peter was fluttering his hands incessantly at the girls as if he were doing some penance to them. They were very serious with him, and seemed to be trying to protect him when later his pansy friends came up and surrounded him. He grew smaller and smaller between the two big motherly madonnas until he was quite drunk again and then he did not seem to exist at all. We left him then. I wondered who would win. They were all very fond of him.

Later we had a letter from him saying how happy he was and how he loved Paris because it was the only place where one could have fun any more. He had changed his address and was living with one of the Italian girls and was thinking of becoming a Roman Catholic because she was one. His letter was full of words like divine and heavenly, and indeed he spoke of all his friends as if they were gods and goddesses.

We had heard about Marius, too, from time to time, and about his successes. There had been riots on his island in the West Indies, and whenever the news crept into the papers Marius's name was mentioned. The workers in the sugar-cane fields were striking for higher pay, and all the landowners were holding out against them except Marius who was on their side. He spoke for them at their meetings and had become an unofficial head of the trades-union that was running the strike. Most of the workers on the island had come out in sympathy with the strikers and Marius was much hated by the other landowners. Sometimes his meetings were broken up by the police and sometimes by parties organized by the landowners. Annabelle's father had been governor of the islands at the time when the strike began and he had tried to settle it and had not been able to, and then he had resigned. Afterwards he lived in this small private house on the island and we heard that he had been ordered home and had refused to come and that his career was finished, but we did not know about this. We went out to stay with him and we arrived at the end of the hot season in the rains.

We went into the town one evening and saw the people standing on the corners of the streets. There was no traffic and nothing to move for, and it seemed that the wooden buildings were material for a bonfire waiting to be set alight. Even the sea was oily, so that it seemed that the water might burn. A group of policemen came down the street with a man handcuffed in the middle of them, and there was no sound except the tread of their marching. Women hung out of the windows of upper storeys as if they were bodies about to arise from graves. It was as if the whole town were waiting for the coming of the devil.

Marius was sitting in the bar of a small hotel, drinking whiskey. There were two young negroes on either side of him who treated him respectfully, like disciples. His voice had a strange accent in it, and when he saw us he came over and was polite. His friends waited for him while he spoke to us, and then he rejoined them and they began talking again. The people at the bar kept clear of him as if the young men were his bodyguard. Marius looked very young, like the captain of a schoolboy's football team. Presently he stood up and left the bar and the young men followed him out in a line.

On the day of the meeting there was a hot wind blowing from the sea and dust hung in the air like ash from a volcano. It clung to mouths and nostrils, and skin became dirty where it collected on sweat. It was a day on which the body becomes horrible. People wore handkerchiefs round their necks and tried to keep still so that their clothes should not rub them. We heard the crowd moving up to the top of the town and the day became heavy so that perhaps one would not have minded dying.

The town was built on a hill with a square at the top where the church and the official buildings lay. The church was a fat square box like a toy with imitation doors and windows and a removable steeple. Steep cobbled streets led down from the square on two sides towards the harbour. On the other sides there was the one motor-road and for the rest just rock. The cobbled streets were so steep that it was sometimes necessary to hold on to a doorway to prevent oneself from sliding. Before the meeting began the police had cut off the motor-road so that the crowd had to climb up the cobbles, and we could see them sweating jerkily through the greasy heat like raindrops running strangely in reverse. Some were carrying banners, and every now and then the bearers slipped and the banners went down in the dust like a sheet falling into an enormous ashtray.

We could not see Marius when we arrived. There was an old negro on the platform and the crowd was making too much noise for him to be heard. Individuals seemed to be shouting quite indiscriminately and yet there was a peculiar solidity about the gathering as if each separate movement was a tentacle spread from the body of the whole. The jerking of a head as it spoke or the clenched raising of a fist seemed to shiver the limbs around it almost physically, and yet one did not know what caused the solitary impulse at the beginning. It was like watching a shoal of fish hanging massed in clear water, the impulse and the effect of the sudden switches of tension were indistinguishable. The crowd was tight, and yet moving, the whole square seemed to crawl. I could see a one-legged beggar beating his crutch ceaselessly against a lamp-post, and the people around him nodding in rhythm to him as if they were dancing. When Marius appeared the bodies switched to him as if he had magnetized them, and he was both the cause and the effect of the impulse. The voices closed into a steady harmony and there was a whistling in the air as if the dusty wind was blowing through the trees. Marius spoke and they listened to him and I do not know if they understood. His voice came clearly through the heavy air and he was saying that there must be no violence, that there was work for many on his estate, and that there was food for all. He said that they would win their fight for better conditions if they stayed together quietly and were patient. He spoke with no rhetoric and with a simplicity that held them. They became calm, and solid, and he had power over them. I did not think it mattered if they did not understand. For a moment, in an emotion of peace, I thought that Marius might be the saviour of the world.

A group of white men, or half-castes, had formed in one corner of the square slightly behind the platform. They wore white shirts and grey trousers and belts of a precisely similar pattern. At a sign from their leader they began to chant, and I remembered the day when I had first seen Marius in London. There the singing had been a thin tuneless wailing in despair against graves: the crowd had not been solid and the air was cold. Now, in the heat, beneath the ash of the volcano, the crowd turned instinctively as if it had been stung. The white men were leaning forwards chanting with a queer artificial jerking of their arms. I had the impression that they were dolls attempting to be sick. They were singing that Marius was a nigger.

Marius heard them and turned to them and I suppose it would not have been right for him to ignore them. He shouted in a voice which carried over the rising hum, "Listen to them and see if they have anything to say worth listening to," and the chant went on with a thousand black heads turned craning towards it: "A dirty nigger, a dirty nigger," and a thousand pairs of yellow eyes coming round in hate. "If I am," Marius shouted, "then what does it matter and is that worth listening to?" One of the white men stretched out a finger and shouted something that was inaudible but which from its gesture was evidently an obscenity. I was reminded of the old woman in Paris dancing with her carrot.

The point of magnetism to which was drawn the direction of the dusty-headed filings of the crowd had now switched from Marius to the group in the corner where the mechanical dolls leaning forwards were vomiting. But Marius still held them back with his voice that charmed and placated, sinking them back into quietude against the spray of hate, and letting the hate wear itself out on the heat of dustiness. The flow of yellow eyes was no more than a murmur, after all the heads were static. He would have held them like this and saved them if the bells of the church had not started ringing.

No one knew why they started or who was ringing them, but when they began there was nothing that could be heard, nothing that could hold them—the direction and the magnetism of the afternoon were scattered and chaos came like the roll of lava through the ashes. It happened quickly—after the first numb intrusion—the crowd breaking up with a strange silent sibilance and the group of white men disappearing and Marius standing alone and important while the mechanical sound rolled on without tune and without order. Fighting began instinctively, immediately, not directed specifically against the white men but just arising spontaneously like the quivering of springs when the tension is broken. It began in groups, like whirlpools, spreading slowly through the square. Then there were soldiers coming up the road carrying rifles and they spread out in a line in front of the church and there was a rush up the steps as the bells beat on and on and the rush went back as it hit the breaker of bayonets. Marius stood with this arms raised to quell them but there was no power any more, no force to stop them, in the sea of black ashes there was no tide and no direction just the boiling of the surface as the spray blew wildly and the line of soldiers came down the steps to clear the square. It was then that the group of white men appeared again, they had got round the back of the crowd and were close to the platform and they were fighting in a wedge getting nearer to it. The line of soldiers went past them and left them driving deeper and deeper in towards Marius, and I went out in the square to see what could be done. I left Annabelle in a doorway, and as I walked I could see her father in front of me punching his way through the crowd with his cigarette-holder jutting up from his mouth and an unlighted cigarette in it, a small dapper man in a panama hat fighting and fighting and making no headway against the arms and legs and fists that surrounded him. I walked through as Marius had done once before, and I saw the white shirts and grey trousers getting up to the platform and pushing at it so as to overturn it and arms stretching upwards to tear at the banners and Marius swaying as if he were walking on water. Then the crowd gathered itself for the last time screaming and broke through the line of soldiers and reached the platform which now seemed to rise up bodily into the air above the black and white heads and the heads were going down beneath the wind of arms and Marius was rising. Then a second line of soldiers spread out by the church and there was an officer giving an order while the white shirts went down and down and the white heads were sinking beneath the black stabs of spray and then the soldiers raised their rifles and fired into the air. For a moment everyone was quiet, they were all kneeling, and as I looked for Annabelle I could see her walking above their bodies like a nurse. She reached the steps of the church as the crowd rose yelling and there was suddenly a crush that seemed to squeeze the last breath out of the daylight and then the soldiers fired again. There was a woman screaming and screaming repeatedly very close to my ear and I could not move my arms and then it seemed that I and those around me were lifted off our feet and carried, unresisting, by the panic of the waves. We were moved in an effortless limp block like flotsam towards the steep cobbled streets that led to the harbour, and as the first people began to go down the screaming rose in a crescendo that fought against the bells and the noise became enormous like a furnace. We went down hill backwards and there were fingers tearing at the woodwork of doors and a sound of cracking as when trees are felled, and always some people coming on top of us like the weight of a glacier. I got my hand round a pillar which supported the front of a house and I clung there with my feet off the ground and bodies moving beneath me and a line of faces jerking close to my own, smooth dirty sweating faces snarling with gold teeth and twisted mouths and breaths like something solid. There was a man beside me clinging to the pillar who had a gold chain round his neck and the chain had been seized by a woman behind him and the metal was cutting into his throat as if he were being hung. His head went back inch by inch and there was a small gold crucifix on the chain which stuck out straight from his Adam's apple like the point of a sword. Then the chain broke and he let go his hold on the pillar and clutched at his throat gurgling and he fell backwards against the woman and they went down on the ground with the crowd going over them. There were bodies on the cobbles crawling and being kicked and then the wave seemed to break and they were all facing downwards and they gave up struggling and were flung forwards wildly like surf. At the bottom they scattered sideways or were pushed or ebbed into the sea. As the last rush came past me the pillar of the house broke and I fell against the woodwork. It seemed that the sky came down in a dust of fire and darkness and then it was quiet. When I picked myself up I saw the house wrecked with a hole in the wall as if a tank had been through it, and at the bottom of the hill by the harbour the muddy water writhing like a vision of hell. But from the square there was silence.

People were drowned in the sea. I walked up the cobbles with a pain in my leg like a cramp and a soldier tried to stop me and I went past him. In the square were soldiers and dirt and the upturned platform. A few policemen were helping to move the injured whose cries came like gulls across the spaces. By the platform were Marius and Annabelle and Mr. Palmerston. An officer was with them. Marius lay in the dust with his legs folded and his hands on his chest. The officer was saying, "It was nothing to do with me." Marius had a large open wound in his stomach and he was not yet dead and I turned away as if to be sick. Annabelle was tearing up her shirt as if to bandage him.

I sat by his head while Mr. Palmerston prayed over him and the soldiers came to watch. The bells of the church had ceased and Marius's eyes were open to the sky with the flies settling on his eyelids. I waved my handkerchief above his eyes to keep the flies away and his face never moved and it was as if his body was not part of him. Mr. Palmerston leaned over him and put his ear close to Marius's mouth but the lips did not speak and then Mr. Palmerston touched his forehead with oil. The flies came to settle on the oil and I waved at them with my handkerchief. Then Marius drew a breath which seemed to come up from his torn stomach past his chest where the hands were folded into his dead staring face and he groaned and closed his eyes and said "I have not loved my beloved." He spoke very clearly and he did not speak again and soon the eyes swam open and the flies settled on them and I did not have to wave at them any more. Mr. Palmerston was praying again and Annabelle covered Marius's face with the shirt that she had torn to put on his wounds.

That evening Mr. Palmerston came to see us and we sat beneath the palm trees while the rain waited. "He is at rest," Mr. Palmerston said. I thought of the big brass bells of the church that had killed him or perhaps had welcomed him. "I do not know how it happened," Mr. Palmerston said.

Later the rain began and we stayed in the house. Annabelle's father lay in bed all day doing crossword puzzles and chess problems from the papers. His cigarette holder had been broken in the riot and he had patched it with sticking-plaster so that it appeared somewhat bent. It was like a limb that has not properly healed.

We went to Marius's funeral. The whole town turned out and the rain ran down like tears across their faces. Mr. Palmerston read the service and the coffin went down into mud. "He should have had a child," Annabelle said. Later we were asked to go through his personal belongings since he had no relations, but there was not much to do. Annabelle found a packet of her letters to him, and she took them. His wife's clothes were hanging in a cupboard and when we shook them the cloth fell away in lumps where the moths had eaten them. I took all his papers and gave the business ones to Mr. Palmerston and kept myself the ones between him and his wife. Mr. Palmerston wanted me to burn them, but I did not do so. All Marius's property went to the Mission which Mr. Palmerston represented. There was nothing further of which the Mission could make use.

One day when the wind stopped Annabelle and I went out in a boat and sailed up the side of the island to the promontory where Marius's house stood against the sea. It was a blue day with clouds like flowers and we landed on the beach where the crabs ran. Annabelle went up to the huge empty house and I stayed on the rocks in front of the palm trees. Below me there were fishes that were striped like silk and weeds that seemed to grow as the water washed them. Annabelle sat on the verandah watching me and I took all the letters that Marius had written to his wife and that she had written to him and I tore them up and threw the bits of paper on the water where the fishes came to nibble at them like bread. Annabelle came down and sat beside me and I put my hand into the water and the water was icy.

We left the house and sailed out onto the open sea and Annabelle sat in the front of the boat with her back to me. I furled the sail and we drifted and there was a terrible ache in my body as if my life had been taken away from me. I lay in the bottom of the boat and watched the enormous hills of the island that arose like sphinxes from a desert, and then I closed my eyes and went back into the centre for the last time and prayed to God and to myself to forgive me. I thought of the last words that Marius had spoken and I knew that they were true for everyone. Memories came in like agonies of the garden and above them all was set the image of Annabelle not far from me with her seldom-smiling face like a swan upon the waters. Above the movement of the sea was a hard dead rock with nothing on it living and nothing on it loving and nothing on it working; and when memories became unbearable I stopped them. I went outwards again because it was the only thing to do and I knelt and kissed Annabelle because it was the only thing to do and I unfurled the sail because it was the only thing to do and we drove towards the land. From the hills above the huge bay the bells of the church boomed out again and summoned us to quietness. The sea was no good for us and we crawled to eternity.

POSTSCRIPT

I re-read this story some sixty years after it had been written; and then I came across the letter from the publisher's reader giving his reasons for turning it down. I thought I could now see more clearly his reasons for doing so, though these might or might not be a good reason for wishing that it might be published now.

The publisher was Rupert Hart-Davis, and his reader David Garnett, who had written to me—

> I have read *A Garden of Trees* with interest and despair. I think it is a failure and that publication in its present form would be a mistake.
>
> The action is always excellently written and alive; the conversation generally bad and dead. Of course belonging to such a much older generation I am not the most sympathetic reader. But I should like to discuss it with you.

I had of course been disappointed, and had argued. Now sixty years later I was feeling I could understand what he meant about the conversation being dead.

At the time of writing, 1949-50, I was in my mid-twenties, and had had a bad stammer since childhood. This had often held me speechless while I listened to what seemed to me to be the often inane conversations of others. As I grew up the chattering political and social world seemed as a whole to be inane; and I wondered if speech might not be part of the curse acquired by humans when they were expelled from the Garden of Eden—or when they descended from being apes in the trees, or whatever. (Might not apes be protected from knowledge of good and evil? Whereas humans have the empowerment of telling lies.)

Anyway, it is true that the young protagonists in my story do not seem very trustful of speech; and the two characters at the centre—Marius and Annabelle—were, I remembered, drawn from two people in real life who at the time seldom spoke, but to whom I and others were mysteriously and strongly drawn. Perhaps now, in this overt age of celebrity, there might be some recognition of the strength of inwardness rather than clamour.

NICHOLAS MOSLEY was born in London on June 25, 1923 and was educated at Eton and Oxford. He served in Italy during World War II, and published his first novel, *Spaces of the Dark*, in 1951. His book *Hopeful Monsters* won the 1990 Whitbread Award. He resides in London.

SELECTED DALKEY ARCHIVE TITLES

Petros Abatzoglou, *What Does Mrs. Freeman Want?*
Michal Ajvaz, *The Golden Age.*
The Other City.
Pierre Albert-Birot, *Grabinoulor.*
Yuz Aleshkovsky, *Kangaroo.*
Felipe Alfau, *Chromos.*
Locos.
João Almino, *The Book of Emotions.*
Ivan Ângelo, *The Celebration.*
The Tower of Glass.
David Antin, *Talking.*
António Lobo Antunes, *Knowledge of Hell.*
The Splendor of Portugal.
Alain Arias-Misson, *Theatre of Incest.*
Iftikhar Arif and Waqas Khwaja, eds., *Modern Poetry of Pakistan.*
John Ashbery and James Schuyler, *A Nest of Ninnies.*
Robert Ashley, *Perfect Lives.*
Gabriela Avigur-Rotem, *Heatwave and Crazy Birds.*
Heimrad Bäcker, *transcript.*
Djuna Barnes, *Ladies Almanack.*
Ryder.
John Barth, *LETTERS.*
Sabbatical.
Donald Barthelme, *The King.*
Paradise.
Svetislav Basara, *Chinese Letter.*
Miquel Bauçà, *The Siege in the Room.*
René Belletto, *Dying.*
Marek Bieńczyk, *Transparency.*
Mark Binelli, *Sacco and Vanzetti Must Die!*
Andrei Bitov, *Pushkin House.*
Andrej Blatnik, *You Do Understand.*
Louis Paul Boon, *Chapel Road.*
My Little War.
Summer in Termuren.
Roger Boylan, *Killoyle.*
Ignácio de Loyola Brandão,
Anonymous Celebrity.
The Good-Bye Angel.
Teeth under the Sun.
Zero.
Bonnie Bremser, *Troia: Mexican Memoirs.*
Christine Brooke-Rose, *Amalgamemnon.*
Brigid Brophy, *In Transit.*
Meredith Brosnan, *Mr. Dynamite.*
Gerald L. Bruns, *Modern Poetry and the Idea of Language.*
Evgeny Bunimovich and J. Kates, eds., *Contemporary Russian Poetry: An Anthology.*
Gabrielle Burton, *Heartbreak Hotel.*
Michel Butor, *Degrees.*
Mobile.
Portrait of the Artist as a Young Ape.
G. Cabrera Infante, *Infante's Inferno.*
Three Trapped Tigers.
Julieta Campos,
The Fear of Losing Eurydice.
Anne Carson, *Eros the Bittersweet.*
Orly Castel-Bloom, *Dolly City.*
Camilo José Cela, *Christ versus Arizona.*
The Family of Pascual Duarte.
The Hive.
Louis-Ferdinand Céline, *Castle to Castle.*
Conversations with Professor Y.
London Bridge.
Normance.
North.
Rigadoon.
Marie Chaix, *The Laurels of Lake Constance.*
Hugo Charteris, *The Tide Is Right.*
Jerome Charyn, *The Tar Baby.*
Eric Chevillard, *Demolishing Nisard.*
Luis Chitarroni, *The No Variations.*
Marc Cholodenko, *Mordechai Schamz.*
Joshua Cohen, *Witz.*
Emily Holmes Coleman, *The Shutter of Snow.*
Robert Coover, *A Night at the Movies.*
Stanley Crawford, *Log of the S.S. The Mrs Unguentine.*
Some Instructions to My Wife.
Robert Creeley, *Collected Prose.*
René Crevel, *Putting My Foot in It.*
Ralph Cusack, *Cadenza.*
Susan Daitch, *L.C.*
Storytown.
Nicholas Delbanco, *The Count of Concord.*
Sherbrookes.
Nigel Dennis, *Cards of Identity.*
Peter Dimock, *A Short Rhetoric for Leaving the Family.*
Ariel Dorfman, *Konfidenz.*
Coleman Dowell,
The Houses of Children.
Island People.
Too Much Flesh and Jabez.
Arkadii Dragomoshchenko, *Dust.*
Rikki Ducornet, *The Complete Butcher's Tales.*
The Fountains of Neptune.
The Jade Cabinet.
The One Marvelous Thing.
Phosphor in Dreamland.
The Stain.
The Word "Desire."
William Eastlake, *The Bamboo Bed.*
Castle Keep.
Lyric of the Circle Heart.
Jean Echenoz, *Chopin's Move.*
Stanley Elkin, *A Bad Man.*
Boswell: A Modern Comedy.
Criers and Kibitzers, Kibitzers and Criers.
The Dick Gibson Show.
The Franchiser.
George Mills.
The Living End.
The MacGuffin.
The Magic Kingdom.
Mrs. Ted Bliss.
The Rabbi of Lud.
Van Gogh's Room at Arles.
François Emmanuel, *Invitation to a Voyage.*
Annie Ernaux, *Cleaned Out.*
Salvador Espriu, *Ariadne in the Grotesque Labyrinth.*
Lauren Fairbanks, *Muzzle Thyself.*
Sister Carrie.
Leslie A. Fiedler, *Love and Death in the American Novel.*
Juan Filloy, *Faction.*
Op Oloop.
Andy Fitch, *Pop Poetics.*
Gustave Flaubert, *Bouvard and Pécuchet.*
Kass Fleisher, *Talking out of School.*

FOR A FULL LIST OF PUBLICATIONS, VISIT:
www.dalkeyarchive.com

SELECTED DALKEY ARCHIVE TITLES

Ford Madox Ford,
The March of Literature.
Jon Fosse, *Aliss at the Fire.*
Melancholy.
Max Frisch, *I'm Not Stiller.*
Man in the Holocene.
Carlos Fuentes, *Christopher Unborn.*
Distant Relations.
Terra Nostra.
Vlad.
Where the Air Is Clear.
Takehiko Fukunaga, *Flowers of Grass.*
William Gaddis, *J R.*
The Recognitions.
Janice Galloway, *Foreign Parts.*
The Trick Is to Keep Breathing.
William H. Gass, *Cartesian Sonata and Other Novellas.*
Finding a Form.
A Temple of Texts.
The Tunnel.
Willie Masters' Lonesome Wife.
Gérard Gavarry, *Hoppla! 1 2 3.*
Making a Novel.
Etienne Gilson,
The Arts of the Beautiful.
Forms and Substances in the Arts.
C. S. Giscombe, *Giscome Road.*
Here.
Prairie Style.
Douglas Glover, *Bad News of the Heart.*
The Enamoured Knight.
Witold Gombrowicz,
A Kind of Testament.
Paulo Emílio Sales Gomes, *P's Three Women.*
Karen Elizabeth Gordon, *The Red Shoes.*
Georgi Gospodinov, *Natural Novel.*
Juan Goytisolo, *Count Julian.*
Exiled from Almost Everywhere.
Juan the Landless.
Makbara.
Marks of Identity.
Patrick Grainville, *The Cave of Heaven.*
Henry Green, *Back.*
Blindness.
Concluding.
Doting.
Nothing.
Jack Green, *Fire the Bastards!*
Jiří Gruša, *The Questionnaire.*
Gabriel Gudding,
Rhode Island Notebook.
Mela Hartwig, *Am I a Redundant Human Being?*
John Hawkes, *The Passion Artist.*
Whistlejacket.
Elizabeth Heighway, ed., *Contemporary Georgian Fiction.*
Aleksandar Hemon, ed.,
Best European Fiction.
Aidan Higgins, *Balcony of Europe.*
A Bestiary.
Blind Man's Bluff
Bornholm Night-Ferry.
Darkling Plain: Texts for the Air.
Flotsam and Jetsam.
Langrishe, Go Down.
Scenes from a Receding Past.
Windy Arbours.
Keizo Hino, *Isle of Dreams.*
Kazushi Hosaka, *Plainsong.*
Aldous Huxley, *Antic Hay.*
Crome Yellow.
Point Counter Point.
Those Barren Leaves.
Time Must Have a Stop.
Naoyuki Ii, *The Shadow of a Blue Cat.*
Mikhail Iossel and Jeff Parker, eds.,
Amerika: Russian Writers View the United States.
Drago Jančar, *The Galley Slave.*
Gert Jonke, *The Distant Sound.*
Geometric Regional Novel.
Homage to Czerny.
The System of Vienna.
Jacques Jouet, *Mountain R.*
Savage.
Upstaged.
Charles Juliet, *Conversations with Samuel Beckett and Bram van Velde.*
Mieko Kanai, *The Word Book.*
Yoram Kaniuk, *Life on Sandpaper.*
Hugh Kenner, *The Counterfeiters.*
Flaubert, Joyce and Beckett: The Stoic Comedians.
Joyce's Voices.
Danilo Kiš, *The Attic.*
Garden, Ashes.
The Lute and the Scars
Psalm 44.
A Tomb for Boris Davidovich.
Anita Konkka, *A Fool's Paradise.*
George Konrád, *The City Builder.*
Tadeusz Konwicki, *A Minor Apocalypse.*
The Polish Complex.
Menis Koumandareas, *Koula.*
Elaine Kraf, *The Princess of 72nd Street.*
Jim Krusoe, *Iceland.*
Ayşe Kulin, *Farewell: A Mansion in Occupied Istanbul.*
Ewa Kuryluk, *Century 21.*
Emilio Lascano Tegui, *On Elegance While Sleeping.*
Eric Laurrent, *Do Not Touch.*
Hervé Le Tellier, *The Sextine Chapel.*
A Thousand Pearls (for a Thousand Pennies)
Violette Leduc, *La Bâtarde.*
Edouard Levé, *Autoportrait.*
Suicide.
Mario Levi, *Istanbul Was a Fairy Tale.*
Suzanne Jill Levine, *The Subversive Scribe: Translating Latin American Fiction.*
Deborah Levy, *Billy and Girl.*
Pillow Talk in Europe and Other Places.
José Lezama Lima, *Paradiso.*
Rosa Liksom, *Dark Paradise.*
Osman Lins, *Avalovara.*
The Queen of the Prisons of Greece.
Alf Mac Lochlainn,
The Corpus in the Library.
Out of Focus.
Ron Loewinsohn, *Magnetic Field(s).*
Mina Loy, *Stories and Essays of Mina Loy.*
Brian Lynch, *The Winner of Sorrow.*
D. Keith Mano, *Take Five.*
Micheline Aharonian Marcom,
The Mirror in the Well.
Ben Marcus,
The Age of Wire and String.

FOR A FULL LIST OF PUBLICATIONS, VISIT:
www.dalkeyarchive.com

SELECTED DALKEY ARCHIVE TITLES

Wallace Markfield,
Teitlebaum's Window.
To an Early Grave.
David Markson, *Reader's Block.*
Springer's Progress.
Wittgenstein's Mistress.
Carole Maso, *AVA.*
Ladislav Matejka and Krystyna Pomorska, eds.,
Readings in Russian Poetics: Formalist and Structuralist Views.
Harry Mathews,
The Case of the Persevering Maltese: Collected Essays.
Cigarettes.
The Conversions.
The Human Country: New and Collected Stories.
The Journalist.
My Life in CIA.
Singular Pleasures.
The Sinking of the Odradek Stadium.
Tlooth.
20 Lines a Day.
Joseph McElroy,
Night Soul and Other Stories.
Thomas McGonigle,
Going to Patchogue.
Robert L. McLaughlin, ed., *Innovations: An Anthology of Modern & Contemporary Fiction.*
Abdelwahab Meddeb, *Talismano.*
Gerhard Meier, *Isle of the Dead.*
Herman Melville, *The Confidence-Man.*
Amanda Michalopoulou, *I'd Like.*
Steven Millhauser, *The Barnum Museum.*
In the Penny Arcade.
Ralph J. Mills, Jr., *Essays on Poetry.*
Momus, *The Book of Jokes.*
Christine Montalbetti, *The Origin of Man.*
Western.
Olive Moore, *Spleen.*
Nicholas Mosley, *Accident.*
Assassins.
Catastrophe Practice.
Children of Darkness and Light.
Experience and Religion.
A Garden of Trees.
God's Hazard.
The Hesperides Tree.
Hopeful Monsters.
Imago Bird.
Impossible Object.
Inventing God.
Judith.
Look at the Dark.
Natalie Natalia.
Paradoxes of Peace.
Serpent.
Time at War.
The Uses of Slime Mould: Essays of Four Decades.
Warren Motte,
Fables of the Novel: French Fiction since 1990.
Fiction Now: The French Novel in the 21st Century.
Oulipo: A Primer of Potential Literature.
Gerald Murnane, *Barley Patch.*
Inland.
Yves Navarre, *Our Share of Time.*
Sweet Tooth.
Dorothy Nelson, *In Night's City.*
Tar and Feathers.
Eshkol Nevo, *Homesick.*
Wilfrido D. Nolledo, *But for the Lovers.*
Flann O'Brien, *At Swim-Two-Birds.*
At War.
The Best of Myles.
The Dalkey Archive.
Further Cuttings.
The Hard Life.
The Poor Mouth.
The Third Policeman.
Claude Ollier, *The Mise-en-Scène.*
Wert and the Life Without End.
Giovanni Orelli, *Walaschek's Dream.*
Patrik Ouředník, *Europeana.*
The Opportune Moment, 1855.
Boris Pahor, *Necropolis.*
Fernando del Paso, *News from the Empire.*
Palinuro of Mexico.
Robert Pinget, *The Inquisitory.*
Mahu or The Material.
Trio.
A. G. Porta, *The No World Concerto.*
Manuel Puig, *Betrayed by Rita Hayworth.*
The Buenos Aires Affair.
Heartbreak Tango.
Raymond Queneau, *The Last Days.*
Odile.
Pierrot Mon Ami.
Saint Glinglin.
Ann Quin, *Berg.*
Passages.
Three.
Tripticks.
Ishmael Reed, *The Free-Lance Pallbearers.*
The Last Days of Louisiana Red.
Ishmael Reed: The Plays.
Juice!
Reckless Eyeballing.
The Terrible Threes.
The Terrible Twos.
Yellow Back Radio Broke-Down.
Jasia Reichardt, *15 Journeys Warsaw to London.*
Noëlle Revaz, *With the Animals.*
João Ubaldo Ribeiro, *House of the Fortunate Buddhas.*
Jean Ricardou, *Place Names.*
Rainer Maria Rilke, *The Notebooks of Malte Laurids Brigge.*
Julián Ríos, *The House of Ulysses.*
Larva: A Midsummer Night's Babel.
Poundemonium.
Procession of Shadows.
Augusto Roa Bastos, *I the Supreme.*
Daniël Robberechts, *Arriving in Avignon.*
Jean Rolin, *The Explosion of the Radiator Hose.*
Olivier Rolin, *Hotel Crystal.*
Alix Cleo Roubaud, *Alix's Journal.*
Jacques Roubaud, *The Form of a City Changes Faster, Alas, Than the Human Heart.*
The Great Fire of London.
Hortense in Exile.
Hortense Is Abducted.
The Loop.
Mathematics:
The Plurality of Worlds of Lewis.

FOR A FULL LIST OF PUBLICATIONS, VISIT:
www.dalkeyarchive.com

The Princess Hoppy.
Some Thing Black.
LEON S. ROUDIEZ, *French Fiction Revisited.*
RAYMOND ROUSSEL, *Impressions of Africa.*
VEDRANA RUDAN, *Night.*
STIG SÆTERBAKKEN, *Siamese.*
LYDIE SALVAYRE, *The Company of Ghosts.*
Everyday Life.
The Lecture.
Portrait of the Writer as a Domesticated Animal.
The Power of Flies.
LUIS RAFAEL SÁNCHEZ, *Macho Camacho's Beat.*
SEVERO SARDUY, *Cobra & Maitreya.*
NATHALIE SARRAUTE, *Do You Hear Them?*
Martereau.
The Planetarium.
ARNO SCHMIDT, *Collected Novellas.*
Collected Stories.
Nobodaddy's Children.
Two Novels.
ASAF SCHURR, *Motti.*
CHRISTINE SCHUTT, *Nightwork.*
GAIL SCOTT, *My Paris.*
DAMION SEARLS, *What We Were Doing and Where We Were Going.*
JUNE AKERS SEESE, *Is This What Other Women Feel Too?*
What Waiting Really Means.
BERNARD SHARE, *Inish.*
Transit.
AURELIE SHEEHAN, *Jack Kerouac Is Pregnant.*
VIKTOR SHKLOVSKY, *Bowstring.*
Knight's Move.
A Sentimental Journey: Memoirs 1917–1922.
Energy of Delusion: A Book on Plot.
Literature and Cinematography.
Theory of Prose.
Third Factory.
Zoo, or Letters Not about Love.
CLAUDE SIMON, *The Invitation.*
PIERRE SINIAC, *The Collaborators.*
KJERSTI A. SKOMSVOLD, *The Faster I Walk, the Smaller I Am.*
JOSEF ŠKVORECKÝ, *The Engineer of Human Souls.*
GILBERT SORRENTINO, *Aberration of Starlight.*
Blue Pastoral.
Crystal Vision.
Imaginative Qualities of Actual Things.
Mulligan Stew.
Pack of Lies.
Red the Fiend.
The Sky Changes.
Something Said.
Splendide-Hôtel.
Steelwork.
Under the Shadow.
W. M. SPACKMAN, *The Complete Fiction.*
ANDRZEJ STASIUK, *Dukla.*
Fado.
GERTRUDE STEIN, *Lucy Church Amiably.*
The Making of Americans.
A Novel of Thank You.
LARS SVENDSEN, *A Philosophy of Evil.*
PIOTR SZEWC, *Annihilation.*
GONÇALO M. TAVARES, *Jerusalem.*
Joseph Walser's Machine.
Learning to Pray in the Age of Technique.
LUCIAN DAN TEODOROVICI, *Our Circus Presents . . .*
NIKANOR TERATOLOGEN, *Assisted Living.*
STEFAN THEMERSON, *Hobson's Island.*
The Mystery of the Sardine.
Tom Harris.
TAEKO TOMIOKA, *Building Waves.*
JOHN TOOMEY, *Sleepwalker.*
JEAN-PHILIPPE TOUSSAINT, *The Bathroom.*
Camera.
Monsieur.
Reticence.
Running Away.
Self-Portrait Abroad.
Television.
The Truth about Marie.
DUMITRU TSEPENEAG, *Hotel Europa.*
The Necessary Marriage.
Pigeon Post.
Vain Art of the Fugue.
ESTHER TUSQUETS, *Stranded.*
DUBRAVKA UGRESIC, *Lend Me Your Character.*
Thank You for Not Reading.
TOR ULVEN, *Replacement.*
MATI UNT, *Brecht at Night.*
Diary of a Blood Donor.
Things in the Night.
ÁLVARO URIBE AND OLIVIA SEARS, EDS., *Best of Contemporary Mexican Fiction.*
ELOY URROZ, *Friction.*
The Obstacles.
LUISA VALENZUELA, *Dark Desires and the Others.*
He Who Searches.
MARJA-LIISA VARTIO, *The Parson's Widow.*
PAUL VERHAEGHEN, *Omega Minor.*
AGLAJA VETERANYI, *Why the Child Is Cooking in the Polenta.*
BORIS VIAN, *Heartsnatcher.*
LLORENÇ VILLALONGA, *The Dolls' Room.*
TOOMAS VINT, *An Unending Landscape.*
ORNELA VORPSI, *The Country Where No One Ever Dies.*
AUSTRYN WAINHOUSE, *Hedyphagetica.*
PAUL WEST, *Words for a Deaf Daughter & Gala.*
CURTIS WHITE, *America's Magic Mountain.*
The Idea of Home.
Memories of My Father Watching TV.
Monstrous Possibility: An Invitation to Literary Politics.
Requiem.
DIANE WILLIAMS, *Excitability: Selected Stories.*
Romancer Erector.
DOUGLAS WOOLF, *Wall to Wall.*
Ya! & John-Juan.
JAY WRIGHT, *Polynomials and Pollen.*
The Presentable Art of Reading Absence.
PHILIP WYLIE, *Generation of Vipers.*
MARGUERITE YOUNG, *Angel in the Forest.*
Miss MacIntosh, My Darling.
REYOUNG, *Unbabbling.*
VLADO ŽABOT, *The Succubus.*
ZORAN ŽIVKOVIĆ, *Hidden Camera.*
LOUIS ZUKOFSKY, *Collected Fiction.*
VITOMIL ZUPAN, *Minuet for Guitar.*
SCOTT ZWIREN, *God Head.*